PRAISE FOR KEVIN J. ANDERSON

"Kevin J. Anderson has become the literary equivalent of Quentin Tarantino."

— THE DAILY ROTATION

"Kevin J. Anderson is the hottest writer on (or off) the planet."

— FORT WORTH STAR-TELEGRAM

"The scope and breadth of Kevin J. Anderson's work is simply astonishing."

— TERRY GOODKIND

"Kevin J. Anderson is one of the best plotters in the business."

— BRANDON SANDERSON

"One of the greatest talents writing today, Kevin J. Anderson is a master of adventures that are filled with dynamic, unforgettable characters."

— SHERRILYN KENYON

FANTASY STORIES
VOLUME 1

FANTASY STORIES
VOLUME 1

KEVIN J. ANDERSON

WFP
WordFire Press

EBook ISBN: 978-1-68057-708-2
Trade Paperback ISBN: 978-1-68057-709-9
Dust Jacket Hardcover ISBN: 978-1-68057-710-5
Library of Congress Control Number: 2024937267
Cover design by Janet McDonald
Cover artwork by Tithi Luadthong "grandfailure"
Kevin J. Anderson, Art Director
Vellum layout by CJ Anaya
Published by
WordFire Press, LLC
PO Box 1840
Monument CO 80132
Kevin J. Anderson & Rebecca Moesta, Publishers

WordFire Press eBook Edition 2024
WordFire Press Trade Paperback Edition 2024
WordFire Press Dust Jacket Hardcover Edition 2024
Printed in the USA
Join our WordFire Press Readers Group for
sneak previews, updates, new projects, and giveaways.
Sign up at wordfirepress.com

CONTENTS

INTRODUCTION

Tell me a story.

It's a game all writers play, an improv act. Some writers are structured; they plan thoroughly, choose carefully, write only what most inspires them, while others are loose and nimble, reacting quickly to run with an idea and meet the challenge at hand.

When J.M. Barrie put the Llewellen Davies boys to bed and they pleaded for a story, he made up tales about Peter Pan and his adventures. A.A. Milne entertained his son Christopher Robin with stories of Winnie-the-Pooh, Rabbit, Owl, and the Hundred Acre Wood.

In my teenage years I spent a lot of time babysitting. Trying to put rambunctious kids to bed and faced with the incessant "Please, can't we stay up just a little longer? Please?" I learned how to trick them by offering a story. "What do you want to hear?" I would ask. They requested Star Trek stories because we had watched *Star Trek* that evening; one time in particular I had to make up a spinoff story from a *Space: 1999* episode. Sometimes they wanted to hear about dragons or magic bicycles.

Any good babysitter—any good *writer*—could fill the bill. This was great training, and I learned how to write a story inspired by a prompt.

In my short fiction career, I often thought of intriguing ideas, independent sparks of stories that needed to be told for their own sake. Other times, anthology editors would contact me, just like those demanding kids in my babysitting years. "Tell me a story about …" for a book on sea monsters, time travel, metaphorical unicorns, dragons, even enchanted garments. Enchanted garments?

All right, I'll take the challenge.

It's what a writer does. You have an idea, and you write the story. If you don't have the idea, you go out and find one. If you keep your imagination well-oiled imagination, by exercising it regularly, the ideas will come—and you always make the best of it.

In my master-class writing workshops I hammer home the lesson that you must always do your best work. There's no such thing as "phoning it in," period. If you are asked to do a story about a magical garment, don't roll your eyes and write a slapdash story—write the absolute best loincloth story you can possibly produce, or don't accept the job.

Whatever you write is bound to be be some reader's first introduction to your work. So, make a good impression.

It's a challenge, and it's a game. What am I going to write today? What story will I play with? What idea needs to be explored? Sometimes it will be fantasy, sometimes science fiction, other times edgy horror. The tales in this volume all fall inside the fuzzy boundary of fantasy, from knights and dragons, to trolls in the modern world, ancient sea monsters, and even cursed loincloths.

Tell me a story, you ask.

Turn the page.

—Kevin J. Anderson
Monument, Colorado
May 2024

The first story I ever sold (for a whopping $12.50) was to the small-press magazine Space & Time, edited by Gordon Linzner. I was a senior in high school. "Luck of the Draw" was about a group of itinerant knights drawing straws to see who would slay the dragon and win the hand of the princess. I liked the idea enough that when I was asked to contribute to an anthology, The Ultimate Dragon, I rewrote the old story from scratch.

Years later, Amazon asked me to write a serial novel for a new program they were launching, and I needed something fast-paced, a story that could be told in installments, week after week, and I kept coming back to this lovable group of rogues, medieval con men selling their services as dragonslayers. I pulled in part of the story from "Short Straws" and some other ideas to write my full novel, The Dragon Business.

But this is where my "paid" writing career started.

SHORT STRAWS

Yes, a dragon was terrorizing the land, so the king had offered his daughter in marriage to any brave knight who slew the foul beast. Same old story. I was new to the band of warriors, but the others had heard it all before. This time, though, the logistics caused a problem.

"We could split a *cash* reward," said Oldahn, the battle-scarred old veteran who served as our leader. "But who gets the princess?"

The four of us sat around the fire, procrastinating. Though I was still wide-eyed to be part of the group—they had needed a new cook and errand runner—I'd already noticed that the adventurers liked to talk about peril a lot more than actually doing something about it. I was their apprentice, and I wanted for us to go out and fight, a team of mercenaries, warriors—but that didn't seem to be the way of going about it.

We knew where the dragon's lair was, having investigated every foul-smelling, bone-cluttered cave in the kingdom. But we still hadn't figured out what to do with the princess, assuming we succeeded in slaying the dragon. It didn't seem a practical sort of reward.

Reegas looked up with a half-cocked grin. "We could just take turns with her!"

Oldahn sighed. "One does not treat a princess the way you treat one of your hussies, Reegas."

Reegas scowled, scratching the stubble on his chin. "She's no different from Sarna at the inn—except I'll wager Sarna's better than your rustin' princess at all the important things!"

"She is the daughter of our sovereign, Reegas. Now show some respect."

"Yeah, sure, she's sacred and pure ... Bloodrust, Oldahn, now you're sounding like *him*." Reegas shot a disgusted glance at Alsaf, the puritan.

Alsaf plainly took no offense at the insult. He rolled up the king's written decree, torn from the meeting post in the town square, and stuffed it under his belt, since he was the only one of us who could read. Alsaf methodically began polishing the end of his staff on the fabric of his black cloak. He preferred to fight with his staff and his faith in God, but he also kept a sword at hand in case both the others failed. Firelight splashed across the silver crucifix at his throat.

Reegas spat something unrecognizable into the dark forest behind him. Gray-bearded Oldahn chewed his meat slowly, swallowing even the fat and gristle without a word, mindful of worse rations he had lived through. He wore an elaborately studded leather jerkin that had protected him in scores of battles; his sword was notched, but clean and free of rust.

I sat closest to the campfire, nursing a battered pot containing the last of the stew, letting my own meat cook long enough to resemble something edible. "Uh," I said, desperately wanting to show them I could be a useful member of their band. "Why don't we just draw straws to see who goes to kill the dragon?"

Alsaf, Oldahn, and Reegas all stared as if the newcomer wasn't supposed to come up with a feasible suggestion.

"Rustin' good idea, Kendell," Reegas said. Alsaf nodded.

Oldahn looked at all three of us. "Agreed, then. Luck of the draw."

I scrabbled over to my bedding and searched through it to find suitable lots. I still preferred to sleep on a pile of straw rather than the forest floor. The straw was prickly and infested with vermin, but it reminded me of the warm bed I had left behind when running away from my home. The straw was preferable to the cold, hard dirt—at least until I got hardened to the mercenary life.

I took four straws, broke one in half so that all could see, then handed them to Oldahn. The big veteran covered them in a scarred hand to hide the short straw and motioned for me to draw first.

Tentatively, I reached out, unable to decide whether I wanted the honor of battling the dragon. Sure, being wed to a princess would be nice, but I had barely begun my sword fighting lessons, and according to stories I had heard, dragons were vicious opponents. But I wanted to be a warrior instead of a shepherd's son, and a warrior faced whatever challenges they encountered.

I snatched a straw from Oldahn's grasp and could tell from the others' expressions even before I glanced downward that I had drawn a long one.

Alsaf came forward, holding his staff in his right hand as he reached out to Oldahn's fist. He paused for a long moment, then pulled a straw forth. His black cloak blocked my view, but he turned with a strangled expression on his face, looking as if his faith had deserted him. The short straw fell to the ground as he gripped his silver crucifix. "But, my faith—I must remain chaste! I cannot marry a princess."

Reegas clapped the puritan on the back. "I'm sure you can work something out."

Alsaf was pale as he shifted his weight to rest heavily on his staff. He nodded as if trying to convince himself. "Yes, my purpose is to destroy evil in all its manifestations. A divine hand has guided my selection, and I will serve His purpose." Alsaf's eyes glinted with a fanatical fury as he strode to the edge of the camp.

"Take care, and good luck," said Oldahn.

Alsaf whirled to face the three of us, holding his staff in a battle-ready stance. "I shall be protected by my unquenchable faith. My staff will send the demon back to the fires of Hell!" He looked at the skeptical expressions on our faces, then changed the tone of his voice. "I shall return."

"Is that a promise?" Reegas asked, and for once his sarcasm was weak.

"I give you my word." The puritan turned to stride into the deep stillness of the forest night, crunching through the underbrush.

It was the only promise Alsaf ever broke.

"For our honor, we must continue." Oldahn held three straws in his hand, thrusting them forward. "Come, Reegas. Draw first."

Reegas cursed under his breath and reached out to grab a straw without even pausing for thought. A broad grin split his face. He held a long straw.

I came forward, looking intently at the two straws, two chances. One would pit me against a scaly, fire-breathing demon, and the other would give me a reprieve. Knowing that the dragon had already defeated one warrior, I decided the princess wasn't so desirable after all. Alsaf had seemed so strong, so confident, so determined. I hesitated, hoping the puritan would return at the last possible moment....

But he didn't, and I picked a straw. It was long.

Oldahn stared at the short straw remaining in his hand. Cold battle-lust boiled in his eyes. "Very well, I have a dragon to slay, a death to avenge, and a princess to win. I had thought it too late in my life to settle down in marriage—but I will adapt. My brave exploits should be sung by minstrels all across the kingdom."

"Our kingdom doesn't have any minstrels, Oldahn," I pointed out.

The old warrior sighed. "I should have volunteered to go first anyway. I am the leader of our band."

"Our band?" Reegas said, sulking in his crusty old chain mail shirt. "Rust, Oldahn—with you gone we aren't much of a band anymore."

Oldahn patted his heavy broadsword and walked stiffly across the camp. It was a beautiful day, and the sun broke through in scattered patches of green light. Oldahn looked around as if for one last time. He turned to walk away, calling back to us just before he vanished into the tangled distance, "Don't be so sure I won't be coming back."

By nightfall, we were sure.

The campfire was lonely with only Reegas and me sitting by it. Oldahn had fallen, and the fact that he was the best warrior in our group (old mercenaries are, by definition, good warriors) didn't improve our confidence. I could hardly believe the great fighter I had revered so much had been *slain*. It wasn't supposed to be this way.

I looked at Reegas, fidgeting in his battered chain mail. "Well, Reegas, do you want to wait until morning, or draw straws now?"

"Rust! Let's get it over with," he said. His eyes were bloodshot. "This better be one hell of a princess."

I picked up two straws, one long, the other short. I held them out to Reegas, and he spat into the fire before looking at me. I masked my expression with some effort. Reegas reached forward and pulled the short straw.

"Bloodrust and battlerot!" he howled, jerking at the ends of the straw as if trying to stretch it longer. He crumpled it in his grip and threw it into the fire, then sank into a squat by my cookpots. "Aww, Kendell—now I can't teach you some things! I meant to take you over to the inn one night where you would—"

I looked at him with a half-smile, raising an eyebrow. "Reegas, do you think Sarna takes no other customers besides yourself?"

Wonder and shock lit up his craggy face. "You? ... Rust!" Reegas laughed loudly, a nervous blustering laugh. He clapped me on the back with perverse pride. "I won't feel sorry for you anymore, Kendell." He drew his sword and leaped into the air, slashing at a branch overhead. "But I'm gonna get that rustin' princess for myself. Maybe royalty knows a few tricks the common hussies don't."

He turned with a new excitement, dancing out of camp, waving farewell.

Alone by the campfire, I waited the long hours as the dusk collapsed into darkness. The forest filled with the noisy silence of a wild night. As the stars began to shine, I lay on the cold ground with my head propped against the rough bark of an old oak. I gave up sleeping on straw in fear that I would have dreams of dark scales and death.

The branches above me looked like the black framework of a broken lattice supporting the stars. The mockingly pleasant fire and the empty campsite made me feel intensely lonely; and for the first time I felt the true pain of my friends' losses. I had wanted to be one of them, and now they were all gone.

I remembered some of the stories they had told me, but I hadn't quite fit in with the rest of the band yet. I was a novice, I hadn't yet fought battles with them, hadn't helped them in any way. And now Alsaf and Oldahn were gone, and Reegas had a good chance of joining them....

Since I had talked my way into accompanying the band, nothing much had happened. Until the dragon came, that is.

Of course, if I had known my first adventure might involve a battle with a large reptilian terror, I might have put up with my dull old life a little longer. My father was a shepherd, spending so much time out with his flocks that he had begun to look like one of his sheep. Imagine watching thirty animals eat grass hour after hour! My mother was a weaver, spending every day hunched over her loom, hurling her shuttle back and forth, watching the threads line themselves up one at a time. She even walked with a jerky back and forth motion, as if bouncing to the beat of a flying shuttle.

Me, I'd just as soon be out fighting bandits, dispatching troublesome wolves, or chasing the odd sorcerer away under the grave risk of having an indelible curse hurled at me. That's excitement—but slaying a dragon is going a bit too far!

I couldn't sleep and lay waiting, listening to the night sounds. At every rustle of leaves I jumped, peering in to the shadows, hoping it might be Reegas returning, or Oldahn, or even Alsaf.

But no one came.

Finally, at dawn, I threw the last long straw on the dirt and ground it under my heel. I had only ever used my sword to cut up meat for the cook fires. I was alone. No one watched me, or pressured me, or insisted that I too go out and challenge the dragon. I could have just crept back home, helped my father tend sheep, helped my mother with her weaving. But somehow that kind of life seemed worse than facing a dragon.

I stared at the blade of my sword, thinking of my comrades. Alsaf and Oldahn and Reegas had been my friends, and I was the only one who could avenge them. Only I remained of the entire mercenary band. I had been with Oldahn long enough, heard his tales of glory, seen how the group worked together as a team. I couldn't just let the dragon have its victory.

Muttering a few curses I had picked up from Reegas, I left the dead campfire behind and set off through the forest.

The forest floor was impervious to the sunshine that dribbled through the woven leaves. A loud breeze rushed through the topmost branches but left me untouched. I knew the boulder-strewn wilderness well, and my woodlore had grown more skillful since my initiation into the band. While we had no serious adventures to occupy ourselves, there was still hunting to be done.

My anxiety tripled as I crested a final hill and started down into a rocky dell that sheltered the dragon's den, a broken shadow in the rock surrounded on all sides by shattered boulders and dead foliage. The lump in my throat felt larger than any dragon could ever be. The wind had disappeared, and even the birds were silent. A terrible stench wafted up, smelling faintly like something Reegas might have cooked.

I crept forward, drawing my sword, wondering why the

ground was shaking and then I saw that it was only my knees. Panic flooded my senses—or had my senses left me? Me? Against a dragon? A big scaly thing with bad breath and an awful prejudice against armed warriors?

The boulders offered some protection as I danced from one to another, moving closer to the dragon's lair. Fumes snaked out of the cave, stinging my eyes and clogging my throat, tempting me to choke and give away my presence. I could hear sounds of muffled breathing like the belching of a blacksmith's furnace.

I slid around a slime-slick rock to the threshold of the cave. I froze, an outcry trapped in my throat as I found the shattered ends of Alsaf's staff, splintered and tossed aside among torn shreds of black fabric. I swallowed and went on.

A few steps deeper into the den I tripped on the bloody remnants of Oldahn's studded leather jerkin. His bent and blackened sword lay discarded among bloody fragments of crunched bone.

On the very boundary of where sunlight dared to go, I found Reegas's rusty chain mail, chewed to a new luster and spat out.

A scream welled up as fast as my guts did, but terror can do amazing things for self-control. If I screamed, the dragon would know I had come, the latest in a series of tender victims.

But now, upon seeing with utmost certainty the fates of my comrades, my fellow warriors, anger and lust for vengeance poured forth, almost, *almost*, overwhelming my terror. The end result was an angered persistence tempered with extreme caution.

Leg muscles tense to the point of snapping, I tiptoed into the cave where I stood silhouetted against the frightened wall of daylight. The suffocating darkness of the dragon's lair folded around me. I didn't think I would ever see the sun again.

The air was thick and damp, polluted with a sickening stench. Piles of yellowed skulls lay stacked against one wall like ivory trophies. I didn't see any of the expected mounds of gold and jewels from the dragon's hoard. Pickings must have been slim in the kingdom.

I went ahead until the patch of sunlight seemed beyond running distance. My jerkin felt clammy, sticking to my cold sweat. I found it hard to breathe. I had gone in too far. My sword felt like a heavy, ineffective toy in my hand.

I could sense the lurking presence of the dragon, watching me from the shadows. I could hear its breathing like the wind of an angry storm but could not pinpoint its location. I turned in slow circles, losing all orientation in the dimness. I thought I saw two lamplike eyes, but the stench filled my nostrils, my throat. It gagged me, forcing me to gasp for air, but that only made me gulp down more of the smell. I sneezed.

—and the dragon attacked!

Suddenly I found myself confronted with a battering-ram of fury, blackish green scales draped over a bloated mass of flesh lurching forward. Acid saliva drooled off fangs like spears, spattering in sizzling pools on the floor.

I struck blindly at the eyes, the rending claws, the reptilian armor. The monster let out a hideous cry, seething forward, fat and sluggish, to corner me against a lichen-covered wall. My stomach turned to ice, and I knew how Alsaf, Oldahn, and Reegas must have felt as they faced their death—

Let me digress a moment.

Dragons are not exactly the best-fed of all creatures living in the wild. Despite their size and power, and the riches they hoard (but who can eat gold?), these creatures find very little to devour, especially in a relatively small kingdom like our own, where most people live protected within the city walls. Barely once a week does a typical dragon manage to steal a squalling baby from its crib or strike down an old crone gathering herbs in the woods. Rarer still does a dragon come across a flaxen-haired virgin (a favorite) wandering through the forest.

Hard times had come upon this particular dragon. Only impending starvation had driven it to increase its attacks on the peasantry, forcing the king to offer his daughter as a reward to rid the land of the beast. The future must have looked bleak for the dragon.

But then, unexpectedly, a feast beyond its wildest dreams! This dragon had greedily devoured three full-grown warriors in half as many days, swallowing whole the bodies of Alsaf, Oldahn, and Reegas.

And so, when the dragon lunged at me in the cave, it was so *bloated* and overstuffed that it could barely drag its bulk forward, like a snake which has gorged itself on a whole rabbit. Its bleary, yellow eyes blinked sleepily, and it seemed to have lost heart in battling warriors. But it snarled forward out of old habit, barely able to stagger toward me....

I won't, by any stretch of the imagination, claim that killing the brute was easy. The scales were tougher than any chain mail I could imagine, and the dragon didn't particularly want its head cut off—but I was bent on avenging my friends and winning myself a princess. If I could just accomplish this one thing, I could call myself a warrior. I would never have to prove myself again.

Alsaf, Oldahn, and Reegas had already done much of the work for me, dealing vicious blows to the reptilian hide. But I still can't begin to express my exhaustion when the dragon's head finally rolled among the cracked bones in its lair. I slumped to the floor of the cave, panting, without the energy to drag myself back out to fresh air.

After I had rested a long time, I stood up stiffly and looked down at the dead monster, sighing. I had won myself a princess. I had avenged my comrades.

But perhaps the best reward was that I could now call myself a real warrior, a dragon-slayer. I imagined I could think of a few ways to make the story more impressive by the time I actually met my bride-to-be.

The monster's head was heavy, and it was a long walk to the castle.

While taking a Japanese history class at the university, I became very interested in the myths, legends, culture, which seemed a very fertile ground for fantasy tales. I read books of the short fiction of Lafcadio Hearn, whose Japanese-inspired fairy tales and ghost stories were rich, clever, and inspirational.

I came home one day from my classes, sat down at my electric typewriter (yes, that's how long ago it was), and wrote this story in one sitting.

I sold it to a well-respected small-press magazine, Grue, and was very surprised some months later when I received a notice that "The Old Man and the Cherry Tree" had been selected for The Year's Best Fantasy Stories anthology published by DAW Books.

THE OLD MAN AND
THE CHERRY TREE

He had lived almost his entire life within the walls of the Buddhist monastery. The priests there told him the Shogun would cut off his head if he ventured outside ever again.

Many years before, his father had been a powerful lord, a *daimyo*. But the Shogun had gone to war with the *daimyo*, ordering that all the lord's family be executed. On the final night, while the father sat bemoaning his imminent loss of his life, the boy's mother had managed to steal away to the nearby monastery with her dearest son. She begged the head priest to save him, to secretly give her some other boy to be executed in her son's stead. The man told her it would be improper for a priest to undertake such a task; but after she offered large sums of money, the priest admitted that the monastery was sorely in need of a second golden image of Amida for the altar. Besides, the boy he had in mind for the exchange was a mere foundling anyway, given over to the care of the monastery however the priests saw fit.

They struck the bargain. The mother kissed her son, then gave him to the priest as he emerged from the monastery with a second boy who somewhat resembled the *daimyo's* son.

Before the priest could take her son into the monastery walls forever, she reached into her robes and carefully withdrew a package wrapped in fine silk. Upon seeing the silk, the priest's eyes opened eagerly. "This is for my son," she said, handing it to the child. "Your father's blade—the sword of a great *daimyo*." She unwrapped the silk to reveal a lovely jewel-encrusted short sword. Gold covered the grip, and fine characters danced on the blade. "You must keep it always by you because it will bring you good luck. When all else has been forgotten, still it will tell you the name of your father—see, it is engraved on the blade. You will learn to read it after the good priest has taught you the characters." The priest's eyes reflected the gold of the sword, and he fervently promised to care for the boy. The mother bowed and disappeared with her false son into the night shadows from which she had come.

The boy grew up in the monastery. The priests soon stopped trying to take his father's sword from him when they realized they would never be able to sell it, not with the name of the rebellious *daimyo* engraved on the blade. And they never made the effort to teach him to read, considering themselves safer if the boy was not constantly reminded of his true identity.

The boy took his pleasure in gardening, caring for the plants and trees in the monastery's beautiful garden. He was especially captivated by a single cherry tree which had been planted by three novices the very morning the Shogun had cut the heads off the rest of the boy's family. The small cherry tree had stood so frail and frightened in the garden, reminding the boy of how he must appear to the other monks.

As the boy grew older, he never shaved his head, or took the vows, nor studied the sutras as did the other novices. He planted and tended his flowers and trees and shrubs in the garden, until the monastery became known for the beauty harbored within its walls. But above all, the boy—now a young man, actually—tended the single cherry tree with all the love he possessed, until it became the glory of the entire garden. In spring the cherry tree would explode with pure white flowers, as if a sweet-scented winter had dropped gently into the monastery garden. At the time, it was said that the blossoms lingered longer on this cherry tree than on any other in all of Japan, and people traveled great distances to gather up some of the fallen petals, which they used for curing the sick and for making love potions.

Sometimes, in secret, the *daimyo's* son would climb up into the tree and look out over the monastery walls which kept him imprisoned. None of the priests had bothered to tell him that the old Shogun had died, nor that the new one did not care about the young man's family name. Instead, he sat up in the boughs under the silver moonlight and looked out to see the wide world he would never be able to explore, listening to the wind in the leaves of his tree and the faint sounds of snoring from the monks' sleeping quarters.

In time, he came to consider the cherry tree his closest and dearest friend. He talked to it as he tended the rest of his garden, and the other novices began to snicker and laugh among themselves about the strange gardener who talked to trees.

So, the years passed. The tree continued to grow, and the gardener continued to grow older. Year after year the white blossoms came, and the *daimyo's* son—now an old man—took no greater joy than in watching the petals drift in the wind. He wept for those that caught like kites on an updraft and escaped, floating down on the other side of the monastery wall.

Each spring many people came to see the blossoms, some even making grand processions all the way from Kyoto. The pilgrims talked among themselves about the exquisite beauty of the delicate white flowers, and of the glowing, honest satisfaction in the face of the old gardener who stood so proudly beside his tree.

And then one year the tree did not blossom.

The other plants in the old man's garden launched forth their leaves and flowers as always, but day after day the cherry tree remained barren, as motionless as a stillborn babe. The people who came to see the tree departed in disappointment—it had once been magnificent, they said sadly, but the old cherry tree had died, and they would have to go elsewhere from now on.

The monks began to talk that they would soon cut down the marvelous tree and burn its wood in the fire.

The old man could not bear to hear this and, recalling the days of his youth, he somehow managed to climb into the tree, searching the branches for buds, any small flickering of life. But the branches were as dry and as barren as the paper on which the monks copied their sutras. The old man saw other cherry trees in the distance, gleaming with their white flowers and scattering petals into the wind. Then his heart knew for certain that the old cherry tree had died, and he threw his arms around the lifeless bole of his only friend, weeping until the curious monks came out and called for him to come down. His legs were weak, but he managed to descend the tree and stood shaking. The monks left him, whispering among themselves, and went back to their work.

As he looked long and hard at the lifeless branches of the cherry tree, the old man decided what he must do. That night, when all the monks slept, he crept out into the darkness of the garden and lifted up one of the flat rocks he had long ago placed around the cherry tree. Under the rock rested his father's jeweled sword, glinting in the light of the dying moon—the colorful silk wrappings had rotted, but the sword was untarnished and as sharp as ever. The old man looked grimly at the blade.

There was one way to show one's utmost devotion, to remove grief and end this life of confinement and pain. Brave warriors followed their lords to death, committing *seppuku* to show their absolute loyalty no matter how their lord had died. And if the warriors could slit their bellies in an ecstasy of pain and honor, couldn't the old man do the same at the death of his dearest companion, his cherry tree? His father's sword was a special sword, the sword of a great *daimyo*, perhaps even containing a little magic. This act would be his final gift to the tree he had loved for so many years.

The old man loosened his robe and squatted down as near as he could to the dead cherry tree. He held the sharp point of the *daimyo's* sword against his stomach, looking down at the engraved characters signifying his father's name—but he still could not read them. The night was cold and crisp, probably the last such night in spring. The noise of the rustling barren branches above sounded to him like a death rattle.

Done properly, *seppuku* would have been a grand occasion—with many priests and faithful companions. But the old man did not have even so much as a white cloth to sit upon. Tradition required that once he had slit his belly, once he had proven his devotion and bravery, his closest friend was then permitted to strike off his head to end the pain. But the old man had no best friend, and so, after he made the deep thrust and long sideways cut, he was forced to bear the pain as best he could, until he could bear it no longer ... and then it made no difference. His blood spilled onto the earth.

The next morning the monks came out into the garden for their tea and found him there. They shook their heads, muttering at how the lonely old man had finally ended his life, but that he had not even done *seppuku* properly. The old gardener had become well-known and many people—bringing their donations—would have come to see the death ceremony. The old man had been very inconsiderate not to let them know of his intentions. Some of the monks came to carry him away and marveled at the beautiful sword they found upon him. No one knew where he had gotten it, and none of them recognized the name of the long-forgotten *daimyo* written on the blade. The monks cleaned the sword and placed it in their treasury.

But that morning, when the sun rose high enough that its rays struck the old cherry tree, something wondrous happened. The wind picked up. A shiver ran through the ground as a silence descended on the garden. Some of the monks dropped their tea, burning their fingers, scowling at each other. They all looked at the dead cherry tree.

The barren branches trembled, as if the old tree were straining with all its might ... and suddenly every branch, even the smallest twigs, brought forth a deep red flower, as scarlet as fresh blood. As the monks watched, gaping in amazement, the tree covered itself with flowers, more than it had ever borne before.

One brash novice crept up to the new flowers in wonder and touched them. He cried that the petals felt wet, then yelped in pain. "It burns! My fingers!" He tried to wipe the moisture off on his robe, then ran to hide inside the monastery.

Word spread quickly throughout the land, and people flocked to see the Blood Tree, as it had been named. The Shogun himself came to see the miracle, and when the monks told the story of the old man who had tended the tree, and of the mysterious sword he had used to commit *seppuku*, another old man from the vicinity recalled the name of the rebellious *daimyo* and how a previous Shogun had executed the entire family. The others remembered how at the same time the monastery had received a generous donation from the wife of the *daimyo* ... and although they could not be certain, many guessed the identity of the gardener.

The Shogun commanded that the monks bring him the ashes of the old man, and they carried out a simple clay urn, bowing their heads in embarrassment that they had not given the ashes a more ornate resting place. The Shogun spoke in his most respectful voice so that all could hear. "If this old man was truly the son of a rebellious *daimyo*, trapped for all his life in the sanctuary of the monastery walls for his own protection, long after it was necessary, I ... I, the Shogun, now pardon him. I set him free so that he need no longer remain inside these walls."

So saying, the Shogun reached into the urn and flung the ashes high in the air, watching as they drifted out to explore the world on their own.

The Blood Tree shuddered, and, with a cracking sound, collapsed into a heap of charred splinters, burned from the inside out. The people gasped, and even the Shogun was amazed.

Many years later, wandering peddlers could sometimes be seen at night, keeping to the shadows, and entering houses where the seeds of dissent had already been sown, secretly offering to sell splinters of the Blood Tree which would cause almost-instant bad fortune and possibly even death to one's enemies.

The Shogun caught several of these peddlers and executed them.

Jules Verne was one of the many classic writers who influenced me when I was young, eager, and dedicated to becoming a writer. As a boy I would curl up in a chair and struggle through big, leather-bound volumes of A Journey to the Centre of the Earth, The Mysterious Island, *and* 20,000 Leagues Under the Sea. *This fascination is reflected in several of my short stories, as well as in my novel* Captain Nemo, *the life story of Nemo and his friendship with Verne.*

When I was asked to write a story based on H.P. Lovecraft's chilling Cthulhu Mythos (another big influence on my writing), I couldn't resist folding Captain Nemo into the story.

What if the Nautilus *encountered some ancient, cursed ruins, deep under the sea?*

<h1 style="text-align:center">20,000
YEARS UNDER THE SEA</h1>

He dreamed of tentacles again.

The battered *Nautilus* cruised listlessly through uncharted waters, its engine struggling, pumps and pistons wheezing like an injured man trying to catch his breath. The hull seams showed the strain of the recent battle, and some rivets leaked water, preventing the armored sub-marine boat from diving deep.

But the dreams of her captain were darker and more restless than the seas around them.

In his stateroom, Nemo's bunk was padded with fine cushions, and he tossed under silken sheets that were fit for a caliph—*stolen* from the corrupt caliph, as was the *Nautilus* and everything else.

In the nightmare, he fought alongside his loyal crewmen against the slimy, thrashing tentacles. Though Nemo's true war was against evil men and their unquenchable thirst for slaughter, the giant squid was a mindless beast of nature. The squid had tried to crush the armored hull in its suckered embrace, and Nemo and his men fought it with cutlasses, harpoons, and daggers, covering the deck with foul-smelling slime and a gushing of black ink like a shadow made out of acid. A well-placed harpoon blinded the monster's eye and penetrated its rudimentary brain, then the wounded creature released its death grip, slipping away from the sub-marine boat and into the sea, taking four crewmen with it.

Captain Nemo and his surviving sailors tended their injuries. The men already had many scars from years of engineering slavery at Caliph Robur's prison camp of Rurapente. After escaping in fire and blood, Nemo had declared his own war on war; nature, however, didn't care about their battle or their pain—the giant squid proved that.

Nemo would not be deterred by storms or by attacking monsters. He tried to rest while Mr. Harding and his engineers repaired the motors. Others caulked and welded hull breaches, reinforcing the seams on the wounded vessel. The navigator steered through the night, looking for some sheltered place where they could put in and complete repairs.

Exhausted and sore, Nemo tried to rest, if only for a few hours, but nightmares of that soulless tentacled creature granted him no peace. Even in sleep, Captain Nemo continued his battle....

Thus, it was a relief when Mr. Harding tapped on his cabin door. "Sorry to disturb you, sir, but we found an island. Looks uninhabited."

Nemo climbed from his bunk, disentangling himself from the silken sheets that reminded him too much of tentacles. "I'm on my way."

Nemo was amazed his navigator had been able to find this bleak and rugged island. With its crescent-shaped cove bounded by black walls that plunged down to the waterline, it reminded Nemo of a claw.

When they encountered the giant squid, the *Nautilus* had been stalking naval battleships in the southern seas, eager to eliminate the bloodthirsty soldiers before they could prey upon innocents. Nemo left any merchant vessel unmolested, but French, British, or Spanish warships were sunk to the bottom of the sea. No mercy. The sailors aboard would have shown no mercy to those they preyed upon: innocent women and children who became pawns in political power plays, like Nemo's own wife and son, like the families of the other engineering prisoners from Rurapente.

Because the seas were so rough south of Terra del Fuego, few sailing vessels wandered far afield for the pleasure of exploring. Now, damaged and limping along, the *Nautilus* had blundered upon a bleak no-man's-land not far from the untouched shores of the Antarctic continent. This isolated, never-inhabited island was surrounded by mist and freezing drizzle.

The sun was only a pale, gray fuzz swathed in mist when Nemo emerged from the hatch with Mr. Harding and engineers named Louart and Fallon. He inspected the glistening hull for traces of slime or pools of blood, but the spray of rough waters had washed the *Nautilus* clean.

Nemo inhaled the salty, mist-laden air, but there was a sour, rotten taint to it. Louart asked, "What's that smell, Captain?"

"This is a sheltered cove," Harding suggested. "Maybe a school of fish ..."

Fallon said, "I remember each year when the alewives would die off and wash ashore. Made the whole port stink."

Nemo did see numerous fish floating belly up on the surface of the cove. "But these are all different species. They wouldn't have died off at once."

Harding got down to business. "No matter, Captain. We're here to make repairs and be on our way."

Nemo gazed up at the sheer cliffs. Seabirds wheeled about, not the usual gulls but black ones that looked like bats. As they hunted in the shadowy mist, their screeches were haunting.

In some trick of the warming dawn, the mist thinned, and hazy light dappled the surrounding cliffs and the mountains inland. Nemo saw more than just boulders and outcroppings: the cliffs were scattered with blocky geometrical shapes, graceful pillars, magnificent but crumbling towers. Even from this distance, with details blurred by fog, the structures looked unspeakably ancient.

"They're ruins, Cap'n!" Fallon cried.

Nemo frowned. "We're off the coast of Antarctica. No civilization ever existed this far south. Even the savages in Terra del Fuego have nothing more than huts."

Louart pointed toward the mysterious city inland. "And yet, Monsieur Capitaine—they exist."

Nemo turned to his second-in-command. "Mr. Harding, I'll let you continue the repairs. I intend to see that city."

Harding never argued. "Suit yourself, Captain. We have plenty of work to do." His bearded face was smeared with grease and his hands were dirty. "I spent hours in the engine room. We'll have to take the motors apart, replace one of the screws. That squid did us a lot of harm."

"Can you fix it?" Nemo asked.

The other man raised his eyebrows. "Of course, we can fix it— we built the boat in the first place. It's just a matter of time."

"Time to explore, then."

Joined by five companions, Nemo took a boat to shore, searching for a safe landing spot against the cliffs. At last, they encountered a cleverly hidden road cut at an angle down the rock, all but invisible except when approached face-on. The wide path was paved with moss-slick flagstones cut from black obsidian. The carved steps were at the wrong height for human legs.

Inland, the strange, bleak island was littered with ruins, white stone structures with trapezoidal doorways that were too low and too wide for an average person. The streets spread out in unsettling angles, and the walls were constructed with a disorienting obliqueness that made Nemo feel as if he were falling when he faced them.

Temples or observatories crowned outcroppings, and huge

columns rose high, but many were broken, strewn about like the bones of prehistoric animals. Boulevards led across a high plateau and then plunged over a cliff edge. Rounded arenas had once hosted some kind of unknown sport or spectacle.

On the lintels of collapsed buildings and an altar of what must have been a temple of worship, or sacrifice, Nemo saw a repeated dot pattern that seemed familiar to him, but he couldn't place it.

Standing tall, dark stone obelisks were covered with strange glyphs unlike any alphabet Nemo had ever seen—a mixture of runes, hieroglyphics, and squiggles. He had learned many languages in his life, and after years of oppression at Rurapente, he was fluent in reading and writing Arabic. His engineers understood the language of mathematics. The language of the ancient engravings seemed an amalgam of all those things.

Even in the gray cold mist Nemo smelled brimstone, and a pall of old smoke seemed hung in the air. These ruins reminded him far too much of Rurapente....

He had been selectively captured in the Crimean War along with other scientists, engineers, and visionaries. The evil Caliph Robur forced them to work in his isolated prison. As the ambitious French engineer de Lesseps carved a channel across the Suez Isthmus that would connect the Mediterranean to the Red Sea, the caliph had commanded Nemo and his fellow workers to build him a warship unlike any the world had seen: an armored vessel to prey upon trade ships that came through the new Suez Canal. He could become the world's most accomplished pirate, the greatest leader, the master of the world.

For years Nemo and his comrades had toiled in slavery. They were rewarded with wives whom they learned to love, even families that gave them a spark of solace in their captivity. Caliph Robur had made the *Nautilus* his fortress, until Nemo and his men overthrew and assassinated him during a test voyage, stole the armored sub-marine boat, and raced to Rurapente to save their families. But they were too late. The caliph's political rivals had already marched upon the secret base and slaughtered everyone....

Nemo could never burn away the images of his return to Rurapente. The foundations of buildings stood like blackened stumps of teeth. The smelting refineries had been caved in, windows smashed, bricks crumbled. The living quarters had been burned to ash and slag. Everything ... destroyed.

The oppressive silence had been broken only by a faint whistle of wind. As he stood there, Nemo had thought he heard the shouts of raiders, the crackle of flames, the clang of scimitars against makeshift weapons, or against soft flesh, hard bone. Screams of pain and pleas for mercy from the desperate slaves, the women, the children—everyone who had endured life at Rurapente. All dead.

And was this place any different?

He and his companions found weathered statues hewn from lava rock, details blurred by time and something more. Together, two crewmen pried loose a stone figure that had toppled face-first into the crumbling gravel and frozen mud. When they lifted it up, Nemo saw not the figure of any man, but a creature with a face that was a hideous mass of tentacles, and eyes that even in the pitted and eroded stone looked as empty and unimaginable as the universe.

Louart paled and made the sign of the Cross, though he had not previously demonstrated any penchant for religion. "It must be one of their gods," said Fallon.

"Or one of their demons," Nemo said.

They continued to explore, studying friezes that depicted the daily life of a civilization inconceivable even to the most fevered opium dream, populated by barrel-like creatures with starfish heads. None of the men spoke, uneasy, awed, and intimidated.

The sour smell of rot was more pronounced as he led the way to the steep path down to the cove. The sun ducked behind the mist again, and gray shrouds thickened around them.

Mr. Harding was on the upper deck of the *Nautilus* waiting for the captain. "Those are ruins even greater than the city of Pompeii," Nemo told him.

The gruff second-in-command scratched his bearded chin. "Then you'll be even more interested in what we found in the cove, Captain. There's an even larger ancient city submerged under the water." His lips quirked in a small smile, "And this one's intact."

When the *Nautilus* had fought its way to the shelter of the natural harbor at night, no one had been looking deep below. As Nemo peered into the deep cove, he could see the shimmering fever-dream architecture of the sunken city. "That city down there has waited a long time for us. It might have been submerged for twenty thousand years or more."

"I don't intend on staying here anywhere near that long, Captain," Harding said. "We'll get to work."

Nemo picked Louart and three other men to don exploration suits and join him. The Rurapente engineers had designed the suits for Caliph Robur, after he lied that he wanted to explore the bottom of the sea; in truth, Robur had needed those suits so his underwater army could augur holes in the hulls of helpless ships.

Nemo gathered the waterproof leather suit, the weights, the buckles, the helmet, and the wrappings that sealed all the seams. As he and his team fastened their helmets and attached the breathing hoses to tanks so they could inhale the stale compressed air, he thought again of his war against war.

The *Nautilus* could have been an unprecedented means of exploration, a boon for science. Before being captured in the Crimea, Nemo had seen much of the world, dared many adventures, but thanks to the smoke and the misery of Rurapente his spirit of curiosity had been snuffed out like a bright ember under a bootheel. Now, though, this ancient and mysterious underwater city intrigued him.

He sank slowly and gracefully toward the bottom. The

pressure of the water closed around him like a squeezing fist, but the reinforced suit protected him. His weights pulled him down until the *Nautilus* was only a strange angular shape that eclipsed the rippling daylight. The other men spread out as they drifted down and landed with slow gracefulness. Together, they turned on their galvanic lights, shining yellow into the gloom.

The buildings of the sunken city were similar to the ruins up above, but here they were better preserved. The walls stood upright and arches gracefully framed entryways into ominous temples.

Taking the lead, Nemo walked with his armored boots on the silty floor, sending up puffs of murk to expose broad flat flagstones. They passed titanic facades, statues, obelisks covered with markings, friezes that depicted the creatures with the barrel-bodies and starfish heads, and another species that were formless conglomerations of bubbles or masses of pseudopods that seemed to be servants or guardians to the starfish-headed creatures. And more images of the tentacle-faced creature from the toppled statue. The arches and rune-encrusted pillars again bore that familiar dot pattern. Perhaps it was something from a book Caliph Robur kept inside the *Nautilus* library.

They spread out to explore, and their galvanic lights bobbed along. The sunken metropolis carried a weight of ancientness, a weariness of years that extended far beyond the twenty thousand years he had suggested. Perhaps these buildings had been erected long before humans had ever populated this planet.

A golden glow flared and then died down, but the suit made Nemo sluggish, and the hazy glow had faded by the time he turned. He felt a chill. He had encountered many predators under the sea, had fought off sharks and a giant squid, but this fear was different and inexplicable.

Louart approached him, signaling with a gloved hand. The two men pressed their face plates together so that when Louart's voice echoed through the thick glass. "Notice, mon Capitaine. No coral, no seaweed, no rubble."

Nemo indicated a cluster of perfectly placed sea anemones

and a large fan of corral, but Louart shook his head inside the helmet. They touched panes of glass again. "Those are intentional —decorations. Something is *tending* this city."

Nemo realized the other man was right. Always when he ventured to the sea bottom, the marine flora was scattered and lush: sponges, shellfish, anchored kelp, and waving fronds of seaweed. Here, though, the cove appeared sterile. He realized that he hadn't seen any fish.

The group spread out again, wary. Nemo shone his light around, found a line of imposing arches that seemed to guide him on. He walked under the first span, and the second, until he saw a domed and thick-walled structure ahead, sealed and armored like a bunker ... or a crypt.

Nemo felt drawn to it, as if compelled. The vault door was barricaded with a complex stone mechanism ... clean, smooth stone. Any normal ruins would have been encrusted with marine growth and cemented shut by coral, but the lines here were razor sharp and clear of debris.

He shone the yellow galvanic beam to illuminate the door. It was covered by a stylized bas-relief that showed a creature with the smooth dome of a skull and baleful red eyes that glowed with inset phosphorescent jewels. The lower half of the creature's face was covered with twisting, curling tentacles.

Though the thing was frightening, Nemo felt a tantalizing tug on his heart that ignited his anger. This thing with the tentacled face symbolized Nemo's own hatred toward those who wrought violence, and it seemed to possess a power to eradicate war. This was something far more deadly than the *Nautilus*, if only he would set it free....

With great difficulty, he pulled himself away and withdrew beneath the looming arches. He could hear his breathing in the helmet, and his heart was pounding like drums. He looked around for his companions.

One figure, Louart, stood close to a tall, ethereal spire of rock carved into delicately balanced segments. The man studied the carvings, then pulled himself to a higher section to see.

Although the sunken ruins were perfectly preserved, they were still fragile with unspeakable age. As Louart placed weight against the joints, the segmented spire wobbled and bent. He pushed himself backward and out of the way as the stone sections collapsed.

The galvanic lights flashed in random directions as the other men backed away from the tumbling stone. Suddenly, the golden glow appeared at the edge of Nemo's vision, brightening and rushing forward. He caught only a glimpse out of the curved helmet.

A swarm of light and bubbles erupted along the corridors of the ancient city. It was a mass of living spheres, like gelatinous blind eyes clumped into a sentient form. All the spheres turned forward, as if targeting the intruder who had knocked down the spire.

Louart saw the thing coming and flailed away. The bubble mass moved so swiftly that it reached the man before the last spire block had tumbled to the ocean floor. The shapeless amoeboid swarmed over Louart. He fought with his arms and legs, but the bubble creature surrounded him and *squeezed*.

Nemo and his companions hurried to Louart's defense, but they were too slow underwater. The ocean was so incredibly silent. Nemo and one other man had spears; the others carried scimitars. The bubble thing continued to contract around its victim, and a sudden splash of red exploded in Louart's helmet, filming the faceplate.

Nemo hurled his harpoon, and it glided through the water, sizzling into the amoeboid thing, puncturing several of the spheres before it disappeared into the mass. But the formless creature rearranged itself, extending pseudopods in other directions. By now Louart was surely dead, perhaps even half digested. The other crewman threw his spear, to no effect.

The bubble thing squirmed along and retreated among the empty buildings of the sunken city. Nemo knew that it could have killed the rest of them, but the creature had retaliated only against the one man who had caused damage.

The other men were panicked, and Nemo pointed upward. His three comrades tore off their weights and floated upward to the waiting *Nautilus*.

Nemo remained in the ancient city, warily looking around. He glanced back toward the tantalizing, armored tomb that he hadn't had the nerve to explore, then he, too, released his weight belt and swam up to daylight.

Even without Louart's body, the *Nautilus* crew held a solemn funeral for him. Afterward, Harding came to stand in the doorway of the captain's quarters. "We've lost too many crew already, Captain."

Nemo sat at his small desk but did not nod. "We would all be dead if we'd stayed at Rurapente. This way, at least we can keep fighting."

"Fight against what, Captain? A giant squid? Some primordial monster in an ancient city?"

"The world is not a safe place, Mr. Harding, and there are other kinds of wars besides the one we chose. We can either give up, or we can continue our fight. This is a setback, but it is not a defeat."

Nemo stared at the books on the shelves, ancient Arabic tomes that Caliph Robur had considered essential—military strategy reports and treatises about the use of bladed weapons, instructional manuals on methods of torture (some of which masqueraded as medical texts). But he thought he remembered seeing something ...

"When will the repairs be completed?"

His second in command stood in cold silence for a moment before answering, "Tomorrow, sir."

"Then let me read tonight."

After hours of paging through documents, he found the volume that contained the familiar dot pattern he'd seen on so many of the ruins. It was a thick handwritten book bound in a curious pale leather. The text inside had been penned in a dark brown ink; all the words were scribed in a trembling hand, as if the author were afraid to put into words the nightmarish thoughts that consumed his brain. *Necronomicon.*

After years as the caliph's prisoner, Nemo was fluent in Arabic, but this writing seemed to be an odd archaic dialect, written by a man named Abdul al-Hazred. Pages and pages of speculations seemed utter gibberish, something concocted in the hashish houses of Cairo or scrawled by a man dying from a madness plague.

According to the mad Arab, the dot pattern was a sign of the Old Ones, creatures from beyond time and space that had settled Earth soon after its formation, long before any natural life had emerged from the ooze. He saw drawings of the starfish-headed things depicted in statues in both the above-ground ruins and the sunken city. The *Necronomicon*'s ravings told how the Old Ones had found a way to traverse the airless chasms of open space, how they had created and enslaved a race of shapeless sentient clusters of protoplasm called Shoggoths that were their servants, their guardians, their caretakers.

The preposterous imagined history laid out a march of epochal events, how a race of tentacle-faced beings—immense and powerful strangers from beyond the stars—had engaged in a great war against the Old Ones, nearly wiping them out, but the Shoggoths and the Old Ones fought back, defeating the octopoid creatures, at least for a time. And the Old Ones had retreated into their cities beneath the sea.

Nemo thought the ruined city on this mysterious island might have been one of those ancient and impressive dwellings of the Old Ones. And the shapeless bubble thing that had attacked Louart—was that a Shoggoth?

The bas-relief carved in the doorway of the armored crypt was much like the octopoid race. The *Necronomicon* named the beings in a word written in blocky letters, as if al-Hazred had dared himself to write the word: CTHULHU.

He closed the book. Rationally speaking, Nemo didn't believe any of it. And yet in a primitive and easily frightened corner of his mind, he thought he knew the answers.

Mr. Harding delivered the welcome news that repairs were nearly completed and the *Nautilus* could be under way by nightfall. The crew let out a ragged cheer. After the death of Louart, the oppressive anxiety that hung over the abandoned island and the ruined city had begun to seep into their psyche like mildew in a dank tomb.

Nemo, however, heard the report from his second-in-command as if it were distant background noise. He wasn't yet finished with this ancient sunken city. The tales from the *Necronomicon* had inflamed his imagination, caught hold of him like an incurable fever.

If he had read the ravings of the mad Arab in the camp of Rurapente, he would have discounted it all, but after what he had seen, not just the statues and cyclopean buildings, but the appearance of the murderous—protective?—Shoggoth that had killed Louart, he knew it had to be real. And that thing sealed in the armored tomb pulled on him like the inescapable current of the fabled maelstrom off the coast of Norway.

"I'm going back down there, Mr. Harding." He raised his voice and glanced at his crewmen at their stations on the bridge. "I'd like three volunteers to accompany me—but I won't require it." He didn't speak further, because he didn't want to be challenged to explain what he was doing or why.

Harding looked skeptical, but he held his tongue. The crew were terrified, knowing what had happened to their comrade, but they were Nemo's men and they would do anything for him. In the end, he had more volunteers than he needed.

As he suited up, Nemo felt preoccupied, his thoughts focused on what he knew was down there. In his life he had fought pirates, been shipwrecked, crossed Africa in a balloon, fought in the Crimean War, and suffered years of imprisonment under a murderous caliph who wanted to be the master of the world. But he doubted he would ever face anything as nerve-wracking as this. His obsession went beyond fear.

In their weighted underwater suits, the four explorers plunged to the bottom of the cove, shining their galvanic lanterns into the murk. They were all more wary now, seeing movement in every shadow, alert for the golden glow of the lurking Shoggoth. The men each carried a spear in one hand and a cutlass in the other, although the previous day's encounter had shown that such primitive defenses were ineffective against the Shoggoth.

This time, Nemo was pulled by an invisible force, like a questing tongue drawn to a broken tooth. He felt a call of that other being whose very image and name exuded awe. *Cthulhu.* The crypt seemed to contain more power than Nemo would need to win his war against war.

The four galvanic beams shone out, illuminating the arches that led to the squat armored building. The circular walls were like low battlements surrounding the sealed temple—or was it a tomb?—of an Elder God.

The other men spread out, holding their spears and cutlasses, on guard for the swarming mass of one of the Old Ones' guardians. But Nemo faced the graven image of the cosmic creature. This being was different from the builders of the ancient sunken city; it might have caused the destruction of the starfish-headed Old Ones. But if so, why would they build a temple to it here? Why honor Cthulhu with such an impressive and elaborate tomb?

He ran his gloved hands along the complex locking mechanism that sealed the crypt door. The stone components were carefully carved and arranged like a puzzle, a mystic trigger built by minds immeasurably superior to his own.

This mechanism was a problem unlike other engineering challenges he had faced in Rurapente, but his hands had their instincts. He applied his mind to the problem, sliding the components sideways, then down, then back into a different interlocking configuration. Something seemed to be guiding him.

He felt the stone door thrum beneath his fingertips, as if an energy inside were building, awakening.

Next to him, the men scrambled backward, and Nemo turned to see if the Shoggoth was coming, but his companions were staring at him, at the temple ... at the door cracking open. What seeped out was not a golden glow, but the opposite—an emptiness of light, a shadow that sucked at the beams of their galvanic lamps.

The water grew suddenly colder, penetrating even his thick undersea suit. The stone door spread wider, and darkness boiled out, along with an ominous emerging figure—a titanic looming shape that seemed much too large to have been contained within the structure.

A current blew Nemo backward like a howling storm wind as the crypt burst open, and the enormous thing with baleful eyes and facial tentacles emerged. The statues had conveyed only a hint of the overwhelming cosmic *presence* of what Abdul al-Hazred had named Cthulhu.

Then Nemo realized what he should have known from the start—that this was not a temple or a tomb ... but a *prison*.

One of his men thrashed in a frantic effort to swim away, but the reawakened Cthulhu turned a horrible, maddening gaze upon him—and the man's struggles immediately ceased. He drifted motionless, struck dead by the mere sight.

The galvanic lamps flashed wildly in all directions as the other two fled. Nemo was stunned and tumbling, trying to reorient himself in the water. He slammed into one of the stone walls and held on for balance. Nemo's mind couldn't contain the immensity of the emerging Cthulhu, a being that had been locked away for twenty thousand years or more beneath the sea.

What have I unleashed?

The water around him suddenly glowed, frothing golden as if illuminated by an unknown and insane source of light. Through his faceplate, he saw a roiling blob of bubbles, a conglomeration of translucent spheres that might or might not have been eyes—it was the Shoggoth returned to continue its attack.

But the formless thing did not pursue Nemo or his companions; instead, it confronted the horrific Elder God. The light in the water continued to grow, and another Shoggoth streaked in from a separate part of the city. Then a third—and four more!

The Old Ones may have been long extinct in this isolated city, but they had left these shapeless but somehow faithful creatures to maintain their cursed metropolis. The Shoggoths did more than just maintain the buildings, arches, and sunken gardens; they were also here to keep the Cthulhu thing imprisoned.

Nemo and his men tried to find shelter behind the enormous facades, unable to do anything but watch. In their scramble away, they had dropped their cutlasses and spears. Nemo's eyes were so blasted that he could barely see details in the glaring light, the masses of bubbles, the thrashing tentacles, and a defiant roar that vibrated through the fabric of the universe.

The Shoggoths swept in and surrounded the powerful, unspeakably evil creature that had emerged from its millennial prison. The formless creatures showed no vengeance toward the *Nautilus* men seeming to regard them as utterly beneath notice.

Nemo and his companions tore away their weighted belts and clawed their way upward, rising toward the distant surface while expecting to be struck dead at any moment.

Below, the battle continued with all the fury of an active undersea volcano. The emerging Cthulhu tore Shoggoths to pieces, ripping the masses of bubbles apart, but the spheres reconverged. The Shoggoths were many, and they had been placed there for the sole purpose of guarding this monster. In a hurricane of golden light and swirling pseudopods, they drove the Cthulhu thing back, unable to destroy it—how does one kill a godlike being that has existed since before time?—but at least the Shoggoths could contain it. They surrounded the ancient monster in a cocoonlike embrace and pushed it back toward the tomb chamber.

Nemo finally broke the surface of the water, and he detached his helmet, gasping. The muffled sounds suddenly grew louder;

next to him, the men couldn't stop screaming. Nemo's own throat was raw, and he knew he must have been screaming as well.

Careless and terrified, they dropped their helmets into the water and climbed the rungs to fight their way aboard the imagined safety of the *Nautilus*.

Mr. Harding stood watching them, surprised and alarmed. "Engines are ready to go, Captain, but what—"

Below, the supernatural storm continued to unleash explosions of light and inky shadows. "We must depart immediately!" Nemo said. "Now!"

Harding didn't argue. Seeing the expressions of absolute terror, not just on the other sailors but on their brave captain as well, the sailors moved more swiftly than they ever had in their lives.

When he spoke, Nemo's voice was torn and hoarse. "Take us away from this island. Far, far away."

The repaired engines hummed, and the sub-marine boat lumbered forward, picking up speed. Beneath them, the cove's deep water looked like a storm of lights and fire, inconceivable colors in a simmering battle that Nemo himself may have triggered ... but one in which he could do nothing to fight on either side.

"What was down there, Captain?"

"Nothing I could understand, Mr. Harding."

The second-in-command gave a small nod, then focused on business, intent on more than cosmic monsters, Elder Gods, or vanished alien cities. "The *Nautilus* is in prime condition again, Captain. Engines at full power. Hull integrity, ramming blades, and reinforced bulkheads all check out. We can continue our mission."

Nemo stared ahead through the dragon's-eye portholes. The *Nautilus* left the mysterious island behind and cut across the water into dark and uncharted seas. His own war against human hatred and bloodshed was an all-consuming struggle, a war so big that he knew it could never be won ... still, the battle had to be fought.

Yet, the war he had just discovered between the Old Ones and Cthulhu was so much vaster, so much more ancient, so much more inconceivable that his own puny struggle against the evils of man seemed laughably trivial in comparison.

But it was his struggle, and it was all Nemo had left. "Yes, Mr. Harding, we will continue our war." He lowered his voice. "Even if it doesn't matter to the rest of the universe."

The *Nautilus* cruised away from the nightmarish island, toward the normal trade routes, continuing the hunt.

EIGHTY LETTERS, PLUS ONE
(WITH SARAH A. HOYT)

Letter #1

September 30, 1872
London, England

My dearest Elizabeth,

I leave this note for you, as the house was empty when I came home to pack. Doubtless you're out enjoying a quaint diversion with your women friends. As for me, I am unexpectedly off to the Suez, my dear. I've been dispatched to intercept a notorious thief who stole fifty thousand pounds from the Bank of England.

The villain is sure to leave the country and use his ill-gotten fortune to live extravagantly abroad. Detectives have been dispatched, one to each major port, and I have been chosen to keep a sharp eye on all British travelers who come through the Suez. I have a clear description of the thief, a well-dressed man with fine manners. Should I find him, I will shadow him till a warrant can be dispatched.

I'm sorry to leave you with nothing more than a note on this, our first anniversary, particularly since you never had the proper wedding you deserved. I still feel a bit of remorse over our brash elopement to Gretna Green, but you know your parents would never have consented to our love match. I still remember how haughtily your mother said that, because I need to work for a living, I should come in through the tradesman's entrance.

I trust you will keep a stiff upper lip while I'm away. The bank has offered a substantial reward to the detective who captures the thief, and I am convinced I'll get him if he comes my way. All that's needed in law enforcement these days is flair. You have to know how to nose these vermin out. And I, of course, I have excellent flair. As I've told you many times, I have a veritable sixth sense for these things.

Two thousand pounds will allow us to buy a better home and to hire a servant to do the house work for you. I know you expect such things out of life. It will also prove to your parents that, though you disobeyed them, you were ultimately right to choose me as your husband.

Meanwhile, I will write to you every day I possibly can. I'm sure you'll hardly notice I'm gone.

Yours, with much love,

Herbert Fix

Inspector, First grade

Letter #9

October 9

Suez, Egypt, Africa

My dear Elizabeth,

Good news! After all these days of waiting, the thief has finally come to the Suez.

Today, when the steamer *Mongolia* docked at the quay in Suez, I spotted a passenger forcing his way through the clamoring and stinking crowd of locals. You would not believe the mob of natives and black Africans that press around every passenger, offering to sell monkeys, unguents, jewelry, and the most grotesque pagan idols. One wretch even had the temerity to offer me some ground mummy which, he said, would strengthen my virile parts! I shudder to think, my dear, of you having to witness such sights.

By great luck, the fellow who came out of the *Mongolia* was in search of a government official. He nosed his way directly to me and held out a passport, for which he wished to procure a visa from the British consul. He was a wiry, dark-haired Frenchman, but he carried an Englishman's passport—his master's. Of course, I immediately glanced at the passport, and the description was exactly that of our thief! I could do no less than try to stop the man.

I told my suspicions to the consul and begged him to delay this man until I could get my arrest warrant. To my great disappointment, however, the consul said that I had no proof the traveler—Phileas Fogg—was guilty of any crime, and that without such proof he could not be detained.

I must therefore follow this rogue to his next stop, which is Bombay. I have talked to his servant, Passepartout—a good sort of fellow, but French and therefore garrulous. The man is convinced his master means to circle the globe to win a preposterous bet. Apparently, the cunning devil made a wager with the gentlemen in his club that he could go completely around the world in a mere eighty days. With my keen intellect, I realized immediately that this outrageous boast is nothing more than cover for his escape with the stolen money.

Hoping to pry more information from the talkative Frenchman, I took him on a shopping expedition to the bazaar. There, merchants offer all types of goods, including a very expensive perfume called Attar of Roses, of which a single drop can be mixed with oil or water to make many concoctions prized by the local ladies. Since you are always in my thoughts, I meant to buy you a dram of it. I also saw a fly swatter made from an elephant's tail, which I thought might amuse you. But, as I'm sure you'll understand, I had scarcely any time for frivolous purchases

Passepartout wished to obtain new shirts and other accouterments for his master. Due to the haste with which they left London, they had brought no more luggage than a carpetbag! Tell me, what man—not a thief and not in possession of fifty thousand pounds—would thus abandon his home and everything in it?

The loquacious Frenchman continually bemoaned the fact that he had left the gas burning in his room and that his master wouldn't allow him so much as a moment to run back to turn it off. This is not the natural behavior of a man who truly intends to return home.

I have applied for a warrant, which should catch up with us in Bombay. My dear Elizabeth, the reward money is as good as ours. I have not had the time to pick up any souvenirs for you just yet, but I am sure to buy you something in Bombay once the villain Fogg has been arrested.

Yours affectionately,

Herbert Fix

Letter #20

October 20th, 1872

Bombay, British India

My dear Elizabeth,

Here I am, once more, fulfilling my promise of writing a letter a day to you. I will also post at once the letters I wrote aboard the steamer.

Unfortunately, we have made such rapid progress—Fogg bribed the owner of the liner to have the engine stoked with extraordinary zeal—that my warrant is not yet with the police here. I am more certain than ever of my quarry's guilt. What man but a fleeing criminal would throw away money in such a way?

Only those who have not had to work for their income view it as of little importance. I know you do not like it when I speak of the extravagance of the lace on your sister's gowns, but were it not for your parents' private, she would surely weigh her expense more carefully and not burden herself with so much expensive frippery.

But worry not, my dear. Soon you'll be able to afford dresses as good or better than hers. In fact, time permitting, I might pick up some fabric in Bombay, which is a city of goodly size and filled with all manner of strange things.

The streets are extraordinarily crowded with dark people attired in cotton robes. On the way to the police station, I saw a man who lay completely at ease upon a bed of sharp nails. Imagine! I also saw a man hypnotize a deadly snake by playing his flute.

I'm rather upset at not having received the warrant yet, but you may be confident in my abilities, my dear. Rest assured— Phileas Fogg, who really has no intention of going around the world, will no doubt remain several days here, which will certainly be sufficient time for me to arrest him. Meanwhile, maybe I'll find you an appropriate gift ... perhaps some silk with which the native women wrap themselves. Something called, as I understand it, a sari.

Oh, I almost forgot to acknowledge that I received your letter, which had been forwarded from Suez to the consulate at Bombay and which, vexingly, made it to town when the warrant didn't.

It is extraordinarily kind of you to say that you'd gladly forego the two thousand pounds for the sake of having me near you again. Your female emotionalism is quite charming, in its own way, but I know you are not serious. If I obeyed you, I have no doubt you'd soon resent our poverty.

And, more importantly, I cannot let the villain Fogg go unpunished.

Bear my absence with fortitude, for I'm sure the arrest

warrant will come soon, and I'll return to you in glory and bearing the reward money that will start your climb back to the sphere you abandoned in order to marry me.

With my regards,

Herbert Fix

Letter #21

October 21st, 1872

Dear Elizabeth,

The warrant is not yet here. I write in haste and frustration. It turns out that Phileas Fogg intended to leave Bombay for Calcutta via the Great Peninsular railway. I was at the point of stepping into another train carriage, when Fogg's servant Passepartout arrived breathless, hatless, barefoot, and bearing the marks of a scuffle.

Though I fear you'll reproach me for my rudeness, I confess that I eavesdropped on the conversation between him and his master. The Frenchman had lost his shoes and barely escaped after violating the sanctity of a heathen pagoda on Malabar Hill—which is forbidden to Christians (or, at any rate, to anyone wearing shoes).

I was, as I said, on the point of stepping into the train carriage when I realized that, rather than waiting for the warrant from England—which might not reach us in time—I could simply find the temple and give the heathen priests the name and destination of their transgressor. Then *they* could press charges.

You see, the British authorities are extraordinarily careful never to offend the native religions—it is part of keeping control over this great uncivilized mob—and therefore, what that fool Passepartout did was an offense before British law. I'll get a warrant for that crime, too, then meet them at Calcutta, and have both men properly arrested.

I will write to you soon and announce the date of my return home with the reward money.

Yours, in haste,

Herbert Fix

Letter #25

October 25th, 1872
Calcutta, British India

Dear Elizabeth,

At last Fogg and his servant have arrived. I was in some anxiety that something had befallen them in the jungle as they crossed the subcontinent. I could not stop thinking of the thief and all those bank notes rotting away in the verdant wildness of India, and my reward unclaimed! I was truly in despair—but now they've arrived at last, and the magistrates had them arrested at the train. Everything was going so well.

Unfortunately, Fogg bought his way out of the situation by posting an exorbitant bail of two thousand pounds, as if it were nothing. *Two thousand pounds*—the same amount that could have made the two of us comfortable for so long, thrown out like so much rubbish!

As I've said before, money that one has not earned is easy to discard.

Sadly, it appears that the thief will escape once more, and I must continue my relentless pursuit, even if it takes me all the way around the world. He is boarding the *Rangoon*, which lays at anchor and is to depart in an hour for Hong Kong.

I have no choice but to follow, despite your half dozen letters imploring me to come home, which I recently collected from the consulate. Again, your letters have safely made the passage, while the desperately needed warrant lingers somewhere on the way. Bureaucracy can be truly exasperating.

My greatest worry now is that Fogg is flinging money about with such abandon that the reward—being a fixed percentage of the recovered money—is shrinking visibly before my eyes.

I'm sure it will still be enough to make you happy.

I shall get him in the British colony of Hong Kong. Fogg and Passepartout are now traveling with a beautiful and clearly genteel young lady they picked up somewhere in the jungles of India. I suspect an elopement, and though you might call it unworthy of me—considering that we also eloped—I should be able to arrest Fogg for *that*, too, because elopement, until sanctified by marriage, can be prosecuted as a crime. I will question Passepartout for details about this woman.

Yours,

Herbert Fix

Letter #37

November 6th, 1872
Hong Kong

Elizabeth,

We are arrived in Hong Kong after much adventure. In your letters you expressed the wish that you could join me in my pursuit. You must realize that this traveling abroad, though exhilarating for a man, would be much too demanding for a delicate woman such as yourself. You are much happier at home.

Just before we landed we met with a hurricane, the greatest storm I've ever seen. It was as if the heavens themselves were on my side, whipping the seas and the wind into a frenzy to delay us. And while I was gripped by the most horrible nausea, I hoped we'd have to turn and run before the squall, which would slow our journey to Hong Kong. This made it more likely the warrant would arrive, and it would also disrupt whatever plans this scoundrel has for escaping the law.

Alas, the vessel braved it, and we made landfall shortly after.

Meanwhile, I learned that the relatives of the mysterious woman are not likely to chase Fogg for besmirching her honor. Auda is a mere native, despite her pale skin—an Indian princess, whom Passepartout and Fogg supposedly rescued from being burned with her husband's body, a barbarous tradition of immolation. Now she is traveling with them.

They have already reserved berths on the *Carnatic*, which was scheduled to depart tomorrow for Yokohama. But I met Passepartout on his way from the quay to his master's hotel, and he told me the *Carnatic* has unexpectedly changed its departure time to this evening instead. The Frenchman was in a great hurry to tell Fogg about it, but I waylaid the simple-minded and naïve servant and got him intoxicated in an opium den, a very common establishment in these parts

The man will sleep for at least a day, till long after the *Carnatic* has sailed. I am sure Fogg will not leave without his man. If my plan succeeds in delaying them, I shall go to the embassy and see if there are any forwarded letters from you.

Yours,

Herbert Fix

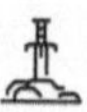

Letter #45

November 14th, 1872
Yokohama, Japan

Elizabeth,

Once more I write in haste. Fogg, having missed the *Carnatic*, engaged a small sail boat, the *Tankedere*—and he allowed me to travel with him. He does not even suspect that I am his nemesis! And Passepartout refuses to believe his master might be a thief. Either he is a wily accomplice, or a fool.

It is maddening to be so near him for so long and yet not to have the warrant that would stop him in his tracks. But there is nothing for it, as we're no longer in British territory. My only hope now is that he'll indeed go around the world in such a fashion hoping to confuse pursuers. I shall arrest him as soon as he lands in England again. Fogg intends to pursue travel to America aboard the *General Grant*.

I've already engaged a cabin in the *General Grant*, and I've now read the latest batch of your letters which, if you'll forgive me, are rather tiresome in your insistence that I return to you at once. I have a job to do. Despite the rate at which this scoundrel is spending the stolen money, think of the renown his capture will bring me, and how much easier it will make my rise in the world.

Only minutes ago, I saw Passepartout being dragged into the boat by Fogg. Passepartout wore a most extraordinarily fanciful oriental uniform, with wings and a false nose which would have sufficed for a family of twelve. People on deck say this is a costume worn in theater for the glory of some god or other. Foolish native habits and abominable idolatry, of course, and one wonders how even a Frenchman could bear to mix himself in it.

While I take a moment to catch my breath, let me tell you something about Yokohama. It is a city of good size, and the native quarter is lit by many-colored lanterns. There are astrologers everywhere using fine telescopes. Scientific instruments to enhance their superstition. Most ironic. For fun, I thought about having a horoscope cast for you—an unusual and exotic gift—but I had no time to delay. I must catch Fogg.

Sincerely,

Herbert Fix

Letter #64

December 3rd, 1872
San Francisco, United States of America

Elizabeth,

We are in San Francisco, the wild city of 1849, with its bandits, incendiaries, and assassins who all came here in the Gold Rush. The city looks more civilized than you'd expect, with a lofty tower in the town hall and a whole network of streets and avenues. It also has a Chinese town, that you'd swear came from China itself.

We found ourselves caught in the middle of some incomprehensible political rally—a dispute for the post of Justice of the Peace involving two men—and soon it turned into a brawl. I could not make heads nor tails of it, nor why anyone would seek to harm anyone else over such a silly squabble. I think these Americans are just hot-tempered.

In the turmoil, I actually protected Fogg from what might have been a disabling blow. Don't worry. Other than my clothes, nothing was hurt. Fogg insisted on buying me new garments, which are of a quality and cut to which even your parents could not object.

In your latest letters you reproached me for my "despicable Opium plot." I must say that you simply don't understand the business of men. Some deeds, though unpleasant, are necessary. Don't concern yourself about the matter any further.

You'll be heartened to know I'm now wholeheartedly working to speed Fogg's travel. Indeed, now that the thief is heading back to England, I am more than glad to help him. The sooner he gets there, the sooner I can arrest him. (And be back home with you, of course.)

And now we are to catch a train on the Pacific Railroad, headed for New York, from where we shall sail for London. I must rush to the train, so I don't lose sight of Fogg.

Herbert Fix

Letter #70

December 11th, 1872
New York, United States

Elizabeth,

Sorry for not writing for two days. Ran out of paper. You'd never believe what we've done in our trip across the United States. We rushed over a bridge mere moments before it collapsed, and in the process we'd gotten up such a head of steam that we didn't even stop until we'd passed the station! Then there was a herd of animals so large that they impeded the movement of the train. We had to wait until the beasts moved before the train could pass. Only imagine! The Americans call them buffalo, though Fogg said that such a classification is absurd. Not sure why.

The wonders of this continent! This world!

At one point, Fogg nearly engaged in a gunfight duel with another passenger, but they were interrupted by an attack from the savage Sioux, who kidnaped three passengers, including Passepartout—which, naturally, necessitated a rescue. Afterward, we caught an express train at Omaha station. Fogg, apparently imagining the demons of justice after him, is not fond of sightseeing, only rushing onward and onward. All the better, for that means I'll collect my reward sooner.

Now we've reached New York at last—but alas the vessel in which we expected to cross the Atlantic sailed forty-five minutes before our arrival. Fogg will no doubt find some boat to purchase or coerce. I very much fear there's not much money left out of the fifty thousand pounds he stole, but I shall still reap fame for apprehending him. Wouldn't you like to be the wife of a hero?

Herbert Fix

Letter #80

December 21
Friday
Liverpool

Elizabeth,

We have made landfall, and I served Phileas Fogg with the warrant, but—how could misfortune befall me so? After all my labors, after pursuing him round the world, I am not to enjoy success. Despite every indication, it appears that Fogg is not the thief after all, for the man who actually stole the fifty thousand pounds was apprehended three days ago, whilst I was traveling!

Worse, that upstart Passepartout punched me when he learned my true purpose in accompanying them on their long journey. Now I am bruised and tired, humiliated, disappointed—but at least I'm home, where doubtless you'll be waiting for me.

Herbert Fix

[On embossed letterhead identifying it as belonging to the law firm of Everingham, Entwhistle and Brown—on the fireplace mantel of Fix's home.]

London
December 18th of 1872

Dear Mr. Herbert Fix,

This letter serves to notify you that your wife, the honorable Elizabeth Rose Merryweather Fix, has returned to her parents' home and is suing you for divorce on the grounds of abandonment.

Our client has further instructed us to inform you that she did not object to your poverty or even your low upbringing, but she cannot forgive your obsession with career at the expense of her peace of mind and felicity. She further instructs us to inform you that you married her under false pretenses, always having characterized your marriage as a love match, when it is clear you love nothing more than your reputation and the pursuit of your own ambitions.

Lord and Lady Merryweather advise you to pose no argument and seek no reconciliation with their daughter, as they have the means to see you dismissed from your employment.

Sincerely

Nigel Entwhistle, Esquire

I've been friends with Sherrilyn Kenyon for more than twenty years. Sherri has written stories for my Blood Lite *anthologies, and we've often discussed collaborating.*

Christopher Golden was given the task of bringing together big-name collaborators for his Dark Duets *anthology (HarperCollins), he asked me who I might have in mind for my partner in a super teamup. The answer was obvious to me, and Sherri readily agreed when I made the suggestion.*

I started with a fascinating premise. I asked her, "Who lives under bridges?" She said, "Homeless people." I said, "And what else lives under bridges?" She thought for a moment. "Oh!"

This story started out as a horror story, but evolved into something much more mythic and far different from what either of us expected.

TRIP TRAP
(WITH SHERRILYN KENYON)

He huddled under the bridge and hid from the world outside, as he had done for as long as he could remember ... No, he could *remember* a time before that, but he didn't like those thoughts, and he buried them away whenever they appeared.

The bridge was old and unimpressive, long ago marred by spray-painted graffiti, mostly faded now. The county road extended from an Alabama state highway and crossed over a creek that was more of a drainage ditch, overrun with weeds and populated with garbage tossed out from the occasional passing car. Brambles, dogwoods, and tall milkweed grew high enough to provide some shelter for his lair.

Skari lurked in the shadows next to piled cans, mud-encrusted debris he had hauled out of the noisome drainage ditch, a bent and discarded child's bicycle (struck by a car). A stained blanket provided very little warmth and no softness, but he clung to it nevertheless. It was *his*. All the comforts of home.

He had a shopping cart with a broken wheel, piled high with the few possessions he had bothered to keep over ... over a long time. He hunched his back against the rough concrete abutment, shifting position. The dirt and gravel beneath him was a far cry from a grassy, flower-strewn meadow he sometimes saw in his dreams. He didn't belong in meadows anymore—just here in the shadows, standing watch at the nightmare gate. He had to guard it. Skari wouldn't leave his post.

The tall milkweed rustled aside, and he looked up at the freckled face of a skinny little girl. "I see you there," she said. "Are you a troll?"

Skari tensed, half-rose from his crouch. Many layers of tattered and filthy clothing covered his skin, masked his monstrous features. The girl just blinked at him.

"What are you doing here?" When he inhaled a quick breath, through the humidity and the odors of the drainage ditch, he could smell the little girl. The tender little girl.

"My brother says you're a troll, 'cause trolls live under bridges. You're living under a bridge," the girl said. "So, are you a troll?"

Yes, he was, but she didn't know that. In fact, no one was allowed to know that. "No. Not a troll," he lied.

She smelled tender, savory, juicy.

"Come closer."

The girl was intrigued by him, but she hesitated. She was smart enough for that at least.

Skari squeezed his eyes shut and drove his head back against the concrete abutment of the bridge. Again. The pain was like a gunshot through his skull, but at least it drove away the dark thoughts. Sometimes it just got so lonely, and he got so hungry here. He'd been thinking about eating children, tasty children ... thinking about it altogether too much.

With a crash through the underbrush, a boy came down the embankment. Her brother. He looked about nine, a year or two older than the girl. Both were scrawny, their clothes hand-me-downs but still in much better condition than Skari's. The children did have a raggedness about them, though, a touch of loss that had not yet grown into desperation. That would come in time, Skari knew ... unless he ate them first.

Next to his sister, the boy made a grimace and said with a

taunting bravery that only fools and children could manage, "I think you're a troll. You smell like a troll!"

Skari leaned forward, lurched closer to the edge of the shadow, and the children drew back, but remained close, staring. "Methinks you smell yourself, boy."

Rather than hearing the threat, the boy giggled. "*Methinks?* What kind of word is *methinks*?" He added in a singsong voice, "Methinks 'methinks' is a stupid word."

Skari grumbled, ground his teeth together. His gums were sore. He picked at them with a yellowed fingernail. No wonder witches ate children. His stomach rumbled. It was sounding like a better and better idea to him.

He wanted to lunge out from the gloom, but he knew the nightmare gate was there somewhere behind him, just waiting for him to let down his guard. Skari had been assigned here to stand watch, *sentenced* to stay here.

For many centuries, evil had bubbled up from the depths of the world, and the nightmare gates through which demons traveled always appeared underneath bridges. Skari couldn't leave his post, had to stay here and protect against anything that might come out. It made no sense to him why a vulnerable spot might appear under this small county-road bridge in northern Alabama, but it was not for Skari to understand. He hadn't felt the evil gate in some time, although there was plenty of evil in *him*.

"How long have you been there, Mister?" asked the girl.

"Longer than you've been alive."

A car peeled off the highway and drove along the county road. Its engine was loud and dyspeptic, one tire mostly flat so that as the car crossed the bridge overhead, it made a staccato *trip-trap-trip-trap-trip-trap.*

"What's your name?" the boy asked, as if it were his turn to dare.

His name. Yes, he had a name. Other people had called him by name, laughed with him, even a beautiful maiden who had once whispered it in his ear. But not anymore. He had no friends, no home, just what he clung to under this bridge where he stood guard.

But he did have a name. "Skari."

"Scarey Skari!" the boy shouted, and the girl laughed with him.

"Come closer!" He was so hungry for those children, so anxious to emerge into the sunlight again, even though it would cause him pain, make him twist and writhe. Skari grew ill from the very thought. It might be worth the pain, though, just for a bit of freedom … or maybe just for a taste of fresh meat.

"Billy! Kenna! Leave the poor man alone."

The two children whirled, startled. They looked as if they'd been caught at something.

Their mother came up, a woman on the edge of thirty, her brown hair pulled back into a ponytail. She wore no makeup, but her face was washed clean. Her clothes also had that worn look to them.

"He's a troll, Ma—he lives under a bridge," said the girl, Kenna.

"He smells," said Billy.

The mother looked mortally embarrassed, rounded up the two as she peered under the bridge where Skari huddled with all his possessions. "I am so incredibly sorry they disturbed you. What can I say?" She hauled the children out of the weeds, maybe to keep them safe from him. "They both flunked home training, but it wasn't from lack of effort on my part."

She sounded conversational, a forced friendliness, as if she felt they had something in common.

"Why does he live under a bridge, Ma?" Kenna asked.

Skari was startled to see the woman hesitate. A bright sheen of tears suddenly appeared in her eyes. "Just be thankful we don't live there."

He heard the unspoken *Yet* in her voice.

"It's all right," Skari said. "They weren't bothering me." His stomach growled, but not loudly enough for anyone else to hear.

"I've been called worse than smelly ... and that by my own family."

"Well, I appreciate your understanding. I'm Johanna. It was nice meeting you."

She seemed uncomfortable, backing down the embankment, protecting her children—and good thing. She didn't want them talking to strangers, especially ones who hid under bridges. Especially trolls.

The air was full of the whine of insects, laden with ozone. Overhead, dark thunderheads clotted. If a downpour came, it would make the humidity more tolerable for a while.

"We need to get back to the car, kids," Johanna said. "It's the only shelter we've got."

"I don't want to go back and sit in the car, Ma! It's hot."

"Been there for days. There's nothing to do," Billy added. "When are we gonna keep driving?"

"As soon as we get gas money. Somebody'll come by."

Whenever Skari saw people, they were from the cars that stopped at the rest area on the highway next to the bridge. It had beige metal picnic tables, trash cans, running water, restrooms, and not much else. Not even traffic. Skari had seen vehicles come and go, and most of them didn't stay long, but now he remembered a rusted station wagon piled with belongings. It had been there a while. He thought he'd heard a loud muffler, a struggling engine, tires crunching gravel, doors slamming—two nights ago? Johanna and her children probably had a hand-written sign on a scrap of cardboard asking for help with gas money or food.

Skari tried to remember how to make conversation. Some part of him didn't want the family to go away ... not yet. "Are you having trouble, ma'am?"

"No ... yes ... maybe."

"Which is it?"

"All of the above. But it's my problem. Don't trouble yourself."

Skari glanced behind him, sensed the nightmare gate. But the barrier was strong, stable—as it had been for many years.

Nothing was trying to get through right now. He ambled closer to her, taking comfort in the thunderclouds that muted the afternoon sunlight.

"We don't got a home no more," Kenna said. "The mean man made us leave."

"What mean man?"

Their mother let out a heavy sigh. "We were evicted. I lost my job a year ago and haven't been able to find another one. I used up my savings, and we're trying to make it to Michigan where my cousin lives."

"Michigan?" He didn't have much familiarity with maps anymore, but he did understand that Michigan was a long way from northern Alabama.

"We'll manage somehow," the mother said. Fat raindrops started to strike the ground. "We just need a little to get by, step by step. If we make it to Michigan, we can have a fresh start." Her expression tightened, as if she had forgotten about him entirely. "We'll find a way to survive."

Before he could stop himself, Skari blurted out, "It's not so bad. You and the girl could live off the fat of the boy for at least three days."

Johanna's eyes widened, and she drew back, startled. Billy thought it was a joke and he nudged his sister. "They wouldn't want me anyway. Girls are the ones made out of sugar and spice and everything nice."

Skari's stomach rumbled. "Don't believe too many fairy tales."

The rain began falling in earnest, thick drops pattering and hissing all around them like whispered laughter. Johanna grabbed the two children. "Come on, back to the car!" She flashed a glance over her shoulder, then ran with a squealing Kenna and Billy off to the rest area.

Skari went back under his bridge, took up his post at the long-sealed nightmare gate, and watched the world as the rain washed the scent of children from the air.

Water ran down the side of the bridge, trickles turning his dank and gloomy lair into a soupy mess. Skari just huddled there. The bugs seemed to enjoy it, though. Even after the storm stopped, leaving only leftover droplets wrung out from the sky, he heard frogs wake up in the creek. Something splashed in a puddle farther downstream. It wasn't yet full dark, but the clouds hadn't cleared.

All the burbling background noise masked the sound of stealthy footsteps, and the fresh rain covered the girl's scent until she appeared. "Mister Skari, are you hungry?"

He was startled. The appetite became ravenous within him. Was she taunting him? He could lunge out right now, grab her before she could run, use his dagger to break her up into delectable pieces, roast her meat over a fire and have a feast. But after the rain, he'd never be able to build a fire. No matter, he was hungry enough to eat her raw.

Skari slammed his head against the abutment again to drive away the thoughts. No, *no*! The hungers, the dark desires had always been gnawing in him, but he could fight them back. He could ... he *could*!

Kenna extended a rumpled white paper sack. "I brought hamburgers. Do you like fast food?"

No, I don't like fast food. I want something slow enough I can catch!

"Hamburgers?" he asked, his voice a croak.

"Somebody gave them to us at the rest area. They're leftovers. Mostly good, but the fries are cold and soggy. I wanted to offer you the last one. Ma doesn't know I'm here." She extended the sack closer, and with a quick movement he might have been able to snatch her wrist. "It's still fine. Only a bite taken out of it."

With a sense of wonder, Skari took the sack and pulled it open. An explosion of wondrous smells struck him in the face. His mouth watered. He was so hungry!

He stuffed the burger into his mouth, fished around with his paws in the bottom of the bag to grab every small, withered French fry. "Thank you," he said, his words muffled around the food. Tears stung his eyes.

He remembered feasting with some of the other warriors, a delicious banquet thrown by the victorious lord after a particularly long and bloody battle. They had slain countless scaly demons that day, driven them back through the nightmare gate and barricaded it under a stone bridge. Skari remembered how much blood there was in the air on the battlefield, how the smoking black demon blood had a sour acid smell, unlike the vibrant freshness of the roasted boar in the lord's firepit, unseasoned meat shimmering with grease. He and his fellow foot soldiers had eaten the celebratory feast, drinking the lord's best wine and his cheapest ale. It was all so delicious!

That was before Skari had failed, before he had been cursed ... before he'd been given this sacred duty.

He finished the food now, licked his crusted lips, and straightened, searching for his scraps of pride and memory as desperately as he looked for more fries.

"Is this your stuff?" Kenna was rummaging in his shopping cart, moving aside the piled possessions he had gathered over the years, decades ... centuries.

He sucked in his breath. He didn't dare let her find his weapons, the spell-sealed dagger. "Get away from there!" The girl jerked back. "You shouldn't be here. Go back to your mother, your family." He raised himself up, and Kenna looked awed and terrified as Skari grew and swelled, an ominous lurching shape under the bridge. She backed away, stumbling in the weeds. Skari lowered his voice, speaking more to himself than to her. "You have a family. Don't forget that."

She ran back to their forlorn station wagon, and he heard her crying, which made his heart heavy. Another stone of guilt, another failure, another thing to atone for. But Kenna had her brother, her mother ... a mother who actually cared for her children.

Skari's mother hadn't been like that. When he'd run away to fight in the demon wars, he'd been cocky, full of false bravado, sure that no nightmare monster breaking out of hell could be worse than the shrewish woman who had beaten him, starved him at home.

He'd been so wrong about that.

For a while, his comrades had become his family. The clerics had blessed them all, the noblemen had armed them, the wizards provided magical talismans with blades dipped in bloodsilver that could strike down demons.

In the first two engagements, Skari had been out of the fray, far from where the monsters boiled out from beneath the bridge. Warlords and armed warriors had fought the slavering demons, while clerics and wizards struggled to seal and barricade the nightmare gate. Skari was terrified, but uninjured—and the war went on.

In the third battle, though, when the fanged and clawed monsters turned, charging into the pathetic group of Skari and his friends, he watched his best comrade Torin die. He was a baker's boy from the same village ... they'd run off together—and Skari saw the demons tear him apart, twisting Torin's arms and legs from his torso like the bones from a well-roasted quail carcass. Another demon had bitten off Hurn's head. The long-haired tanner's apprentice had feminine features and a cocky smile, and the fanged monster had opened its hinged jaws, engulfed the boy's entire head, bit down, then spat it out amidst a gout of foul breath. Hurn's head had struck Skari right in the chest.

He didn't remember dropping his sword or running screaming past all the other soldiers. Many hundreds of human soldiers had died that day, but the demons were driven back at an incredible cost of brave blood. Skari, though, was captured by the lord's men, found to be a coward, sentenced to be executed by a headsman's axe. But he was given a choice—a choice that he hadn't known was so terrible. The wizards offered him the opportunity to become the guardian of a sealed gate, to be made immortal, to stand watch in case the nightmare hordes ever tried to break free again.

Babbling, Skari had agreed. He dropped to his knees weeping, begging them to make him a guardian. He had not known that choice would be worse than simply dying.

Skari had lost his family, his friends, everyone and everything. He had been alone for centuries, moved from bridge to bridge when it was deemed necessary, when a new vulnerable spot appeared anywhere in the world.

"Your job is to protect mankind," the wizard had said.

The lord who stood before him had a grim, heartless face. He had lost a hand in the last battle. He had seen Skari run in terror from the monsters, and Skari knew he had earned his isolated eternity. His crime was not so great that he deserved hell itself, but bad enough for him to be sentenced to this purgatory. His fate, his *job*, was to protect humans against evil ... even though his close proximity to the nightmare gates had twisted him, too.

He could never let the evil escape again. He couldn't let it get to Johanna and her two children.

He turned to the bridge wall behind him where he could sense the simmering gate. It had been quiet, silent, but he dare not let his guard down. Dare not leave ... dare not have hope. He clenched his filthy, scabbed fist and hammered against the hard wall. "I hate you!" Nothing was worse than to be trapped alone where you didn't want to be.

While he kept the nightmare gate guarded, he thought of Kenna and Billy, homeless, penniless, cast out by a "mean man," vulnerable to human predators and unkind fate. Even if the demon wars were over, the darkness of human society was heartless, too. At least the demons were obvious enemies, and they could be defeated.

His thoughts kept going to the woman and her children. How could he defend against the troubles Johanna faced? The family was like the one he'd never had. Maybe that was another part of his punishment: to feel such helplessness after he'd begun to sense a connection. But what could he do?

We just need a little to get by, step by step, Johanna had said. *If we make it to Michigan, we can have a fresh start.*

As he thought of them, he sighed. They were the ones he

fought for. But if he simply ignored their very real, though not supernatural, plight, he might as well let the evil behind the nightmare gate eat them. It would be like running away from the battlefield, a coward again.

He went to his cart and dug through his cluttered possessions, the detritus and treasures piled and packed there … until he found the last two things he had from his original life in another time, another world: a thick gold medallion, one small ring, and a handful of silver coins, spoils from his first battlefields. The trinkets had amounted to a fortune even then, an even greater one today.

For centuries, he'd kept them safe. Now, they would help a young mother and her children reach safety.

It was full night now, and the nightmare gate seemed strong, stable. He sensed no whispers of evil back there, only emptiness. But he did feel the pain and the need of Johanna and her children.

Halfhearted rain began to fall as he trudged to the parking lot of the rest area. The station wagon was dark, closed up for the night as the family huddled there for shelter, safer and warmer than under a bridge. It was the only vehicle there. A single, white mercury light shed a pool of illumination over the picnic tables. A metal sign peppered with divots from shotgun pellets said NO OVERNIGHT PARKING—STRICTLY ENFORCED. But no one had bothered to enforce it for days.

Shambling forward, a looming shadow surrounded by deeper shadows, Skari approached the driver's side window and thumped on it. He heard a startled gasp from behind the glass, the children stirring. He saw a glint of the mother's eyes; she was concerned, ready to fight. In the darkness, they would be able to discern his gargantuan size, but unable to see his ugly twisted features, his scabrous skin.

He held up the pouch. "Didn't mean to scare you, ma'am. I just thought this would help you get on your way."

Johanna rolled down the window just enough for him to push the pouch through. She took it, and he turned, not wanting to speak with her, not waiting for her to see what he had given them.

Skari ambled back into the night, hurrying before any demons could discover the unguarded nightmare gate, before he would have to endure the mother telling him "Thank You."

No more than an hour later, as he sat in the damp gloom of his lair, Johanna, Billy, and Kenna appeared under the bridge, walking closer. They weren't afraid of him. The mother held the sack with the medallion, the ring, the old coins. "I can't take this."

"Yes, you can. Those things do me no good, but for you they can make the difference. Buy yourself a new chance." He tried to remember how to soften his words with humor. "It should keep you from having to eat the boy for at least a week."

She laughed, and her brow furrowed. "It'll keep us from living under a bridge." The boy and girl gathered closer, and they all looked at Skari. Johanna's face was tight, and he saw tears in her eyes. "This is the nicest thing anyone's ever done for us. Thank you."

The little girl burst forward, threw herself against him, and hugged him tight. "You're not a monster."

Billy nodded and said strangely, "You're saved. I'm glad we didn't have to kill you."

No sooner had the boy spoken than pain shot into Skari's body. He hissed as it burned through him, screaming through his muscle fibers. His skin began to boil and turn color. Underneath his layers of old, encrusted clothing, his body twisted in a spasm. He bent over, threw himself against the bridge abutment, and his mind rang with terror.

Were these people escaped demons? Had they come here to attack him? He staggered into his shopping cart, grabbed it. He had to get the bloodsilver dagger, defend himself, defend the world—but the cart crashed to one side.

Unable to stand the pain, Skari doubled over, dropped to the muddy, garbage-strewn ground—

And shrank in size. Confused, Skari looked at his hands that were no longer gnarled ugly paws. They were hands again. Human hands. He flexed his arms, pushed himself to his feet.

The mother and children stood before him, watching, but their eyes didn't look evil. In fact, they seemed glad ... relieved.

"The demon wars were over long ago," said Johanna. "The nightmare gates are permanently sealed, but after all this time, the *guardians* themselves have become dangerous."

Billy added, "Not only were you immortal, you became inhuman, too—so close to the darkness that it found a home in you."

"We've been sent to find the last few remaining trolls, to test them," Kenna said in a voice that did not belong to a little girl. "To see if they need to be destroyed, or if they have learned human decency and compassion. You, Skari, are one of the last. We were afraid for you."

Instead of the eyes of a little boy, Billy's eyes were hard and ancient. "But you convinced even me."

"You are free now," Johanna said. "The world is safe from demons ... and it is safe from you."

Kenna grinned, and her eyes sparkled. "We release you from your post."

Growing up in rural, small-town Wisconsin left its mark on me. I was surrounded by hilly fields of corn, cabbage, or soybeans; I climbed trees and rode my bicycle into town on errands. My neighbors were all cousins, and many of my friends were farmers. Over the course of my career, as shown in the contents of these collections, I've written many stories set in the weird Wisconsin town of Tucker's Grove.

I did this story of two quirky characters, a pair of warm-hearted circus freaks from a traveling carnival, people who want to fit in, and they see the homey small town as a place where they might find acceptance. But since I remember so many times from my youth when I was the "weird kid" who read books and comics, who wanted to be a writer, I knew that it wasn't so easy to find acceptance if you weren't just like other normal people.

There's a bittersweet tone to this tale, because while I found much of that environment supportive and heartwarming, I also experienced how unwelcoming and narrow-minded they could be to anyone who didn't fit into their neat mold. Sometimes it can be a circus....

JUST LIKE NORMAL PEOPLE

Pestilence had spread across the acreage adjacent to the road, through the hilly cornfields half a mile back, and all along the barbed wire fence lines. It looked as if the Grim Reaper had flown over at midnight and shaken the bad blood off his scythe blade, letting droplets poison the ground.

After years of producing nothing but horrors as crops, the farmer and his family had split up and fled Wisconsin in their separate directions, abandoning the land to seek a normal farm and a normal life.

For a pittance, Collier & Black's Traveling Circus and Sideshows had rented one of the vacant fields.

As the sun thought about setting and the muggy air hoarded its heat, the roustabouts set up tents and rides and midway games and concessions. The sideshow wagons pulled into their slots. The birds and bugs had quieted down for the afternoon; mosquitoes would soon be coming out in full force.

A few people from Tucker's Grove had driven by in old pickups on the county trunk road, slowing down to take a glance, then speeding up as they saw the surly looking strangers pitching the tents and stringing the lights—not the type of people normal folks wanted to be seen with. Some farmhands might finish their chores and creep over to get a preview after dark, but most would wait until crowds and daylight made it safe to look around....

Two of the sideshow freaks hiked away from the main activity with their own peculiar gaits, heading toward the blighted cornfields, as if drawn there. The two had been together a long time, and they knew how to walk side by side, adjusting to each other's pace. Scarecrow remained silent, while his companion jabbered, as always.

"Something ain't right around here," said the Raven, indicating the sick and stunted trees along the fence line with his stubby arm. He scampered ahead with a birdlike gait, jerking his elbows behind him and up in the air. Cocking his head, he added, *"Rawwwkk!"* for good measure.

The Raven's grotesquely outthrust face made him look like a surly bird. During shows he wore a costume adorned with black feathers, but even without the plumage his dark skin, his mannerisms, and his raucous voice kept him in character. In cut-off trousers for the humid heat, the Raven's short legs looked like drumsticks. His large eyes glinted black as he jerked his attention from one sight to another. "You know where we're going?"

Beside him, Scarecrow sighed. "No. I just want to be away from the sideshow for a while. I'm tired of getting stared at everyplace we go."

He looked into the rows of weirdly rotten corn: freakish corn, as misshapen as he and the Raven. Purple-gray blobs of smut oozed from the cornstalks. One of the ripe ears had split open, showing sharp kernels like the yellowed teeth from an old skull.

Scarecrow shambled along, flopping his many-jointed arms and legs in the choreographed jittery walk he had learned to master. Tall and gangly, he wore patchwork clothes, mussed his blond hair, and seesawed too much as he moved, like his namesake from *The Wizard of Oz*. But his sunken skull-face and dead-man's skin made no one look at him as a lovable buffoon.

All summer long as the circus worked its way across the Midwest, both he and the Raven would wander around the midway before and after their scheduled appearances in the sideshow tent, handing out leaflets, fascinating the towners, and steering them toward particular shows. The two freaks were comic relief, horrid enough to titillate the customers into wondering what *else* might be lurking inside the sideshow tent.

Today though, with the roustabouts doing all the setup, Scarecrow and the Raven took the opportunity to blow the show for an evening. But Scarecrow wasn't certain if he wanted to come back. What, after all, would they really be leaving behind?

They passed a dead chokecherry tree so gnarled that it looked as if a huge hand had crumpled it. The bark writhed in the heat, contorting into silent screaming faces. The tall crabgrass hissed like a pit full of snakes. Virginia creepers had twisted into the rusty barbed wire fence, snapping the posts with slow violence.

Keeping his voice neutral, Scarecrow gestured into the cornfields, toward the low hills. "Let's go straight that way. The farmhouse should be over there."

He plunged into the rows of sharp, drooping cornstalks. When his arm brushed one of the ripe ears, the kernels burst like a line of boils, splattering yellow pus onto his patchwork clothing. A very odd place indeed.

The Raven leaped into the field, knocking down stalks and flapping his stubby arms. "Look! I'm doing your job for you, Scarecrow!"

He startled several crows, which flew toward the sanctuary of trees along the fence line. Through the fluttered blur of black wings, one of the crows appeared to have two heads.

Scarecrow watched but said nothing.

The dirt lane ended at a cleared yard where the nameless farmer had once lived. An old, dilapidated barn stood near the toppled carcass of a windmill, but only a foundation with burned timbers, broken glass, and scorched ground marked the former location of the farmhouse. The floor had caved in, showing the cellar to be an empty pit.

Scarecrow stared. The air was silent. He heard no birds. The sky bled orange with sunset, and the breeze died down.

"Over here!" the Raven said, hopping up and down beside the hulk of a tractor. One giant wheel had slumped off its axle and fallen to the ground. Black oil oozed from the crankcase into the dust. The rest of the body sagged under its coating of rust.

Flopping his arms and popping his knee joints, Scarecrow ambled over to the tractor. Behind it, a wide rake had been attached, the kind with hundreds of detachable tines used to roll new-mown hay into a long swath that a baler could scoop up. The rake was blood-rust brown, with globs of dust-clotted grease cementing it to the hitch of the tractor.

"Here, here!" The Raven cocked his head and jerked his protruding chin to indicate the rake's claws.

Though dead weeds and clumps of crabgrass covered the farmyard, every scrap of vegetation had been erased in a circular swath extending outward from the rear of the tractor, as if the plants had pulled up their roots and fled.

Scarecrow could not bend down the way other people did. Instead, he marshaled all of his joints and *folded* himself down closer to the ground, wrapping his body into a tighter package so that he could see.

One of the detachable tines was strikingly different, oozing a rainbow-colored light like an oil slick on a dirty parking lot. It was a smooth metal claw, a talon of steel designed to rip into the dirt and tear the soil free for the crops—but this one *felt* different from all the seemingly identical tines on the tractor rake. He touched the cold, weirdly slick metal, the center of the whirlpool of strangeness here. The curved tine seemed to pop off in his hand, jumping into his grasp as if it wanted to be free of its attachment. Scarecrow held it up to the failing light of sunset.

"What is it, Scarecrow? What did we find?"

Scarecrow could feel the fundamental oddness of the piece of metal. Was it a freak of nature? Had it been fashioned from a meteorite fallen from the sky? Or had it been dipped in human blood? Or forged by a blacksmith with murderous thoughts in his heart?

"Something that doesn't belong here," he said, caressing its edge with an extra-long finger. "I wonder if the farmer even knew about it."

Scarecrow held it as he stood up, unfolding and straightening himself, snapping joints into place until he was reasonably sure his body would hold him upright. Scarecrow could not understand it himself, but he felt a kind of affinity for the anomaly, the out-of-place metal. Something that normal people would never understand. "I think I'll take it with us."

The Raven looked toward the darkening sky, at the burned-out ruins of the farmhouse, at the distant field where the traveling circus had set up. "Shouldn't we ... get back?" he said. He cocked his eye at the dead spot on the ground, performing none of his antics now.

Scarecrow had no interest in returning just yet. "No." He nodded toward the barn. "Let's spend the night here."

Oil-stained rags had been tossed next to rusty coffee cans filled with equally rusty nails. Three empty bottles of Southern Comfort lay label-up in a corner. The upper loft held a dozen old bales of hay, their fresh green-tan turned gray with age.

The Raven scrambled up to the rafters and tucked himself into a V-brace, brushing fat spiders out of the way and wrapping one stubby arm around the beam. He stuck his distended face into his armpit and fell fast asleep.

Scarecrow lay down on the hard-packed dirt floor. He tossed and turned, finding little comfort, but enjoying himself nonetheless just to be spending a night away from the circus tents, the freaks' trailers, and the curious towners.

He clasped the prong-shaped piece of odd metal to his chest, as if it were a treasure, rubbing his many-jointed fingers along the slick surface, like Aladdin rubbing his lamp.

Scarecrow couldn't doze off: his mind crackled with images of the small Midwestern towns the circus had pulled through on its summer circuit, the homey, isolated villages so pleasant and so peaceful, the elm-lined main streets with white Victorian homes, the tire swings in the front yards, the town square with the hardware store and the drugstore and the independent grocer.

Scarecrow remembered in particular the churches, from the high-steepled Presbyterian or Lutheran buildings to the Catholic churches with long purple-prosy names. In Tucker's Grove, as the circus trucks and wagons passed down Main Street, the signboard in front of the Methodist church had caught Scarecrow's eye. "Sunday Service—All welcome." The phrase in quotes denoting that week's sermon read, "We are all God's children!" It struck him with the force of a hammer blow.

All welcome. He wondered if he could believe it. *We are all God's children!*

Scarecrow knew about the towners who came to gawk at the sideshows, laughing and pointing their fingers, saying the same crude comments—he and the Raven had to endure, continue to look freakish because that's what the towners paid to see. But after diverting themselves with the circus, the normal people could go to their normal homes, play their normal card games, listen to their normal radio programs, go to their normal churches.

He drifted on the surface of sleep, with vivid images sprouting in his mind like a bumper crop, and he saw *himself* without his freakish exterior, clothed instead in a normal body. He could have been a steadfast farmer, tall and blond like many of the Nordic settlers of the area, hardworking. He would have suntanned skin, and dirt under his fingernails, and a huge appetite for a home-cooked meal after a day working out in the fields or in the barn. He could have been a pillar of the community, not a leader but just a wholesome, honest worker like these other good folk.

Into his dreams came the Raven, too, but without the defective body-costume his genes had forced him to wear—Raven might have been an eccentric but friendly shopkeeper, maybe running the drugstore or the hardware store, a good-humored stout man who took in strays, fed birds, let kids build a treehouse in the big elm in his front yard....

As dawn brightened the sky, he felt his heart ready to burst with genuine longing and envy. Scarecrow knew he had seen what he and the Raven were really like inside, their true worth—and he was certain the townspeople would see it, too.

Scarecrow picked up a rock and hurled it toward the rafters. It clattered and bounced around the thick beams. The Raven awoke with a squawk and fell to the ground. Some instinct made him flap his stubby arms, as if he had forgotten that he couldn't fly. He landed with a thud and turned a somersault, opening and closing his mouth in silent gapes like a blind chick. "Whaaaaat?!"

Scarecrow tucked the wondrous metal tine into his patched pocket as if it were some sort of treasure; he was sure it had something to do with his vision, a funhouse mirror that brought reality into a clearer focus.

"Come on," he said. "It's Sunday. We're going to church."

They entered Tucker's Grove amid stares of horror, fear, and amazement—but Scarecrow and the Raven were used to stares. They had spent over an hour walking along the country roads, shuffling in the dandelion-choked gravel by the shoulder. A pickup truck roared by, and the driver hurled an empty beer can at them, which banged and clattered on the pavement.

Tucker's Grove Welcomes You! read the sign at the town limits, adorned with emblems of the various civic clubs, the Lions, the Rotarians, the Optimists.

The two companions passed along streets of quiet houses, then up Main Street, where the shops were all closed for Sunday morning. Above their heads, squirrels chattered in the branches of the elm trees. The center of the town drew Scarecrow like a magnet. The curved metal piece in his pocket pulled him along.

Finally, they stood on the well-maintained sidewalk of the white-washed Methodist church. Scarecrow imagined monthly church get-togethers, families spending a Saturday afternoon weeding, mowing the church lawn, trimming the bushes. A true sense of community and home, the way Scarecrow *should* have felt back at the circus and among the other sideshow people.

He touched the curved tine in his patched pocket. It felt slippery and cold even through the fabric, strange, unusual, wonderful…. Maybe he would offer it as an unexpected gift to the kind pastor in charge of this church, set it gleaming in the middle of the offering plate as it was passed from hand to hand. Scarecrow and the Raven could settle down, become part of Tucker's Grove, fit in like real members of the community.

The early church service had already begun. The congregation sang an opening hymn in a group voice that blurred the melody and the words. The organist lifted the singers along with the force of the music.

Scarecrow opened the door just as the congregation fell silent for the opening prayer. Most of the people did not turn around, focused on the service, thinking that perhaps some oversleeping member had arrived a few minutes late.

But children dressed in stiff, uncomfortable clothes squirmed to look at the freaks, eyes widening to the size of plates. The rest of the congregation did not notice until the pastor himself raised his head from the beginnings of a prayer. His jaw dropped, and he stopped in the middle of a word.

Scarecrow unfolded his long arm and then unfolded his index finger, indicating the outside. "All welcome," he said. His voice cracked.

This startled the pastor, and his expression changed, as if he found himself trapped by his duty. "Please find a seat," one of the ushers whispered. Scarecrow felt no warmth or welcome from the words.

The pastor raised his hands to the rest of the congregation. "Shall we continue our prayer?"

The people in the pews mumbled along, reading the words of a preprinted prayer in their bulletins. Scarecrow and the Raven went to the empty back pew closest to the door. The ushers stood at attention, perhaps hoping the two would go away. Tentatively, showing some fear, one usher handed Scarecrow a mimeographed bulletin that listed the order of hymns and prayers, a program for the sermon and offertory and benediction.

The pastor was a gray-haired man, clean-shaven, with wire-rimmed glasses that looked sharp on his face. Deep lines around his mouth made him appear to be pursing his lips like a chimpanzee. He finished his prayer and called out the next hymn just after the two newcomers sat down. Scarecrow sighed and went through the process of unfolding himself again to stand up. His many joints ached after having spent the night on the hard dirt floor.

Using his long fingers to shuffle through the pages of the hymnal from the pew pocket in front of him, Scarecrow located the proper hymn before the end of the first verse. Beside him, the Raven jostled and fidgeted, making harsh singing noises without paying much attention to the words.

The congregation members surreptitiously found excuses to turn around and glance at the two. A fat little boy picked his nose and flicked a booger toward the Raven, who lunged forward to catch it in his distended mouth. In the pew in front of them, a prim family shuffled toward the aisle, moving one row up and squeezing in with the already-crowded people there. The pew ahead of Scarecrow and the Raven stood empty, like a barrier between them and the others.

Scarecrow felt a stab of disappointment. They had both joined the circus because the normal world would not accept them, but the small Wisconsin towns had seemed so different, so welcoming, like a place from a fairy tale. An illusion.

The pastor began to read a passage from the Old Testament. It had something to do with demons and the devil walking among men, but Scarecrow found himself staring dreamily at the walls adorned with paper butterflies that had been cut out and finger-painted by Sunday School children. A bright poster said JESUS LOVES ME!

The pastor began his sermon, but his thoughts rambled, and Scarecrow could determine no point to the lecture. The pastor stuttered and lost his place several times, frequently glancing back toward the two newcomers. A sheen of sweat stood out on the man's forehead. Scarecrow felt a heavy ache in the pit of his stomach. Apparently, not everyone was welcome after all.

Raven fidgeted against the hard, wooden pew that was not conformed to his lumpy back. As he squirmed, he made cheeping noises that sounded too loud in the sanctuary.

The sermon ended, and the ushers marched up the aisles to take two offering plates from the pastor's extended hands.

Scarecrow fidgeted, realizing that neither of them had any money—but he took out the wondrous, otherworldly tine from his pocket. It would be a strange offering, but it would be magical. Something these people had never seen before. Maybe that would make everything better.

As soon as the Raven realized what the offering plates were for, he hopped to his feet, jerking his elbows up in the air. "Whaaat? They want us to pay?" He looked down at Scarecrow with his black-lacquer eyes. "It ain't even much of a show!" His voice was raucous and loud enough for everyone to hear. "Cheat! Cheat!"

A man stood up three rows in front of them. His face was livid below his greased hair. His suit had gone out of style a decade before. "I've had just about enough of this ... this sacrilege!" He seemed pleased to have an opportunity to use the portentous word. Several others spoke their agreement.

The ushers stopped their offertory and uncertainly marched toward the back, glancing at each other as if they had never dreamed they might have to act as bouncers. Soon most of the congregation was shouting.

The pastor banged his hands on the lectern for quiet and turned his attention to the freaks. "I think it would be best for you two to leave now," he said. His voice was low and menacing. "You've caused enough trouble in my church."

As he gripped the slick tine with his overlong fingers, Scarecrow heard an echo in his head, shadows of words, as if he could see into what the self-controlled pastor was actually thinking, the phrases the man really wanted to shout.

We hate you! You're too ugly, too strange! You are not wanted here. Go back where you belong, despicable freaks! You're loathsome. You're not NORMAL like we are.

Scarecrow stood, slowly unfolding himself from the hard pew. His long legs made him appear to be rising, rising, like a cobra from a snake charmers basket. The Raven hopped onto the pew seat, standing up and glaring at the congregation with his vulture-like face. Saying nothing to the pastor or the people, Scarecrow nodded to his companion, unable to express his disappointment. "Come on," he said, "let's go."

The Raven gave an excited caw and leaped over the back of the pew to the rear aisle. As they walked toward the church door, adjusting to each other's gait again, Scarecrow expected the people in the sanctuary to cheer. The larger usher followed them to the door, but the other merely stared in silence.

All welcome! If any sideshow in Collier & Black's tried such blatant false advertising, Scarecrow thought, the owner would be locked up for fraud.

⚔

The morning was fresh and full of sunshine as he and the Raven stepped outside. Behind them, the door closed, and Scarecrow heard the click of the lock. Muffled through the walls, the organist threw herself into playing a hymn so that the whole congregation could heave a joyous sigh of relief.

With the church barred behind them, Scarecrow and the Raven stared out at the masked town of Tucker's Grove. Few other man-made sounds came to them: an occasional car driving by, some people working outside, three children playing. Several blocks away, the Presbyterian and the Lutheran church would be having their services; Catholics would be at Mass. He and the Raven would have received a similar reception no matter where they had gone. *All* normal people *welcome.*

Slowly, feeling it cling to his fingers as if it had been coated with drying slime, Scarecrow pulled the metal tine out of his pocket. The curved shape gleamed like a claw in the humid air. The idea came into his mind, but he couldn't tell if it came from himself or ... something else.

The Raven hopped a step back. "Whatcha gonna do? Whaaaat?"

"I'm giving them a gift," he said. "A glimpse of something—a show like they've never seen before."

Scarecrow bent at the knees, extended his long body forward, and stretched his arm down to the ground. He thrust the sharp metal end into the manicured lawn with a sound like an ice pick going into meat.

He hesitated as other, innocent images came to him: church socials with kids and their parents, old people, teenagers laughing and working together, children squealing as they jumped into piles of leaves, bankers and dentists pulling up weeds, housewives serving up orange drink and almond windmill cookies to everyone. He thought of the congregation praying for each other when they grew sick, helping out when times were hard, laughing together at church craft fairs or bake sales or ice-cream socials.

Scarecrow dug the tine into the ground again, as if stabbing a sacrificial knife into the chest of a victim. He pulled the curved piece along as he took a step backward. The lawn and the dirt parted like flesh in a rotten fruit.

With his strangely sharpened vision he saw the tine open a bloody furrow in the earth, splitting the grass and leaving a pulsing red-purple wound that glittered with shadows. Heat and a lava-light rose from the gash with an odor like the breath from a furnace cooking spoiled meat.

"Follow me," he said, listening to his instincts, to what the unearthly artifact *wanted* him to do. He wondered at the destruction at the old farmstead, what sort of poisoned life the farmer had had and how he had been unable to bear seeing the veils slashed away.

With the Raven keeping his distance, Scarecrow worked his way backward across the lawn, ripping the gash open wider. He turned the corner and passed under the stained-glass windows, pulling the furrow along with him. Inside, he heard the pastor reading a passage from the New Testament.

One step at a time, Scarecrow scribed a bloody ring around the church, where all were *not* welcome. When he had dragged the scarlet tip across the clean cement of the sidewalk to meet the beginning of his circle, he thrust the tine into the dirt like a nail holding the ring together. That would be his offering to this congregation.

When he let go of the tine and stood all the way up to survey the raw furrow he had made, he saw nothing other than a scratched line in the dirt.

Inside, the pastor raised his voice in benediction, and the organist played the postlude as the churchgoers buzzed with conversation, no doubt tittering over the excitement they had experienced that morning.

Scarecrow and the Raven stood out near the street under a tall oak tree. "Watch," Scarecrow said.

The doors flew open, and four rowdy—but well-dressed—children burst out, crossing the invisible boundary, and brought themselves to a standstill. Other congregation members strolled out looking smug and self-important as they chatted about their business, the crops, the weather.

A broad-shouldered and jowly man caught sight of the two freaks standing on the sidewalk in front of the church. His face turned florid, and he pointed at them while grumbling to another deacon beside him. Like bouncers in a roughneck bar, they strode forward as the other people emerged from the church.

"Uh, we should go!" the Raven said, flapping his arms in alarm.

"Go!"

But Scarecrow remained where he was, rigid and watching. His vision sharpened, darkened—and as the people crossed the line he had drawn in the soil, he watched their masks peel away. He snapped up his awkward head and stared at details he had not seen before.

—The little bald pharmacist, with the twinkle in his eye and sugar-free candy for little kids, who added a little "extra" to some of his prescriptions for people he didn't like, giving them an attack of diarrhea.

—The tallest boy in the choir, desperately clean-cut, out in the darkness of the milking barn with three of his friends, whispering "Hold her steady! Hold her steady!" as he thrust his erection inside the confused cow. The others would each have their turn, after the first had "loosened her up." They had made a pact among themselves never to tell anybody....

The crowd stopped in their tracks, milling about. Some people screamed at what they saw in the faces of those they had known all their lives. Some were appalled by their neighbors, while others were repulsed by *them* in turn. It was a regular freak show.

—The old woman who fed stray dogs hamburger laced with ground glass to "teach them a lesson for pooping on her yard."

—The Sunday School teacher who had been planning how to invite several of the young boys over to his house, where he could have some "fun," the details of which he himself had not yet decided.

—The unmarried bank teller who took a vacation each year to visit mythical relatives in Milwaukee, though her primary objective was to hang out in pool halls and pick up as many city men as possible, preferably two or three a day. Last time she had come back home to Tucker's Grove with syphilis....

As Scarecrow watched, he felt more than vindictiveness or revulsion—he sensed an eerie fascination at these flaws and shames of others. He realized with a start that this must be what the spectators experienced when they came to look and point and titter at the freaks in the circus. He pitied them.

Hearing the babble of frightened commotion, the pastor himself strode out of his church. He looked around, saw the freaks on the outer sidewalk, and then he marched forward, taking charge, intending to throw them off the church property. And then he crossed the line.

—The pastor added false backs to the drawers in his dresser, where he kept bras and panty hose, negligees, and other items of women's clothing he liked to try on and model for himself in front of a tall, bordello-style mirror. Even this morning, as the pastor gripped the lectern, flecks of bright whore-red nail polish clung to his cuticles.

The congregation members turned on him like a wolf pack, shrieking in horror at yet another exposed small-town secret.

As Scarecrow and the Raven turned to leave the screams and commotion behind them, he could still see the shadows of the real people here, the fat women and the ugly men, the pimple-faced teenagers, scarred and retarded people who had no other place in the world. They had turned their scorn upon Scarecrow and the Raven—misfits even worse than they—upon whom they could dump their own shame and revulsion.

"It's only right for them to know just how normal they really are," Scarecrow said.

He also realized that the previous night's rose-tinted dream—him steadfast and hardworking, Raven good-natured though eccentric—was not how things *might* have been without their freakish exteriors ... but how the two truly appeared in their hearts.

As they walked away, Scarecrow hesitated once, looking back toward the church. He had left the wondrous tine behind, thrust into the dirt. The artifact pierced the masks all people wore, and he could imagine its incredible power.

If he took it with him back to the circus, he would be able to see Collier and Black for who they really were—harried businessmen full of bluster but caring deeply for their show—or the big-hearted fat lady, or the game hucksters who sometimes gave the most wonder-filled kids an extra chance at the games, or the cook who always did his best to help them get by....

No, Scarecrow decided he didn't need the tine after all. He might not be a perfect judge of character, but he knew his friends well enough. He felt the empty pocket of his shirt. The skin on his chest tingled where it had touched the tainted metal.

Scarecrow and the Raven walked without shame down the

main street of Tucker's Grove as the day grew brighter and warmer. "If we hurry, maybe we can catch the show before they pack up and leave," Scarecrow said. "I don't think there's any particular need for us to part company with them."

"Nope," said the Raven, who hopped ahead, excited. "Nevermore!"

Early in my career I got heavily involved with the small-press community and fanzine community, where ambitious publishers used the equivalent of stone knives and bearskins to produce their own journals or magazines. Some of them were photocopied and some were mimeographed, while the really ambitious ones were offset printed.

During those days, I met a lot of fan writers. We were all trying to learn how to do this "writing thing," exchanging information and tips, teaching one another how to write, because any one of us had only a few small pieces of the puzzle. Back then, I collaborated with a lot of writers, because it was like a game, and we each learned so much by writing a story together. One of us would have an idea, the other would develop it, and we would send sections back and forth.

Did I say stone knives and bearskins? It may be hard to imagine now, but we would literally type up our pages on paper, make photocopies, and then send the package through the mail. (Yes, in an envelope with a stamp.) Then the other person would have to retype those pages and edit along the way, add their new sections, and send it back to the coauthor. It was not a fast way to produce a story, but I did it. Again and again.

"Laeth-eth and the Trolls" is one of those early collaborations, a story written with Star Trek fanzine writer Patricia M. Spath. This story is an odd mix of amusing medieval fantasy, like my other stories "Short Straws" and "Skeleton in the Closet" (another early collaboration with fellow writer Ron Fortier), both of which also appear in these collections. Laeth-eth is a misfit, clunky, and downtrodden seventh daughter who will do anything to keep herself from being sent off to a nunnery—and then the story took a really dark turn.

Pat wrote all the funny, flirty parts, and I, of course, did the darker stuff. The story was published in my old standby small-press magazine Space & Time.

I admit "Laeth-eth and the Trolls" is uneven, but upon rereading it, I felt the tale had a powerful punch, so I'm including it here.

I never met Pat Spath in person; we only corresponded, and I learned through the science fiction fan community that she passed away in 2019. I'm glad to be able to bring this one back into print.

LAETH-ETH AND
THE TROLLS
(WITH PATRICIA M. SPATH)

The cursed sunlight turned her flesh to stone, trapping all thoughts and memories within a petrifying brain. One final sentence lay frozen for eternity in her consciousness: I am not a troll!

As the centuries passed, moss crept over the fossilized forms of three trolls and one woman. A procession of seasons weathered the stone, breaking it down, exposing her memories one at a time, the oldest ones first....

The Mother Superior sat like a misshapen shadow by the hearth, absorbing the warmth of the crackling fire with all the enthusiasm of a succubus in a monastery. Blue circles shone beneath the old woman's baggy eyes, highlighting the wrinkled mass of her face.

Lord Montehaute twiddled his thumbs, supervising the disposal of Laeth-eth, his seventh daughter. After having dealt away the first six over the years, he had mastered the daughter-barter technique and made himself far richer in the process. The eldest daughter had received the richest and handsomest suitor-cum-spouse; the next five had all received husbands with landholdings and physical appearances according to the daughters' positions within the siblinghood. But for his youngest daughter Laeth-eth the world offered no lord under ninety with more than a thimbleful of land or title.

Simply stated, the law of the land dictated that Castle Monte Cliff could have only one "Lady of the Manor." And, as the last daughter by his first (and only Church-sanctioned) marriage, Laeth-eth still filled that legal position. But lately, Montehaute's mistress, the Lady Melantha de Costa, had been growing more and more insistent. To the nunnery Laeth-eth would go.

The dried prune of a woman leaned closer to Montehaute and spoke in her rasping voice. "My Lord, we have discussed all essentials save one. Is the Lady Laeth-eth still, er, untouched by man? I ask only because, you understand, absolute purity is the strictest requirement set by the 'Sisters Who Search for the Holy Purple Robe Which Our Saviour Jesus Christ Wore as He Died on the Cross for Our Sins' nunnery. Celibacy is a great and wearisome burden. I, myself, have many times been sorely tempted by the pleasures of the flesh. But we must be strong."

Lord Montehaute had seen morel mushrooms more beautiful than the appallingly unattractive Mother Superior, but he said nothing. He pushed his bony back hard against the chair, allowing a thin smile to twist the lips above his ratty gray beard. "Mother Superior, you have seen the dubious beauty of my Laeth-eth. I assure you she has never so much as *seen* a naked man, not to mention coupled with one!"

"Then, my lord, I am pleased to accept your fine daughter as a member of our Sisterhood. And your gift of a seven-foot-tall, finely wrought gold-plated crucifix is also a most welcome addition to our meager chapel."

"Six foot tall," Montehaute corrected forcefully.

"Oh yes, yes of course. Shall we give the Lady Laeth-eth a few days to get over her joy of becoming a member of our convent? Shall we come for her, perhaps, in four days' time?"

"That would be most agreeable, Mother Superior. And I shall

inform my lady Melantha that our own wedding plans may proceed apace."

Both the old woman's and the old Lord's faces glowed with ecstatically smug expressions.

And Laeth-eth knew full well what was going on. "Damn, damn, damn!" she muttered to herself, slamming the heavy wooden door and almost extinguishing the massive candles in the hall. "Christ's blood! I will not rot in a dank, gloomy nunnery just so Father can legally frolic with his concubine!"

She cursed herself for not having spent more time trysting with the less-attractive (hence more desperate) knights; then perhaps she would have disqualified herself from the "absolute purity" of the Sisters Who Search....

Then a delighted expression splattered itself across her face.

"Oh, Welby!" she crooned in (she hoped) a sensual voice. "Do come here a moment."

Laeth-eth sat in the arbor, hidden by the softly rustling green leaves. It would do for a romantic spot.

The strapping and very-flaxen-haired son of the castle gardener stood up from the garden patch, interrupted in his weeding chores. Welby looked around in bafflement. Laeth-eth knew that if he didn't return to work in a moment, Welby would probably forget the job he had been asked to do. The castle gardener kept Welby's chores simple, for his son had been blessed with the brains of an empty suit of armor. What he lacked in mental capacity, however, Welby overcompensated for with sheer brawn.

"I'm here, Welby. In the arbor." Laeth-eth swallowed a little, then unbuttoned her bodice to reveal the valley between her convexities. She pulled at one sleeve, exposing a flecked shoulder.

Welby crashed through the arbor and looked at her with a happily expectant grin. "Yes, my lady?"

She smiled, closed her eyes shyly, and began to rotate her shoulder in a seductive manner.

"My Lady, are you in pain? Does your shoulder vex you?"

Laeth-eth sighed to herself. "My shoulder is perfectly fine, Welby. Perhaps if ..." She raised her skirts to uncover a nicely curved ankle attached to a regrettably large foot. She winked at him.

A look of profound befuddlement wrinkled his forehead.

Laeth-eth then made passionate kissing motions and slowly licked her lips.

Welby's expression of concentration could not have been more intense. "My Lady, shall I fetch the Lord Montehaute? Perhaps he can summon a chemist to aid your affliction?"

He lifted a massive knee, ready to trot off faithfully to the castle. Welby was a good sort, and absolutely devoted to the Lord's family. So were the Lord's hunting hounds. And at times it seemed that the hounds grasped things Welby couldn't. Laeth-eth rose quickly and grabbed his shoulders.

"My dear Welby, I have an illness only *you* can cure. My father seeks to send me away to a nunnery. But I will be saved only if ... only if you will *deflower* me!"

Welby stared at her with his mouth slightly open. She saw his mental distress as he seized his head and rocked back and forth. "My Lady, your words make my brain ache! You are *wearing* no flowers!"

Plan two.

The atmosphere in the Boar's Bristle and Hoof felt as thick as three-day-old milk. Laeth-eth had once smelled the stench of burning corpses, victims of the previous winter's fever, but she had never dreamed how foul living bodies could smell.

A wall of seven empty beer steins stood across the table,

separating her from the slab-of-masculinity she had cornered. Grund, one of the Lord Montehaute's men-at-arms, seemed finally to be feeling the effects of his ale. It had been hours, but now his bloodshot eyeballs began to sway.

Grund burped at her across the table. She decided it was time.

"Grund, do you find me attractive?"

A few moments later she found herself following his weaving steps up a ladder to the loft above the inn's great room. She cringed slightly, afraid Grund would lose his grip on the rungs and come crashing down on her like a knight at the tilt. But he made it, and grasped her hand in a stumbling chivalrous action to help her up. He sucked at her knuckles and declared with slurring words, "I am privileged to aid you in your dilemma, my lady."

Grund began to undo his tunic, failed to comprehend the knots, and tore the seams instead. As he removed his trousers, Laeth-eth discreetly looked away after catching only a glimpse of his very hairy legs.

She began to loosen her own bodice, and turned toward him, smiling hesitantly.

Grund collapsed in the hay with a crash and almost immediately began snoring, leaving a pleased and satisfied grin on his face. His breath reeked of ale, and no amount of shouting or slapping from Laeth-eth would rouse him. She kicked him angrily in the ribs and cursed.

Plan three.

For one of the most traveled roads in the Lord Montehaute's demesne, it certainly didn't have much traffic. So far only a shrunken old tinker had wandered by. And after sitting on a fallen log for hours upon end, her posterior had begun to feel the effects of the knobby bark. The supposedly haunted Nightwoods simmered and hummed around her in the late afternoon. She didn't really want to remain here much longer.

At last she saw a knight riding toward her, a knight she

recognized from Castle Monte Cliff. Sir Fernando de Chanson the Incredulous rode a horse that seemed to be eternally weary. Both man and steed had seen better and younger days, and the pair now approached middle age in unison. The mare had always been gray, and Sir Fernando's hair was changing color to match.

As they came slowly down the road through the forest, Laeth-eth put on her best Maiden-in-Distress expression. She plucked out a few eyelashes, and stinging tears began to run down her cheeks.

Sir Fernando de Chanson the Incredulous, as befitted his title, could not believe his eyes. In all probability, he had not rescued a fair maiden for many years, though the definition of "fair" might need to be stretched a little to include Laeth-eth. No one disputed the fact that she was still a maiden. That was her entire problem.

"My Lady Laeth-eth!" he cried, squinting his eyes in the green forest dimness and pulling his horse to a halt. He dismounted, but not without his share of effort. Laeth-eth attempted to aid the noble knight, but he declined her assistance. With a grandiose gesture and creaking armor (or perhaps a creaking spine) Fernando bowed deeply. "What do you here in these haunted Nightwoods? Are you not aware that Fosboe the Horrific and his hideous band of trolls lurk herein, waiting to capture young maids and devour them? There is great peril!" The knight looked around nervously, as if afraid that he might be asked to do something about the trolls. "May I be of some service?"

"I sincerely hope so." Laeth-eth began to tell her tale of woe, adding a little extra woe for good measure. Fernando listened without comment.

"So, most honorable sir, would you not say that mine is, indeed, a dire situation? And do you not agree that it would be a truly honorable and heroic deed to rid me of my *burden*?"

"My most lovely Lady," Fernando said quickly, "I'm afraid I have been pledged to a Quest at the very moment. I must fly to the Tor de Costa in order to escort the valuable dowry of your honorable father's wife-to-be. I dare not tarry, on my knightly honor, for the treasure must be delivered four days hence."

"But, sir, I assure you it would not take long!"

Fernando fumbled with his mouth a bit, as if trying to think. "Dear Lady Laeth-eth, it would be an honor and, no doubt, a pleasure to lead you from childhood into womanhood, but even if my body were capable, it would be dishonorable outside the sacred bonds of matrimony."

Laeth-eth stood and glared at him. The sun rested near the horizon, and she had no more time or patience. "Sir Fernando, it is your knightly duty to help a *maiden* in distress. And if you rid me of my maidenhood, you will no longer be bound to obey me if, for instance, I were to demand you go into these Nightwoods—at dusk—and singlehandedly rid the land of the troublesome troll band lurking within."

Sir Fernando's face turned the color of rancid butter, and he swallowed. "You make a most convincing argument, my lady."

He began to undo the straps binding his Brigandine doublet, then the gauntlets, vambrace, couter, rerebrace, and pauldron, all the armor protecting his upper body. Laeth-eth regained her seat, pulled her skirts up around her calves and between her thighs. She rested her chin in the palm of her hands. The sun began to set.

As the darkness and night sounds crept closer to the path through the dense woods, Sir Fernando grew more and more nervous. She could see sweat breaking out all over his body. The mare stood as if exhausted, munching on weeds. At last the knight had stripped down to the final piece of bodily protection, his crotch plate. But as he prepared to remove it, a rumble of thunder crashed across the storm clouds on the distant horizon. Fernando slumped, then fell to his knees.

"Oh good Lord Jesus Christi, I am most ashamed of my actions. I cannot honor your request as promised, fair Lady. God does not approve of such a sin. Please, Lady." He began to sob.

Rolling her eyes upward in disgust, she said scornfully, "Perhaps you should consider reclothing yourself, sir. You have only nine hours until daylight, and this is a much-traveled road."

At this point she finally threw Operation Deflower to the wind and stormed off into the dense Nightwoods.

Time for Operation Run-and-Hide-in-the-Forest-for-the-Rest-of-Your-Life.

Darkness had fallen, but the gloom within the Nightwoods did not seem to change. The trees grew too close together, grappling with each other to gain a small modicum of sunlight. The heavy underbrush hunched as if trying to pull down trunks for the moss, mushrooms, and termites to devour. The ground beneath Laeth-eth's feet squished with every footfall. The entire area smelled of dank earth.

Her imagination became cluttered with all manner of things inhuman, unnatural, and just plain spooky. A thrumming din echoed through the air as countless insects set up a banshee symphony. She knew that she should be worried about the finer points of survival, such as finding a place to live, things to eat, and water to drink; but for now the hidden spectres in an unknown and supposedly haunted forest occupied all her attention. She tried to tell herself that any demon she encountered here could be no more distasteful than the human men she had met thus far. But the hairs on the back of her neck prickled and threatened to stand on end at a moment's notice. She could understand why fearful travelers might imagine hideous trolls lurking in the Nightwoods.

Trolls, like the one who now stood before her, glowering through a bulky brow and showing one snaggled fang.

Even in the dim light he was ugly. She gulped, and decided the best course of action would be not to have gone into the Nightwoods in the first place. Since this was not feasible, she stared instead, and the troll gawked back, probably as repulsed by her as she was by him.

The troll's skin reminded her of the grayish-green of a peeled fish. His bald head was lumpy and blockish, as if a child had tried to make a clay bust of an ugly man and had given up in the middle of the job. A bumpy reptilian ridge ran from his eyebrows to the top of his head. He stood over eight feet tall, with muscled arms as thick as tree trunks. And he carried a very nasty-looking club.

"Don't ya know these here be the woods of Fosboe the Horrific?" the troll said in a voice that would turn back a thunderstorm.

She forced the tremor out of her voice. "Yes. And you must be Fosboe? I'm very pleased to meet you."

He reached out with an immense arm, and for a moment she thought he was going to shake her hand—until he grabbed her with splayed fingers that nearly circled her waist and lifted her up. He tucked her under his arm like a log for the fire. Laeth-eth squeaked, but dared not struggle. He could probably crack her ribcage as easily as he could squish a berry.

"Does ya know what day of the week it be, Lady?"

The forest reeled under her vision as she felt torn between the urge to faint and the urge to vomit. "Wednesday," she said weakly. "Let me go!"

"Gosh darn it!" Fosboe grumbled, carrying her along through the thick forest. "Can't eat white meat on Wednesdays."

The three trolls had built a greasy-smelling campfire, and the smallest troll busily roasted shelf-mushrooms on the coals. Fosboe plopped her down next to a gnarled tree trunk and, with movements remarkably fast for such a massive creature, tied her securely to the tree. Behind the campfire, a small pile of treasure and some scattered weapons gleamed in the firelight.

"This here be my brother Buboe, and this be my brother Sludge." Fosboe pointed to the other trolls seated on large boulders by the fire.

Buboe, the littlest troll, quickly grabbed a wooden placard on which someone had written "Today is *not* Wednesday!" Buboe shook the sign up and down, imploring the others to read it.

"Aww, cut it out, Buboe!" Fosboe rumbled. "Buboe don't talk much. He's not mute—he just don't like to talk."

Buboe sat back down and seemed resigned to eating shelf-mushrooms instead of fresh human meat. He reached into the fire with his bare calloused hands, tossed a mushroom to Sludge, and began to eat one for himself.

"Hey! Not before you says grace!" Fosboe glared at his brothers until they all bowed with abashed expressions on their faces. "Thankee, Gawd!" all three shouted in unison, then fell to eating. Buboe's voice was very high pitched and womanish, and Laeth-eth thought she knew why he kept quiet most of the time.

Fosboe continued to talk. "And Sludge, here—we call him that because he carries a sludge hammer."

Sludge stood up and proudly showed off a massive stone mallet. He twirled it once and brought it crashing down on the vacant boulder next to the fire, turning the boulder to gravel. Sludge wore a tattered eyepatch on the wrong eye, and thus couldn't see much of what was going on.

"You brick-brain!" Fosboe roared and buffeted his brother on the side of the head with enough force to knock down an oak tree. "That was my boulder!"

Sludge sulked away. "Sorry, Fos."

Laeth-eth had never known the true meaning of *noise* until she had heard the three trolls snoring. Though she tried all through the hours of forest darkness, she could not break free of the rope binding her. Instead, she spent her time thinking up an absolutely fabulous plan for her survival.

"Be it morning yet? Be it Thursday?" Sludge yowled.

"It always be so damn dark in these woods, who knows if it be morning?" Fosboe mumbled through his sleep.

"Close enough!"

"Oh, all right! Buboe, stoke up that fire. Let's get breakfast going."

Laeth-eth looked into the most desperate, hunger-filled eyes she had ever encountered. And the pit at the bottom of her stomach became bottomless. She hoped her assessment of the trolls' intelligence had not been too far from the mark.

"But you can't eat me." Laeth-eth hoped her voice carried just the right mixture of mock sentiment, concern, scorn, and confidence.

"But we *can* eat you!" gloated Sludge. "Besides, who asked you?"

"You doesn't have any say in the matter!" Fosboe said.

Buboe jumped up and down with his "Today is *not* Wednesday!" sign.

Laeth-eth kept up her sweet, confident voice. "I'm just warning you for your own good, you boulder-heads! Look." She nodded to two large moles on her shoulder. "Do you know what these are?"

"Two dark spots?" Fosboe guessed. The other trolls didn't speak.

"Idiot! This is the Sign of the Black Asp. When I was just a baby, the deadliest of all demon serpents crept into my cradle and sank his fangs into my shoulder, right here! I burned on the verge of death for days, but since I was a pure baby, and since I had been bitten at the height of the full moon, I survived and grew up to be cursed with this mark. That most deadly of all venoms is still surging through my veins, and it fills every morsel of my flesh. If you tried to eat me, you'd swallow the venom. *Then* do you know what would happen?"

All three trolls gulped and looked at her, horrified. They shook their heads in unison.

She lowered her voice to an ominous whisper. "First your skin starts to fester, er, even more. Then it begins to peel off in large chunks. Then all contact with gold and jewels becomes increasingly painful to you. All your teeth fall out, and fungus starts to grow inside your belly until it slowly, *slowly* eats away all your insides. It is excruciatingly painful, and by the end you'll be crawling out into the sunlight on purpose just to end your agony."

The trolls backed away from her, muttering among themselves.

"But please, it is too horrible for me to carry this burden inside me. Even when I am dead and buried, the worms won't go near my body for fear that they might catch the venom themselves. Please, end my life now, so I don't have to bear it any longer. Just be careful not to let one drop of my blood touch you ... or else."

None of the trolls seemed the slightest bit eager to do the deed.

"You have been sent here!" Fosboe cried in a trembling voice. "Because we be sinners, all three of us?"

That was a turn she had not expected. "Yes! Yes, indeed! And if you do not untie my arms immediately, your penance will be far worse."

The trolls scrambled forward in an awkward semblance of anxiety and dread.

If it hadn't been for the almighty ruckus caused by the Mother Superior of the Sisters Who Search ..., the Lord Montehaute would have been perfectly happy to announce the disappearance of his beloved daughter Laeth-eth and left it at that. However, the Mother Superior had dearly set her sights on the promised gold crucifix and had forced Montehaute to action.

Grund and two others of the Lord's men-at-arms had each been given five gold pieces and the promise of ten more if they succeeded in finding Laeth-eth. Or fifteen more if they *didn't* succeed after a day's search. (The latter part remained confidential, of course.) Grund took a small keg of ale from the castle kitchen and, with his two companions, trudged out of sight into the Nightwoods, intending to spend the day in thoughtful conversation on a woefully limited range of topics.

Meanwhile—

Laeth-eth had reached an uneasy truce with the trolls. They

avoided her like the plague, which was not too far from the mark, and she had decided not to press her position. She felt reasonably confident they would not harm her for the time being. Above all else she did not want to go back to her doom at the nunnery. And if she remained here, what could be better protection than the awful trolls? Maybe, just maybe ...

She had taken one of the smaller rusted swords from the pile of weapons, in case she happened to find a rabbit or squirrel or something similarly furry and potentially edible. The trolls didn't like her digging in their precious treasure pile, but she had left the jeweled scabbard there and sworn to return the blade. Fosboe and his brothers knew perfectly well a mere sword could do no harm to crusty troll flesh. Laeth-eth wandered from the troll camp that morning to look for berries, but after several hours her search had been, literally, fruitless.

Until she stumbled upon Grund and his two companions.

Laeth-eth cracked a twig under her foot, and Grund belched from the ale, and both looked up to see the other across a small clearing.

"Aw, rust! There she is!" Grund swore.

"Go 'way! And don't come back!" one of the other men-at-arms shouted.

"No, you fool!" Grund hissed to the others. "If she runs away and goes back to the castle, we may as well hang ourselves now and save the Lord Montehaute the trouble!" Grund drew a dagger and lurched to his feet. "Let's get her!"

Laeth-eth froze for an instant, then stumbled backward before she had sense enough to run. The other two men-at-arms fanned out on either side as Grund charged toward her like a sun-struck bull.

"Fosboe!" she shouted. "Sludge! Help!" Not much of a chance, but at least it let Grund and his goons think she had reinforcements coming.

Unfortunately, through all her formative years, Laeth-eth's teachers had insisted on showing her the wonderful aspects of embroidery and court dancing and had sorely neglected her physical training. Within minutes Grund had cornered her, leering at his victim. The other two guards crouched on either side.

Laeth-eth held her rusty sword in both hands, like a club, and the three men laughed. Grund smiled, ignoring the potential danger of the sword, and lunged with his short dagger. Laeth-eth spun, deciding not to engage him with the unfamiliar blade, and instead planted a heavy kick with one of her overlarge feet. She felt her heel crunch into the delicate masculine equipment which she had earlier hoped to put to a different use.

Grund gasped as he crumpled into a fetal position. "Lowly bitch!" he wheezed.

Before she could think further, she swung the sword down at his exposed back. The blade struck his ribs with the delicious feel of cutting meat. She almost smiled as he cried out.

"The wench sliced me!" Grund screamed as he tried to roll away. "Get her!"

But the other two men-at-arms stood frozen with gaping mouths. Two towering trolls stood in front of them like petrified nightmares—Fosboe with his deadly club and Sludge with his granite hammer. The trolls swung their weapons, and the men-at-arms fell like broken trees.

Grund whimpered as he felt his pain and slowly realized what had happened. Laeth-eth planted one of her feet on his ribs and rolled him over on his back. He looked at her in fear for a moment, then regained an infuriated composure. She placed the sword point at his throat. He cursed at her, but lay motionless.

Laeth-eth felt anger, betrayal, and excitement welling up inside her, searing like lightning through her brain. "Grund, you are about to give me more pleasure than you have ever given any woman."

For a moment, Grund probably thought he would escape with a lesser punishment. Then the blade came down on his neck.

Laeth-eth had never imagined that her first sight of a naked man would be like this. Grund rolled in a bizarre pirouette over the fire as Buboe turned the crank, roasting the man-at-arms on a spit. Fire licked Grund's flesh, sending the smell of cooking meat into the forest air. Grease dripped and spattered in the fire.

Laeth-eth watched Grund's headless body, feeling a strange excitement within her. Her belly snarled and cursed, reminding her she had not eaten in an entire day. A jolt of hunger made her consider tasting human flesh. But her inhibitions rapidly drove that thought away, chasing it with revulsion. *That flesh is far more venomous than my own could ever be*, she thought. Fosboe and Sludge delighted themselves with the gold coins they had found on the men-at-arms.

"I've brought you a great deal of meat, and treasure," she said to the trolls. "Are you happy?"

The three trolls cheered her, and she smiled. Laeth-eth no longer felt helpless against the people who had cast her away, torn her from her life at Castle Monte Cliff, forced her to live in the Nightwoods with these hideous trolls. But she had begun to realize the trolls were no worse company than the humans in her acquaintance.

"Would you like for me to bring you much more treasure? Gold and jewels to outshine the entire pile you have now?"

Buboe jumped up and down in delight. Sludge shouted his approval. But Fosboe narrowed his eyes. "Be this not some sort of *temptation*?" The other trolls stopped suddenly, as if they had seen through to Laeth-eth's true purpose.

"No, no. By coming to rescue me today, you have passed all tests. You are no longer sinners and can rest easily." Laeth-eth felt a new sort of camaraderie with the trolls, joined against the humans who had betrayed and tried to murder her. "Now I'm simply asking as a friend—how would you like to get some more gold? An entire wedding dowry from a fine noble family?"

She sat upon the same fallen log, but facing the opposite direction. Once again, late afternoon had arrived, and the sky was a muddy soup of gray clouds. Accompanied by three servants and one donkey laden with gem-filled golden urns, Sir Fernando de Chanson the Incredulous pulled his exhausted gray mare to a halt and rubbed his eyes again in disbelief. "My Lady Laeth-eth, you are *still* here?"

She smiled and stood up. "Of course, Sir Fernando. I've been waiting for you to return. I want you to see a surprise."

On cue, Buboe gave a high, womanish shriek and leaped out of the branches overhead to land squarely on the path in front of Sir Fernando's horse. Underbrush exploded out of the way as Fosboe the Horrific and his brother Sludge stormed out of the Nightwoods on either side.

Deciding this would be as good a time as any, and better than some, Sir Fernando's aged mare uttered a slight neigh and gave up the ghost, collapsing lifeless with a crash of unsettled armor. The three servants vanished like pigeons in a panic, scattering in different directions through the wood.

Sir Fernando toppled from his fallen mare and landed on his back in a muddy pothole, trapped like an overturned tortoise in the prison of his cumbersome armor. Laeth-eth lost no time pouncing on him, ripping off his helmet and laying Grund's dagger against his exposed throat.

Sir Fernando swallowed hard, and his Adam's apple made the blade bounce up and down. "My Lady, it seems you have changed your attitude toward the laws of the world and the ways of chivalry."

Laeth-eth laughed. "Indeed I have! Those things profited my life none, but the dowry of my father's whore will profit me a great deal."

Her fingers felt electric, and she liked the sensation of dominance, power, control. She enjoyed seeing the great and noble knight in a subservient position, the knight who could have solved her dilemma before, but had refused for his own petty reasons. In a way, Fernando had insulted her more powerfully even than Grund had. The man-at-arms had at least been willing; Sir Fernando had flatly refused her.

"My noble knight, I realize you do not crave a valiant heroic death on the field of battle. I hope you are satisfied now, lying helpless in the mud with a woman pinning you to the ground. Indeed, you will not enjoy a heroic death."

She watched through fiery eyes as her eager hands drew the blade across his veins, slitting his throat. A jet of blood struck Laeth-eth as she leaned over his dying body, and she found it warm and soothing.

The celebration fire had died into a glimmering stupor as the sultry light of day tried to break through the canopy of the Nightwoods, and failed. Buboe lay with his head pillowed by a pile of sharp-edged gems, but didn't seem to mind. He snored softly. The half-eaten, overcooked carcass of Sir Fernando de Chanson the Outsmarted lay on a rack above the ashes of the fire.

Laeth-eth looked at the three trolls and curled her lips in a smug grin. They looked on her in a decidedly more favorable light now, almost worshipful. When she had finally told Sludge to put his eyepatch on the other eye, thus enabling him to see much better, the one-eyed troll forgot himself and gave her a big hug. No one had ever hugged her so sincerely before, and her ribs still ached from the experience.

She was confident now. Laeth-eth the Spurned. Laeth-eth the Avenger. Laeth-eth the Terror of the Countryside, who preyed on all those who had wronged her. She laughed a little to herself. The next step was obvious.

"Tonight, my brothers, we shall destroy my father's wedding celebration! Neither he nor the Lady Melantha de Costa will ever forget their wedding night. I, however, am going to enjoy it a great deal."

The trolls looked at her with wide eyes. "But we be not strong enough to take an entire castle!" Fosboe cried.

Laeth-eth frowned. "Do you doubt my leadership? Look at all I've done for you—are you trolls, or are you cowards?"

"No, no—we be not cowards! We don't like people—we be confined in these Nightwoods by the curse of the Lord Gawd, else we turn to stone in the sunlight!" Fosboe moaned.

"We'll wait here for you, though. Help when you come back," Sludge suggested.

"Pah!" Laeth-eth snorted, spitting away the last of her patience. "I'm more of a troll than you are!" And, as if to prove it, she tore a hunk of stringy meat from the carcass of Sir Fernando and thrust it in her mouth. "I'm going by myself, then. See if I ever help you get treasure again." She stormed off into the woods. "I have to take care of some business of my own."

"Oh, Welby! I'm here in the arbor!" Laeth-eth called, trying to keep the razor edge out of her voice. Dusk swallowed up the brightness in the arbor. The leaf shadows reminded her of the comfort of the Nightwoods.

"Lady Laeth-eth!" she heard Welby cry. As she listened to his crashing footsteps as he ran eagerly toward the arbor, she readied herself with a hard smile frozen on her face.

Welby trotted around the corner of the leafy alcove and grinned broadly. "My Lady! I thought you had run away! And now you're back! And safe! Oh, I'm so glad!"

Tears crawled out of his eyes and streamed down his cheek. She began to laugh, and he grinned even more. The ecstasy on his face could not have been plainer.

It probably took him a moment to feel the narrow dagger she thrust into his chest.

For a long, slow instant his expression remained unchanged, and then a look of confusion followed on the heels of his grimace of pain. "My Lady?" he gasped.

Laeth-eth twisted the dagger and thrust it deeper. Welby slowly dropped to his knees, pulling the knife handle from her fingers. He looked up at her like an ox which had just been stunned by its owner—betrayal and innocence and absolute confusion melted together on a face that had become the texture of candle wax.

He fell forward, and Laeth-eth laughed quietly to herself. Her eyes had narrowed in the confines of the Nightwoods, becoming hard as crystals. She retrieved her dagger, filled with electric elation at felling another of her enemies. She had been wrong to trust and obey them all her life. Now she was master.

Inside of her, the last shreds of humanity shattered and tinkled into nothingness, blown away by the night air that carried with it the rich smell of Welby's blood.

The withered Mother Superior huddled naked on the cold stone floor, looking like a wrinkled mass of old leather. She whimpered as Laeth-eth stood over her, smiling with hatred. Laeth-eth had barred the heavy wooden door from the inside, and the Mother Superior's screams would never be heard by anyone who cared enough to help. At the sight of Laeth-eth's bloodied dagger, the old nun probably had no volition to scream either.

Slowly, enjoying the distaste she saw on the Mother Superior's visage, Laeth-eth donned the nun's bulky habit, pulling the wimple down over her head to conceal her young face. The old nun had been simpering in the empty meeting chamber, grumbling about her loss of the promised golden crucifix due to the disappearance of Lord Montehaute's seventh daughter. Laeth-eth could not have found a better disguise.

"I hope you're quite cold on that stone floor, Mother Superior," Laeth-eth said happily. "If I'm lucky, you may even catch pneumonia. For the time being, however, I consider it a worse punishment to keep your soul trapped inside such a loathsome body. By lying there naked and helpless, perhaps you'll be fortunate and find a knight who's drunken enough to be tempted."

The Mother Superior cringed back into a corner. "May God's curse fall upon you!"

Laeth-eth managed to tie a gag around the nun's mouth. "As my own curse has already fallen on you, vile Sister! You have destroyed far more lives than I ever shall."

She slammed the heavy door behind her as she prowled out into the familiar passages. Midnight had arrived, and she could still hear the continuing revels of the Lord Montehaute's nuptial celebration. But the walls seemed close and forbidding around her, and she missed the dark comfort of the Nightwoods. Even the flickering torchlight hurt her eyes, and she stayed in the shadows for her own comfort as well as for concealment.

As she entered the vast banquet hall, Laeth-eth did her best to act the part of the sour Mother Superior. Most of the guests wallowed in a drunken haze by now anyway, and would have failed to notice anything amiss had she strode in completely unclothed. The remainders of the wedding feast sprawled on the vast plank tables: whole joints of beef, entire roast boars, roast fowl, bread, honey in the comb, fruits, and nuts.

Laeth-eth didn't feel hungry. She had already eaten.

Sparkling candlelight filled the hall, and the newly-legitimized lovers sat at the main table upon chairs elevated slightly above those of their guests. Laeth-eth's narrowed eyes watched as the couple laughed and touched each other. It was sickening.

You have forgotten about me quickly, Father, and you have taken your whore to wife quicker still, Laeth-eth thought. *But my vengeance will be just as swift, and not soon forgotten.*

One of the more sodden and outspoken guests hauled himself from the floor back to his chair. He raised his goblet and overturned it in what might have been meant as a toast. "My Lord Montehaute! My Lords and Ladies! Is it not *yet* time for the Game to commence?"

A roar of approval echoed throughout the room, and Laeth-eth's heart quickened. Her hand tightened on the hilt of the dagger beneath her habit, but the pulsing anticipation failed to burn the sweat from her palm.

The Lord stood up and gave a lengthy speech, much of which Laeth-eth and the other guests ignored. Four burly men, each latching onto the chairs of the bride and groom, lifted them up and marched slowly around the massive table before placing them on the fresh rushes in the center of the hall. The Lord Montehaute stood from his chair. "The game of blindman's chance will commence!"

The smug new Lady of the Manor also rose from her chair, and two of her servants undid gold chains attaching the long, embroidered train to her pale blue gown. One servant placed a velvet cloak about her shoulders as a throng of female guests stormed toward the center of the room. Laeth-eth joined the group of cackling women.

In the meantime, the Lord had been blindfolded by his own servants, and spun around enough that he'd had time to lose his bearings and find them again. Laeth-eth knew the game: blindfolded, her father would now have to search through the throng to find his lady-love; if he failed to find her, he forfeited his "first" night in bed with her. To make the game more entertaining, the women dispersed throughout the large hall as the Lord began his search.

Grabbing at thin air, he moved forward until he laid hands upon a rather stout woman with the face of an old chicken. After a quick and fumbling examination, the Lord dismissed her and blundered on. He pushed aside lady after lady in favor of the next. Laeth-eth bided her time. And the game dragged on.

The Lord finally laid his hands on Laeth-eth's shoulders. He traced down her sleeve, and she allowed him to take her hand in his. The Lord gently kissed her knuckles, as a chuckle ran through the crowd. They had never expected the Mother Superior to tolerate even this much. He touched her wimple, and almost dismissed her offhand ... but then he ran his hand along her cheek. He suddenly stiffened.

"Yes, Father." Laeth-eth's whisper was too soft to reach any but his own ears. The Lord Montehaute quickly reached up to grasp at his blindfold.

And with a dead heart she thrust Grund's dagger into his chest. He gasped, not believing the fate that had befallen him. The Lady Melantha de Costa shrieked and ran toward her new husband as he melted to the floor like a discarded scarecrow.

With all the boldness of a madwoman, Laeth-eth ripped off her disguise and laughed. The guests were mortified. Through the crowd rippled a steadily growing whisper: "It is Laeth-eth!"

Then she fled the hall.

Up until now, her thoughts had centered completely upon vengeance, and the sweetness of watching her father fall dead in front of all his guests. She kicked herself for not having given at least a passing thought to her own escape. As she stole through the halls, she heard the clamoring shouts announcing the murder of the Lord Montehaute. Drowsy-looking guards stumbled toward the dining hall. Some passed her without stopping, and one even recognized Laeth-eth and shouted a greeting as he ran by. She did not acknowledge him.

Luckily, intoxication had rendered many of the guests useless in the search, and Laeth-eth managed to remove herself from the castle within an hour. As she crept through the darkened courtyard and passed through the arbor, she saw Welby's dew-covered and stiffening body in the milky moonlight. Laeth-eth paused a moment over the fallen gardener's son, gloating, until she heard a sound from the castle outbuildings, which made ice water trickle down her spine.

The guards had unleashed the Lord Montehaute's hunting hounds.

Laeth-eth ran as a spirit possessed. Now she could have used the aid of her troll allies, but Fosboe and his brothers had probably already forgotten about her. Cowards—she considered them a disgrace to the race of trolls.

She had never trained her body to take so much exertion in one day. Less than a week before, she had been sleeping on feather mattresses and exercising nothing more than her mind.

Today she had murdered two men, wrestled the clothes off a nun, walked the great distance from the Nightwoods to the Castle Monte Cliff ... and now she had to run back. Her legs ached, her lungs burned, and her mind raced.

The hounds howled as they surged to the pursuit. Laeth-eth had seen them tear their prey apart many times. And even if she managed to escape the hounds, guards would be following close on the heels of the pack.

At last the fringe of the Nightwoods loomed ahead. On the boundary she saw three trolls waiting for her, shouting for her to run. Laeth-eth almost stopped in confusion, then ran faster. In her haste, she had failed to notice the changing color of the sky, but her troll allies had not. Blood-pink tinged the eastern sky, shooting arrows of pale dawn-light into the darkness.

"She ain't gonna make it," Buboe moaned shrilly.

"And the sun's gonna come out. I, for one, be not about to risk myself for the likes of her," Fosboe said.

Sludge squatted and watched, holding his fingers in his mouth, either biting his nails or picking the black from between his teeth.

Laeth-eth made for the woods as the sun seeped over the watercolor horizon. The hounds came after. Buboe began to jump up and down like a frog, while Fosboe and Sludge screamed for her to hurry. Fosboe and Buboe stepped back slightly, folding themselves deeper into the gloom and safety of the Nightwoods. Sludge waited a moment longer, as if to acknowledge a debt to the friend who had fixed his eyepatch.

The sun had risen almost a quarter of its width over the horizon. Laeth-eth's skin felt as if it were being scalded, and steam curled from her flesh. Her joints stiffened. She couldn't understand why, but she had no time to wonder over it. At the time when she most needed haste, her movements became sluggish.

Fosboe and Buboe tried to pull their brother into the safety of the darkness. Laeth-eth had almost forced her stiffening body within the protection of the Nightwoods. Sludge extended his hand toward her, and she reached for it, only to see his fingers turn to stone. Her own arm had a gray, muddy tinge.

The sun broke from the horizon, and a great wind stirred the trees, breaking the canopy of the Nightwoods and letting a destructive blast of sunlight penetrate the gloom. Laeth-eth heard a ghostly voice, a medley of accusations from many different people: Grund, Sir Fernando, the Mother Superior, Welby, her father.

Fosboe, Buboe, and Sludge writhed in agony as the sunlight did its work. Laeth-eth screamed as she felt herself petrify. "I am not a troll!"

Yes you are, claimed the spectral voice. And that thought remained with Laeth-eth for all eternity, for her brain turned to stone around it.

The hounds arrived in the clearing with the guards close behind. But the smell of a passing thunderstorm hung in the air, clinging to the four stone figures. Nobody seemed to know what to do.

In the end, the Lady Melantha—now mistress of the entire castle —had her bards write a song about it. The troll statues, along with the stone Laeth-eth, remained for all to see.

Clockwork Lives, *written with Neil Peart—the legendary drummer and lyricist for Rush—is probably my favorite of all my books. Set in the same universe as our steampunk fantasy novel* Clockwork Angels *(based on the Rush concept album of the same name),* Clockwork Lives *is even more ambitious, I think, a sort of steampunk* Canterbury Tales *all connected by a frame story. Finishing the manuscript was one of those times when, as a writer, I felt that everything just worked right. When Neil read the final manuscript, he wrote me, "KJ, this is surely your finest work."*

Because I love all the stories in Clockwork Lives *so much, and because they are all interconnected, it's difficult to choose just one representative tale per collection. But this one, "The Sea Captain's Tale," is one of my favorites, showing my fascination with maritime legends. How does someone who grew up in the farmlands of Wisconsin and has spent more than two decades living in the heart of the Rocky Mountains get so interested in the sea? Maybe because it's so far away and mysterious.*

Attentive Rush fans will find a dozen or more Easter eggs in this story from Neil's lyrics.

CYGNUS: THE SEA CAPTAIN'S TALE
(WITH NEIL PEART)

On my first sea voyage, a man jumped overboard in the middle of the night. He was laughing the whole time until the waves swallowed him. That was how I knew something else was out there.

By the time the other sailors threw ropes and life preservers into the water, it was much too late. They shone coldfire lanterns down on the placid waves, but the man did not call out for help—not once—and we saw no sign of him in the dark and moonless night.

Captain Macallan looked disgusted. He let the other sailors take out boats to perform a perfunctory search, calling out their comrade's name, but they received no response. Finally, the steamer sailed on.

"He didn't fall overboard, Captain," I said, jarring the man out of his disturbed thoughts. "He jumped on purpose."

The captain narrowed his eyes, measured me. "The angels got him," he said. "The angels of the sea."

Then he went back to his stateroom and locked himself inside.

I grew up in Heartshore, a small fishing village south of Poseidon City. My father was a fisherman, and I learned to walk on a deck before I walked on land. I fell asleep each night with the sound of the waves as comforting as my mother's breathing. The sea called to me, and when my father saw me gaze out at the waves, he clapped me on the back. "You're a born fisherman!"

But that wasn't enough for me. The fishing boats from Heartshore rarely lost sight of the coast, and my gaze stretched farther—beyond the horizon. Heartshore was a warm and lovely place, but I wanted adventure!

I set off to find my fortune when I was old enough to sign aboard a cargo steamer—which is not very old at all. I ran away from home and went to Poseidon City, where I loitered around the port until I found a steamer looking for a crew. I would receive almost no pay, but the captain promised "a wealth of experience." Only two days after I arrived in Poseidon, I was crossing the sea in a ship full of metals, minerals, and alchemical powders for export to Albion.

Sailors whispered about the angels beneath the sea, beautiful women who could play a man's heartstrings like a musical instrument. I suspected they were just stories meant to tantalize or alarm a gullible new shipmate. I had grown up with fishermen, after all, and I knew about stories that were never meant to be believed, no matter how well told. But the undersea angels didn't sound like the usual tall tales; in the sailors' voices I heard as much fear as wonder.

And then that man jumped overboard in the middle of the night. Maybe he had seen the angels for himself, or believed so with a fervor that verged upon insanity.

For the rest of that first voyage, I stared over the edge of the steamer, looking in vain. I would go out at night and listen, trying to hear their mysterious song. But the sea kept its secrets, and I heard no ethereal voices beautiful enough to drive a man mad.

Not that time at least.

The steamer arrived in Albion to dock in Crown City. I was wide-eyed with wonder, the only one aboard who hadn't been there before. The other crew laughed and joked, telling me about sights I could see or incredible items I could purchase (many of which I didn't even understand, but I nodded sagely anyway, pretending to be mature beyond my years).

Standing on the deck, I jabbered about how I wanted to see the Alchemy College, Chronos Square, the Mainspring Hub where all the steamliners came and went, the majestic Watchtower that was said to be a mile high if it was an inch—and most of all, the Clockwork Angels.

But the captain put his hand on my shoulder, more like a vice grip than a paternal pat. "To a gullible boy like you, Crown City is more dangerous than a hundred undersea angels. Be careful. We set off at high tide on Wednesday. With all those clocks in Crown City, you'll have no excuse to be late. Better you stay close to the ship. You can always see more next time—if you come back for a second voyage." He gave me a sad smile that suggested just how unlikely it was that a young and unproven deckhand would be back.

I listened, though. I saw wonders, exactly as I expected, but I remained cautious, kept much of my money, and I kept my head about me. Leaving the Albion coast behind when we sailed back home that Wednesday, I counted my blessings as I looked at the hung-over misery of my fellow sailors: the swollen eyes, chipped teeth, and bruised faces from dockside brawls, the empty purses that had been full with their entire pay for the trip.

I didn't have to see or do everything the first time, because I knew I was meant to be a sailor, and I would be back.

After an uneventful voyage, we returned to Poseidon City eight days later. As I walked down the gangplank and into the city, I could tell from the look in Captain Macallan's eyes that he expected me to run home to Heartshore, settle into a typical life as a fisherman, and tell stories about the great adventure I'd had when I was young. I had no intention of doing so.

I had seen almost nothing of Poseidon City the first time,

however, since I'd straightaway joined the steamer's crew. Now, I sampled restaurants; I got into trouble, and I got out of it; I was robbed, but not before I had spent most of my pay anyway, so the cost was more to my pride than to my financial situation.

And when it was time, I made my way back to the steamer and walked aboard with my head held high. Much to the surprise and approval of Captain Macallan, I signed my name in the crew book for the next voyage to Albion.

After four days at sea, I did hear the music—more urgent, more beautiful, and more compelling than anything I had ever imagined.

I was asleep in my hammock belowdecks, off duty, and I sensed the presence dancing on the edge of my dreams. I woke in the darkness to the decidedly unmusical snores of my shipmates. The only light came from a half-shuttered lantern in the corner near the piss pot. The songs I heard came from the other side of the hull, at the waterline—and I knew I had to see for myself.

I swung out of the creaking hammock, careful not to wake anyone. With the voices of angels ringing in my head, I crept out on deck. Something told me I needed to keep this a secret. The undersea angels were calling to me and me alone. They had chosen *me*—none of the other sailors. I needed to hear their music for myself. It was an experience that could be cherished but not shared.

The night was black, without a moon, and I saw a pearlescent glow on the waves, rippling at the stern of the ship. The music came louder inside my head, an aria sung by voices that could never have come from human throats. Leaning on the rail, I stared down into the water, where I saw swimming figures—beautiful sleek forms with feminine curves and pearlescent skin.

Seeing that I had answered their call, the figures bobbed just beneath the surface. I could make out one angel, her face crystal clear, her features achingly beautiful. Her wings were made of iridescent scales, and they flapped like fins and drove her along. The angel easily kept pace with the steamer's engines.

My heart felt as if it would burst out of my chest. My throat went dry. I *ached* for her.

She looked up at me, her eyes wide and bright, her smile longing. She spread her gem-like wings as if to fly beneath the waves. She opened her arms to reach out for me. She wanted me! She *needed* me. She called to me to join her.

I felt a rush of hope, a sense of self-worth greater than I had ever experienced. It would be so easy just to swing over the side of the steamer and drop down into the sea. She silently promised me a kiss ... and an infinity more. Tears were pouring down my face. I *needed* this!

"Hey, you! Lad, what're you doing? Get away from there."

My life was shattered, the hypnotic manacles broken. The song jangled in my head as if a trapdoor had opened beneath an entire orchestra. When I felt strong hands grab my arm, I thrashed and struggled like a wild beast.

By the time I managed to look overboard again, the glow had vanished from the water, as had the angels beneath the sea. They were gone. They no longer wanted me—at least not tonight.

I had missed my chance.

The ocean remained silent for the rest of the voyage, and when I explored Crown City, even the wonders of that fabled place seemed flat. The Clockwork Angels were just inferior artificial contraptions, not remotely as beautiful as the angels I had seen in the sea....

In time, I became a true sailor instead of just a boy who wanted to run off to sea. I crossed the ocean over and over and again, growing wise in the ways of the tides and the weather. In a few years, with his appreciation and a heartfelt recommendation, Captain Macallan allowed me to transfer to another ship, where I would be groomed as first mate.

I kept longing for that elusive music, searching the sea and the wind for the songs of the angels. Though I sometimes heard it, the marvelous women never came close. They must have been haunting other ships and other sailors less prone to disappoint them. I yearned for them, but they did not answer me.

Eventually, though, I found another way to break that elusive call: The only thing stronger than the unrealistic longing of a fantasy love is a *real* love and a family, and ties that bound me to solid ground instead of the sea.

Each time my ship returned to Poseidon City, I frequented the dockside taverns, but I felt most at home at a particular inn with a flying swan on its signboard, the Cygnus Tavern. The common room was no different from other inns; the food and the ale no more special; but a young woman named Selise caught my eye, and I caught hers.

Selise and her brother Rickard ran the Cygnus Tavern together because their rotund old father had a heart condition that prevented him from doing heavy work. Selise was smart and beautiful, quick with a joke or just as quick with a barbed insult when a rude customer deserved it. Something about the set of her eyes, the curve of her cheekbones, made me think of angels beneath the sea—and when I realized that fact, I went from being smitten to being in love.

While I sat in the Cygnus Tavern like a mooncalf, Selise would find a way to brush my shoulder or stroke my arm when she thought no one was looking. Each time my ship steamed away to Albion, I held my memories of her like a jeweler polishing and re-polishing a precious gem, and on each trip back to Poseidon City, I spent the days thinking about when I would see Selise again. That proved to be a cure from the seductive call of the angels.

Finally, at the start of a long storm season, which the weather diviners claimed would be the most severe in decades, I decided to stay behind and give up the sea. I had saved up my pay, because with dreams of Selise to occupy me, I had little need to spend my wages on carousing, though I did occasionally buy exotic treasures that I brought back to Selise.

In Crown City, I had bought a ring of the Watchmaker's gold, and when I returned to Atlantis, I purchased the most beautiful fire opal from the quarries of Endoline. It seemed a perfect balance—a gem from Atlantis, a gold ring from Albion, since the two continents pulled me back and forth, with the ocean in between. I intended to give that ring to Selise as a memory of my life as a sailor, the life I would be giving up for her.

Before the hearth in the Cygnus Tavern, I went on bended knee and asked Selise if she would marry me. The late-night crowd of drunken sailors fell into a hush as they realized what I was doing, then let out a roaring cheer when Selise accepted my proposal. From behind the bar, her brother gave me an approving nod, since he had measured me a long time ago.

When the rough storm season came, I was settled in my new home, landbound, a happy newlywed working in the tavern along with Selise and her brother. I felt no regrets; in fact, I barely thought of my former shipmates at all until they came back into the Cygnus Tavern when they returned to port.

A year later Selise's father died, not unexpectedly, but in Nature's odd sense of balance, she discovered she was pregnant soon afterward. Selise eventually gave birth to a healthy, red-faced boy who could squall with hurricane force. We named him Aiden. Selise was a good mother, and I thought I was a good father. The baby grounded me and anchored me. I learned the joys and the exhaustions of being a parent.

My shipmates came and went all year long, telling their adventures, which I knew were mostly lies, but I listened with an increasing wistfulness. Those days seemed so far away. Before long, my baby boy and my wife, both of whom I loved so much, who anchored me, began to feel like genuine anchors dragging me down.

The sea called to me.

I fought it for a long time, strengthening my resolve when Aiden took his first steps, or said his first words, but each time I left the tavern to go out on errands, I took detours to the docks and just stared at the ships, the names painted on the bow, counting which ones I knew.

I watched the brotherhood of sailors as they laughed and joked, singing chanties while they hauled crates, then went out to carouse in the town. They were alive and energetic, full of the moment instead of long-term plans. Back at the Cygnus Tavern, I saw only a horizon composed of everyday days.

Oh, how the sea called to me.

Rickard saw the different look in my eyes, the glances I gave the sailors in the tavern. "You are going to hurt her," he said to me in a low voice, and I was startled at what he had realized—what I, myself, had been unwilling to admit.

I held on as long as I could, but Selise already knew long before I found the courage to talk to her. "It will be just one more voyage," I promised her, a promise that I fully intended to keep. But Selise knew I wouldn't.

"Come back to me," she said. I could tell Selise was heartbroken, but she wouldn't surrender to tears. "As long as I know that, I can stay here. I have a home and a good business, my brother and his family to keep me company. I won't be the only sailor's wife in Poseidon City. That's how it is. Just don't make me a sailor's widow."

Several captains offered to take me aboard as part of the crew, and I chose my ship carefully. I kissed my wife and held her so tightly and for so long that I almost changed my mind. Almost. I hugged my three-year-old boy and swung him around so that his memory of me would be laughter and smiles.

Then we sailed off for Albion.

The sea was a calming influence on me. I had satisfied my hunger, and now I could relax, like sipping a glass of fine brandy after a delicious meal. The ocean was calm, and the passage both ways was uneventful—so uneventful, in fact, that when I brought my pay back to the tavern, I suggested that I make just one more voyage. I hadn't been gone that long—only a month—and I had barely gotten the taste of a sailor's life again. Selise was resigned but not surprised.

Then it became a third voyage, a fourth, and a fifth. I would stay home for a week in port, help as needed around the tavern, spend time with Aiden and Selise. The Cygnus Tavern prospered, and my family wanted for nothing.

On my seventh voyage, though, the angels beneath the sea called to me again, sang to me, and set their hook in my heart. That irresistible pull dragged me out onto the deck at midnight, stumbling, like a fish being reeled in. The songs swelled inside me, the voices like diamonds and honeydew. They sang to me of wishes that could indeed come true and of the tyranny of unfulfilled dreams. They moved me. How they moved me!

I tried to be silent as I went out on deck, for I wanted no interruptions, no sailor on the night watch to stop me as had happened before, but I felt as if I'd lost my sea legs. My knees were wobbly—though it didn't matter to me because when I joined the undersea angels I could fly with them beneath the water, maybe even sprout my own pair of iridescent wings.

I saw them swimming beside the ship, goddesses of light beneath the waves—wings spread, arms outstretched, mouths open and filled with promises. It would have been so easy to slip overboard and be with them. So easy ...

Although the temptation was like a storm front, I chose to resist. I thought of my anchor, my Selise, my Aiden, my family, my home, the Cygnus Tavern. Under the onslaught of the angels, my lifeline felt as thin and fragile as spider silk, yet I clung to it nevertheless. I cherished Selise's face, remembered running my fingertips along her cheek, kissing her lips.

Yet the angels still called me.

I remembered my laughing boy, swinging him around in my arms to make sure he remembered me when I was gone. Was that how he would remember me forever, if I went with the undersea angels now?

No!

I tried. I fought. I felt drunk with desire as the song resonated in my head, in my heart, and in my soul. The angels in the water spread their arms. They sang. My lifeline stretched and frayed, and I knew I was lost. I could not resist.

Suddenly, another sailor was beside me, grinning like a madman. His eyes were wide, delirious. Laughing, he leaped over the rail into the sea.

In that moment the spell was broken. I watched the man disappear beneath the waves. The angels enfolded him, and for a moment their iridescent wings looked sharp and dark, like shark fins.

I came to my senses, yelling, "Man overboard! Man overboard!" But it would be no use. The angels had wanted me—or they had wanted *someone*, and they were satisfied with the companion, or the victim, they had received. I was shaken, heartsick, and terrified because I knew that if they ever made that call again—and oh how I wanted them to!—I would not escape.

After that ordeal, I hurried back to the safety of home. *Home*—the word meant something more to me again.

Those dark and tantalizing fears out in the sea had burned me, changed me, and when my steamer finally returned to the Poseidon City harbor, I could not get off the ship fast enough. I raced to the Cygnus Tavern, found my beautiful Selise and my laughing boy Aiden, swept them both up in a hug, and promised I would stay with them from that point on.

For months, I took solace in the daily routine of the inn—working the bar, sweeping the floor, dealing with customers, performing chores. At night I held my wife and slept soundly, though occasionally I was haunted by nightmares—and sometimes seductive dreams—of the angels beneath the sea. But *Selise* was my angel, and the call of family was far stronger than the call of the sea.

I managed to keep that promise for more than two years.

I would carry Aiden on my shoulders, but as he grew older he insisted on walking beside me. We spent days at the docks watching the steamers, seeing the cargoes they brought in from distant Albion, watching the crates of exotic gemstones and alchemical minerals delivered from the mines inland.

I told the boy of my seafaring adventures, and Aiden was enthralled, just as I had been as a boy in long-forgotten Heartshore. I described Chronos City and the Clockwork Angels, careful not to mention those far more dangerous angels in the sea.

But as my life's pendulum swung back the other direction and the balance shifted again, the terrors of those feminine voices disappeared into memory. I never doubted what had happened to me that night, but the call of the sea tugged in the opposite direction, pulling me away from my home and out to that compelling expanse of ocean.

Selise saw the yearning in my eyes and in my heart, and she knew what I was thinking. She had never understood the pull on a sailor's heart, but she understood *me*, and she knew that I would be miserable if she didn't let me go. "I would rather have you part of the time than lose you forever," she said. "Find a ship, do a voyage or two until you get it out of your system, then come back to me and stay for a time."

Selise made me promise to stay home during the dangerous storm season, and I agreed to the condition, but I understood there were greater dangers out in the sea than mere storms. I knew what lay beneath.

Before I set off again, I prepared myself. When I signed aboard another steamer, I knew how to protect myself.

I had paid a blacksmith to craft me a pair of manacles.

I did not hear the singing of the angels again for two more years, by which time I was captain of my own small ship. And the next time the ethereal music throbbed in my head and in my soul, I locked the manacles around the rail and around my wrist. To keep me safe. The keys were in my cabin, and my first mate had his instructions.

In the pale moonlight, I gazed down at the painfully beautiful women with their iridescent wings, their beckoning arms, their beseeching expressions. They insisted that I join them—and more than anything else in my life, I wanted to do just that. I longed to jump overboard.

But the manacles held me back. I fought and struggled, unable to think straight, and when I reached out for memories of Selise and Aiden and the cozy Cygnus Tavern, the angels' tone changed. They became angry, *jealous*. They did not like to be defeated. I had failed them, betrayed them, tricked them—and I thought I had betrayed myself.

I thrashed against the manacle, bemoaning my helplessness, wondering why I had been so foolish. Then other sailors ran down the deck toward me, grabbed me and held me even as I struggled. My wrists were raw and bloodied.

But the singing fell silent. The frustrated angels vanished, leaving me alone.

When I came to my senses again, I embraced the memory with great satisfaction, reveling in the experience. The angels were like a dangerous drug, but my resolve and my love for my family was stronger than the pull of that addiction. The manacles had bit into my wrists, but I was alive.

Though many sailors talked about the angels beneath the sea, and some claimed to have seen or heard the calling, no one had escaped them unscathed as I had.

After time and tribulations, I found a satisfactory story balance, a stable point between the pull of the sea and the pull of my family back at the Cygnus Tavern. It seemed appropriate when I learned that in ancient times Cygnus the swan was also a god of *balance*. What could be more fitting?

I would sail during the trading season, stay home during the storm season. I was reliable and competent, and eventually I became captain of a larger ship.

My son grew to be a sturdy lad who helped his mother and uncle at the tavern, but he also sneaked off to the docks to watch the sailors. Selise and I eventually gave Aiden a little sister, an adorable copper-haired girl we named Cythia—all blue eyes, sparkles, and freckles, as much of a joy to our family as our son had been.

When I sailed back and forth across the sea, the crew indulged my peculiar habit of staying out on certain nights manacled to the rail, so I could stare at the water with my head cocked just so, listening hard into the whooshing silence. Some thought I was eccentric; others thought me mad.

Five more times over the years, the angels came to me, calling with more and more urgency, and though I wrestled with the manacles, I could not detach them. I endured, and I adored, and I recovered from the pain of bruised wrists with the euphoria of the music I had heard and the beauty I had seen.

I became the captain of the *Rocinante*, a majestic ship with a thick hull and a wide beam that could ride through any storms. Our fighters could fend off the Wreckers if need be. I had the respect of my fellow captains, and I had my quiet, perfect home at the Cygnus Tavern. The best of both worlds.

Cythia grew into a spunky girl who stopped clinging to her mother's skirts and learned how to get into trouble all on her own. Aiden became a headstrong young man with dreams of his own, so I was not surprised when, coming home from a voyage, I found Selise in tears and a shadow over the tavern.

"It's those stories you put in his head! You and the other men in the tavern." She clenched her fists and pounded my shoulders. "Aiden ran off to sea! He signed aboard a steamer to work as a cabin boy. He's gone!"

With a heavy heart, I held Selise as she let her anger rush out like the retreating tide. I had seen the look in our son's eyes, and I knew the call of the sea was strong in him. "He'll be all right," I reassured her. "Just as I was. It's in his blood. If you understand me, then you understand Aiden."

She was weak and shaken, and I knew she had been crying for days. "All that we can do is wish him well. It's what he wants." I made her a promise that I knew I truly would keep. "When he comes home, I'll take him aboard the *Rocinante*. He could work as a ship's mate with me. There's no need for him to be on a strange ship. We'll be together, and we'll both come home to see you."

She brightened, as if that thought had not occurred to her. I continued to hold her. "He'll be safe with me," I lied.

I learned the name of the steamer Aiden had joined—a good vessel and a good captain, so I knew my boy was in satisfactory company. It would probably take a voyage or two before I could find him, work out an agreement with the captain, and bring my son aboard the *Rocinante*, but it would happen.

As my ship headed back out for Albion, the air took on a sour smell as of something dead. A red tide—a poisonous bloom of algae that sucked all life from the water like a spreading bloodstain on the waves.

A pall settled over the crew, and I gave orders for the *Rocinante* to keep going at full steam, anxious to make our way through the ocean sickness as swiftly as possible. But the red tide went on and on, and we hadn't found the end of it even by sunset.

Late that night with a full moon overhead, I couldn't sleep. I felt an uneasiness in my mind as if the angels were singing to me again, but this time in an off-key dirge. I ventured out onto the deck, heading to the bow where I could be alone. The stars looked down as I fastened my manacle to the rail, just in case.

Before long, the sea took on a luminous character, the phosphorescence that preceded the appearance of the undersea angels, but this time it was a sickly red glow, filtered through the algae and the belly-up fish bobbing in its path.

The angels began singing, and I heard them in my heart. I tugged on the manacle chain and looked over the side of the steamer. The beautiful forms appeared, oblivious to the death around them, spreading their iridescent wings as they looked up at me with unearthly eyes. Their song was as powerful as always, but compelling in a different way—not as seductive, not as jealous. Not as angry. This felt...*victorious*, as if the angels were somehow satisfied at last.

I strained against the manacle, and the metal cuff bit into my wrist, but the pain didn't jar me out of the hypnotic trance.

The angels swam together at the waterline, glorious, yet also terrible. When they saw me gazing at them, they *laughed*, and the music broke off inside my head. Two of the angels swam away with a flash of their undersea wings, leaving only one behind.

I was baffled. I had withstood their advances for so many times, and they would no longer try to tempt me. The last angel looked up at me. *We don't want you.* Her voice was an insidious whisper within my brain. *We don't need you.*

She began to stroke away from the *Rocinante* before she laughed again.

We have your son.

Then the angel dove beneath the water, leaving me there, chained to the rail and unable to escape the heartbreaking news. I sobbed until dawn.

I still have the manacles, but the angels have stopped calling to me, singing to me. They are satisfied with what they took, and now the sea, for all its mysteries, is just an empty book.

I'm known for writing giant, complicated novels with intertwined storylines and a large cast of characters, multi-volume epics that have consumed the paper from many trees. But sometimes I like to stretch my creative muscles in the other direction, seeing just how short I can write. These efforts can turn out to be extreme, micro-fiction of only a few words, like:

"Cliché"
Once upon a time, they lived happily ever after ...
But then they woke up, and it was all a dream!

Or,

"Letter of Resignation"
Dear Mr. Escher,
I quit. I just can't take it anymore.
Your housecleaner

Or another one,

"Tea Time Before Perseus"

The lonely Medusa sat inside her ever-growing statue garden. She waited for more company to arrive, hoping that today there might be a chance for some conversation.

While clever vignettes, those don't comprise an entire story.
The following piece was inspired by the memory of my parents

frequently forgetting the two-hour time difference after I had moved away from home, leaving Wisconsin for a job in California. They would often call at odd times, not realizing it was still very early in the morning for me, or that I wasn't home from work yet. "Time Zone" uses that as a springboard for a Twilight Zone-style story.

TIME ZONE

I had just gotten home from work, ready to start dinner for myself, when the phone rang. It wasn't even 5:30 yet, but the dinner hour is exactly when phone solicitors like to prey on customers. I answered with a "Hello" that was more like a sigh.

"Ronnie! Are you all right? We're so worried!" Not a salesman, then—my parents, back in Wisconsin.

I had moved to California only a month ago, and my parents seemed as lonely as I was. They often called just to hear my voice.

Right after college I had taken a job for a large company in the San Francisco area. I was a young man living on my own for the first time, far from home. My fiancée would follow me in six months, but for now I was solo, except for babysitting her dog, a fat and snorting pug named Beau that she loved for reasons more unfathomable than the reasons why she loved me. Beau greeted me now with far more exuberance than I wanted, demanding attention while I concentrated on the phone.

"Of course, I'm all right. I just walked in the door from work. Did you forget about the time change again? I'm not usually home this early." My parents lived in rural Wisconsin, had never traveled farther than the adjacent states, and certainly never left the country. Their business was local, never had to worry about calling New York or Los Angeles. "You're two hours earlier, remember?"

"No, the earthquake!" my mom said. "It's been on the news non-stop."

My dad broke in, talking on the extension. "A major quake. San Francisco is leveled. We couldn't get through—the phone lines have been jammed for more than an hour, but we tried and tried."

I looked around my intact townhouse. "Everything's normal. No earthquake."

Beau snorted and farted, wagged his tail so forcefully that his entire body wobbled. I bent over to pat him on the head, hard.

"We're watching the report on Fox right now," my dad said. "Total devastation. We thought you were hurt. We couldn't get through."

I thought about fake news. My parents have often been duped. "No quake, honest. Not even a little devastation."

My mom was crying. My dad was tense. "I'm reading the crawl right now! Magnitude 6.0 earthquake hit the East Bay at 5:35 PM."

I looked at the clock on the wall. "It's not even 5:35 yet. You're forgetting the time change again. You're two hours ahead."

At my feet, Beau whined and then began barking, much more agitated than his usual excitement about my lukewarm affections. Then he began to howl.

"I'm so glad." Mom's voice still sounded strangled with disbelief. "I don't know how to explain it."

I tried to shush the dog, but Beau was going crazy.

"Nothing to worry about, Mom." I wondered what other crackpot conspiracy theory would set them off next.

The clock hit 5:35.

The ground started to shake beneath my feet.

H.G. Wells's The War of the Worlds *made me want to become a writer. When I was only five or six years old, my parents let me watch the classic film of* The War of the Worlds, *and it changed my life. That was the type of thing I wanted to write! I was so moved, inspired, and fascinated by the story that I couldn't get it out of my head.*

And I've used Wells as an inspiration for much of my writing. This story is one of the most obvious results of that, featuring a young H.G. Wells and his own (fictional) inspiration for the horrific Martian invasion.

SCIENTIFIC ROMANCE

Late after dark on a chill November night, young Wells followed T.H. Huxley up to the labyrinthine rooftop. The air felt damp, tinged with a clammy mist, yet the sky overhead was dark and clear and sparkling with stars.

The meteors would begin falling soon.

The minarets and gables of London's Normal School of Science provided nooks, crannies, gutters, and eaves where students could hold secret meetings, perhaps rendezvous with young girls from the poorer sections of South Kensington. Wells doubted, though, that any of his classmates would climb to the sprawling rooftop for the same purpose as his teacher and mentor led him now.

Huxley's creaking bones and aching limbs forced the old man to move slowly along the precarious shingles. Wells knew better than to offer the professor any assistance. Huxley finally found a spot against a gable and eased himself down. Leaning backward, he propped his head up and stared into the depths of the universe.

"Is this your first meteor shower, Herbert?" Huxley asked. "The Leonids are a good place to start. We should see about twenty per hour."

Wells, at only eighteen and much more limber, struggled to find his own comfortable observation place. "I've seen shooting stars before, sir," he said, "but I've never actually ... studied them."

Huxley gave a wheezing laugh. His voice sounded strange to Wells, a private conversational tone instead of the forceful oratory for which he had become famous across England. "From what I can see, young man, you study every facet of life with those quick and darting eyes of yours."

Wells blushed, then ran a hand across his face to hide his embarrassment. His unkempt dark hair fell over his forehead, and his moustache showed gaps where the whiskers hadn't yet filled in enough.

He fidgeted, working himself into an awkward squat, holding onto a gutter for balance. Huxley intended to stay out here for hours, but the conversation interested Wells more than his personal comfort. Ideas made mankind superior to other creatures ... and superior men had superior ideas.

The flash in his peripheral vision took him completely by surprise. "There!" he shouted, gesturing so rapidly that he nearly lost his precarious balance on the angled roof. A streak of brilliant, white light shot overhead then evaporated, so transient it seemed barely an afterimage on his eyes.

"The first meteor of the night," Huxley said with a smile, "and you spotted it, Wells. I'm proud of you. But of course, your eyesight is much better than mine."

"But your eyes have seen more things, sir," Wells said, then hated the reverential tone he had let slip.

"Don't flatter me," Huxley warned. The old man's wit and intellect were as bright as the sun, but his personality remained acerbic and abrasive. Wells would tolerate any number of rebukes, though, for the insights the professor had given him during his biology lectures.

Even now, Huxley fell comfortably into the role of teacher. "Make note of the meteorites we see this evening, and you will be able to envision their radiant point in the constellation Leo."

Wells settled back to continue watching. Bright in the western ecliptic, the ruddy point of Mars hung like a baleful eye, not twinkling, though the other stars around it glittered and flickered.

He shivered from the chill in the air, then tapped his foot, always moving, trying to get warm. Due to his severe financial situation, Wells was underweight and scrawny ... even cadaverous, if one were to believe his roommate and friend, A.V. Jennings. On Tuesdays, the day before weekly pay for the scholars, Wells occasionally could not afford lunch, and Jennings would take him out to fill up on beefsteak and beer so that they could return replenished to the workbench in Huxley's laboratory.

Wells's wardrobe was meagre, consisting of grubby dark suits and worn celluloid shirt collars. His thin jacket was insufficient against the chill of the November evening, but he had no desire to go back inside the school building.

A second meteor appeared overhead like a line drawn with a pen of fire, eerie in its total silence. "Another!"

Around them the city of London made its own nighttime noises. Horse carts and black cabs clopped quietly by, while prostitutes flounced into dim alleys or waited under the gas streetlamps. Across the park, in the boarding house at Westbourne Grove where he and Jennings shared a room, Wells knew the other residents would be engaged in their nightly carousing, brawls, singing, and drinking. Here, high above it all, though, he enjoyed the peace.

Within moments a third meteor passed overhead, far from the trivial human concerns around him. This shooting star was larger and louder than the others, sputtering. Mentally tracing the fiery line back to its origin, Wells saw that the meteor radiated from a point in the sky not far from Mars itself, almost as if the red planet were launching them like sparks from a grinding wheel.

"Do you ever imagine, Professor Huxley, sir," he said as an intriguing idea formed in his mind, "that perhaps these flaming meteors are signals of a kind, even ships that have crossed the gulf of space?" Wells had had many outrageous ideas since the age of seven, and he often spoke his speculations aloud, sometimes to the entertainment of others, sometimes to their annoyance.

Huxley shifted position, looking over at his student with keen interest. "Ships?" His eyes held a bold challenge, as did his tone. "And from whence would they come, Wells?"

Wells rose to the occasion. "Why not ... Mars, for instance?" He indicated the orange-red pinpoint of the planet. "According to theory, as the solar system cooled, each planet became hospitable to life in relation to its distance from the Sun. On Mars, therefore, intelligent life could have begun to evolve long before any such spark occurred on Earth."

At the mention of evolution, Huxley perked up—just as Wells had known he would. The professor had spent his life as a proponent of Darwinism, had debated buffoons and ill-educated orators in so many forums that Huxley became infamous as "Darwin's Bulldog."

Another shooting star passed overhead, as if to emphasize Wells's point.

"Martians," Huxley said with a wry smile. "Interesting. And what do you suppose a Martian would look like?"

Wells folded one leg over the other, in spite of his precarious rooftop position, and restrained himself from answering instantly. Huxley did not suffer foolish or glib answers. "I would suppose that since the Martians are a much more ancient race, they would have minds immeasurably superior to our own. Their bodies would be composed almost entirely of brain."

Two more faint Leonid meteors danced overhead unnoticed. Wells uncrossed and recrossed his legs.

"And what would such beings look like?"

Wells frowned, letting his thoughts flow. "Natural selection would ultimately shape a superior being into a creature with a huge head and eyes. He would have delicate hands, tentacles perhaps, for manipulating tools—but his mentality would be his greatest tool."

"An interesting exercise, Wells. You have quite an imagination." Huxley leaned forward from his cramped position against the gable, scooting across the roof tiles so that he could speak in a low, hoarse voice to his protégé. "But why would Martians want to come to our green Earth? What is their motive?"

Wells was ready for that one. "Mars is a dry planet, cold and drained of resources. Our world is younger, fresher, more vibrant —filled with all the things they have lost over the course of their evolution. Perhaps even now the Martians are regarding this Earth with envious eyes. They might even be drawing up plans for invasion."

As a boy, Wells had studied military history, staging mock battles in the park, and observing the movements of one historical army against another. But an interplanetary war was beyond his comprehension.

"A war of the worlds?" Huxley actually chuckled at this. "And you believe that such superior minds as you propose would engage in an exercise as trivial as military conquest? You must not consider them so evolved after all."

Wells kept his thoughts to himself, for he had suddenly realized that perhaps Thomas H. Huxley was a bit naïve himself.

In his life, Wells had seen the gross divisions of the upper and lower classes and how each fought amongst the others for dominance. His sweet, hard-working mother had sent him off to be apprenticed to a draper, where he had labored as a virtual slave. After escaping that fate through his own calculated incompetence, Wells had lived with his mother where she was the head domestic servant in a large manor, and she had commanded the workers beneath her. His angry father had once been a gardener, but for years had found no better employment than occasional cricket playing....

The hierarchy remained, no matter what their social standing, powerful and powerless. It proved to Wells's satisfaction the Darwinian basis that all humans had been predators at some time in the past.

Wells answered his professor carefully. "If the Martians are a dying race," he said, "it would be survival of the fittest. The

Martians would see Earth ripe for conquest, humans as inferior cattle."

"Survival of the fittest—I'll concede that point, Wells," Huxley said. "We must hope the Martians do not invade." He shifted back to his former position, where he watched for further Leonids.

The two sat in silence, looking into the clear sky. Wells shivered, partially from the cold, partially from his own thoughts.

They watched the stars fall as the red eye of Mars blinked balefully at them.

The following day, in the bustling laboratory section of Huxley's biology course, Wells felt feverish. He wondered if he had caught a chill from the previous night's vigil.

Nevertheless, the sounds of clacking beakers, the smell of old chemical experiments, and the chatter of students engaged his mind. He soon became totally absorbed in the setting up of microscopes and experimental apparatus for the morning's exercise.

One of Huxley's assistants—a demonstrator who delivered occasional lectures when Huxley himself was too ill to speak— prepared the laboratory activity. As if he were a prize French chef, he presented a pot in which he had prepared an infusion of local weeds and pond water. The resulting murky concoction was infested with numerous fascinating microbes.

Wells's workbench partner, A.V. Jennings, was the son of a doctor. He received a small stipend, which allowed him much greater security than Wells, though they both lived in an unpleasant boarding house an intellectual world away from the high atmosphere of Huxley's lecture hall.

Now, while Jennings set up their shared microscope on a narrow table against the windows, Wells went forward with his microscope slide to receive a drop of the precious infusion, as if it were some scientific communion. He carefully slid a cover slip over the beer-colored droplet and returned to where his partner had finished preparing the apparatus.

Under watery light shining through a veil of gray clouds, Wells focused and refocused the microscope. Jennings had a sketchpad, as did Wells, to record their observations. Wells feverishly sketched the alien-looking creatures he observed: protozoans of all types, alien shapes with whipping flagella, hairlike cilia vibrating in a blur ... blobby amoebas, various strains of algae.

As Wells scrutinized the exotic creatures swarming and multiplying in the tiny universe of a drop of water, he felt like a titan. His looming presence stared through an eyepiece to observe the tiny struggles of pond microorganisms....

Wells realized that the other students had stopped their conversations and stood at attention, as if a royal presence had entered the room. Professor T.H. Huxley had deigned to visit his laboratory this morning.

The intimidating, acerbic old man strode around the various workbenches where his students diligently studied the infinitesimal animals they found on their microscope slides. Huxley nodded approvingly, made quiet sounds but little conversation, and moved from station to station.

When the great man came to where Wells stood proudly beside his microscope, Huxley said in a gruff voice, "Morning, Wells." The professor bent over to study their slide, adjusted the focus ever so slightly as if it were his due. "Lovely euglena you have here under the light." He made another noncommittal sound, then moved on to the other students.

Wells stood looking after his mentor, disappointed. Huxley had made no mention of their shared experience with the meteor shower, their imaginative conversation. He had come here for no purpose other than to scrutinize his insignificant students ... in the same way that Wells and Jennings had been studying the microbes.

His cheeks flushed, and the cool feverish sweat swept over him. He extended his imagination farther, wondering if other powerful beings might even now be scrutinizing Earth in the same manner, curious about the buzzing and swarming colony of London.

The hair on the back of his neck prickled, as if he could sense the probing eyes watching him from afar.

He was startled to find Jennings regarding him oddly. "You don't look at all well, Herbert," he said. Jennings reached over with practiced ease and touched Wells's forehead. "In fact, you're burning up." He frowned. "I think you should go home and rest before this grows more serious."

The fever caught hold with nightmarish strength, and Wells fell into a labyrinth of delirium fostered by the powerful resources of his own imagination.

He saw meteors falling and falling, huge cylinders accompanied by green fire that blazed across the sky. The interplanetary ships crashed to Earth, pummeling England like quail shot.

In the great impact craters where they settled and cooled, the cylinders opened up to reveal that they were warships from the red planet, carrying hordes of invading Martians—hugely developed brains with tentacled limbs evolved under a lower gravity.

Their vast mentalities had turned toward the conquest of Earth. The most insignificant of these extraordinarily developed creatures had a military intellect far superior to the combined genius of Napoleon and Alexander the Great.

Using their whiplike appendages, the Martians built war machines, clanking metal things on tall stilt-like legs that surpassed even the imagination of Leonardo Da Vinci.

The clanking machines strode about the English landscape like the industrial contraptions he had seen among the dark factories of the dirty towns where he had worked as a draper's apprentice. But these machines were equipped with weapons, powerful heat rays that burned everything in sight.

Hot like Wells's fever.

And overhead the meteors continued falling, falling....

When the fever finally broke, Wells awoke in his narrow, lumpy bed to find Jennings tending him, laying a cool rag over his forehead. A patch of bright, hot sunlight spilled through the window, warming his skin.

Wells croaked, his voice uncooperative, but he spoke quickly, not wanting his roommate to get the best of him with a first witticism. "What now, Jennings?" he said. "Are you practicing to become a doctor like your father?"

Jennings smiled. His eyes were red-rimmed, as if he hadn't gotten much sleep. "You've had quite a time of it, Herbert. Been sick for days, feverish, haven't eaten a thing but a bit of broth I managed to acquire for you."

"Worst of all, you've missed three of my lectures," said another voice.

Weakly, Wells managed to prop himself up enough to see another man standing in the small, stuffy room. T.H. Huxley himself.

"Since you are one of only three students who has so far proved worthy of a first-class passing grade," the old professor said, "I wanted to see why you were so rude as to forsake my class." Huxley's voice was stern but subdued, as if he were restraining his normal booming tone only with great difficulty.

"Not to worry, sir," Wells said. "I'm sure Jennings took good notes."

It embarrassed him that Huxley had to see how lowly his student lived. The room in South Kensington had a crowded, squalid appearance, with too many brutish noises that carried through the walls as other boarders came in drunk at all hours. The air was cold—no one had brought up coal for some time—

and smelled rank from unemptied chamber pots sitting out in the hall.

The professor maintained a mock stern expression. "I should have been quite disappointed had you died, Wells. Though you are only eighteen, I see great potential in you."

Huxley paced the room as if searching for something significant to say. Wells waited for him. "Quite humbling, isn't it?" the professor finally said. "A superior creature such as yourself, highly evolved and possessed of a grand intellect—laid low by something as crude and insignificant as an Earthly germ."

Wells gave a wan smile in response. "I'm sorry, sir. I shall try to prove my evolutionary superiority henceforth."

Huxley sighed reticently and paused at the door, ready to leave. "You may wish to know, Wells, that I have decided this will be my last semester teaching. I've spent far too many years trying to show everyone the obvious truth, and I shall give it up and retire out of sheer exhaustion."

Distraught, Wells cried, "But, sir, there's so much more we can learn from you!"

"I have wasted far too much time and energy in debates with fools over the correctness of Darwinism. I've earned myself a rest. But I will need someone to carry on, eventually."

Huxley opened the door, adjusted his hat, and frowned back at his sick student. "With your imagination, I think you can make something of yourself, Wells," he said. "Don't disappoint me."

Then Huxley left, heading out to far more pleasant surroundings on the other side of the park.

Wells leaned back into his bed while Jennings stared at him in awe. "That was quite a benediction, Herbert."

Wells lay back and closed his eyes, dizzy with residual weakness from the fever. But his mind was already whirling and spinning, filled with a thousand thoughts.

"I think I'll rest for a bit, Jennings," he said.

After all, he had to restore his health before he could begin his life's work.

Ah, Dungeons & Dragons! What an influence on my life as a fan and a writer.

I first discovered D&D when I was in college. A group of us played a game every Sunday night, and our dungeon master, whom I met in a creative writing class, was Kristine Kathryn Rusch, who would go on to become a very successful and award-winning novelist herself.

Those weekly games captivated my imagination. At a time when I had read The Lord of the Rings, The Sword of Shannara, *and* The Chronicles of Thomas Covenant the Unbeliever, *D&D was the purest distillation and the greatest expansion of everything I loved about fantasy fiction. Our weekly campaign, in fact, inspired Kris Rusch's first novel,* The White Mists of Power, *as well as my first fantasy trilogy,* Gamearth, Gameplay, *and* Game's End *(recently republished as the HexWorld Trilogy).*

So, yes, Dungeons & Dragons has been very, very good to me. I even had a beer with Gary Gygax, the original creator of the game, at a gaming convention where I was the author guest of honor, and I worked as a consultant for Wizards of the Coast on one of their game expansions.

Given that background, I was delighted to contribute a story to a new Dungeons & Dragons anthology. I was offered my pick of their D&D universes. Which one to choose? I settled on the exotic Dark Sun universe and wrote a minotaur gladiator story, an unabashed celebration of the fantasy genre.

BLOOD OASIS

Seawater moved against the hull planks like a lover's whisper. The yellow sun of Athas was bright, and a westerly breeze stretched the *Horizon Finder*'s sails, guiding the three-masted carrack toward the seaport of Arkhold.

Unexpected spray whipped up from the bow, and Jisanne laughed. She had untied her long brown hair, letting it blow loose and free. She drew a deep breath with a sense of wonder that these sailors did not feel. They didn't understand how lucky they were to be here.

Captain Hurunn, a wealthy minotaur merchant with a large gold ring in one floppy ear, said, "A long voyage, a full cargo hold, even a net overloaded with fresh fish—time for me to settle down and enjoy my profits." Even when he was in a good mood, Hurunn's voice sounded like a gruff growl. From what little Jisanne knew from her brief previous visits to this glorious time, she doubted the minotaur captain would ever settle down.

With gentle reverence, she touched the opalescent crystal mounted to the compass stand. "The navigation crystal always finds its way back here." She was never sure how clearly the ship's captain and crew could see or hear her.

Hurunn snorted. "It's what the navigation crystal is for—to guide its owner home. It's a simple enough spell."

Jisanne shuddered at his casual attitude, forcing herself to remember that these people did not automatically hate and fear magic users, regardless of whether they were defilers or preservers. Whatever disasters had robbed Athas of this beauty had not happened yet. The world was still fresh and alive, as it had been before its possibilities were stolen.

The *Horizon Finder* entered the mouth of the harbor, and crewmen gathered on deck, waving at the numerous fishing boats, feluccas, and galleys. They were all anxious to get back to port.

High above, the elf lookout yelled, his already-thin voice even more high pitched. "To arms—sea serpent off the stern! It's following us."

As the crew scrambled to snag harpoons and bows, a fearsome triangular head rose up, streaming seawater from its golden scales. Its hinged jaw dropped open to reveal long fangs. A short distance away, a second monster rose up.

"That's *two* sea serpents, not one," Hurunn growled. "I need a better lookout for my next voyage."

The pair of serpents glided toward the *Horizon Finder*, intent on attack. Seeing the swollen net of still-squirming fish suspended by a rope and winch above the stern, Jisanne had a sudden realization. "The fish—the serpents want the fish."

"Of course they want the fish. They always want the fish," the minotaur said, not overly concerned. "I was hoping we'd make it all the way to Arkhold, but these waters are infested with cursed sea serpents. A small enough price to pay."

With a deep bellow such as only a minotaur could manage, Hurunn commanded his sailors to swing the boom over the water. The sea serpents pressed closer to the dangling net, snapping at the spray in the carrack's wake. "Dump the catch!"

As twitching fish rained down, the serpents frolicked in the water, greedily feasting. From the rails, the sailors jeered at the monsters, and Hurunn complained—out of habit—about the money he'd just lost. The breeze picked up, blowing the ship safely into port and leaving the sea serpents behind.

Ahead, Jisanne stared at the thriving city. The fortress of a forgotten order of ancient knights sat atop the highest point overlooking the blue harbor. People had gathered down at the docks to welcome the sailing ship. A few ambitious traders even took small boats out to meet the *Horizon Finder*, hoping to strike a sweet deal with Captain Hurunn before he came to the quay.

The minotaur handed Jisanne a flask of wine. "Here, to celebrate. Myself, I don't drink the stuff." He snuffled through his bull nose. "Clogs my sinuses."

She took a swig of the richest, headiest wine she had ever tasted. Everything seemed so unreal.

As the carrack tied up to a long stone quay, Jisanne saw the colorful market stalls full of fresh fruit. Musicians played instruments, their competing tunes a raucous clash of sounds. Jisanne took another drink from the wine flask and glanced down at the pristine navigation crystal. Tears stung her eyes. She didn't want to lose any of this, but she knew—

As the scene around her faded, the moist salty air in her nostrils became harsh, sour, and dry. The puffy clouds in the sky shimmered into high blowing dust. The skirling music and the babble of marketplace sounds turned into the moan of desert wind.

"No!" But her cry was just a whisper, words lost in time. Jisanne clutched at the fabric of the world, digging deeper into the arcane magic, not caring where she found the power to hold on for just a few moments longer, but it was no use.

The blue ocean, the lush harbor, the vibrant city were all swallowed into dust. The waves became dunes, the horizon only an empty basin of powder, the Sea of Silt. Exposed by scouring winds, chains of ivory vertebrae and skulls with chipped fangs marked the long-desiccated carcasses of sea serpents. The minotaur captain, his elven lookout, and the rest of the ship's crew didn't notice they were vanishing. *She* was slipping in time, not them.

That Athas, that golden age, was long gone.

Jisanne dropped to her knees on the deck of a skeletal wreck against a crumbling stone quay. Overhead, the bloated red sun was like an angry coal. The ancient flask of wine in her hand was as parched as the landscape. Next to her, propped up by a flat stone, sat a clay bowl half-full of her dark, drying blood; the dull shard of the navigation crystal was immersed in the liquid.

Jisanne felt weak and alone, drained. She had used defiling magic by drawing on her own life force, not caring about the cost of her spell. She had restored the lovely, Eden-like landscape of Athas for a time ... too short a time.

And now she had to face reality again.

The crowds cheered in the stands of the Criterion Coliseum, whistling, calling for blood. The spectators were all the same, regardless of their social status: powerful templars in special travertine seats near the sand of the arena, aloof patricians who whispered about Balic city business in between bloody combat matches, and unruly commoners crowded in higher seats under the hot red sun.

They roared their approval when Koram strode out of the gladiators' gate, wearing his white ceremonial sash with the sign of Dictator Andropinis dyed in red; he hated the sash, but was required to wear it. He adjusted his armor made of sheets of petrified wood, then looked at the stands with passive disgust. These same people had cheered for him when he was elected a praetor of Balic, and they had likewise cheered when he had announced his plans to liberalize the city's laws. Later, when the scheming foreign Praetor Yvoluk, darling of Andropinis, disgraced him on false charges, the fickle crowds had cheered just as loudly. Then, after Koram had been shaved bald and thrown into the Criterion to battle monsters, they'd cheered again, expecting him to die ... and now they cheered each time he emerged victorious.

No one had expected him to survive for seven months in the arena.

The people of Balic would cheer for anything, Koram thought, *so long as blood was involved.* He felt no further loyalty toward them; he had already paid enough. Praetor Yvoluk had seen to that. Koram's wife and young son were already dead, worked to death in slave camps.

Emerging into the ruddy afternoon sunlight, Koram turned slowly and raised his bronze-inlaid ivory sword. Metal was extremely scarce, and good blades even scarcer; most of the other fighters considered him lucky to have a strengthened and embellished sword. But Koram would never consider himself lucky; he had earned this with blood.

As praetor in charge of the arena, Yvoluk could have warned him what sort of beast he would be fighting this day, but the evil templar liked to keep his surprises. Koram would defeat the opponent just the same. Otherwise it would be surrender.

The spectators continued to whistle and stomp. Koram stood in the shade of the stretched awning that covered the noble seats and part of the sand-covered fighting ground. In the pits below, handlers would force animals and monsters onto elevating platforms and turn them loose through trapdoors in the sand.

Koram heard the rumble of machinery, felt the sand tremble at his feet, and prepared himself. Since being sentenced to the Criterion, he had faced Thri-Kreen packs, drays, a Raaig soulflame, two Goliaths, and numerous human warriors. Koram had slain them all because it was the only way for him to survive. He was lucky; he was skilled; he was determined. But he knew Praetor Yvoluk would give him no way out. He had not yet figured out how to kill the praetor for what he had done, but he kept trying to think of a way.

Koram saw something move beneath the arena floor, stalking him ... a burrowing creature that sensed the vibrations of his movements. Koram stood absolutely still. Bored, the spectators in the stands shouted out catcalls, but he didn't budge.

In his special box, Dictator Andropinis sat on his throne under the awning, picking at his fingernails. He seemed an elderly man with a thin face and an intent expression, but he was not intent on the gladiatorial combat before him. When the dictator addressed his people, he exuded power. The sorcerer-king of Balic claimed to have been duly elected to his position several centuries ago—and who could gainsay him? Andropinis attended gladiatorial combats out of a sense of duty, not any real interest. Over the many years of his reign, the dictator had seen, and caused, enough death. Right now, he merely appeared bored.

Bursting out of the arena sand, a trio of gray-skinned anakores spat dust from mouths filled with needle-sharp teeth. Koram identified a large female with a hunched back and a line of thick, knobby protrusions, and two smaller, younger males with smoother hides and gleaming eyes. Anakores hunted in packs, and they would be a formidable team fighting against him.

But he didn't need any assistance. He fought alone.

The first of the younger males lunged toward Koram, and he slashed with his ivory-and-bronze blade. The anakore swung a clawed hand, blinking its black eyes as if unable to see anything but dust, but its wide, flat nose smelled him. As Koram danced away, the vibrations of his footfalls were enough to guide the monster.

The second male circled around and dove in as his companion retreated. Koram spun easily on the loose sand, jabbing again to drive the monster away. Then the older female let out a roar that sounded like an avalanche in a cave. In traditional anakore hunting behavior, one would knock a victim to the ground, while others plunged forward to finish him. The female thundered toward him.

But it was a different ploy. Her challenging bellow had distracted Koram long enough for the two males to dart forward, attacking him from both sides.

He easily decapitated the anakore on his left, and the creature's body kept sliding forward with its own momentum while the head went in a different direction. The other male crashed into him, but Koram slammed his armored shoulder into the monster's body, knocking it to the sands. With a quick, hard thrust, he skewered it through the chest.

The crowd cheered, but Koram did not acknowledge them. Dictator Andropinis continued to study his cuticles, never even looking at the combat.

The female howled and hurled herself at him like a boulder from a catapult. Koram barely had time to recover his balance and lift his sword. As she lunged forward, he swung hard, and the bronze edge of his blade cut the anakore's shoulder. The creature dove again, burying herself in the sand and leaving only a spot of dark blood on the stirred sand.

Koram turned in a slow circle, alert. The two males lay dead on the sand, twitching. He wondered who had caught these creatures in the wild and dragged them here to die in the coliseum. Everything died here, sooner or later.

Some gladiator showmen would have drawn out the battle, making the bloodshed last for most of the afternoon. The people saluted them as heroes, celebrities; those fighters reveled in the attention. Koram, though, didn't care about anyone watching him. He had killed two of the monsters, and he would dispatch the third just as easily.

The female anakore sprang out of the dust again with barely a ripple. Without a flourish, Koram slashed and cut a deep, painful gash along the monster's side. The female reeled, bleeding profusely, and staggered back, retreating from the gladiator. She stopped by the two dead bodies of the younger anakores, swayed, and moaned.

Koram stalked forward, but the female did not fight him. In barely comprehensible words, she touched the blood from her deep wound, then looked at her dead companions. "Merrrrrrrrcy." She dropped her head toward the slain males. "My fammmilleeeeee."

He hesitated, suddenly understanding. Anger and sickness rose up in him like bile. No one had given any mercy to his family, and he knew he could do nothing for this monster. The female would die here soon enough.

"The only mercy here is a quick death," he said, too quietly for the audience to hear. And without further spectacle, he drove the point of his blade through the monster's chest, ramming it all the way to the hilt to be sure of the kill. He jerked his sword back out, letting the anakore die without more pain. The big female collapsed beside the corpses of her sons.

The crowd applauded the speedy dispatch of the three enemies, but their response was lukewarm. Without bothering to cut off the monster's head as a trophy, Koram stalked back toward the gladiators' gate and out of the sun. He was finished for the day.

The lean, bearded templar stood under the stone arch, his face dark with anger. As Koram walked into the shadows of the tunnels, Praetor Yvoluk struck a hard backhand across his sweaty face. "Fight harder, worm dung! Perform for the people—earn another day of your worthless life! You make our opponents seem weak and nonthreatening when you kill them so quickly." His voice was heavily accented; Yvoluk had come from the east, an exile from another city, but he had made a powerful position for himself here.

Koram just looked at the man who had caused him so much pain. "Why don't you face me yourself in the arena? Then I would show you how much I want to fight."

Yvoluk raised his hand, threatening to strike him again, but Koram merely strode past and headed to the large underground cells where the gladiators lived. It was not, and would never be, his home. But it was all he had.

Koram had been optimistic once; he had wanted to help the people of Balic. In the showy democracy espoused by the sorcerer-king, ordinary citizens were supposed to have the freedom to speak; they were allowed to run for the office of praetor, whether or not the Council of Patricians or Andropinis approved. Koram had been so naive, so foolish.

An "unapproved" candidate who managed to be elected praetor met with an unfortunate accident before long. In his own case, Koram had asked too many questions in the first two months, and Yvoluk had orchestrated his downfall, disgracing him with false charges, turning public opinion against Koram (who had been their favorite only weeks before). Though there was no proof, the people did not believe Koram's vehement denials. He was arrested and stripped of his rank. His wife and son were sold to slave raiders for a long march to Tyr, where they died within weeks. Koram was thrown into the gladiator arena, where he did not have the good sense to die. Seven months later, he continued to fight and kill.

His fellow warriors sulked in their rooms, brooding over their fates. Some oiled their muscles or strapped on armor in preparation for upcoming matches in the arena. A pair of dwarves sparred enthusiastically to hone their fighting skills. A newly captured Goliath hunkered on a stone seat in his cell, rocking back and forth, holding his knees; the half-giant's misery was even larger than his body. An insectoid Thri-Kreen tracker, separated from his two psychically bonded partners, sang poetry through his mandibles to drown out the Goliath's moans; the sandy, chittering Thri-Kreen claimed to be a nihilistic philosopher, and he accepted his undoubtedly short life as a gladiator.

Koram had befriended none of his comrades. They would be pitted against one another when monster combatants were in short supply, and if Praetor Yvoluk happened to notice that Koram cared for any particular gladiator, he would take great pleasure in arranging for a death match.

Koram sat on a stone bench and used oil, sand, and a scraper to remove the blood and grit from his skin. He no longer noticed the scabs and scars; all of his motions were mechanical. Another fight, another day.

Before he could lie back and rest on his pallet, however, a call to arms echoed through the barracks beneath the Criterion. Dimly heard through the stone-block walls, the crowds in the stands roared with a sound that was definitely not cheers.

The gladiators stood, looking around in alarm; even the moaning Goliath climbed to his feet, keeping his head and shoulders bent so as not to strike his shaggy head against the ceiling. The two sparring dwarves stopped and listened. They recognized the sound of the alarm. "Balic is under attack."

The Thri-Kreen nihilist changed his song. "Today, our deaths may come in a different manner, but it is death nonetheless." Koram knew that the Thri-Kreen had been renowned as one of the most skilled trackers in his tribe, but his skills were wasted in the arena.

Though the guards had taken his sword, Koram painstakingly strapped his petrified-wood armor back on. Alarms continued to sound outside in the city, gongs and bells ringing. He didn't hurry.

With a clatter of boots and armor, soldiers marched along the stone-tiled tunnels, led by a dark-visaged Yvoluk. The Goliath wrung his hands together and lurched out of his chamber. "Praetor! What is happening?"

Yvoluk's expression soured, as if an olive pit had caught in his throat. "The Skull Wearer leads an army of beast giants to the walls down by the estuary. They've destroyed one of the Dictator's forts on the Dragon's Palate, and now they mean to take the city of Balic." At a signal from the praetor, the guards lashed their whips, making loud cracks against the stone walls. Yvoluk continued to shout. "Gladiators, our beloved Andropinis demands that you defend the city. You will be armed and sent to the walls. You are our bravest fighters. You will save Balic!"

"Why should we?" Koram asked. At another time, he would have been ready to leap into action, but his city had failed him.

Yvoluk curled his purple lips in a tempting smile. "You need incentive? Drive back the beast giants, and I will ask Andropinis to grant you your freedom. Fight for us this day, and you need never fight in the Criterion again!"

The Goliath made a delighted sound, while the sparring dwarves squared their shoulders and grinned. The soldiers handed the gladiators their familiar weapons and rushed them out of the barracks and into the city streets. Koram intentionally wadded the sash that marked him as a fighter for Andropinis and left it behind on the bench in his cell.

The Thri-Kreen tracker matched Koram's pace, leaning over to whisper, "Do you trust Praetor Yvoluk to follow through on his promise?"

"As much as I would trust a footpath across the open Sea of Silt."

Behind them, the Goliath moaned again.

From across the city, soldiers were mustering toward the wall that overlooked the dry estuary where hundreds of faded, dusty silt skimmers tied up to the docks. Yvoluk led the hapless gladiators to the top of the stone barricade, confident in his power.

A deafening tumult thundered from the harbor below. Koram and the gladiators gazed down upon a large army of towering monsters. Hundreds of beast-headed giants waded the silt shallows, slogging through parched, pale depths that would have drowned any man. The giants' heavy armor weighed them down, but they plodded ahead, stirring up clouds of fine dust. Their heads were a menagerie of ferocious creatures, fanged feline predators, reptilian saurians, bloodthirsty lupine monsters, sharp-beaked birds of prey.

At the lead of the encroaching army stood a dominating figure, a huge giant with a necklace of skulls that dangled from a thick cord at his throat. The most fearsome of the beast giants, Skull Wearer supposedly drew power from the spirits of those he had slain—and he had slain many. With legendary animosity toward the civilized inhabitants of Balic, he had led many previous raids against the city, but Koram had never seen an army like this before. Dark energy thrummed around the giant leader as he let out a roar of challenge; the hundreds of beast giants marching through the silt echoed the shout.

"Skull Wearer has long hated Andropinis," Yvoluk said. "You must protect our sorcerer-king and save Balic!"

Below, the beast giants reached the docks, ripped the silt skimmers free of their moorings, and smashed the hulls. Pressing their shoulders against the pilings, two reptile-headed giants shattered a sturdy dock, tearing it down. The attackers swarmed forward in a frenzy, wrecking all of the boats.

Most of the silt sailors had evacuated as the enemy army approached, but a last few men ran toward the gates, desperate to get inside. The Balic guards refused to open the reinforced barriers, despite the ever-increasing pleas. Beast giants grabbed the frantic sailors and battered them into ooze against the wall.

Skull Wearer shouted another challenge for Dictator Andropinis. More giants pressed forward like the waves of a long-forgotten tide. It seemed impossible that anyone could protect the city against such an invasion; Koram could see that he and his comrades would all die in the first line of defense. He glanced at the dwarves, the Thri-Kreen tracker, even the miserable Goliath; they all realized the hopelessness of their position as well.

Yvoluk raised his hands, filled with enthusiasm. "This will be your greatest battle—for the glory of Andropinis and Balic." The praetor stepped to the edge of the wall, gesturing toward the giantish hordes below. "If you survive this day, you will have your freedom. I promise." He seemed to expect cheers.

Koram reached out, gave the man a hard shove, and toppled him off the wall into the press of giants. Yvoluk flailed as he fell, too astonished even to scream.

Koram had acted without thinking, sure he was dead either way. "I am through fighting for your benefit."

Seeing his action, the other gladiators immediately came to the same conclusion. The Goliath rose up and battered soldiers on either side of him, toppling them off the wall. The Thri-Kreen laughed in surprise and delight, clacking his mandibles as he turned on the astonished guards, and the two dwarves began to fight.

In response to the unexpected turmoil above, the beast giants pounded on their shields, then hammered on the gates with stony fists like battering rams. A volley of spears arced upward, shafts as thick as small trees, and struck into the crowded guards and spectators.

The gladiators continued to fight atop the wall, throwing the

Balic soldiers into chaos. Skull Wearer summoned the magic he had drawn from the ghosts of his victims, unleashing a dark thunderstorm of power against the harbor city.

Before long, Dictator Andropinis arrived with his escort, shouting out his own spells as he drew power to defend Balic. The air itself began to crack and tremble, the surrounding trees and plants shriveled and died, the ground turned black as all energy was sucked away.

In the confusion, Koram turned his back on the front lines, waved his bone-and-bronze sword to chase panicked soldiers and citizens out of his way. Some of his gladiator comrades fought anyone and everyone with great glee, giving their last great battle performance; others scampered away, seeking a place to hide.

Koram felt not a flicker of guilt for abandoning his city. He thought of the female anakore and her two sons—his latest victims. He thought of his own family, killed through treachery. He had killed enough. He would not shed his blood to protect the sorcerer-king or his duplicitous citizens, nor would he stay and revel in the city's destruction.

He was done.

Koram made his way to the far exit gates that were not yet blocked. Before long, the city's back gates and side entrances would be clogged with citizens racing into the hills as they realized the true desperation of their plight.

He would set out into the wilderness and find his own path of survival. Considering what he had been through, he knew he would fare better alone under the dark sun of Athas than amidst the treachery of Balic.

Living aboard the petrified skeleton of the *Horizon Finder*, Jisanne had the city ruins to herself. No caravans or silt schooners came this far south. Arkhold received no visitors except for the rare and foolish adventurer in search of forgotten treasures. Knowing how people were likely to treat a magic user,

Jisanne hid whenever she saw a stranger; more often than not, the perils of the abandoned city drove them off before she had to worry.

Jisanne was on her own, just as she wanted to be.

However, the desiccated place provided little for her survival. She caught rodents and lizards to eat; she set up scattered cisterns to hoard the reluctant droplets of water that rained down twice a year. But it wasn't enough, and she had to venture out on regular supply expeditions.

As the red sun lumbered over the grainy horizon, Jisanne stood on the ruins of the stone quay, facing the expanse of the Silt Sea. Her voice hoarse from thirst, she shouted a summoning spell for a floating mantle, one of the mysterious but gentle beasts of the deep wastes.

Her hands trembled and her head throbbed as she called upon the power. It would have been so much easier, so much faster, to steal the life energy of the surrounding flora and fauna, but Jisanne refused such shortcuts. She knew in her heart that the excessive and indiscriminate use of that sort of magic had wrung Athas dry. By using the navigation crystal, she had been able to visit the lush past, and she knew what the defilers had done to a healthy world.

Magic users were widely hated across Athas. All her life, Jisanne had tried to preserve the life of the world, never harming anyone, and yet, when her abilities were discovered, the people of Balic had punished her. As a hermit, far from any people, Jisanne was much safer. But the pain of her loss did not go away.

Answering her summons, the floating mantle appeared in a blurry brown corona of dust. The jellyfish-like creature drifted on the thermals, trailing thin tentacles to the silt. It hovered at the end of the stone quay, then lowered its enormous body to the ground so she could mount.

"Thank you for coming." Jisanne had no idea if the creature could understand her. Securing her sacks, pots, and supply pack, she climbed onto the leathery dome, grasping the ridges and nodules. Air flaps vented gas as the floating mantle exhaled, then rose into the air and propelled itself along, carrying her away from Arkhold and across the impassible expanse.

She ventured to the more fertile, and more dangerous, highlands of the Dragon's Palate as rarely as possible. The Palate was close to Balic, and she never intended to go back home again. That was where happiness had been burned out of her—not by any defiling magic, but by human hatred.

Years ago, Jisanne had lived in Balic with her older sister Selanne; Selanne had a husband and two fine daughters. Unmarried, Jisanne helped wherever she could, often secretly drawing upon the power of the living to ease their existence. But Jisanne was a preserver, not a defiler; even though she knew full well the difference between the types of magic, most common people didn't understand, didn't try, or didn't care. And she wasn't cautious enough.

Jisanne had ignored the rumors about her, the whispers when she and Selanne walked through the forum market, the way other people shunned their house. Oblivious, she had gone out one day to pick olives in a grove near a crumbling noble estate. Returning home at sunset with a full basket, she had found her sister's family murdered, the house burned. The mob had scrawled hateful words in the ashes—they had mistaken *Selanne* as the magic user.

Before they could come for her too, Jisanne had fled. She did not stop until she had reached the end of inhabited territory, and even then she kept going all the way to Arkhold. The mummified port city seemed the perfect place for her. However, time had not lessened the pain of her massacred loved ones. Those nightmares remained as vivid as the navigation crystal's visions of ancient Athas....

The floating mantle brought her to soupy mud flats at the shore of the Dragon's Palate. A thin stream trickled down from the foothills, where the scrub forest thickened. *That would do.*

She landed the docile beast near a dryer patch of thick grasses and slid down its rubbery curved back. When she released it from her spell, the jellyfish creature floated away from the mud flats, heading back out to the silt barrens. Her quest here would take some time and require a great deal of caution. The steep mountains of the Dragon's Palate were inhabited by ferocious beast giants; fortunately, a military outpost from Balic kept the giants busy.

Jisanne filled her water containers upstream, then placed the heavy jugs in a subtly marked cache, which she could retrieve before she headed home. Then, with empty sacks tied at her waist, she explored the forest in search of edible berries, roots, mushrooms, fruits, and herbs.

A pang of loneliness stabbed her, but she had fended for herself so long. Only once had Jisanne let down her guard and trusted a stranger in the Arkhold ruins—and that lapse had nearly killed her. She had revealed herself to a half-elf treasure-seeker who had looked so friendly, so earnest. The lone adventurer had captivated her with his story, his passion, and Jisanne had shown him the navigation crystal, revealed what the world of Athas had once been like.

Jisanne had been so desperate for companionship that she'd believed him—until he stole the crystal. She pursued him and used her magic to make the pouch drop unnoticed from his waist. As the thief ran away from her with mocking laughter, taking a shortcut out onto the sands, a tentacled Silt Horror grabbed him before he even realized his danger. Hearing his screams, Jisanne felt no sympathy. She retrieved the navigation crystal from where it had dropped to the ground and held it tightly. From that point on, Jisanne hid whenever she saw a human visitor.

As she filled her sacks with edibles from the forest, she took comfort in knowing the navigation crystal was hidden in a small pouch tied on the inside of her breeches. She had to exercise great care to avoid detection from the marauding giants on the island; their main lair was to the north, closer to Balic. She was safe here, where she could hear, and hide from, the crashing approach of any plodding giant hunter.

She did not, however, notice the trap set by the band of feral halflings.

As she'd foraged, the small wild-eyed savages had stalked and surrounded her in utter silence. The halfling hunters scuttled ahead, lying in wait with their ropes and nets, and then they sprang.

The vicious little men hurled bolos at her, several of which missed, but one caught around her leg, and another struck her head, wrapping around her neck.

"Fresh human! Tender human!"

"Take her back to the village."

Jisanne clawed at the bolos—and then the halflings dropped a net on top of her. They pounced, driving her to the ground.

"Bring her to the other captives."

"If we have any left!" The last comment was met with cackles of laughter and howls of disappointment.

A stocky leader thumped his chest in triumph and hefted a sword made from a giant's sharpened femur. "Another victory for Borodro!"

"But we *all* caught her, Borodro—" whined one of the younger halflings.

With a slash of his giant-bone sword, Borodro decapitated the complainer, and the severed head continued to whistle and grimace as it rolled on the dry leaves on the ground. The leader gave a snort. "Look, Delfi keeps complaining even without a body." The halflings' initial gasps of horror turned to laughter, cheers, and grumbling stomachs. "Bring his body back to the village." They seemed satisfied with that.

Jisanne thrashed in the net, struggling to tear the tough strands. She didn't waste energy or breath demanding to be freed, since that would do no good. Everyone knew the cruelty of halfling raiders and slavers. She tried to work an escape spell but failed; she was already weak and had used much magic to summon and control the floating mantle. She needed time and concentration.

"Tenderize her," said Borodro, "then let's get back to the village."

The halfling hunters fell upon Jisanne with sticks and clubs.

She covered her head to protect herself, but the blows were too many....

Some time later, she awoke, a mass of pain, trussed up and carried along, as the halflings whistled their satisfaction. Jisanne clamped her bruised lips together to keep from making a sound. She heard shouts and cheers from more halflings ahead as they arrived at the village, a ring of stone houses that surrounded a stone pyramid.

Halflings were notorious slavers, and Borodro had said he kept other human captives, though none were readily visible. The halflings dumped her into a small, filthy pen with walls made of twisted thorn branches. Her hands and ankles remained bound.

Jisanne tried to concentrate so she could gather magic, draw power slowly from the surrounding plants and trees, perhaps even from the halflings themselves. If she garnered strength gradually, she might not alert the vicious little men to what she was doing.

She could have just ripped the power from the fabric of the world, stealing as much life force as required, but even to save her life Jisanne was reluctant to destroy herself in another way by turning to the corrupting magic. The only time she truly defiled nature was to activate the navigation crystal, and that was ... necessary. For now, she would find another way.

The halflings left Jisanne in the pen, focused on other interests now, jabbering and chuckling. "I'm hungry."

"They better not have gnawed all the bones!"

"Save me a tender piece," Borodro said. The other halfling hunters dumped the decapitated body of their comrade on the trampled ground. "And start cooking Delfi. Throw in a lot of garlic so he doesn't taste so gamey."

Jisanne realized that there were no other captives. Several human carcasses—mostly picked clean—were being roasted over a bed of orange coals near the stone pyramid. The returning hunters rushed over to the cookfire and squabbled over the remaining meat.

She felt a sickening wrench in her gut. Halfling cannibals were the worst.

Sweating, in pain from her contusions and cracked bones, Jisanne closed her eyes and began to concentrate on scraps of magic, pulling together any possibilities for her escape. She didn't have much time.

Koram walked away and never looked back at the Balic skyline. He did not listen to the mayhem as Skull Wearer and his beast-giant army hammered the walls, did not flinch as sorcerer-king Andropinis fought back with arcane magic. He heard explosions, screams, a loud ripping roar ... and he kept walking. It was no longer his battle; perhaps it had never been.

With his sword he cut the mooring rope of a fully stocked silt skimmer, then set sail out into the estuary. As a youth, in happier days in the great walled city, he had learned how to guide and levitate the skimmers on his impetuous adventures in the surrounding area. Now, though, this was no mere lighthearted expedition. He would never return.

The hot, dry breezes blew him past other coastal villages, then he turned east into deeper silt, crossing to the hazy highlands of the Dragon's Palate, where he hoped to live off the land.

After he beached the silt skimmer at sunset, Koram set up camp in the trees; he slept little, with his back against a sturdy trunk, as he listened to creatures stalking the night. He had no plan, no goal—and it felt liberating. Before, he had lived for his family, for his city, to make a better existence for all the citizens of Balic. He had worked hard and dedicated himself to people he cared about. And after his disgrace, he had been forced to fight and kill for people he hated.

Now all that was gone, the good and the bad. He owed nothing to anyone. He would heal, he would survive, and one day perhaps he would find something else to believe in.

Next day, he continued to explore the island, finding the ruins of a Balic fort whose inhabitants had been slaughtered, probably by Skull Wearer's giants. He picked through the wreckage and took what he needed, but he did not want to stay at the site of a recent massacre.

Continuing his explorations, he encountered a commotion ahead, shouts and snapping branches. He heard the halfling warrior party crashing through the forest long before he saw them. He decided they must be bad warriors to be so noisy and obvious ... and then he realized they were chasing someone.

A young woman burst out of the trees, running wildly; long brown hair streamed behind her. She looked battered and exhausted. When the woman saw Koram, they both froze. He had not intended to save anyone, and she looked just as reluctant to accept his help, but the yips, howls, and high-pitched curses of the pursuers drove her toward him.

"Halfling cannibals," she said, heaving great breaths. "I used my magic to escape ... not much left now. And no time."

"Magic?" Koram tightened the grip on the hilt of his sword. "I have no love for defilers."

"I'm not a defiler. I'm a survivor—so far. You'll come with me if you hope to survive."

Bounding forward with a speed and agility that belied his stocky body, the halfling leader raced out of the trees, waving his ivory sword. He skidded to a halt, his eyes bugging out as he saw the armored gladiator, then he yelled back to the trees. "Hey, hurry up! I've caught another one!"

Brazen with confidence, the woman whirled to face the bearded halfling. "Leave us, Borodro—and maybe we won't kill you."

Borodro laughed. "I have fifty followers right behind me!"

"I counted forty-five," she said.

He paused to tally them again in his mind. "More than enough."

Since he had done nothing to provoke the halfling hunter, had made no sign of even choosing sides in the dispute, Koram was taken off-guard as Borodro threw himself forward like a rabid animal. With fierce and unhindered sword work, the feral halfling landed the first blow and chipped one of Koram's petrified-wood armor plates.

As a gladiator, Koram had fought many different opponents, and so he adjusted his combat technique accordingly. His arena fighting skills took over, automatic and without mercy. He had not meant to fight again, did not want to get involved in this squabble ... but he could not simply ignore this woman. If he had fought back earlier, if he had defended his family against the guards who came to take him, maybe he could have saved his wife and son. Koram parried the halfling's sharpened-femur sword with his own bronze edge, hammering so hard he splintered the giant bone. Borodro hesitated in surprise at the ferocity of the blow.

With a curled fist, Koram smashed the halfling leader in the nose, drawing forth a surprised yowl and a burst of blood. As the enraged Borodro threw himself against the gladiator again, Koram impaled him on his sword. The halfling collapsed, wailing as his blood poured out.

In the dense trees nearby, the remaining forty-five halfling pursuers heard their leader's death scream, then raised their own voices.

Koram held his sword and stood his ground; he did not even know who this woman was, but he was certain he could never defeat so many halfling cannibals.

The woman yanked a small pouch from her breeches and unwrapped it to reveal a rough shard of crystal. She looked up at Koram, wild-eyed. "No way around it now. I can use Borodro's life force before he dies, and I'll probably have to drain a dozen trees, too. But it's either defiling magic, or we both die."

Anger flared inside him. "I refuse to be part of defilement."

On the ground, Borodro coughed blood and wheezed out a death rattle. Wearing a grim expression, the woman knelt next to the dying halfling, working her hands around the crystal. "Normally I would use my own blood, my own strength, but this creature has already taken enough lives." She spat in the halfling's face to express her loathing, then she looked with greater sympathy at Koram. "You saved me. I'll save you. I'll take you to … a better place."

As she summoned the power to activate the crystal, Borodro wailed and writhed, then shriveled to dust. The grasses and weeds on the ground withered as the circle of defiling magic spread, drinking life energy from anything it touched. Tall trees turned brown, creaking, splintering.

Koram yelled at her, "I do not want—"

Then the first members of the halfling hunting party charged forward out of the trees waving their weapons. They all looked hungry.

The crystal in her palm glowed as she finished her spell.

The world shimmered—and they were both in a different place. Koram's next breath tasted of moisture, life, flowers, and leaves. Nearby, a brook tumbled over mossy rocks on its way downhill. The shadowy monster-infested forest was now asparkle with birdsong and gentle breezes. Even the sun in the sky was bright yellow, rather than a dull bloody red.

He stared in awe, then looked at the woman, demanding explanations. "Where have you taken me?"

The magic user shuddered in disgust at what she had done. The rough crystal in her bloodstained palm emitted a yellowish glow. "This is Athas … our world, before the sorcerer-kings and corrupt magic users wrung it dry."

"How did we get here?" The gladiator looked around, worried that Borodro's cannibal halflings had followed them through time. "How do we get back?" He had not intended to stay with this woman. The wounds and memories were still too fresh in his mind and heart, and he did not want to cast his lot with a stranger. It would not be fair to her, or to him.

The woman—who told him her name was Jisanne—looked down at the strange glassy shard she held. "Ancient sailors used this navigation crystal to take them home. *This* time period, this version of Athas, was the home of a powerful ship's captain." Though her skin was covered with bruises and she walked with obvious pain, Jisanne set off down the slope, following the stream. "I've brought us here. Look around you. Are you so anxious to be back in your harsh world?"

He found the fresh, green, *living* landscape remarkable ... but its very strangeness was intimidating. "I have lost my family, and lost my interest. Little matters to me anymore. But I will ... stay with you until I'm sure you are safe."

She regarded him with a hard expression. "I have taken care of myself for a long time, and I don't need a protector." She drew a deep breath. "But you are here with me now. I prefer this time and place, when the world was young and healthy—but my magic isn't strong enough to make it permanent. Come, we don't have much time."

Koram followed her down the slope to a wide blue river course—clear, swift-flowing water dotted with colorful sails of trading ships, oared dromonds from the city guard, even pleasure craft. He recognized it. "This is the estuary!"

"The way it once was." Jisanne led him along the shore. "This is how Athas was meant to be."

His heart felt leaden, wishing his wife and son could see this. "I suppose if we are trapped here ... I would not complain." He could make a new home here, a new life far from his memories.

"It won't last." Jisanne scanned the shore, looking for something. "I stole life energy for this spell. Defiling magic is the only way to activate the navigation crystal, and it will fade soon enough."

He was uneasy with her casual use of the corrupting power, but he also knew that otherwise he would be dying right now, his body pierced with halfling arrows and blades. Jisanne had saved both of them. He owed her a debt of gratitude.

When he had turned his back on Balic, he had severed all ties, washing his hands of the evil government that had destroyed his family and the fickle people who had shown him no loyalty, no support. Though he had little to live for, once he'd left the arena, he did not want to die. Given time, perhaps Koram would find a reason that meant something—and someone who deserved it.

After they had rushed along through the peaceful forest, Jisanne let out a happy cry and hurried through the underbrush to a small rowboat tied to a drooping tree trunk. "Come, we must head south as fast as we can, while the spell lasts. Unless you'd rather travel across the silt?"

Though he didn't know what she meant, her urgency was plain. Koram climbed into the boat, took the oars, then guided them out into the fast-flowing estuary. "Where are we going?"

"South—to Arkhold. To my home."

After a lifetime of considering desolation to be the normal state of the world, he marveled at the bounty of water, the moisture in the air, the fractured-gold flashes of sunlight on the river's ripples. As he rowed vigorously, water splashed on the caked dust and blood on his skin; it felt cool and strange as the fresh breezes dried it quickly. A strange stirring occurred in his chest, and the weight on his shoulders seemed less heavy. Koram began to feel *alive* again.

As they made good time along the current, Jisanne told him her story, and he shared his own. She didn't seem at all astonished to hear of Praetor Yvoluk's cruelty or how the fickle people of Balic had so easily turned on him. They had done the same to her. Jisanne explained how ancient sorcerer-kings had abused dark powers, draining the world year after year, spell after spell, war after war.

"Defiling magic did this to Athas—and now I have used it to bring us back to a time before the world was destroyed." She shook her head in disgust at herself. "Ironic, isn't it? In order to visit an Athas untainted by the parasitical magic, I need to drain more life force from the land."

"Either way, we are here." Koram rowed as hard as he could, carrying them far down the watercourse. They traveled for many leagues before the magic weakened. As Jisanne felt it fade, she urged him to pull the boat to the shallows.

With a wrenching disappointment, they watched the green shore and blue current curl and evaporate, changing from a verdant Eden to a barren brown wasteland. The Athas he was used to seeing. He felt suddenly hollow and lost, and he had to bite back a cry of disappointment.

The small boat ground ashore and fell apart with the sudden weight of age, disintegrating into dry and ancient splinters. The two found themselves in the rocks on the edge of a bone-dry canyon. "We'll have to walk from here. Arkhold isn't far," Jisanne said.

He hesitated, looking around at the stark rocks and dry desert. "I did not intend to stay."

She looked uncertain. "You saved my life. I prefer being alone, and I never said I wanted company…. But stay and rest. You can find your own path tomorrow."

Together, they trudged back to her skeletal ship, the dry docks, and the silt-buried old harbor city. He gave a gruff answer. "No place else to be."

⚔

Dust-shrouded Arkhold was dead, empty … and peaceful. When she and Koram reached her makeshift home aboard the *Horizon Finder*, Jisanne fell into a deep, exhausted sleep. It took days for her to recover from the magic she had used, and so Koram did not leave. He tended her, brought her food and water, and kept watch against the ever-present dangers of the desert.

She could not shake the disheartened realization of how willingly she had turned to defiling magic to summon the past centuries of Athas. When possible, she would use her own blood to work the spell, drawing upon willingly surrendered life energy to trigger the crystal. A spell could be more permanent if not forced and stolen—but she had to use what she could. Jisanne knew she would do it again. Every moment she experienced in that long-lost period was worth the sacrifice, even if she had to steal the energy from other living creatures. It could rapidly become too easy …

The gladiator from Balic wanted nothing from her, put no obligations on her, posed no threat. She had come to this place intentionally, hiding from her past; the other strangers she had encountered here were greedy, driven, dangerous. Koram, though, had cut himself off from the strings that bound him to his city, and he had let the hot winds of circumstance blow him wherever they wished. And they had brought him to her.

While she continued to recover, Koram trudged off into the rugged land nearby. He returned a day later with three large iguanas he had caught, a pouch of leathery-shelled turtle eggs, and several wrinkled gourds that held water. If not for him, Jisanne doubted she could have survived.

For his own part, he also seemed to be healing just by staying with her in the empty quiet. The two kept their distance from each other, kept their silence, but eventually they talked more, surprised to find how much they were alike. Though the man carried no happiness within him, at least he seemed to find an inner contentment being here. In the evenings he would sit with her, and gradually opened up, talking more and more.

"I had to shut out all of my pain and anger just to survive in the arena. But I don't like to be so empty. When you showed me the past, you made me see how healthy this world once was ... and could be again. Maybe my life can become whole again as well." He hung his head. The bristles of hair had begun to regrow from his shaved scalp. "I will hold onto that hope."

With a wistful sigh, Jisanne thought of the glorious, vibrant past. "If we could return there, I would turn my back on all of Athas without a second's regret ... the way you turned away from Balic."

Koram made a rumbling sound in his chest. "I would do it in a second."

The peace could last only so long.

Just as the first flames of dawn scorched the Sea of Silt, a bellowing voice echoed through Arkhold. "Gladiator Koram, come out and meet your master—and your death! The smell of your treachery makes you easy to follow."

Belowdecks in the petrified old sailing ship, Koram recognized the voice, a sound that had come from beyond the grave. He leaped off his pallet and grabbed his sword, but did not have time to strap on his armor. Koram said to Jisanne, "Hide here. He doesn't want you."

She sat bolt upright, her eyes wide. "Who is it? Who tracked you here?"

"Praetor Yvoluk. He survived somehow. I suppose a soul as twisted as his cannot be easily crushed." He hefted his bone-and-bronze sword. "If I kill him, I'll be back."

Jisanne took out the navigation crystal, drew a deep breath. "I am strong enough to use magic again. Let me help you fight him."

"That would be a waste of your life. Yvoluk has already taken my wife and son. That is enough." He stalked off and climbed the ladder out of the hold. He no longer felt empty and aimless. If he was going to face a hated enemy again, at least now he had a reason to fight.

He did not hear Jisanne whisper under her breath, "And *I* lost my sister and her whole family because I wasn't there to protect them."

Emerging onto the open deck, Koram saw a silt dromond bearing Balic's flag. Powered by a psionic helm, the large ship hovered above the dust, separated by less than a meter from the *Horizon Finder*'s starboard bow. In the fleet maneuvers of Dictator Andropinis, Koram had seen these fearsome ships glide across the desert like giant sharks in the sky.

Smug, Yvoluk stood on the dromond's bow next to the Thri-Kreen tracker who had also fought in the Criterion arena; the chittering Thri-Kreen bobbed his rounded head, his faceted eyes gleaming in the bright daylight. "You see, Praetor—I told you I could track him." In his segmented limbs, the Thri-Kreen held the rumpled sash of Andropinis that Koram had left behind in his cell. Five more Balic soldiers stood behind them, armed and ready to fight.

When the tracker saw Koram's angry scowl at the betrayal, he shouted to the other ship. "It makes no difference. If we'd been pitted against each other, you would have killed me or I'd have killed you. It is nothing personal."

The words were dry as they came out of Koram's mouth. "I won't hold any sympathy or any grudge. My grudge is with Yvoluk."

The praetor's laugh sounded like splintering wood. "And my grudge is with *you*. You cast me to my death, but magic cushioned my fall. Unluckily for the beast giants, they have a strong life force. Using it to power my magic was as easy as poking a hole in a wineskin. I was nearly buried among the corpses I had slain." Behind him, the five warriors drew their blades and bows, ready to attack, but Yvoluk motioned them back. He seemed proud of what he had done.

"I crawled out of the zone of death just as Dictator Andropinis cast his own spell from the wall above. He unleashed so much defiling magic that he felled dozens of giants, not to mention several hundred of his own citizens. He called up a lava storm in the estuary, enough to send Skull Wearer and his minions fleeing. I barely scaled the wall myself." The praetor shook his head like a disappointed parent. "But you had already run away, Koram. You gave us quite a chase."

"Then I will save you further trouble. When you forced me to fight opponents in the Criterion, I had no reason to kill them. Now, though, I have all the reasons I need." Koram bent his powerful legs and sprang across the gap from the *Horizon Finder* to the levitating dromond.

Jisanne was already rallying her magic as she emerged onto the deck. She saw Koram land on the adjacent silt dromond to face his enemy, yelling, "Fight me, Yvoluk! I have waited long enough for this."

The Balic templar just laughed. "And why should I bother

fighting you when I have others to do so?" He motioned for his fighters, and three of the men nocked arrows to bowstrings; the other two lifted their short swords and crouched to charge.

With anger roiling through her, Jisanne stepped out of the shadows and began to work her first spell. Drawing energy from all around her in a quick rush, she felt the tension build within her. Her need justified whatever means she might employ, even defilement—fast, powerful, and deadly magic. "Leave us alone!"

Spotting her, the Thri-Kreen tracker gave an alarmed squawk and his small antennae lifted, twitching. "Koram sent a defiler against us!"

With instinctive terror, Yvoluk's warriors fired their arrows without any command from the praetor. Three shafts leaped out from twanging bows. One of the arrows clattered on the *Horizon Finder*'s deck—but the other two struck Jisanne, one in the left side of her chest, the second in her abdomen. The impacts drove her backward.

With a howl, Koram thrust his sword deep into the traitorous Thri-Kreen's back, piercing the tan chitin; the Thri-Kreen's lower set of legs folded, and he fell to his knees, dragging Koram's sword with him, caught in the insect's hard shell. "Ah, so this is how it ends...." He whistled through his mandibles.

Jisanne gasped as her spell died around her. She tried to keep uttering the words, but only blood came out of her mouth, not the rest of the incantation.

With a barked command from Yvoluk, the soldiers fell upon Koram, five against one. Even as he struggled to tear his sword free from the Thri-Kreen's body, the warriors swarmed over him, thrusting and stabbing.

Lying in a pool of her own blood on the deck of the *Horizon Finder*, Jisanne saw an image of her sister's family cut down by mob hatred against magic users. Yes, she did know how to use arcane magic, and now her own blood gave her all the power she needed to finish the spell.

The silt stirred beneath the levitating dromond. A line of ivory vertebrae moved in a serpentine ripple, and a pair of ribcages lifted up through the sand. Balanced on puzzle-pieces of stacked bones, two saurian skulls dropped open hinged jaws to brandish sand-worn fangs. The long-dead sea serpents both roared, a dry rasping sound that scratched through their hollow throats. Once so majestic as they glided on Athas's long-forgotten seas, the fossilized monsters now loomed over the levitating dromond. Jisanne clenched her bloodied fists, drove the monsters into action.

Yvoluk's warriors looked up and screamed, scrambling away from Koram. The praetor stared in awe, craning his neck up at the giant fanged skulls, then frantically worked his own spell to protect himself—but before he could finish, one of the skeleton serpents darted forward and chomped down. Lifting the bleeding templar in the air, the serpent shook him from side to side, bit him in half, then tossed the severed body off the dromond. Yvoluk was still gurgling as he sank into the silt.

Jisanne crawled to the side rail, lifted herself up, and extended a red hand toward Koram. On the levitating dromond, he was a patchwork of deep wounds, bleeding from numerous slashes and cuts, many of them surely fatal. She tried to call his name, but her lungs were filled with blood.

Koram dragged himself to the bow and somehow found the strength to make a staggering leap back to the *Horizon Finder*. Jisanne attempted to catch him, and they both tumbled together. One of the arrow shafts snapped off inside, and the pain blinded her.

Even without her magical control, the skeletal serpents continued to attack the dromond. Ivory skulls smashed the planks, broke the hull, shattered the rails. The serpents seized the terrified Balic soldiers in their jaws, tossing bodies over the side or leaving them strewn across the deck. The dromond crashed, running aground onto the stone quay.

Jisanne and Koram held each other, barely hearing the screams and the mayhem. Drowning in the pain, she felt the magic fade. The twin sea-monster skeletons raised sinuous bone necks as if in a salute, then crumbled into ivory shards in the dust.

Jisanne knew she was dying, and beside her Koram grasped her hand. His wounds looked even worse than hers. "Do you have the navigation crystal?" he said. "Take us back ... to when Athas was alive."

With an effort she removed the dull-edged object, wet fingers fumbling with the strings of the pouch. "The defiling magic won't last. It destroys. It is what drained this world."

He leaned closer, his breath rattling. "Then I give you my life energy willingly—take it! I'd rather die there than in this place."

Jisanne cupped the navigation crystal in her palm. Each breath was like broken glass caught on fire; the arrow deep in her stomach was a grinding spear of ice that twisted in her guts. "Maybe with my life force, too, it will be enough to seal the spell permanently."

Koram could barely hold his head up. He was fading quickly. If she didn't act soon, the opportunity would be wasted.

Jisanne clenched her fingers around the crystal. Previously, she had filled a small bowl with her own blood, just enough to work the arcane magic. Now there was so much blood, but she felt so weak ... and Koram was so weak.

She pulled the spell from her own core, stronger than ever before. Jisanne used everything she had, and everything Koram had. She scraped both of their existences until they were bone dry and empty, she pulled on any life force around them, the waning energy of the dying guards, the small burrowing creatures in the ground, every faint flicker she could find. Even the sand and dust turned dark. She had never called on so much life force to fuel her magic.

Her vision faded into static and grit, and she could see only the crystal in her hand. Jisanne tried to hold onto it, but the object dulled, then crumbled into small shards and glittering dust in her hand.

Destroyed.

Jisanne collapsed, feeling the weight of Koram beside her but no life there, and no life inside her either....

Then the deck began rocking beneath them, and the bright

sun beating down seemed to have a different quality. The air Jisanne inhaled was moist and salty—and as she sucked in a lungful, she realized that the arrow wounds no longer hurt. The spell had worked after all!

With a loud snort, a deep voice grumbled at them. "I see you are back, lady magic user—and you have brought a fighter, too. He looks strong enough, but lazy. Lounging around on the deck—hmmf!" The minotaur captain stood over the two of them.

Koram picked himself up, touching his bare chest and searching unsuccessfully to find his deep wounds.

"Are you going to sleep all day?" Hurunn put his powerful hands on his hips. "This ship has places to go—I am not running an inn at sea!"

Jisanne got to her feet and looked off the starboard bow to see the beautiful harbor city of Arkhold with its whitewashed buildings on the hills, the large marketplace down by the docks, the colorful sails of small fishing boats.

"We are glad to be here, Captain," Jisanne said. She felt more solid now than ever before, more *real* in this time.

Koram was amazed. "Please let us stay."

"All right, I won't throw you overboard just yet." The minotaur turned and stalked back toward the bow. "Just make yourselves useful."

Because they had surrendered their life energy voluntarily, they had twisted the nature of the defiling magic, and the navigation crystal had incorporated them into the past, into its memory of "home." Maybe they were really here, or maybe it was only a recorded vision that had an objective and persistent reality of its own. Either way, it didn't matter.

"This is our permanent place now, Koram," she said, convinced as she stood beside him. "We both made it so. This spell will never fade." They faced the sun—the golden yellow sun.

This is a very mythic story, dealing with powerful archetypes, the many aspects—and obligations—of Death. It was an experiment in structure for me, one of the more unusual and literary short stories I've written. And maybe even a little sympathy for the Grim Reaper himself.

DARK ANGEL, ARCHANGEL

The train thundered toward him, its sharp light pinning him like a spear. He stood in the center of the tracks facing it, not moving. Defiant. Impotent. The night seemed to laugh around him.

He opened his arms to greet the onrushing locomotive, waiting for its juggernaut embrace. In its glowing headlight he saw a glimmer of what humans called Heaven.

And then the train passed through, leaving him unharmed. He turned to watch the train rumble into the distance. It always happened the same:

He remembered leaping off a high rooftop to fly like a dark angel toward the pavement below. The wind was cold on his face, ruffling his hair as he soared down and down ... then he landed with a ballerina's grace on the night sidewalk below. Unharmed. Even his hair dropped back into place.

And again: Pressing the pistol against his temple, he squeezed the trigger with genuine nonchalance. His ears rang with the explosive gunshot, and he turned to look at the bullet hole on the wall.

He wasn't going to die—that had never been an option. But he knew that if he kept trying, the new incarnation of Death would appear. She would want to taunt the predecessor who had failed in his duty. When commanded to make the human race extinct, he had refused. But the new Death had no such qualms.

Suddenly, she stood beside him on the moonlit tracks. A shroud of pearly mist hung from her beautiful shoulders. Her hair glinted like spun quicksilver. "Why do you torment yourself so much? You know I won't let you die." The White Lady's voice was a tangled mix of sarcasm and sincerity.

"Don't I have the right to be fascinated by Death, after half a million years of doling it out? Let me talk with you. You have to stop what you're doing."

He had been the Dark Angel, the Grim Reaper, flaunting his power in front of human beings until his masters, the aurorae who hung shimmering above the world, decreed another mass extinction, as had happened several times in the Earth's past. But the Grim Reaper had developed a fondness for humans over the millennia, and he would not wipe them out as ordered. So, the aurorae stripped him of his title.

He glanced into the clear night sky above the train tracks, but over the years he had purposefully made his way down to lower latitudes, where the aurorae rarely showed themselves. They hung in shimmering curtains from the Earth's poles, charged particles from the All-Father Sun that spiraled in the magnetic field-lines, auroral beings so alien that inquisitive human scientists regarded them merely as interesting electromagnetic phenomena. The aurorae doled out nourishing energy to their servants, such as himself and the White Lady.

She regarded him now with scorn. "You gave up your duty. This species is scheduled to end. How can you be sentimental after all this time?" She laughed like broken glass and threw her glowing garments back into an unfelt breeze. "*I* listen to the aurorae. I know what they expect of me."

He opened his mouth to speak, but she held up one nailless finger, showing no vestigial remnants of the claws of lower animals. "Because of the respect I used to have for you, I'll listen. Briefly. Come with me as we talk. I've got work to do tonight."

The old woman lay on sterile hospital sheets, waiting in silence as she felt the tumors growing, squirming, fighting inside her. Veins stood out on her neck with the effort as she kept her lungs rhythmically filling and emptying.

Her eyes remained open, and she watched the White Lady who sat in the shadows of her room. "If breathing is so difficult," the White Lady asked, "why not just stop?"

And the old woman did.

As she walked beside him, the White Lady appeared genuinely concerned for him, but she didn't understand. "What happened to you? Why do you care anyway? You've done many routine extinctions. It's the order of the universe."

The order of the universe? That wasn't the reason at all. The aurorae could not survive in a static environment, and so they forced constant flux, constant change, and turmoil on the world. "The aurorae asked too much this time."

One of his predecessors had been Death when the aurorae ordered the obliteration of most dinosaur species to which he had expressed an attachment. That incarnation of Death had hurled an asteroid whistling and flaming through the atmosphere. He had summoned up volcanoes, earthquakes, and in the end, he had devastated the world, wiping out thousands upon thousands of species, out of defiance.

It had driven him insane, turned him into a gibbering mass of random energy. The aurorae were forced to imprison him under the ice of the polar caps where they could watch over him.

And now that the aurorae had decreed the extinction of human beings, he thought he understood how his predecessor must have felt.

The Lady laughed at him. "Mankind's been dominant for half a million years, and their time has come. The aurorae know." She shook her head with a flirtatious toss of her beautiful hair. "I don't see why you're making such a fuss."

"It's different. *They're* different. Humans are … special, in a way. Listen to me." He dropped his voice and leaned closer to her. "I know something our masters overlooked."

The rabbit twitched its nose in the cool night air, looking up into the darkness just in time to see the White Lady swoop down on owl's wings, talons extended to plunge into warm blood.

The White Lady remained aloof. "And what is the redeeming virtue of humanity that *you* know but even the aurorae don't understand?"

He didn't want to fight her. He was weak now, and she was strong. And if she defeated him, all would be lost.

"Humans are *afraid* of Death, and this gives us power. That's why the aurorae need to get rid of them, so that you and I remain weak." He paused to let the idea sink in. "The lower animals have a self-preservation drive, but their fear of dying is just instinct. Humans, though, spend their lives obsessed with Death, worshiping it. I watched people die beside their hunting fires at the dawn of time. I listened to emperors, warlords, and slaves. I took each dying soldier away from his comrades."

He opened his hands to her. "Don't you see? Their constant preoccupation gave us form and substance. You choose to appear as beautiful Lady Death in her white garments to seduce the doomed with promises of Paradise. *I* always preferred to come as the Grim Reaper."

He waved his hands in front of himself, and his human form dissolved away. He stood cloaked in tattered black garments full of the mustiness of tombs; the skin peeled away from his face, leaving a leering skull with honeycombed eye sockets and rattling teeth. In his bony hand he clutched a scythe, razor-sharp and bloodstained in the moonlight. Its long wooden handle was slick and polished smooth from aeons of use.

The White Lady stood dumbfounded to see the transformation. "But you've been stripped of your position! How—?"

The Reaper's voice sounded like dry autumn leaves. "The aurorae don't know everything. I still hold much of my power, even after you thought I was banished. Humans gave me a shape, an idea to conform to. Before their race began to think, Death was nothing more than an abstract, lurking fear. Our predecessors had no names. They remained formless, weak, just a brooding force that came and went, taking lives with them. But human fear and superstition built *us* into something more powerful." He raised his scythe high and pointed a finger of ivory bamboo at her white shrouds. "Look at us now!"

She spoke in an exasperated voice, "What difference does it make if I appear as the White Lady or as some shadowy force? I am Death, and I am the most powerful force in the universe."

"You're only a tool. A pawn of the aurorae, to bow and scrape to them."

She crossed her arms over her chest, and the Reaper remembered how full and fresh the new power had once felt to him. He saw that the White Lady would not listen to him. She didn't care, and humankind was doomed.

He had to stop her. He threw back his black hood and turned to face her, holding his Deadly sickle in a combat stance. She laughed again, still not taking him seriously, but the Reaper gave her no time to prepare. He leaped forward and swung his scythe.

The three teenagers had managed to get themselves so drunk that, one of them claimed irreverently, they wouldn't need an undertaker to embalm them. The driver found it difficult enough to keep the car on the road, not to mention on his own side.

The two full-moons of dazzling truck headlights hurtled toward them, and it took the teenaged driver too long to recognize the threat. But somehow, he managed to swerve at the last instant, bouncing the car into the ditch and careening back up onto the road as the truck's horn bellowed back at them.

The teenagers giggled and drove on, thrilled but unconcerned at their close brush with Death.

The White Lady stumbled backward and looked up at him in awe. "You can't!"

He lunged again, but she dodged, focusing her strength. In her pallid hand appeared a dove with heavy claws and a cruel beak. She flung the bird at the Reaper, and it swooped at him with a fire in its holocaust eyes. The dove's claws skittered on his bony face, and its beak tried to crack the Reaper's skull.

Someone else was dying. It couldn't be him.

He clutched his chest, but his heart refused to follow the clockwork commands of his brain. Shadows rushed through his bloodstream into his head. He fell.

His wife frantically rubbed his wrists, pounded on his chest, and tried to breathe in his mouth ... all the treatments that worked on TV. Finally, she had the sense to call an ambulance. The shrieking vehicle arrived after an eternity as his heart, duty-bound, still tried to perform.

Paramedics pushed the frantic wife away. They had arrived in time. It wasn't too late.

"No," said the White Lady, echoing in his ears, "it's not too late." His heart finally surrendered and stopped forever.

She crawled back to her feet as the Reaper snatched at the attacking dove. With the swiftness of unexpected Death, he caught one of its wings in his skeletal grip and hurled it back at the Lady. Then he stormed after her down the railroad tracks, swinging his scythe. He could not let her recover, because she was much stronger than he was.

Overhead, the sky began to glow as the distant aurorae noticed the battle.

He slashed the White Lady's gossamer garments. Desperation and elation added strength to his swing.

Her lungs were ready to explode. Her starved blood had used all the oxygen, and now her eyes turned glassy under the murky water. The girl saw the White Lady swimming behind her eyes, urging her just to breathe deeply one more time.

Yet the girl refused, struggling against the tangle of old barbed wire on the bottom of the lake. Tears came out of her straining eyes to be washed away in the surrounding water. Darkness took chunks out of her sight.

As the last morsel of hope died inside her, years of underwater exposure took their toll on the rusted wire, and the girl broke free with only the inconsequential cost of torn skin.

The light of the All-Father Sun beckoned her to the surface. And she knew she would make it—by a miracle.

The dove attacked him, but the Reaper felt rejuvenated. He reached up and blasted the bird to a cinder.

The White Lady held her ground, raised her hands to the brightening auroral sky, and new power sang through her. When the Reaper struck again, the scythe glanced off her immortal flesh.

This time he staggered, tasting despair in his mummified

throat. The White Lady moved toward him, glowing brighter. Even her garments seemed alive.

The Reaper swung his curved blade, channeling his remaining power into one final attempt. The scythe struck the granite flesh of her throat and almost, *almost* cut. The long wooden handle that had lasted five thousand centuries broke in two.

The White Lady leaped on him with a vampire's embrace.

Each sleeping pill looked like a tombstone in her hand. She had stopped counting how many she'd swallowed, and still she swallowed more. The White Lady urged her on.

The nagging fear of Death, the persistent drive to stay alive—to live without David, without a future, without love—shouted in her conscious mind. No. Nothing mattered any more. Nothing. The Nothing of Death.

But doubts assailed her, begging her to give life one more chance. Her hand weighed a thousand pounds as she reached for the telephone. She managed to punch two numbers before the pills stopped her.

The White Lady laughed. And the telephone receiver dropped to the floor.

The Reaper lay crushed on the railroad ties and looked up at her with his hollow eye sockets, trying to evoke sympathy. "Please don't," he whispered. "Think of what you're doing!"

The White Lady placed her hands on her hips, and her eyes held the inferno of mankind's future. He had made his stand, and failed, but he felt something final brooding inside him. There was one remaining thing he could do.

"Your victory isn't complete, Lady." He clasped the broken halves of his Deadly sickle to his own breast. "The humans gave us things even the aurorae don't know."

He summoned the shreds of his power, remnants he wasn't sure he possessed until now. No defeat for him, no imprisonment in the polar ice caps, no torment as the aurorae stretched his soul across the Earth's magnetic field-lines and flayed him as infinite punishment for his betrayal.

The mystery opened itself to him, and the Grim Reaper embraced his own Death.

The White Lady was taken by surprise as he crumbled into glittering dust. The spangles of the Reaper's soul—free now, even from the aurorae—spiraled like dust motes into the future.

She stared. He shouldn't have been able to do that! The aurorae claimed they had stripped him, and he should have been so weak....

Overhead, the sky brightened as the aurorae absorbed energy that streamed from the All-Father Sun as the slumbering star awakened in the upswing of His eleven-year cycle.

She looked up at the sky, but the aurorae offered no answers. She began to wonder—how much did they hide from her?

The White Lady loved her new power as Death. If she did exterminate the human race, what would her existence be like without the fears that gave her form?

She thought of the Reaper and how he had somehow escaped his punishment. She thought of their dark formless predecessor; he had caused the mass extinctions at the end of the Cretaceous Period, and he now seethed in his prison under the ice caps.

The aurorae had promised her that eliminating the human race would be so easy. The White Lady had events to set in motion, antagonisms to build. Perhaps a new plague, perhaps a nuclear holocaust, perhaps another asteroid strike. Maybe she would wait and think about this.

For now, she would enjoy and ponder her power.

She was in no hurry.

And now for something a little lighter. You never know what strange subject an anthology editor might pick, but any good writer fires up the imagination engine to see what might come to mind.

I was invited to contribute a short story to an anthology called Pandora's Closet, *fantastic stories about magical garments. Garments? Given all the possibilities, I decided that the most entertaining story would be about an enchanted loincloth....*

LOINCLOTH
(WITH REBECCA MOESTA)

All alone in the props warehouse on the back lot of Duro Studios, he made his case to Shirley in his mind, rehashing the argument they had had the night before. This time, though, he was bold and articulate, and he easily convinced her.

Walter Groves opened another one of the big crates and tore out the packing straw mixed with Styrofoam peanuts. "Not exciting enough for you, am I? You don't feel fireworks? I'm too sedate—not a man's man? Think about it, Shirley. Women say they want nice guys, the shy and sensitive type, men who are sweet and remember birthdays and anniversaries. Isn't that what you told me you needed—someone just like me? You've always despised hypocrites. But what do you do? You fall for a bad boy, someone with tattoos and a heavy smoking habit, someone who can't keep a job for more than a month, someone like that last jerk you dated, who treated you rough and left you out in the cold.

"But I loved you. I treated you with respect, drove you to visit your grandmother in the hospital, and fixed your computer when the hard drive crashed. I got out of bed when you called at three in the morning and came to your apartment just to hold you because you had a nightmare and couldn't sleep. I gave you flowers, dinners by candlelight, and love notes—not to mention the best six months of my life. 'Someday, you'll regret it. Maybe not today. Maybe not tomorrow, but soon'"—he pictured himself as Bogart in *Casablanca*—"you'll realize what you threw away. But I won't be waiting. I'm a good man, and I deserve a wonderful woman who values me for who I am, who appreciates my dedication, and wants a nice, normal life. Go ahead. Have your shallow, exciting fling with Mr. James Dean in *Rebel Without a Cause*. I'll find someone sincere who wants Jimmy Stewart in *It's a Wonderful Life*."

Scattering straw and packing material, he pulled a long plastic elephant tusk out of the prop box. The faux ivory was sharp at one end and painted with "native symbols." He glanced at the label on the box: Jungo's Revenge. After marking the name of the film on his clipboard, he listed the stored items beneath the title. He sighed.

If only he could have come up with just the right answers last night, maybe Shirley wouldn't have dumped him. If only he could have been tough like Mel Gibson in *Braveheart*, confident like Clark Gable in *Gone with the Wind*, or romantic like Dermot Mulroney in *The Wedding Date*. Instead he had squirmed, speechless with shock, his lower lip trembling as if he were Stan Laurel caught in an embarrassing failure. Walter had made no heartfelt appeals or snappy comebacks; those were as much fiction as a script for any Duro Studios production.

Shirley had grabbed her stuff—along with some of his, though he hadn't had the presence of mind to mention it—and stormed out of the apartment.

Sharon Stone in *Basic Instinct*. That's who she reminded him of.

The large, black walkie-talkie at his hip crackled, and even through the static of the poor-quality unit, he heard the lovely musical speech of Desiree Drea. Her voice never failed to make his heart skip a beat, then go back and skip it all over again. "Walter? Mr. Carmichael wants to know how you're coming with the props. He needs me to type up the inventory."

"I ... um ... I—" He looked down at the box, searching for

words, and seized upon the letters stenciled to the crate. "I'm just now up to *Jungo's Revenge*. I've finished about half of the work."

As Desiree responded, he could hear the producer's voice bellowing in the background. "Jungo! It's all worthless crap. Trash it."

The secretary softened the message as she relayed it. "Mr. Carmichael suggests that it's of no value, so please put it in the dumpster."

"And tell him he damn well better stay until he finishes," the voice in the background growled. "We need that building tomorrow to start shooting *Horror in the Prop Warehouse*."

"Tell him I'll do what needs to be done," Walter said, then clicked off the walkie-talkie, though he would gladly have chatted with Desiree for hours. He didn't have anything better to do that evening than work, anyway. He was very conscientious and would finish the job.

Chris Carmichael—producer of low-budget knock-off movies. The Jungo ape-man series, a bad Tarzan knock-off, had skated just a little too close to Tarzan's copyright line. The threatened legal action had caused the films to flop, even though they were direct to video. Walter had seen one of them and thought that the movies were bad enough to have flopped all on their own, without any legal difficulties to help them along. If anything, the publicity had boosted the sales.

He pulled out the other plastic elephant tusk, then some ugly looking tribal masks, three rubber cobras, and a giant plastic insect as big as his palm that was labeled "Deadly Tsetse Fly." Walter shook his head. He had to agree about the worthlessness of these props. There wouldn't be any collector interested in even giving them shelf space. If there had been enough fans to generate a few collectors, the Jungo franchise might never have disappeared.

Near the bottom of the crate he found a rattle, a shrunken head, and another tribal mask, but these props were far superior to the others. They looked handmade, with real wood and bone.

The shrunken head had an odd leathery feel that made him wonder if it was real. He shuddered as he took it out of the crate.

It seemed unlikely that Chris Carmichael, a tightwad with utter contempt for his audiences as well as his employees, would spend money on the genuine articles to use as props. Maybe a prop master had purchased them online or found them in a junk bin somewhere. Beneath the last of the witch doctor items, at the very bottom of the crate, he found a scrap of cloth that made him smile as he pulled it out and brushed off the bits of straw that clung to it.

A leopard-skin loincloth, the only garment Jungo the Ape Man had ever worn in the films—all the better to show off his well-developed physique, of course. Walter tried to remember. According to the story, Jungo had killed a leopard with his bare hands when he was only five years old and had made the loincloth out of its pelt. Apparently, the loincloth had grown along with the boy. Maybe the leopard had been part Spandex.... Jungo was probably the type of man Shirley would have fallen for —wild, tanned, brawny, and barely capable of stringing together three-word sentences. Walter groaned at the thought.

Now Desiree was another story entirely. Even on the big studio lot, they often crossed paths. He saw her in the commissary at lunch almost daily—because he timed his lunch hour to match hers. She was strikingly beautiful with her reddish-gold hair, her large blue eyes, her delicate chin, and when she smiled directly at him, as she had done three times now, it made him feel as if someone in the special effects shop had created the most spectacular sunrise ever.

But Walter still hadn't gotten up the nerve to ask if he could sit and eat with her. He was a nobody who did odd jobs around the lot for the various producers. Some of them were nice, and some of them were ... like Chris Carmichael. The man was Dabney Coleman in *9 to 5*, or Bill Murray before his transformation in *Scrooged*. Carmichael had put in a requisition and Walter had pulled the card: One man needed to clear prop warehouse. It was really a job for four men and four days, but Carmichael always slashed his budgets to leave more money in his own expense account. Carmichael didn't even know who Walter Groves was.

But Desiree did. That was all that mattered.

He gazed at the leopard-skin loincloth, hearing Shirley's words ring in his head. "You aren't a man's man. You don't let yourself go wild." He sniffed, trying to picture himself in the role she seemed to want him to play. What if Desiree felt the same way? What if all women thought they wanted a nice man but were only attracted to bad boys?

He picked up the witch doctor's rattle and gave it a playful shake, then put it down by the mask and the shrunken head. Even though she had hurt him, he wasn't the type either to put a curse on Shirley, or to transform himself for her into a muscular hunk of beefcake like Jungo. He would have needed an awfully large special effects budget to pull that off. Walter held up the leopard-skin loincloth to his waist and considered the fashion statement it would make. It looked ridiculous—even more so in contrast with his work pants and his conservative windowpane plaid shirt.

"If I wore this, what would Desiree think?" Would it convince her that he was a wild man, or would she just think him pale-skinned and scrawny? All alone in the prop warehouse, he had no particular need to hurry up. Carmichael, who never noticed anyone's hard work, had already said that the props were junk.

Before he could change his mind and think sensibly, Walter unbuttoned his shirt and peeled it off. Taking a deep breath, he slipped off his shoes and trousers and tied on the loincloth. He surveyed the effect, looking critically at his skinny chest, thin arms, white skin, and the leopard-skin loincloth. He cast a skeptical glance at the witch doctor mask. "Exactly how did I expect this to bring out the wild man in me?"

Then something happened.

His heart began to pound like drumbeats in his ears. His skin grew hot and his blood hotter. He felt dizzy and then very, *very* sure of himself. The worries and confusion of his life seemed to float away like soap bubbles on the wind. His attention focused down to a single pinprick. Everything was so clear, so simple. He had worried too much, *thought* too much, suppressed all of his natural desires. He drew a deep breath, kept inhaling until his chest swelled. Then on impulse, he pounded on his proudly expanded chest. It felt good and right.

He didn't have to worry about the prop inventory or about Shirley. She had made a bad choice, and she was gone. He no longer needed to think of her. Outside the sun was bright. He was a man, and Desiree was a woman. Everything else was extraneous, a distraction. He was a hunter and he knew his quarry. A real man relied on his instincts to tell him what to do.

He let out a warbling call, broadcasting a defiant challenge to anyone who might get in his way. Barefoot, he sprinted like a cheetah out of the prop warehouse and onto the lot. He had seen where Desiree worked. He knew where to find Chris Carmichael's trailer. His vision tunneled down to that one focus.

He streaked past the people working on various films. Someone made a catcall, but most of the crews ignored him. Employees at Duro Studios were accustomed to seeing axe murderers, Martians, barbarians, and monsters of all kinds.

Chris Carmichael's headquarters were in a dingy, gray-walled trailer on the far end of the east lot. The success of a producer's films earned him clout in the studios, and Carmichael's track record had earned him this unobtrusive trailer and one secretary.

Desiree.

Walter yanked open the door and leaped in. He hadn't decided what to say or do next, but an ape-man took matters one step at a time. He reacted to situations, without planning in excruciating detail beforehand. Instead of startling Desiree at her keyboard and the producer on the phone, he blundered into a shocking scene that would have made his hackles rise if he'd had any. Carmichael stood with both hands planted on his desk, crouched like a predator ready to spring. Desiree shielded herself on the other side of the desk, trying to keep it, with its empty coffee mugs, framed pictures, and jumbled stacks of scripts, between herself and Carmichael.

He leered at her, moved to the left, and she shifted to the right. She was flushed and nervous. "Please, Mr. Carmichael. I'm not that kind of girl."

"Of course, you are," he said. "If you didn't want to break into pictures, why would you work in a place like this? I can make you an extra in my next feature, *Horror in the Prop Warehouse*. Ten-seconds screen time minimum, but there's a price. You have to give me something." Now he circled to the right and she moved left.

"Please, don't do this. I don't want to file a complaint, but I'll call security if I have to."

"You do that, and you'll never work in this town again."

Before she could reply, Walter let out a bestial roar. He wasn't sure exactly what happened. Seeing red, he acted on instinct, and charged forward. He grabbed the producer by the back of his clean white collar, yanked him away from the desk, and spun him around. As he spluttered, Walter the ape-man landed a powerful roundhouse punch on Carmichael's chin and knocked him backward into the chair he reserved for visiting actors.

Startled, Desiree gasped, but Walter was already on the move. He bounded over the desk, slipped an arm around her waist, and crashed through the screen of the trailer's open window, carrying his woman with him. The rest was a blur.

When he could think straight again—after the witch doctor's spell, or whatever it was wore off—he found himself on the rooftop of one of the backlot sets, sitting next to Desiree, his lips pressed against hers. With a start, he drew back. Her hair was rumpled, her cheeks flushed, and she wore an expression of surprise and amusement. "That was a bit unorthodox, Walter," she said, "but you were amazing. You saved me when I needed it most."

"What have I done?" Walter glanced down at the loincloth, flexed his sore knuckles, and knew with absolute certainty that he would soon die from embarrassment. He was sitting half-naked on a roof at work and had just made a complete fool of himself in front of a woman he had a genuine crush on. "I'm sorry. I'm sorry!" He scuttled backward, stood to look for a ladder or stairs, and quickly found an exit. "I didn't mean to hurt you. Mr. Carmichael's going to get me fired, for sure."

"Who, Chris? He has no clue who you are," she said. "Anyway, I'm going to hand in my own resignation. I've had enough of that man."

"I ... I need to put something decent on. I can't understand what got into me." He felt his cheeks burning. His legs wobbled, and his knees threatened to knock together. Some ape-man!

Before Desiree could say anything more, he bolted, cringing at the thought that someone else might see him this way—that Desiree *had* seen him. He was sure Jungo never had days like this.

By the time he got home, Walter was consumed with guilt. He felt flustered, exposed, and too embarrassed for words. He couldn't believe what he had done, prancing around the lot in nothing more than a loincloth, crashing into the producer's trailer offices. He had punched out Chris Carmichael! Then, after jumping through a window with Desiree, he had somehow whisked her off to a rooftop and *kissed her*! He was the very definition of the word "mortified." To make matters worse, Walter had gotten dressed again, called in a friend to finish clearing out the warehouse, then slunk off the lot, taking Jungo's loincloth with him. He could justify this, since Carmichael had made it clear that the props could be thrown into a dumpster.

He sat miserably in his empty apartment—without Shirley— and wondered how he could possibly make it up to Desiree. He didn't much care about Chris Carmichael. The man was a cad, but Walter himself had stolen a kiss from Desiree, practically ravished her! Considering the power the loincloth had worked on him, he could easily have gotten carried away. In the process of saving Desiree, he had proved that he was no better than that jerk of a producer.

And Walter had just left her stranded there, on the roof of the movie set. No, no, that wasn't Walter Groves. That wasn't who he really was. Though he wanted nothing more than to crawl under a rock, he knew what he had to do for the sake of honor. He had to go find Desiree and beg her forgiveness.

For a long time, he stood in the shower under a pounding stream of hot water, rehearsing what to say until he knew he couldn't put it off any longer. Every moment he avoided her was another moment she could think terrible things about him. He dried his hair, dabbed on some aftershave, and put on his best dress slacks, a clean shirt, and a striped blue necktie. This was going to be a formal apology, and he wanted to look his best. Pulling on his nicest, though rarely worn, sport jacket, he rolled up Jungo's loincloth and stuffed it into the pocket. Though it didn't make any sense, he would try to tell Desiree what had happened, explain how the magic had changed him somehow into a wild man, someone he wouldn't normally be.

After dialing information, then searching on the Internet, he tracked down a local street address for D. Drea. He knew it had to be her. Gathering his resolve, he marched out to go face her. He didn't need the crutch of a loincloth or some imaginary witch doctor's spells to give him courage to do the right thing. He would do this himself.

On the way to her apartment, he didn't let himself think, forcing himself onward before the shame could make him turn back. He had to be like Michael Douglas in *Romancing the Stone*, not Rick Moranis in *Little Shop of Horrors*. Nothing should disrupt the apology. Leaving his cell phone in the car, he walked to the door of her apartment, raised his hand to knock, then hesitated. He wasn't thinking clearly. He really should have brought flowers and a card. Why not go to a store now, buy them, and then come back?

He heard shouts coming from the other side of the door, followed by a scream—Desiree's scream!

He froze in terror. What should he do? Desiree was in trouble. Maybe he should run back outside, get his cell phone and call 911. He could bring the police here, or better yet, pound on her neighbors' doors and find someone who was big and strong. She screamed again, and Walter knew there could be only one solution. He tried the knob, found the door unlocked, and barged in. He found Chris Carmichael already there, reeking of cheap cologne and bourbon.

"Leave me alone," Desiree said. She held a lamp in one hand, brandishing it like a club.

Carmichael let out an evil chuckle. "Now that you no longer work for me, we can have any sort of relationship I want. There are no ethical problems."

She raised the lamp higher. Walter stepped forward, outraged but quailing at the idea of a fight. When Desiree saw him, her eyes lit up.

Carmichael turned.

Walter blurted, "Hey, What-what's going on here?" He wished he could hide or, at the very least, run back out of the apartment and return to do a second take of the scene. He needed to be a tough guy, like Dirty Harry in *Sudden Impact*— "Go ahead, make my day"—and the best he could come up with was a Don Knotts-worthy "Hey, what's going on here?" He groaned.

Carmichael recognized him, and his eyes grew stormy. Ignoring Desiree for the moment, the larger man lurched toward Walter, grabbed him by the shirt, yanked his tie, and drew Walter closer to him. "You're that little freak that sucker-punched me in my office, aren't you? Where's the spotted underwear?"

"I-I-I don't need it."

"You'll need an ambulance is what you'll need."

Indiana Jones would have done something different. He would have punched the villain, starting an all-out brawl, but as Carmichael lifted him and twisted his tie, he could only make a small *meep* sound.

"You put him down," Desiree cried, and Walter's heart lurched. She was actually defending him!

Carmichael laughed again. "You can't even save yourself. How do you expect to help this mouse?" He pushed Walter up against the wall, clenched his fist, and drew back his arm, as if cocking a shotgun.

Walter was sure his head would go straight through the drywall. "Wait. Wait, please." He swallowed and drew a deep breath. "If you're going to do this, let me face it like a man. I ... I'd like to use the restroom, please."

Carmichael blinked, then gave him a knowing smile. "Oh, afraid you're going to wet yourself, eh?" He let Walter slump to the floor. "Sure. Why not? Desiree and I were just enjoying an intimate conversation. We can wait."

He glared at her and she sat down on the sofa, not sure what to do. Walter scurried into the bathroom and closed the door, his mind spinning. Maybe Desiree kept a gun in the bathroom, perhaps taped behind the toilet tank, like in *The Godfather*. But he found nothing there and a quick search of the drawers and the medicine cabinet revealed no other weapons he could use to save the day.

He stuck his hands in his jacket pockets and his fingers brushed a patch of sleek fur. The loincloth. It was his only chance.

Walter burst out of the bathroom wearing nothing but the scrap of leopard-skin. Barefoot and bare-chested, his mind filled with the thoughts of a hunter. Testosterone and adrenaline pumped through his veins and he let out a wild yell, pounding on his chest. His hair was a mess, his eyes on fire. Seeing his enemy, the producer, he lunged toward him like a hungry lion attacking a springbok. Walter felt total confidence and did not hesitate.

Chris Carmichael, who used his position of perceived power to intimidate people, faltered. When he saw Walter leap toward him, he suddenly reconsidered what he'd been about to do.

Walter let out another roar. His lungs seemed to have twice their normal capacity. "*My* woman!"

Carmichael had probably never been challenged before. A producer, even a bad producer of second-rate movies, could boss people around in Hollywood. But Walter the ape-man, wearing nothing but his loincloth in Desiree's apartment, had no doubt that he himself was king of the jungle. Carmichael turned, took several steps in retreat, then paused. Through his hunter-focused gaze, Walter watched his prey, preparing to throw himself on the man if he made a move in the wrong direction.

Desiree decided for both men, though. As Carmichael started to turn back, she lifted her lamp, and smashed it on his head. He crumpled to the carpet like King Kong falling off the Empire State Building. The rush in Walter's mind drained away, and he found himself standing naked in Desiree's apartment, except for the ape-man's loincloth. He shivered, and goose bumps appeared on his arms. "What did I do this time?" he said, looking down at the producer with dismay.

But Desiree was close to him. Very close and very beautiful. "You protected me, Walter. You saved me." She slid her arms around his waist and gave him a hug. "You're my hero."

It was not the magic of the loincloth that made his heart start pounding again. "You-you don't mind?" he asked in surprise.

"I'll show you how much I mind in just a minute." She stepped away and looked down at the unconscious Carmichael. "But first, help me take out the garbage. We'll put him in the hall and call the police." Walter and Desiree rolled the man like a skid row drunk into the apartment hallway.

Desiree closed the door, locked it, and turned to face him. Suddenly he felt as if he were the prey and she the hungry lioness.

He gulped. "I'm really a nice guy most of the time. But I can be bad, if I need to be."

"Walter, I *like* that you're a nice guy. It's the first thing I noticed about you, even from a distance. You may not have known I was watching, but I've seen you hold doors for other people, help them carry things when their arms were full, loan them lunch money, listen to what they say. Most of the time, that's exactly what women want. It's what *I* want. But women are ... complex creatures. So once in a while we also like a bit of a wild man. You seem like the best of both worlds to me."

"You may never be safe," he pointed out. "What if Mr. Carmichael comes back? I don't think he'll leave you alone."

With a lovely smile she led him to the couch and sat him

down. "In that case, maybe you'll just have to stay here to protect me."

There was a stirring in the loincloth, and he felt very self-conscious. "Maybe I should get dressed in real clothes."

"No, Walter. You stay just the way you are." Desiree leaned over to kiss him.

In our Dragon Award-winning alternate history novel Uncharted, *Sarah A. Hoyt and I created an alternate American frontier where magic actually works. When Lewis and Clark crossed the Mississippi to explore the vast American West, they found a land filled with mythical beings, dinosaurs, water serpents, shaman magic, and ghosts.*

Before the novel's release, we wrote a new story in the same universe as a teaser, which Baen Books published on their website. Sarah and I decided to tell the tale of a Catholic missionary wandering the wild and magical West, who encounters strange things in the land of Yellowstone that test his faith.

I was good at the storytelling part, but I had to rely on Sarah for all the Catholic details. This is the first time "Father Avenir and the Fire Demons of Yellowstone" has appeared in print form.

FATHER AVENIR AND THE FIRE DEMONS OF YELLOWSTONE
(WITH SARAH A. HOYT)

The tall spare man walked as though pursued. In fact the pursuit mostly came from within.

His name, given to him by water and the holy chrism, in the rites of his father people, the name he would get called by at the last rising was Pierre de Toussaint D'Avenir. The other name his long-dead mother told him had been given only by her in the secret of the tent, late at night, in the rites of the tribe she'd been taken from as a child was Tatanka, which meant Bull. His mother had told him that meant he wouldn't retreat from anything. But, born between worlds, sometimes he wondered if he'd ever done anything but retreat. Or advance.

When you walked alone, it was sometimes difficult to know in what direction you went.

Since shortly after his father had dropped him off at school in St. Louis, at six years of age, he'd cleaved to the Word of God, the rites of the Catholic Church as an anchor, in a madly shifting world. In a world of conflicting ideas, a world of conflicting visions, in a world in which the old gods had come to life, manifesting their chaotic ways, interfering with human life and making people their playthings, a God who had sent his only son to die for the world was all he clung to.

That was why he'd become a priest of the holy mother church, taking the Word far beyond the Mississippi River and over the Continental Divide. And yet, in a world where the Pope—if there was still a pope—and the rest of the church had been broken off from the Americas, this left him yet once more trapped between the worlds, a man who believed in rites and ceremonies most Christians in America disdained.

He'd taken to the wild lands, then, to take his faith with him where he need not question the wisdom of serving a Universal Church that was no longer universal.

In the wild, breathtaking landscape, he walked, in buckskin pants and tunic, his wild waist-long black hair, increasingly streaked with white, blowing in the wind, his beard long and only intermittently trimmed by his own knife. His increasingly more tattered cassock, he kept with all his other possessions on his back, bringing it out only when he had to perform rites for those who asked them of him. A few natives, but mostly men like him, the product of Native and European. And yet they needed him. Perhaps even the natives needed him. No one knows how the seed will grow once spread.

He knew he looked odd, as a priest of the mother church, and that he was inadequate. But everyone was inadequate, in these wild times, and many of the other priests had lost their way, degenerated into ways of idolatry and sorcery. Or turned their back on the church and embraced some other sect of Christianity.

Father Avenir, or perhaps Tatanka, would have retreated into the chaos of power and desire to control the future too, if he could. Or he'd have joined the more powerful Protestant sects from the North. But it was not in him. That nature, perceived or created by his mother at his tribal naming stood, firm, steady, facing down threats with lowered head, ready to charge.

In a manner of speaking, of course. Mostly he ranged all over the unexplored arcane territories filled with scattered and Native tribes, all of whom, needed to hear the Word of God.

Now, more than ever, they needed to hear that in the world of spirits and supernatural creatures as inconsistent and wild as themselves, there was a rock to cling to. *For God so loved the world he sent it His only son.*

In the changed world fifty years after the Sundering, when Mr. Halley's comet had exploded over the Earth and forever separated America from the Old World, Father Avenir's beliefs had become even more potent and necessary.

But all the unleashed magic had also made manifest the powerful Native gods as well. What should have been preaching to scattered tribes, sitting around their campfires and sharing food, had become more than talking to them of his faith, of the man who was God and who required nothing more of them than their faith. It had become fighting demons and visions. Sometimes literally. Father Avenir feared it would become a war for souls.

He had wandered for the past fifteen years of his life, embarking as a missionary. Up the Missouri River, heading across the Great Plains, and up into the mountains trending ever northward where his father had once hunted; where his mother had carried him on her back. It had been scary then, twenty years after the Sundering. It was scarier now. More beautiful too, but scarier. The younger generation of Shamans didn't rely only on the legends of their forefathers. They had visited worlds of the spirit. They had talked to Coyote and flown with Raven. They had seen River Serpents and been attacked by Canotti with their magic arrows.

Sometimes you needed miracles to convince people beguiled by Shamans. And he would not do sorcery. He would not risk his connection to Him Who'd Redeemed the World. Sure, he'd heard of the land of the dead where one lived as the tribes did here. But what place had he there, a half breed that he was? He had to go to the God that claimed all peoples. Or nowhere.

He spoke English, French, and a half-dozen or so Native tongues, and often the words got mixed up in his mind because he spent so much time wandering alone and talking to himself. But now, at last, after hearing stories from the tribes, he knew about a great, powerful wizard, an evil force that seemed to be draining energy from the land, destroying numerous tribes, bringing back the dead, summoning monsters—all to strengthen the wild arcane territories and fight against the white men in the East.

Father Avenir felt that he had at last come to his most important battle. He trudged along on foot, crossing a ridge and working his way through sparse pine trees and larches, until he looked down at the wide and smoking valley below, where heat shimmered, where steam and spray wafted up into the air, bringing with it a sulfurous taint. He could hear the hiss and grumble in the forest silence. The Shoshone had told him of this place and sent him here. A land where the rivers ran hot and cold within feet, where the stone was yellow, or mud bubbled up from the ground and geysers roared with hot steam like a dragon's breath expelled into the air.

Father Avenir reached to his chest, fumbled with his buckskin jacket, and touched the hand-carved wooden cross that hung on a leather thong around his neck. It gave him strength, and he would need it to face the demons ahead. Father Avenir had once intended to purge the demons, to show the power of God and convince the tribes of the power of Jesus. Now, he just hoped he would survive. He reached for the rosary, strapped to his belt so he could count the beads as he walked.

> *Áve María, grátia pléna,*
> *Dóminus técum.*
> *Benedícta tū in muliéribus,*
> *et benedíctus frúctus véntris túi, Iésus.*
> *Sáncta María, Máter Déi,*
> *óra pro nóbis peccatóribus,*
> *nunc et in hóra mórtis nóstrae.*
> *Ámen.*

"*Hóra mórtis nóstrae,*" Father Avenir muttered to himself, and sighed. He hoped indeed that Mary and the Angels would be there to receive him at the hour of his death, but sometimes he worried.

Maybe the things he'd done—small acts from his small magic, to avert death; to convince a tottering believer, had damned him already.

Nothing he could do but continue. *Grátia pléna*, he'd been told the Mother of God was, and he'd have to trust in her full grace to intercede with her son on his behalf.

He walked ahead, finding his own trail, his feet carrying him forward before he could let any doubts assail him. All his life he had conquered his questions and survived persecution. From the Natives who considered him a stranger, from the whites who considered him a Native, from the pagans who considered him mad, from the Protestants who considered him evil.

Just because America had been severed from the rest of the world, that he was in any way cut off from Jesus, Mother Mary, or the Holy Spirit. Surely God was stronger than any magic he could imagine.

The air was chilly, the clouds gray and overcast above. The tall larches swayed back and forth whispering, not a threat, but like a frightened child whispering a prayer. Avenir straightened and kept walking.

Far ahead on the other side of the valley, with a loud hiss, a geyser gushed, shooting a plume of super-heated water and steam high into the air. The sound shattered the silence and he flinched. He heard other gasping fumaroles, exhalations of poisonous gas belching up from the ground. A slurry of mud and ash bubbled up, growling like some witch's cauldron. He closed his eyes, prayed more loudly, and kept walking.

He'd known of this place, of course, or at least his mother had told him of it. It had been all heated water and natural gases. Now, he had been told, it had become something else.

Near the edge of the valley, he paused to make his preparations. A thin stream trickled down the hillside and he knelt beside it. The water ran slowly, and a thin scum of chemical residue had gathered near the banks.

Father Avenir removed his pack and opened it, withdrawing his empty bowl used for his own cooking, his potages, and also for washing, even shaving when he felt so inclined. For now, though, it would serve as a basin to hold the water. He dipped the bowl in the stream and went through the motions of blessing it. Far better for a battle such as this against arcane demons and the minions of Satan himself, to use holy water blessed by the Pope himself, but no drop of that precious fluid existed any longer in all of the Americas. But every priest, who had been ordained by another priest, in a line stretching back to the apostles, had after all been given the power to cast out demons.

Hadn't the seventy-two sent out, according to Luke, come back reporting *"Lord, even the demons are subject to us in your name!"*

Setting the holy water aside, he prepared himself. In a clean handkerchief in his pack, he carried the wafers, purchased from a house in St. Louis who claimed to make the consecration bread in a way acceptable to the church. Father Avenir doubted it. Over the years, whenever he went back and bought it, he found it was yellower and contained more seeds. But it would have to do. As would the wine he poured from a small bottle to a willow bark cup.

He'd set out with French wine and a silver cup, fifteen years ago, but neither had escaped the rapacity of the first Native tribe to whom he'd tried to preach. Now he used some kind of berry wine purchased from the tribes, usually in exchange for furs, and a willow bark cup he'd made himself.

It didn't matter. By the words of the consecration, they'd become the body and blood of that most powerful act of sacrifice that had redeemed the world.

He spread a clean piece of suede on top of a large rock, balanced the offerings on it, donned his cassock, and started the holy service.

He didn't open the Bible. He remembered the readings for the day, and as he boomed the holy words, in Latin, from memory at the wild land, it seemed to him a hush fell over it, as though it listened. And why not? Hadn't St. Francis preached to the fish? Not that he was a Saint, much less that powerful a Saint.

He did the whole service and consumed the flesh and the blood of the Son of God, willing himself to become one with him, possessed of his strength.

He put away his implements and folded up the clean suede piece. He pulled out the wooden cross and let it hang proudly on his chest. He ran his fingers through his beard and his tangled hair, but he was not going to a debutante's ball. Moses himself, wandering through the wilderness, had looked no worse. When Jesus was tempted by the devil, he had not fretted over his appearance. Father Avenir's heart and soul was what mattered.

He filled the battered, but serviceable, old aspergillum with the newly-blessed water. He took his battered old copy of the Holy Bible and held it in his hand, pressed it against the black tunic at his chest, then he raised himself to his feet, looking ahead into the smoke and fumes as another angry geyser blasted not far from him.

"I come to pray," he said aloud. "Fire demons, you will bow before the Word of God." His voice was soft, but the challenge was clear.

He had no doubt that the supernatural forces lurking out in this damaged raw wound on the landscape would hear him. They would bow before his faith, and he might let them live. Even angels themselves could fall from heaven and creatures such as these that manifested the superstitious beliefs of the unconverted were all part of the universe that God created, and if they could be brought to heel, controlled, made to give their service to the Holy Word, then perhaps they could be useful. Father Avenir had seen countless inexplicable things in these arcane territories. It was not his purpose to question the wonders of the changed world, and he didn't dare question his faith.

He was in no hurry, and he had to be completely prepared. He reached for his belt, grasped the beads and took the time to say the full rosary, feeling its strength build up within him, like the most powerful magic spell. Then he let the rosary beads drop from the belt again as he made his final preparations.

Leaving his pack and his fur coat behind where he could

retrieve them if he survived this confrontation, or where scavengers could find them if he didn't, Father Avenir strode ahead. One man alone carrying the strength of God himself, walked out into the blistering valley of fire and smoke. He could smell the bitter brimstone in the air and the fumes stung his eyes, but they were tears of joy and determination. This was not just a wild landscape, no mere uncharted territory of interest to explorers and prospectors. Father Avenir's life had prepared him for this. And in defiance, he inhaled deeply of the sulphurous fumes, knowing he was about to enter hell itself. For had it not long been believed that hell exhaled sulphur? In the New World would that not be literal?

The tribe had called themselves the Snake People, or in their own language, the Shoshone. They had once been a large tribe with many villages and much trade throughout the mountains, but in recent years, with the growing evil force that had corrupted the magic from the land, many of the Shoshone had been possessed, their minds stolen away so they could be servants of the dark controlling force. Many of their villages had been burned to the ground, destroyed by incomprehensibly evil attacks, fiery demons summoned by the Black Spirit himself.

Now, the Shoshone were scattered and desperate, packing up their possessions and moving about. Their strong warriors forced to form raiding parties to take food and supplies from settlements even weaker than their own.

In his wanderings, Father Avenir suddenly found himself confronted by a sturdy warrior, with long black hair and a fierce-looking spear. He and another warrior were on horseback, and they rode out of the trees like bandits pouncing on the wandering priest. Father Avenir had found himself in many such perilous situations before, but he had the Word of God as a shield and a calm demeanor, as well as the fact that he had no possessions anyone would want to take except for some dried meat and old acorns that were much too hard to chew and could only be boiled and mashed into a paste that was somewhat edible. Father Avenir smiled at the dour-faced warriors and said a Latin prayer for them, speaking greetings in English, French, and several of the local Native tongues.

The lead warrior straightened, cocked his chin. "A priest? A shaman of the White God?" He sniffed skeptically. "And how strong is your God?"

Father Avenir straightened and showed all the confidence he could summon. "My God is strong. He created the world and the whole universe."

The warrior let out a gruff laugh. "All gods say that, but at least our God, Coyote, admits that he sometimes plays tricks on us."

Father Avenir formed a stern expression. "My God does not play tricks." He clutched the cross at his chest. Though, really, who but a God with an odd sense of humor would create a child half-white half-Native then give him the religion of a sect whose leader had been removed from this reality?

The warrior gestured with his spear and the second warrior brought his horse around. "I am Cameahwait," said the lead warrior. "Ride behind my companion. We want you to speak with our shaman. The Snake People need strength. Perhaps you can succeed where our shaman failed."

They led him to a new village that was small and sparse. The people had cut down saplings and built new huts, covering them with skins that looked old and tattered. Father Avenir thought they had salvaged their possessions and moved from place to place. They built up fires and Cameahwait called out introducing their guest, calling for the women to cook and share their food which consisted of a few rabbits, squirrels, and trout from the streams.

Father Avenir accepted their hospitality, though the people looked at him with both fear and suspicion. Avenir nodded to them, smiled, and gestured his blessing. He made the sign of the cross and the Shoshone people flinched as if he were summoning some great magic. But he was benevolent, sat on a log near the cook fire as they brought out food. He still wasn't certain why he was here, but as always, he accepted the chance to speak about Jesus Christ and spread the Word. He had an acceptable familiarity with their language. His mother had been captive among them as a young woman. And he knew enough similar words in other tribal tongues that he could patch together ways to tell even the more esoteric concepts. But the women who served him were not his audience. Cameahwait and several other warriors from a scattered raiding party also kept their distance, and the few rambunctious children running among the trees avoided him.

Father Avenir sat alone, eating, until another man emerged from an isolated structure, a wiry man with an immediate weighty presence about him, clumpy, scrabbly hair, and a feral demeanor. He strode forward, partially bent over as if he couldn't decide whether he was a man or a wolf. He wore a loincloth, stained moccasins up to his ankles, and the rich, silvery pelt of a coyote wrapped around his shoulders with the head still intact, lolling to the side. The shaman came forward, his eyes locked on Father Avenir's, and he took a seat immediately across the fire staring at the priest. Something about the shaman's presence changed movement in the air and the acrid smoke from the campfire drifted about and burned Avenir's nose and eyes. He blinked away and gestured, made the sign of the cross, and somehow the smoke drifted off in a different direction.

The shaman grinned as if this were some kind of test of wills. "My name is Dosabite," said the shaman. "You are a priest of the white men. You bring their Bible from across the great water, long before the Sundering."

"I am a priest," Avenir admitted. "I bring the Word of God. I follow the words in the Bible, the traditions of the apostles, and the dictates of the Holy Father from Rome." He held up his Bible, knowing that the Shoshone and none of the other Native tribes had any written language. "God's Word is preserved here forever. It is great magic."

"So you say," said Dosabite. "But if your God is so strong, why hasn't he defeated the evil spirit that is draining these lands? Stealing our warriors, raising revenants from the dead as his minions."

"Perhaps the fight is just beginning," Avenir said. He had heard whispers and rumors, stories told in terrified voices, but these Shoshone seemed to have a first-hand experience with the evil supernatural attacks.

"We shall see how strong your God is," said the shaman, and he picked up the coyote head and placed it firmly on his own, adjusting it and tugging it down as if it were a helmet. The sharp teeth stood out across Dosabite's face. The flaps of fur hung over his ears with pointed canine tufts of their own rising up. The dead eyes of the coyote were like dark holes, but the priest stared at them. The spirits of the world were just the spirits of the world. They had no power over the eternal.

Father Avenir had been trained by other priests in St. Louis when he was just a young man. He had learned how to read and learned how to preach, and he had become impassioned and convinced of the truth of the Word. He had been born after the comet came, after the magic shifted. He knew that many spells and folk magic worked, and that some people exhibited great powers, most prominent of which was probably the great wizard himself, Benjamin Franklin. Father Avenir had some small ability with magic himself, though he preferred not to learn spells and only trust his faith to guide his power. Because learning spells was confessing there was a magic greater than God's power, and he would not do that. He felt it was his purpose to spread the Word of God in the arcane territories where the tribes had heretofore had no opportunity to learn about Jesus, or David and Goliath, or how Jeremiah stopped the sun in the sky, or how Moses parted the Red Sea. These were stories greater than any Native myths, and they were true.

As he faced the shaman over the campfire in the Shoshone settlement, Father Avenir made his case, told his impassioned tales to Dosabite, who listened to them without skepticism. And when he was finished, even though Avenir had little interest in hearing it, the shaman reciprocated by telling of the trickster God, Coyote, a powerful spirit whose works could be seen every day in the natural world with incomprehensible coincidences, unexpected problems, but also miracles.

"Only God creates miracles," Avenir said. "The rest is just magic, which is lesser. My mother told me all those tales when I was little. They're not miracles, but the works of magic and spirits."

"Only fools insist on one explanation," retorted the shaman.

As they both ate and talked, Dosabite talked of the tribulations of his people, how they had been driven from place to place by the evil spirit abroad in the land, by fire demons who burned villages, and then he told Father Avenir of a place to the north in the mountains where the anger and evil bubbled forth from beneath the ground, where it cracked open the land of the yellow stone, where true evil could be confronted. "If your God is strong enough," Dosabite said.

Something about the shaman's words intrigued Father Avenir. "I would see this for myself," he said. "My mother told me of the place, but not that there were spirits there."

"I do not doubt your stories or your God," said Dosabite, "In these days with the magic saturating the land, and the beliefs and fears of all tribes feeding it, one would be ill-advised to doubt any God."

With a flare, sparks swirled up from the campfire and Father Avenir blinked, leaning back as he crossed himself. The smoke drifted in front of his eyes again and then the sparks died away to a low glow of embers and he looked across at the shaman, shocked to see that the coyote skin covering Dosabite's head had changed. The jaws were longer, settled into place. The eyes were fire with a golden glow. He was Coyote, the head had become part of him. The shaman's tongue lolled out between long, sharp teeth and he made a chuffing, feral sound before he leaped up from the log and bounded away from the campfire, leaving Avenir alone and clutching his Bible.

Around the steamy, smoking basin, Father Avenir saw a pristine wilderness. Towering evergreens, rolling hills, mountain peaks under an overcast sky. During his long trek from the village of the Snake People, following the directions the shaman Dosabite had given him, the priest had headed into the lush wilderness, far from where even the remaining tribes would go.

Avenir feared the looming evil presence that supposedly was growing, engulfing all of Arcane America beyond the Mississippi and the Missouri, and he fought for strength within himself, knowing in his heart and in his soul that he himself might have to be the warrior to defeat that presence. An inadequate warrior, for such a great battle.

He'd fasted and he'd prayed, and he sang the old hymns he'd learned in the church in Saint Louis, his voice echoing, strong, off the landscape and ringing a strange susurrus from the local magic.

> *Pange, lingua, gloriósi*
> *Córporis mystérium,*
> *Sanguinísque pretiósi,*
> *Quem in mundi prétium*
> *Fructus ventris generósi*
> *Rex effúdit géntium.*

Let the spirits and magics hear of the king born of a virgin, who'd shed his blood for men. Let them tremble.

As he entered the hellish landscape, though, of curling steam and foul-smelling smoke, he could feel the power simmering within the earth, an angry strength that was fierce, independent. His voice silenced, slowly.

He strode forward, his right hand wrapped around the cross hanging at his chest. The Bible was snug against him, tucked between his arm and his side giving him comfort and strength. The holy water in the aspergillum was a potent weapon, but secondary to his faith. The brimstone stench swirled around his face, but he strode forward, breathing deeply, showing no fear. Yes, when the comet had exploded and sundered America from the rest of the world, that event could have swept the remnants of Eden along with all the stranded white settlers in the east that might have been the hope of the righteous. Perhaps Arcane America held the gates of hell, but hadn't Jesus himself said they would not stand against the church? Even if all that remained of the church in this desolate place was Father Avenir, he had been ordained by men ordained by the apostles who'd broken bread with Jesus. And he'd sanctified himself for this battle.

The hollow breathy roar of a fumarole broke open to his left, gushing fumes and hot gases from beneath the earth, like the laughter of a monster. Avenir could feel the pull of his enemy ahead, though; a strength that made the ground throb. Despite the surrounding tall pines in the thick forest here in the basin, the chemical exhalations had bleached the ground, covered it in white powder, killed off many of the trees so that they stood bent and brown, withered from the poison within the soil. Another geyser erupted, spouting hot steam, and a jet of water, high overhead.

The priest would not be intimidated. He trudged onward muttering the words under his breath,

Verbum caro, panem verum
Verbo carnem éfficit:
Fitque sanguis Christi merum,
Et si sensus déficit,
Ad firmándum cor sincérum
Sola fides súfficit.

He realized that mumbling was not good enough, he sang the words, *TANTUM ERGO SACRAMÉNTUM*.

Venerémur cérnui:
Et antíquum documéntum

Novo cedat rítui:
Præstet fides suppleméntum
Sénsuum deféctui.

Genitóri, Genitóque
Laus et jubilátio,
Salus, honor, virtus quoque
Sit et benedíctio:
Procedénti ab utróque
Compar sit laudátio.

Then followed it with the twenty-third Psalm, his favorite:

Dominus reget me et nihil mihi deerit, In loco pascuae ibi me conlocavit super aquam refectionis educavit me, Animam meam convertit deduxit me super semitas justitiae propter nomen suum, Nam et si ambulavero in medio umbrae mortis non timebo mala quoniam tu mecum es virga tua et baculus tuus ipsa me consolata sunt, Parasti in conspectu meo mensam adversus eos qui tribulant me inpinguasti in oleo caput meum et calix meus inebrians quam praeclarus est, Et misericordia tua subsequitur me omnibus diebus vitae meae et ut inhabitem in domo Domini in longitudinem dierum.

He didn't know enough Latin to catch the nuances. The priests had taught him Latin, of course, so he could read the Holy Word as it came from the ancients. But he thought perhaps they hadn't been very well taught, the great teachers and great books of learning having been lost in the Sundering. They sometimes told him they didn't understand a word. And yet, he knew the Psalm spoke of God walking with him—as he'd walked with David—and setting a table for him in the presence of his enemies. How many times had Father Avenir been safe where he shouldn't be? How had he survived in hostile territory these many years? How but for the grace of God?

The geyser field seemed cowed, or was that just his imagination?

He took heart, though, and trudged forward, shouting, "I bring the way, the truth, and the light. I can feel your evil presence here. I can smell the lake of fire and eternal damnation, and I am not afraid."

He squeezed the cross, felt its well-smoothed wooden sides press into his calloused palm. "Come and see me. Face me. Or are you afraid?" His lips were cracked, his throat was dry, and it burned from the caustic fumes. His eyes stung, and water welled up within them, but it only purified his vision. Mud pots bubbled like lava on either side of them, but he did not waver in his forward journey. He had remained steadfast in his faith all his life.

He had argued with the numerous Protestants, defended himself for being a papist, for still obeying the Holy Father in Rome even though no one knew who that might be now. He had been mocked and ridiculed, shunned, robbed, beaten. But Father Avenir had survived. Each such incident was a trial that God inflicted upon his missionary, and if he had to die while serving his mission, his Lord, then that would only assure his passage into heaven. Martyrdom might, in fact, be the only way he got to heaven.

A geyser erupted close to him. He saw the piled, powdery white crystals around the crater that looked like a maw in the ground. Scalding water rocketed up, spreading out and drenching him in a hot downpour. He felt the water steam in his tangled hair, soak his tattered black tunic, but he stepped forward, blinking away the distraction. A new hole blasted in the barren, brownish white ground in front of him, cracking open, sending gouts of foul-smelling steam, and Father Avenir stopped. It was like a thunderstorm of smoke and sulphur and blisteringly hot vapors.

And he saw shadowy shapes, twisted inhuman forms, damned wretches, like souls who had been cast into hell itself. They lurched up, barely taking shape, looming closer as if to attack him, or at least stop him. Father Avenir cried out, then uttered his prayers again in Latin. He'd been told there was power in the old words. He crossed himself and the shadows backed away, hiding within the folds of noxious steam that continued to waft upward in curtains. But the hideous dark figures were not avoiding the priest, not cowed by his prayers, rather they backed away as if in deference, as an escort to ... something far worse.

The silhouette in the steam and smoke approached: a towering muscular figure that loomed a full foot above Father Avenir's head, and even so, its back was hunched as if beaten. The priest didn't flinch, but looked up as the figure strode forward, pushing aside the obscuring veils as if impatient to be seen. Avenir watched a wide, coal black, cloven hoof step forward, improbably balanced on the rough, blasted ground, brick-red skin covered with knobs and scabs. A bare wide chest, like a blacksmith who worked on a forge of souls. A long, barbed tail lashed from the base of the creature's spine, like a terrible weapon. Then the demon loomed forward to show black horns on his head, evil slitted eyes, a face that should have been beautiful, but was instead a sculpture of diamond hard fury.

"Lucifer," Father Avenir said, "fallen angel."

The devil laughed out loud, a sound like a crack of thunder. The ground rumbled and boiled. More geysers erupted, belching steam and smoke like a regal fanfare for the king of the damned.

"If that is what you wish to call me. I've appeared this way to comfort you."

"To comfort me?" Avenir was aghast. He held his Bible up. "I draw no comfort in seeing you, Satan."

The thing laughed again. "You draw comfort in the affirmation of your beliefs. You see this place as hell and so you expect the devil himself. I am here exactly as you wished."

"I wish you to be gone," Avenir said. "In the name of the Lord God Almighty, I banish you from this arcane world. These lands are not yours."

The looming Satan twitched, but that seemed to be the extent of Father Avenir's power.

"But I am these lands. I am part of the spirit of these mountains, the forests, the rivers. There is also much anger in this land and it manifests here, boiling to the surface. You can see it all around you. With the coming of the comet, the magic was reinforced and released. It made all this possible." Lucifer reached up with hands outstretched, the fingertips adorned with long, black claws. "The magic here belongs to the land and the people. And your magic, too. I feel the strength within you, Tatanka, the bull man, he who will not be moved." The devil leaned closer, and the priest could smell its foul breath, which reminded him of a long-abandoned abattoir. "You are part of me as well," Satan said.

"No!" the priest yelled back.

"Can't you feel it? The simmering power in this land makes all things possible. The gods of the Native tribes have regained their strength, become real and tangible. No one of their Shamans can deny what he sees with his own eyes, and neither can you." His long, barbed tail thrashed with impatience.

Father Avenir choked. The brimstone smell was suffocating. "You have no power over me. You're as subjected to God's power as I am."

The devil back-handed him across the face, striking hard with his wide knuckles that felt like stones. The priest tumbled to his knees, felt the blood oozing from a gash in his cheek, but he still kept his grip on the Bible. "Yes, evil is real, I've never doubted that," Avenir said, "but that doesn't mean you can't be defeated."

He pulled himself to his feet again, remaining defiant. He wondered what the Shoshone shaman would have seen if he had come out to this geyser. Surely Dosabite would not view the devil like this. What would other tribes have seen?

"I will drive you from this place," Avenir said.

Lucifer huffed. "I *am* this place."

The priest surprised him, pulled out his aspergillum and, without warning, muttering a prayer in the back of his throat, enhancing the blessing, he hurled the holy water at Satan's chest. With a bright flash, the steam erupted white and pure, somehow driving away the mists and the curtains of steam from the fumaroles, the geysers, the exhalations from the mud pots.

The devil roared, looked down at his chest in shock, as a great smoking hole ate its way through his chest, devoured his heart, dissolved his brick-red stubbly body. Satan himself broke apart, shattering into thousands of small dissolving pieces, like a smashed sheet of ice that broke apart and melted under the hot sun.

Striking down the devil seemed to settle the ground around him. The earth beneath his feet ceased its rumbling. The geysers faded, the hot water droplets pattering to the caked ground all around him, and the mists cleared. A breeze whipped away the strongest rotten egg stench and he saw a slice of blue sky overhead, widening.

Father Avenir laughed and clutched the Bible against the cross over his heart. And yet, he waited. The Great Deceiver was after all that. He waited to feel an exhilaration in the earth itself, a lifting of the weight of evil, a cleansing of this great scarred valley.

But instead, the powerful force that throbbed inside of him, tugging like a magnet pulling him along, remained just as strong —and it came from ahead of him. "I banished you," he said in a hoarse voice, but he still felt the power, the anger.

A voice resonated in his head, no longer the thunderous, booming male voice of Satan himself, but a female voice. A woman's voice at once benevolent and deadly like all the protective mothers in the world, speaking in unison. "You banished that part of me that was within yourself, but I am still here."

The force tugged at him, and he staggered forward between the, now, quiescent geysers, walking along the valley floor. "I want to see you, and you need to see me. You have killed your Satan, and I applaud you, but I am not the same."

Her voice was tantalizing, and though he fought it, it seemed to put him in a trance. The aspergillum was empty, and he had no more Blessed Water. But he had his Bible and he had his cross. He stopped resisting. The smell of brimstone was thinner now and he did not feel as threatened, though the female voice that throbbed from the ground, that came from somewhere ahead, mixed in with other faint steam, seemed more powerful than even the hulking Lucifer. This, he realized, was his real opponent.

The spirit of this valley of fire demons, the vengeful fury of the arcane lands made manifest.

Up ahead, he saw the flat, circular bowl of a small lake, like a shimmering irregular mirror. Exhalations of steam drifted up, and as he approached he saw that the waters were absolutely still, not stirred by the wind, nor by fishes. This pool was a conduit, the source of the voice, the entity that lived within this large and strange valley. The waters were scalding hot. He could sense that even as he came closer. The ground was bleak and barren. The lake itself was dead and yet full of colors, as if someone had drowned a rainbow there. Chromatic rings of blue and copper, bright green with tendrils of yellow spread out beneath the water; pigments that highlighted the lake bed.

"Come closer," the voice said. "Look into me so that I may see you."

"I will show you the Holy Cross," he said, and stood on the shore feeling the heat. He held out his wooden cross and looked down to see his reflection in the perfectly still surface, and yet the vision went deeper, changing him to a younger man, then an older man. His face changed, and his appearance shifted in the reflection, not just from himself but to Dosabite, then Cameahwait, then numerous other natives he had seen; his beloved priests back in St. Louis, who'd taught him Latin and the Word. His mother, smiling at him and crying when she'd left him at the school in St. Louis. His father, his blue eyes bleak, his mouth set when telling him he was leaving him here so that he'd learn not to be a savage. A beautiful Native woman he'd loved before he realized his calling was to the church and celibacy. It was a blur of shapes, memories, figures.

"Why do you tempt me?" he said.

"I remind you. That is all. I need you to understand that I am not evil, just different, just as you are different from the ways and the beliefs here in the wilderness."

"I bring my beliefs with me," said Avenir, forming words of defiance. "I was baptized. I am a priest. I bring the Word of God."

"You were baptized in the civilized world, foolish man."

A stir of ripples circled the throbbing chromatic pool. Steam drifted higher, but Avenir continued to peer closer. He leaned over, feeling the pull of the shimmering water, the iridescent colors.

"If you wish to serve in these wild lands, if you are truly a missionary, then you must be baptized here." The heat of the water rippled up nearly blistering the skin on his face.

"You would kill me," he said. "You would trick me."

"I have no need of tricks," the pulsing voice of the wild said. "I know what I am, and I sense the goodness in you, the passion for truth and eternity."

The voice echoed in his head and Avenir felt a warm honey drifting through him.

"I find it exhilarating," the voice said.

"I have my mission," he said. "You will not sway me from it."

"I am trying to help you," said the voice. "You cannot bring your civilized ways out here; so you must adapt your ways to the spirit of the land. There is evil here, even I know it," said the voice, thrumming as if in an undertone of fear. "Before this battle is over, there will be many strange alliances. Are you willing to take the risk? Will you be strong enough and baptize yourself here as well?"

Father Avenir shivered, despite the pounding heat all around him. "I cannot," he said. "I will not forsake what I believe."

"I did not ask that of you," said the woman's voice. "I asked you only to trust ... as you ask the natives to trust you, to believe your words, now believe mine." Her voice echoed louder, and he cringed, but he couldn't press the sound away. "I'm not saying I'm a rival of your God, nor that I am the sole creator. But I am a powerful part of His creation, and you cannot deny me."

The colors in the chromatic pool were tantalizing, the water itself seemed perfect, pristine, inviting. Father Avenir was sore and weary, his hair caked from the smoke, and grit, and dust of countless days alone on the trail and in camp. "I will need the strength," he said. "I come from the civilized world, but I am part of this one. I don't ever intend to go back, any more than America can return to the rest of the world."

When he had faced the manifestation of Satan, Father Avenir had felt fear, but this was not so simple or clear. This was dread and uncertainty, yet longing as well. He did know he was alien here in these arcane territories. He remembered seeing Dosabite and how he had shifted into the form of Coyote. There were things here that Father Avenir could never explain, but questions were only doubts until they were answered.

He was like those early apostles going out into the wild tribes. Unless the Bible was wrong—and that was impossible—then in those days too spirits and magic had walked the land. Had the Catholic missionaries not told some of the local gods they were now something else, and integrated them into their tales and their belief so that the spirits themselves converted, and a legend of Jupiter became a tale of St. John, or a story of Diana became the most holy story of St. Catherine?

He was not a fool. He understood how that had happened, the Catholic belief encircling and purifying the pagan one. But could one do that unless one accepted it and became part of it? His mother was Native. He was part of this land. Surely he could touch the spirits and make them his own.

Before he could change his mind, the priest pulled off the tattered black tunic and set it on the ground beside the edge of the hot pool. Then he set down the Bible and aspergillum, removed his boots, his buckskin breeches, and stood there naked, alone in the wilderness, just as he had been in his first baptism. The female voice remained silent, but he could feel the presence there. And he looked down at the hot pool, knowing that the water was scalding, near to the boiling point. It was deadly—yes, it would kill him, just like a martyr being boiled in oil, back during the days of the inquisition.

He would die, and his body would float here, unseen by the Shoshone or any white trappers. His flesh would be boiled off his bones, which would then sink to the bottom. Father Avenir would be forgotten. He would die.

But he chose not to believe that. His own faith was strong, just as when he had destroyed the vision of the devil. Had not Daniel walked out of the furnace alive?

The female voice, the presence of the land of the yellow stone throbbed upward to enfold him, to protect him. He closed his eyes and gritted his teeth. If his faith was too weak, he did not deserve to live anyway. Father Avenir fell forward and plunged into the hot pool. The shock flashed around him. The water embraced his skin and his hair. He nearly gasped, but fought back his feelings. The only thing he kept was the wooden cross on the thong around his neck, and it floated around him as he drifted in the hot pool, like a lifeline.

The water burned and tingled, enfolded him, scrubbed his skin, soaked his hair—but he lived. He floated there, wrapped in the blanket of his own faith, and of the strength that the magic in this land gave to his beliefs. Yes, he was strong enough to do this, and now he would be baptized in the ways of the wild as well as the ways of the white man. He was terrified for a moment, but then he was cleansed. He was accepted. And after a long moment, the female voice in his mind said, "Yes, it is as I thought. I know you now Tatanka, Bull of heaven, Rock of all Saints, Father of the Future. You may go, and you will be remembered."

Father Avenir staggered out of the scalding water and stood with steam drifting away from his reddened skin. He looked utterly clean, scrubbed, his skin pink, his hair fine and soft as the water evaporated. He turned and looked back at the rainbow colors submerged in the pool. He had answers to the mysteries that were strongest, while the other questions remained just as powerful, but not quite so urgent. "Thank you," he muttered, realizing that whatever that spirit was, she also understood some part of the love of God as he did.

With painstaking care, Father Avenir dressed himself again, but even his stiff and dirty clothes could not take away the feeling of purity inside him now.

With his pack and his furs, the priest trudged away from the land of the yellow stone and the steaming geysers. He needed several days alone just to think about what he had experienced, to accept it and to assess the new powers that he had acquired. The epiphany that made him different now, not just a priest from the white man's world, but also fundamentally a part of these arcane territories. A part infused with the strength of the creator and of his son who died for the world. He was now, as he'd been at birth, both Native and European, both wild and civilized. But for the first time he accepted both. He was Tatanka Pierre de Toussaint D'Avenir. He wanted to tell the shaman, Dosabite, everything that had happened, but he was in no hurry. Perhaps Dosabite could only perceive part of it. But even that part would help.

He made his way through the mountains, camping each night, finding food for his supper, or going hungry when he found none. Finally, one day in the long shadows of late afternoon, two riders came upon him in the forest; long-haired warriors whom Avenir recognized instantly, Cameahwait and his companion. The warrior chief looked strained and saddened, not the cocky raider who had first met the priest some weeks before.

"You are the Catholic priest," Cameahwait said. "We have searched for you."

"Yes, you know me," he said. "I am Father Avenir. I am Tatanka Pierre de Toussaint D'Avenir."

"Sacagawea sent me to find you. Her husband has been struck down by the great wizard. His spirit is gone, and she has requested a priest for the last rites."

The other warrior said, "We've been searching for days."

Father Avenir stood, placid. He brushed off the front of his furs. "I will accompany you. That is my duty as a priest. But, who is Sacagawea?"

"She is my sister," said Cameahwait, "taken from us as a child by raiders. She is back now, though. She is traveling on an expedition with a group of white men, led by Captain Lewis and Captain Clark."

"An expedition?" Father Avenir asked.

The second warrior was impatient. "There is no time for questions. Come with us. Make haste."

Father Avenir agreed and mounted up behind the second warrior. "Take me to them and I will do my duty as a priest." He also understood more, but he had many questions. Maybe his own revelations could be shared not just with the Native tribes, but with others back in the east. "I look forward to speaking with these Captains, Lewis and Clark."

When I was a new writer, I once attended a small writing workshop led by science fiction legend Damon Knight. I submitted a short story about a medieval con man making fake Splinters of the True Cross to prey upon gullible villagers. Damon announced, in front of all the other writers, "This story is totally screwed up, but you do show some talent as a writer." I never rewrote it, but years later Rebecca and I contributed a story to an anthology centered around Renaissance Faires. I thought it might be an opportunity to revamp that Splinters of the True Cross idea, and Rebecca ran with the concept, and we worked out the following story.

Oh, and I also incorporated the original con-man idea into my fantasy comedy The Dragon Business.

SPLINTER
(WITH REBECCA MOESTA)

S omething about the Renaissance Faire beckoned to him like the sound of a hundred sirens luring a lonely sailor from the sea. In spite of the nearly hundred-degree heat of a California summer, he never tired of the beauty of it all—the jostling crowds in brightly colored clothing, the noisy parades of "royalty" and minstrels, the jugglers, the candlemakers, the serenity of a young mother with ample breasts exposed suckling a newborn child as if it were the most natural thing in the world. He loved the spectacle of a hundred different kinds of entertainers and artisans and food vendors, all putting on Elizabethan micro-performances minute by minute, doing their utmost to lure money from the cash-fat pockets of the faire-goers.

And it was those cash-fat pockets that brought Wil to these open-air festivals year after year. He never tired of the magic of thousands of bodies jostling together, muttering loudly, kicking up dust ... never noticing the slender young man with the wispy beard and peasant clothing who expertly and discreetly relieved them of their excess valuables. Pickpocket, thief, rogue, highwayman—after all, that was a legitimate part of the time period, too. Certainly, more authentic than either the churro or cappuccino seller.

It wasn't long before the first opportunity presented itself. Wil had learned to recognize those opportunities while he was still in high school, furtively watching for an unguarded purse or backpack; by now his instincts were so well tuned he hardly had to think about it. He had just passed the booth from which he'd shoplifted his own costume two years earlier, when he came upon a couple in casually elegant street clothes. They were having a heated discussion just outside a palm reader's tent.

"Why not?" the young woman said. "Are you afraid she'll tell us we should get married, after all?"

The young man scoffed. "Come on, they only say what they think you want to hear, anyway."

Quickly assessing the situation—it was important to be a good judge of character—Wil deduced from shoes, hair, makeup, and demeanor that the young woman would be carrying the money. *I'm even doing them a favor,* Wil thought. *A few arguments about money will give them a more accurate sense of their marriage compatibility than any palm reader could.*

He conveniently joined a cluster of people passing by, allowing himself to be crowded into the arguing couple. It took only one brief bump and a mumbled "Excuse me" to liberate an expensive Tumi wallet from the young woman's equally expensive Dooney & Bourke leather purse.

A little farther on, Wil ducked between two booths to determine the value of his acquisition. He was immediately impressed with himself: $281 in cash, and the wallet itself would fetch a good price at the local flea market. Wil tucked his prize into an interior pocket of his billowy brown knee breeches and moved on with a spring in his step. He would dispose of the credit cards, of course. Too easy to get caught using stolen cards.

And he didn't plan to get caught. Ever.

The next two hours proved considerably less satisfying. Discouraged, Wil bought a roasted turkey leg, then removed the pewter tankard he wore at his belt and had it filled with chilled ale. He sat down to eat on a bench in a small amphitheater where two jugglers were throwing knives at each other while making witty banter.

After polishing off his lunch, Wil tossed the turkey leg bone to the ground, not even bothering to look for a trash can. If someone scolded him about it, he could argue that his gesture was certainly truer to the Renaissance spirit than using a trash can was. If it really bothered some do-gooder, let *him* dispose of it. Wil had never believed in much except himself ... and he'd gotten over himself long ago.

Wil headed up a rocky, hay-strewn path, his eyes beginning their automatic sweep. His vigilance was quickly rewarded when he spied a middle-aged man with a chest-length salt-and-pepper beard counting out bills from a leather pouch at his waist. One of the bills fell to the ground and was caught by a hot breeze and blown a few feet behind him onto the path. Noting that the foot traffic was light and no one else was watching, Wil bent smoothly for the merest second, plucked the bill from the ground and continued up the path before the bearded man even had a chance to turn and look for the fallen money.

Wil passed a tarot card reader and a cluster of college students singing madrigals beside a fake wishing well. At the glassblower's tent, he spotted a man in his mid-thirties making a purchase. He wore safari shorts, a golf shirt, designer sunglasses, and sockless leather loafers. A grade-school-aged boy and girl pranced impatiently beside him. A quick glimpse told the pickpocket that the man's wallet contained enough cash to pay Wil's expenses for weeks.

"Come on, Dad! You promised we could see the storyteller."

"And that's just what we're going to do." The man slid his wallet into the front pocket of his shorts and accepted a wrapped package from the glassblower. Wil hung back and decided this man might be worth following.

The man began herding his children up the path. "Why'd we have to buy Mom another glass unicorn?" the boy said.

"We get her one every year, Evan, whether she can come or

not. It's not her fault Grandma broke her hip," the girl answered. "What a stupid question."

"Now, Orli, don't call your brother stupid."

Wil gritted his teeth as he watched Perfect Family Guy, more determined than ever to interject a little bit of gritty reality into the pampered PFG's perfect life. Wil was an old hand at rationalizing to himself. He had been making up excuses and explanations for so long that he had almost come to believe them. Almost.

They came to a small pavilion, where half the floor was littered with hassocks and colorful overstuffed cushions on which children sat or reclined. A man with a leathery face and white shoulder-length hair walked among them, telling stories. Wooden tables running along one side of the breezy tent held books bound in hand-tooled leather. The sign over the pavilion said, "Tales of Glorye."

Wil watched as Orli, Evan, and Perfect Family Guy seated themselves on cushions. Pretending a casual interest, Wil entered the pavilion and began browsing the books. The storyteller spoke in a rich, expressive voice. Wil let the words wash over him, but his concentration was focused on PFG.

When the tale ended about ten minutes later, many of the listeners came up to drop money into a hat beside the old storyteller. Most of the audience left, but Wil's three marks lingered to ask questions. He suppressed an impatient sigh, picked up another leather-bound book and leafed through it, pretending to admire the meticulous hand lettering.

The storyteller plopped the hat full of money onto a table not far from Wil.

"So, what happened next?" Orli asked the old man. "I mean, after the knight went back and told the King."

"Ah, now that's a much longer story."

"Do you have a book that has the story in it?" PFG asked.

"Over here on the table." The storyteller moved closer to Wil and selected a thick tome with a burgundy leather binding.

Perfect Family Guy showed it to his daughter. "Say, aren't you worried about leaving all that money just lying on the table?"

Finding the comment particularly ironic, Wil glanced over to see the old man smile. "I find that when you take care of the really valuable things, everything else takes care of itself. That's why I keep everything that's truly valuable to me right here in this pocket," he said, patting the left side of his leather breeches.

"I can admire that philosophy," PFG said.

"Look," Evan said, pointing at the pages of the book. "There's the story he told today."

"And two stories that come before, and three that come after it," Orli said. "Daddy, can we get this?"

PFG stroked his daughter's hair. "It would be the perfect souvenir."

Wil gritted his teeth again. *Perfect.* The very perfection of this family was driving him insane.

"Let me wrap that for you." The storyteller moved to Wil's right, reached under the table, and came up with two sheets of heavy paper that looked handmade.

The children began looking at the books on another table. PFG got out his wallet and began counting out the money. When the storyteller laid the sheets of paper on the table and began wrapping the book, Wil saw his chance. The pocket that held the old man's "true valuables" was within a foot of Wil's hand, so he clumsily dropped the book he had been looking at. Pretending to reach for it, Wil awkwardly bumped the old man with his hip, at the same time slipping his right hand into the pocket and apologetically steadying the storyteller with his left hand.

The whole maneuver took less than a second. Wil felt an uneven lump in the pocket, something strange—but just as his hand closed around it, a searing pain shot up his arm. It was like nothing he had felt since the age of ten when he'd lost control of his bicycle going down the driveway, veered into the neighbor's yard, fallen, and ripped his leg open on a sprinkler head.

With another jostle, Wil snatched his hand back and bent to

retrieve the fallen book. He fumbled around, momentarily blinded by the pain and sucked in a sharp breath.

The old man put a hand on his back. "You all right, lad?"

For a panicked second, Wil wondered if the old man knew he'd been pickpocketed, but when his eyes focused on the kindly face, he saw no suspicion. "No, I, uh … sudden migraine." He put a hand to his head. "Probably the heat."

He handed the book back to the storyteller. As quickly as it had come, the scorching pain subsided, but Wil's hand still throbbed as if he had slammed it in a door.

Perfect Family Guy was beside him. "My wife gets migraines. They can get pretty nasty. Maybe you should lie down somewhere in the shade."

"There's plenty of room on the cushions," the old man offered.

"No," Wil said a little too quickly. "Thank you. I, uh, probably should take some medication for this. It's out in my car." Damn. Now that both men were so solicitous of him, Wil stood little chance of slipping in under their radar.

The storyteller regarded him with solemn eyes. "I hope you feel better really soon. Sometimes there's a trick to it."

"Do you need help out to your car?" PFG asked.

"Thanks. I'll manage." He left the pavilion, cursing himself for attracting so much attention from two potential marks. Surely, he could have toughed out just a little bit of pain when he stood to profit so much. Already the searing stab had receded to a mere pinprick in his mind. It had been foolish weakness, but he would not call attention to himself again.

Once he was out of sight of the pavilion, Wil hurried to put as much distance between him and the two annoyingly helpful men as possible. Safely on the other side of the faire, he scanned the crowds once more for opportunities. *This is easy.* He struggled to focus. *You're a natural.* But nothing felt natural right now.

He was filled with a sensation that was simultaneously pleasant and unpleasant, a fizzy alertness of the mind not unlike the way he felt when, after an all-nighter, his body replaced sleep with pure adrenaline. Wil forced himself to move into the flow of shoppers and sightseers.

There. Wil saw his opportunity. A young woman with hot-pink polish on the nails of her manicured fingers and pedicured toes was pushing a baby carriage. The mother stopped and bent to comfort the child as it continued to wail. Her attention was fully focused on the brat and not on the purse dangling from the stroller's handle.

He moved in. This was almost too easy. A simple swoop would do it.

His hand dipped into her purse, but the moment he touched the wallet, a lightning bolt struck the index finger of his right hand, shot through his wrist, traveled up his arm, and spiked into his brain. He simultaneously jerked his hand away and fell to his knees. The young mother looked up in alarm, her concentration startled away from her child who, also startled, stopped crying for a moment.

"Sorry," Wil gasped. "I tripped."

"You okay?" She moved around to the back of the stroller, darting a cautious glance down at her purse.

"Yeah, I'll be fine." Wil forced himself back to his feet and dusted off his breeches. "Good as new."

He backed away and lost himself in the crowd. That had been close. Damnedest thing about his hand, too. In a patch of bright sunlight, he examined his finger. It still stung, as if something small and sharp was embedded in it, but he could see no burn or blister, no cut, no sliver, *nothing*. Yet the pain—the pain in his hand, his arm, his head—had been real. He frowned. Maybe it was a pinched nerve, or maybe he really was having a migraine.

Wil always kept a bottle of ibuprofen stashed in his glove compartment, so he headed out the front entrance, remembering to get his hand stamped for re-entry. The parking lot offered no shade at all, and Wil considered waiting for the "shuttle," a wide, canvas-covered horse-drawn wagon that ferried attendees to and from their cars for tips. But the wagon was at the far end of the lot, and Wil didn't want to wait.

By the time he got to his battered '83 Dodge, he had worked up a substantial sweat. He got the bottle of extra strength pain reliever, took twice the suggested number, and washed them down with a grimace and a swallow of the flat, and by now hot, soda he'd left open in his car.

He rolled down the windows and took a short nap in the front seat to give the analgesic time to work. By the time he woke up it was late afternoon. The faire would be closing in a couple of hours, and parts of the parking lot had already begun to empty out. Wil felt greatly refreshed, in spite of the heat, and decided to get back to work.

He got out of his car and strode through the lot in the general direction of the entrance. As he walked, he glanced through car windows, looking for wallets, merchandise, purses left behind by faire-goers in the "safety" of their locked cars. For the most part, he ignored the older cars, like his, which usually weren't worth the trouble. He also avoided anything too new and too likely to have an alarm. Within ten minutes he had found one with a purse on the floor of the passenger side, "hidden" underneath the morning paper.

He grinned. "Haven't lost your touch, Wil."

All the doors were locked, of course, but he easily found a substantial rock that would remedy the situation. After a quick glance to make sure no one was around, he hefted the rock and swung it toward the window.

Several seconds later, Wil opened his eyes to escape the blinding white explosion in his head. He found himself flat on his back in the dirt, still grasping the rock. The slicing, stabbing, burning pain that grated up his arm was less intense now, but still impossible to endure.

When he dropped the rock, the pain finally began to subside. He hauled himself back to his feet, looked at the car window, and blinked in surprise. The window was not broken. Not even a crack. But he couldn't have missed—not with the force he'd used, not at such short range, and yet ...

Carefully, afraid of triggering the terrible pain again, he

picked up the rock, this time with his left hand. He swung with all his might at the window—

Bam! Flat in the dirt again. Wil's head pounded as if a grenade had gone off in his right ear, and his right arm felt as if an elephant had walked across it. He whimpered—something no one had ever heard him do. He wondered if he might be having a heart attack. Wouldn't that be the left arm? It was hard to think.

His fingers let loose of the rock, and he lay on the tire-flattened grass until the pain had subsided to a mere pricking in his right index finger. He brought it up to his face and studied it again, but still found nothing.

Something was very wrong with him. Wil didn't have medical insurance, but there was a first-aid tent inside the faire. He could describe his symptoms, maybe have them examine him. At least it would be free.

He got up slowly, not even bothering to brush the dirt off. It might add an air of authenticity when he explained his symptoms, make the first-aid workers take him more seriously. On his way to the entrance, much to his chagrin Wil passed the Perfect Family waiting to take the wagon shuttle back to the parking lot. The wagon was coming, the horses clomping forward, the people pushing closer to get a seat aboard.

Wil hoped to walk past the annoying family unnoticed, but Perfect Family Guy saw him right away and managed to look genuinely concerned. "Hey, how's that migraine doing?"

Wil's first instinct was to lie, but what was the point? "I thought it was gone, but it seems to keep coming back."

The little girl, Orli, trotted out in front of the wagon, grinning. "Look—what pretty horses! Where's the video camera, Daddy? Can you take a picture of me with them?"

Two rowdy young boys began to clatter against each other with wooden swords they had purchased as souvenirs.

PFG nodded his sympathy toward Wil. "Could be one of those cluster headaches, I suppose. They come and go, and they can be as bad as migraines." Wil made a noncommittal response and stepped around the crowd, wanting to be away.

A younger boy, frustrated at being left out of his brothers' sword fight, pulled out his "Renaissance souvenir" pop gun and pointed it at them. "I'll get you both!" He fired the pop gun, augmenting the sound with his own yell, "BLAM!"

The hot and tired horses responded to the noise. Startled, they flinched in their harness, snorted, and lurched forward. Orli was standing right in their path, still waiting for PFG to film her with the video camera. The wagon driver wrenched at his reins, the horses lifted their hooves, and the girl shrieked.

Because he had been trying to get around the crowd, Wil was closest to where the girl stood. He jumped forward, knocked Orli out of the way, smashed into the nearest horse, and fell to the ground. Before he could roll away, he felt a hammer strike his chest. The girl had fallen backward to sprawl in the dirt and had already begun to sob, but the weeping came more from startlement and confusion than from severe pain. Wil, on the other hand, thought he might have cracked a rib or two.

The wagon driver backed the wagon up several feet and jumped down from the buckboard, and other people hurried forward to Wil and the girl. The horses snorted, as if embarrassed by the incident. Orli continued to cry softly, and her father quickly checked to make sure she was uninjured before moving to take a look at Wil. "Wow, that could've been bad! I don't know how to thank you. Are you all right?"

Surprised was the first thing that came to Wil's mind. He had acted completely without thinking, with no regard for his own safety. Stranger yet, he felt very little pain. "Fine." And he found it was true. His entire body was suffused with a pleasant tingling sensation. "Better than fine. I'm great."

Perfect Family Guy still looked concerned. "Could just be endorphins and adrenaline talking. You'd better have a doctor check you out."

A distant part of his mind seemed aware that his body was hurt. He pulled open the loose neck of his muslin peasant shirt and looked inside. A red flush of bruising was already beginning to appear beneath the skin. How odd. After the inexplicable agony he had experienced several times today—each time while trying to ply his trade—now he felt euphoria when he should *really* be hurt. And he'd only been trying to help someone, after all. There was definite irony in that: invisible pain after trying to steal, and a feeling of well-being when trying to help, despite a visible injury.

Wil's eyes narrowed as the thoughts flashed through his mind. *Was* it irony, or was this something more sinister? It had all begun after he'd tried to pick the storyteller's pocket. Had the old man done something to him, administered some sort of drug or hypnotized him?

He smiled up at the PFG. "You're probably right. I'll head back inside to the first-aid tent."

Perfect Family Guy still looked concerned. "They won't be able to do much in there. You might need an x-ray. Do you have insurance?"

Wil shook his head. PFG pulled out his wallet and removed a business card. "Here's my card. If you end up needing to see a real doctor, I'll make sure that your expenses get covered."

"Thanks." Wil glanced down at the little rectangle of paper, then put it in his pocket. *Bentley Watson-Taylor III, Attorney at Law.* "I hope I won't need it. I'm just glad Orli's okay." A tingling rush of good feeling started in Wil's hand and swept up his arm and through his body.

"Thank you, mister," Orli said, and gave him a hug. "I hope you're going to be okay."

Wil knew the hug against his sore ribs should have hurt, but he didn't even wince. "I'll be fine. You just stay out of trouble."

Back at the entrance he showed his hand stamp, went through, and headed toward the storyteller's pavilion.

On the way, he tested his theory. He tried to pick a pocket and received a fresh jolt of pain. Then, after helping an older woman push her husband's wheelchair up an uneven slope and position the man where he could watch a troupe of players perform humorously abbreviated Shakespeare plays, Wil felt the rush of euphoria again.

The old storyteller had definitely done something to him.

When Wil reached the pavilion, the old man had just finished spinning a tale and the few late-afternoon audience members left quickly. Wil walked straight toward the storyteller, stepping over the scattered cushions. The leathery face registered recognition and concern, but no surprise.

"What did you do to me?" Wil demanded. His voice was rough with mixed emotion.

The old man considered the question. "I shared something with you, as I do with all who listen to me. How is your headache? Are you feeling better now?"

Wil felt an acid spurt of frustration burn in his stomach. "You know it wasn't a headache, and no, I'm not feeling better. You tricked me."

The old man's expressive eyebrows climbed a millimeter up his forehead. "How so?"

Wil cast about for an answer. He wasn't sure how he'd been tricked or what had been done to him, but he traced the strangeness back to *here*, in this tent with gauzy walls and cooling breezes, and this enigmatic man from whom he had tried to steal something of "true value."

"You ... you tricked me by saying you had something valuable in your pocket."

The old man nodded soberly. "You heard that, did you? That is true. I carry what I value most in my pocket. But how is that a trick?"

Wil seethed inside. Wasn't the answer obvious? "Because you knew I'd hear you, and that I'd try to find out what was in your pocket."

"Ah." The storyteller's voice was barely a whisper. "And ...?"

"*And?* When I touched whatever was in your pocket, it gave me a jolt of some sort. It hurt so much I let go and fell to the ground. That's how you tricked me. What was it? Some kind of trap?"

"I admit, I did speak the truth in your hearing, yet no one can choose what another person will do with the truth once they hear it. I did not make that choice for you."

Wil couldn't believe his ears. Was the storyteller actually implying that this was all his own fault? "Oh, no you don't, old man. You still did something to my hand, and I'm betting you know how to undo it. Every time I try to practice my ... business, my hand, my arm, my body, my brain, *everything* hurts like hell. Well, fine. You made your point. Picking pockets is bad. Stealing is bad. I get it." He raised a fist. "Now make it stop or I'll—"

An excruciating pain sizzled up Wil's arm and blinded him for a moment. As soon as he lowered his arm and forced his fist to relax, the agony began to fade. "For God's sake, just make it stop."

"Make it stop? For God's sake ..." The storyteller looked troubled. "Let me tell you a story—it's what I do. Please, sit down."

Wil wasn't sure why, but he sat. And listened.

"In the time of the Third Crusade, the Year of Our Lord 1190, many brave knights, greedy lordlings, and hapless soldiers traveled across Europe by boat or by foot, in order to secure the Holy Land from the evil Turks. Some crusaders truly felt a calling from God, but the real reason for most of the lords and commanders—third and fourth sons without lands to inherit— was to capture new domains to rule. Other knights simply came for the chance to fight, to kill the infidel, to find glory on the battlefield.

"One such knight—let us call him Roderick the Brash—led his soldiers into battle, cutting his way through Turkish lines to establish a foothold in Jerusalem. There, while attempting to occupy the ancient holy city, Roderick came upon a kindly old leather worker, who went by the name of Julius. The leather worker did good deeds for his neighbors in Jerusalem, without giving thought to whether they were Christians, Moslems, or Jews. He claimed to have been a centurion in the Roman army in the time of Jesus Christ."

Wil scoffed. "That would have made him over a thousand years old."

The storyteller simply looked at him. "It's a story. Would you like to hear more?"

"As long as there's a point."

"Julius himself was present at the crucifixion and had come into possession of a fragment of the True Cross, and a Splinter from this remarkable artifact had kept him alive for so long. Though he wasn't wealthy, the leather worker had sufficient means to meet his needs and was content. No doubt he experienced the same euphoria you did when you performed a selfless deed."

"That's a stretch. Are you telling me—"

The old man calmly went on. "When he learned that Julius the leather worker had such a treasure, this holy relic, Roderick the Brash came at night into his shop and demanded to see the fragment. Julius told him the story I just told you. And then Roderick struck him down with his sword and took the fragment for himself."

The old man's gaze was distant, and his voice hitched. After a brief pause, he reached into the pocket where he kept his treasure, where Wil had felt the first sharp sting. He withdrew an oddly shaped and unimpressive lump of very old wood, less than two inches long. "When the fragment encounters someone who needs its ... assistance, it shares a part of itself. A Splinter.

"Roderick the Brash had great need of it. After touching the fragment, Roderick attempted to ignore the message of the Splinter. He continued to fight and kill until the pain became so overwhelming it rendered him unconscious, and his men left him for dead on the battlefield. After that, Roderick had no choice but to change his ways. He performed his penance for many centuries, made his way through the world, and found his own contentment. And, over the years, the fragment grew smaller, bit by bit, as it found others who needed it."

Wil's impatience mixed with wonder, annoyance, and indignation. "So, I'm supposed to believe that you're a knight named Roderick the Brash, who lived during the Third Crusade? And that I've got a Splinter of the True Cross stuck in my hand?"

"I simply told the story." The old man gave him a noncommittal look. "Believe what you wish."

Wil blew out an angry breath, looking at the lump of wood. It wasn't the least bit impressive. "If I believe that's a real holy relic with magical powers, and an invisibly small Splinter is embedded in my finger, then I'd also have to believe that I no longer have free will. I'm just a rat in a maze, and God is some sort of cosmic experimental researcher dispensing either treats or electric shocks, depending on whether or not I do what He wants."

The storyteller did not answer the accusation directly. His pensive gaze seemed to look through Wil. His eyes seemed very, very old. "There are many possible interpretations—some harsher than others. Some say that the Splinter is a sort of ... conscience for anyone who has discarded the conscience that God gave them. But I don't believe that.

"Others believe that because the cross is a symbol of sacrifice, a Splinter of the True Cross might bestow peace and happiness for every deed that is selfless or sacrificial, while selfish acts are rewarded only with pain."

The storyteller paused. "But I don't believe that either. All of my experience and knowledge have led me to conclude one thing, that a Splinter is distilled truth. No more, no less."

Wil wanted to object, to interrupt and call the man's words bullshit. He didn't believe in Biblical morality or in miracles and had never felt a need to go to church. He had certainly never let himself be bound by superstition. But something kept him silent.

"Each Splinter senses the good or bad potential of a person's actions, then gathers those effects, concentrates them into the *now*, and transmits the truth back to its owner. If a thief takes a wallet, he causes financial injury to the person he steals from. He also steals some of that person's time and robs him of his feeling of safety. Like a pebble dropped into a pond, there are ripple effects."

Wil rubbed his forefinger but felt no twinge of pain. "Now you're getting pretty esoteric."

"It is concrete enough. Perhaps the thief's victims would not have enough money to buy necessities for themselves or their families. Imagine that a person needed to fix the brakes on his car.

If there wasn't enough money to fix the brakes, and the brakes failed, then a terrible accident could result. All these things factor together and are condensed by the Splinter into a single manifestation of pain, great or small. In the same way, a kind or unselfish deed helps both the giver and receiver. The Splinter concentrates consequences, intensifies truth."

"But ... but, if I believe you, then you've just taken away my livelihood!" Wil squawked. "That's how I survive. You don't have any right."

The storyteller smiled. "Imagine what the ruthless warrior Roderick the Brash must have experienced. How difficult it was to give up hatred, pillaging, and violence, stranded in a hostile foreign land, suddenly prevented from looting and killing.... Still, he learned to get by. So can you."

Wil squirmed. Something about the old man's interpretation rang uncomfortably true. "So, is there anything I could do to get rid of it? Short of amputation? I mean, if I did a lot of good deeds would it go away ... and leave me in peace?"

"I have met a few people who tried amputation. Strange, no matter how much they cut off—finger, hand, arm—the Splinter stayed inside them, as if it were in their blood. Perhaps you stand a better chance of finding peace if the Splinter remains in your finger."

The old man began to stack up his fine tooled-leather books. With a callused finger, he rubbed the intricate designs and workings, smiling at the craftsmanship. "It's not so hard to learn a new trade, given a little incentive, although you might find it comforting to revisit ... familiar surroundings from time to time."

Outside the tent, criers were announcing the closing of the Renaissance Faire for another day.

Wil just stood, unsettled, staring at the storyteller, not knowing what to do. "This is impossible. You don't really expect me to change who I am and what I do for a living just overnight, do you?"

"No, my friend. But you will have plenty of time. After all these centuries, who would know better than I?" He paused for a moment, holding up one of his ornate books. "You might discover talents you never knew you possessed. You already have quick hands, sharp eyes. Think about what you could become."

The old man's words were too much to absorb all at once. Wil had to let the implications sink in, and questions piled up in his mind. "I have plenty of time ...?" Then, as he began to consider the possibilities, a familiar pleasurable sensation tingled in his hand. "You mean I could be a fine artist, a poet, a rock guitarist, even a surgeon? How would I choose?"

A small smile flickered at the corner of the storyteller's mouth. "Why choose? You could do them all. But use your abilities to help people, and you will find contentment."

The pleasant warmth seemed to be growing stronger. "Well, I guess I've always wanted to see other countries. Maybe I could join a service organization and travel while I learn some job skills —new ones, I mean—and some foreign languages."

Now the tingle seeped from Wil's hand into his entire body and, for the first time in memory, he felt a true sense of wonder.

Again diving into myths and legends, I was intrigued by the tales of great kings who hadn't really fallen in battle, but were hidden away, magically sleeping and waiting to return when the world needed them, like King Arthur or Frederick Barbarossa.

"Heroes Never Die" is a story inspired by my kindly old farmer neighbor, Mr. Reindahl, who lived alone in his big white farmhouse. He wouldn't talk about his past, wouldn't say if he'd ever been married (though I did see a framed black-and-white portrait of a pretty woman on his desk). I often went over to his house and helped him out with farm chores, but he wouldn't let me go anywhere in his house beyond the kitchen.

A curious kid had to wonder what secrets a man like that might have in his past....

HEROES NEVER DIE

He awoke after seven centuries of God's Slumber, with the vision still burning inside him. He remembered leading his army across Europe, fighting against the Infidels and sending great sacrifices of blood to the Divine Creator; he remembered trying to cross the swollen and churning river ... and he remembered drowning. It had been cold and mysterious.

Now he lay in a hidden cave, motionless on a stone table, placed there by some elder race. His heavy red beard had indeed grown completely around the table, just as the Legend had decreed; and as he sat upright, with painful slowness, he clearly recalled the geas, the relentless mission the Angel had placed on him. He was destined to save the world, to unite the Holy Roman Empire into the grand Christian kingdom. He was a legend come back to life, he was a hero who could never die.

After nearly 700 years, Frederick Barbarossa returned to the world.

Danny sat comfortably against the cardboard box which contained books, knick-knacks, and an old pair of shoes. With her usual amount of consideration, his mother decided she needed to unpack that box next, even though dozens of them still cluttered the new house. He tried to ignore her by intently watching superhero cartoons on the portable black and white television. Static and fuzz-balls of light danced across the screen: the reception out here wasn't nearly as good as it had been in the city, and Mom said they would never be able to get cable again.

"Come on, Danny—move!" she snapped, and he absently scooted out of the way. Danny had helped her with the unpacking —the new house had so much more room than the old apartment —but he had quickly lost interest. The superheroes rescued him from boredom every afternoon; he still didn't know how to tell time, but some inner clock always told him when cartoons would be on.

"Who do you think the next one will be about, Mom?" He didn't take his eyes from the TV, didn't really notice when his mother paid no attention to him. "I hope it's Spiderman he's my favorite!"

Mom picked up the box with a tired sigh. Danny waited impatiently for A Word From Our Sponsor to be over.

"Danny, come and open the door for Mom." She stood by the door, ladling the box in her arms, balancing it against her left thigh.

"Just a minute."

"Danny—now!" she snapped.

He got up and listlessly opened the door for her, with his full attention still fixed on the television. "Aww, it's only Captain America anyway."

A few moments later she reentered the room with a box containing encyclopedias, volumes A through J-K, which his dad had purchased "for when Danny goes to college."

"Why don't you go play outside?" she said, throwing some of her frustration at him. Dad would have watched superheroes with him ... Dad sometimes even bought him comic books to look at.

"Outside, Daniel!"

"But, Mom, don't you want me to help you?"

She pushed a sweat-curled strand of hair out of her eyes and managed a small smile. "No, Danny. Mom can do it by herself. Why don't you go and explore our big back yard?"

"Okay ..." he said, after a long pause.

He let the screen door slam behind him even though he knew he wasn't supposed to. (Dad said the previous owners had purchased a piece of land bordering a patched and bumpy country road and had erected an out-of-place tri-level house, with beautiful landscaping and young trees standing in small islands of flower beds.) Behind the house, rows of corn stretched to infinity like green corduroy on the hills. But rusty barbed wire fences set up a barricade behind and to one side of the yard—farmers were like wild animals, marking off their territory. Off to the other side a narrow alfalfa field separated them from the run-down farm of Mr. Rossa, their closest neighbor.

Danny's new yard had still not been sufficiently explored, but the mere fact that it was his own yard made it a great deal less interesting than the neighboring farm. He began to run across the alfalfa field.

He knew the old farmer lived alone, renting out his remaining fields to younger, more ambitious farmers who called themselves "agricultural engineers." Mr. Rossa's drab house was old and peeling white; the yard was infested with clover and dandelions, and the weeded-over driveway was almost indistinguishable from the rest of the yard. In front of the house lay the carcass of an ancient tractor, decaying into rust as if it had collapsed there and died, with the weeds growing up to surround it, looking for new footholds among the crumbling gears and sprockets.

This was the way old farms were supposed to be.

Prismatic light reflected from the crystalline stalactites, making even the air seem to sparkle. He saw with some amazement that time and dampness had turned his armor into a thin coating of reddish soot on

his body. Alongside the stone table, the Angel had provided him with a heavy white robe and sandals.

He looked for his sword, his one true friend through a thousand battles. The blade still gleamed, unnotched and razor sharp, untouched by the centuries, protected by the Angel. The waters of the Calycadnus River had washed away the bloodstains and had brought eternal life to the jewels on the hilt. Seeing his sword, his companion, he felt happy again.

He used the blade to chop off all but a span of his red beard, leaving the rest to lie in long coils on the cave floor. He washed himself in the hot spring at the back of the grotto, donned the robe and sandals, and lovingly picked up his sword. The Angel would not help him again, would never so much as contact him whether he succeeded or failed. He went bravely to the mouth of the cave and prepared himself to go out into the world at last.

The giant old trees fascinated Danny. The thin saplings in his own yard were too small even for him to climb ... but these! They had to be at least a hundred years old. Huge, gnarled, and chapped trunks with a circumference larger then he could embrace, oaks and box elders with abundant knobs and sucker branches for footholds. Danny had seen trees this big in parks, of course, but his parents had never let him climb them. Only once, with one of his babysitters, had he been able to. He had told his mother how much fun it had been, looking down from so high. They had never had that babysitter again.

Danny stood in front of the challenge of the first tree, looking up into the sea of leafy branches, the hidden world high above the ground. He circled the trunk slowly, contemplating, and then grabbed a clump of small branches, hoisting himself upward. He jammed his left sneaker against a bald lump on the trunk and fought with his fingers in the wide cracks in the bark, trying to find another handhold.

He reached up to grab a real branch, not a twig, and climbed again, wedging his foot into the first handhold. The tree seemed to cooperate now, offering many branches to assist him. His fingers were sore and raw, and his arms were tired, but this was wonderful! The air was still, and he could hear birds somewhere higher in the tree. He went up to the next branch and looked down to see how far he had climbed. This was triumph! This was scary! He felt like Spiderman.

Above him, one branch jutted out, tantalizingly out of his reach. He shimmied out farther on the branch, reached up, stretching, feeling like he would fall at any moment, and then grabbed the branch. Danny inched himself forward, then stopped, panting, as high as he could go.

And that's when he knew he would never be able to get down.

He felt his heart stop cold; he had thought only grown-ups knew how to sweat. He moved his eyes slowly down to where his sneaker balanced on a small bulge, and he couldn't move it. Danny felt like crying, and somehow knew he was going to.

"There's a little branch below your left foot. If you rest your weight on that, you can come down—no trouble at all."

Danny was so startled he almost fell from the tree. Below him, with hands on his hips and peering up into the tree, stood a large, old man with a huge, bushy beard, scowling and squinting as if the sun were in his eyes. Danny knew it must be Mr. Rossa and tried not to look at the farmer's fierce expression as he searched for the small branch. He found it, but it was too small, and too far away for Danny to even consider reaching.

"It's too far!"

Mr. Rossa hemmed and bit on his lip, running his fingers through the thick mass of his beard. "Just a minute—I'll get you down. Just you wait right there!"

The old farmer jogged out of sight. Danny waited, and waited, and felt like he was going to cry again. What if Mr. Rossa had called the police? He shivered and wished he were back home watching cartoons.

Mr. Rossa reappeared, puffing and carrying a weathered gray ladder. Danny held his breath and waited as the farmer tried to maneuver the end of the ladder up into the mass of branches. He heard the thump as the ladder banged against a branch and came to rest, just a little below him.

"Now can you climb down?" Mr. Rossa looked up at him expectantly.

Danny saw the ladder, just below him, but his fingers were cramping and wouldn't let him release his hold. He knew he could easily reach the ladder, but his body didn't.

"No." His voice sounded thin and small.

"All right then ..." Mr. Rossa grunted. Danny heard the ladder creak as the old man began to climb up. The farmer made puffing sounds as he ascended, rung by rung, muttering to himself probably out of habit rather than in anger at Danny.

"Come on, now, can you reach? That's a good boy. Come on." Danny saw that Mr. Rossa was just below him, reaching up with a hand that was strong and calloused, not the least bit arthritic and frail as his grandmother's had once been. Danny looked down into the old man's eyes—deep, ancient eyes, older than he could imagine, filled with more knowledge and more memories than Danny could ever hope to know, or want to know. He felt that the distance to the bottoms of those pupils was far greater than the distance to the ground.

"All right then." Mr. Rossa broke the trance and climbed two rungs higher until he could easily pluck the boy from his perch. Danny shivered until Mr. Rossa stood firmly on the ground again after a long and toiling descent from the rickety ladder. And then the fear piled up on him, expressing itself in long sobs. He bawled and clung to the old man's neck, burying his face deep in the bushy, streaked beard. It was a tangled brownish-gray color now, but all the rampant red hairs dotted throughout testified that it had been a flaming scarlet color once.

He didn't notice the old man stiffen. Mr. Rossa stood for a long time, holding the boy, and then finally pulled Danny away from him and set him back on the ground. "Come on now—it's not all that bad. Come on, stop your crying."

Danny sniffled, but the sobs had already begun to fade. The

old farmer looked at him intently, frowning, and suddenly Danny realized Mr. Rossa wasn't going to yell at him for climbing his tree. "Now, young man, you'd better introduce yourself. I don't think I've seen you before."

"I'm Danny ... I—" His voice convulsed with a leftover sob, and he managed to point across the alfalfa field. "You live next to us."

Mr. Rossa smiled, and the crow's-feet around his eyes folded together. "Ah! And does your mother know you're here?"

Danny wiped his eyes, nodding his head in a diagonal way, not knowing if the old man would interpret it as a yes or a no.

Mr. Rossa stood for a long time, inspecting Danny but also looking slightly uncomfortable. The old man opened his mouth several times as if to say something, but he seemed reluctant. "Would you like to stay here a while?" The farmer ran a finger slowly down his bearded chin, pursing his lips, as if trying to think of something that might interest a five-year-old boy. "I was just going to look at some old books in my attic."

Danny looked up at the old man, then past him at the farmhouse standing ancient and spooky even in the bright afternoon. All the tears vanished, evaporated and forgotten, as his eyes lit up. "Yeah!"

"Come on, then." Mr. Rossa strode toward his porch door with a strange mixture of firmness and pride in his steps, seeming to show that he was more than just an old farmer.

He came down out of the desolate mountains, protected from the cold by his own immortality, carrying only his beloved sword as a support. The path was winding and complex, the beginning of the long road his mission would require him to travel.

All those centuries ago, he had united the squabbling German principalities, fused them into an empire like Rome, and called it Holy. He crusaded against the Turks and sacrificed to his God. He would have won, but the Angel and the rushing waters of the river had taken him too soon.

And even after seven centuries of slumber, it never occurred to Barbarossa that he might have been forgotten.

Gray patches of naked, weathered wood stood out where the old white paint had chipped from the porch door and fallen to the grass. The door squeaked as Mr. Rossa pulled it open, gesturing for Danny to enter. The boy's eyes were wide as he entered the farmhouse, I breathed deeply and smelling the fuel oil, the dark and musty shadows....

And up in the attic, the trapdoor groaned loudly, to Danny's delight, as Mr. Rossa grunted and heaved it up, letting it crash backward to the attic floor. It seemed perfectly right to Danny that the old man had brought a candle with him, instead of a flashlight, to light their way.

"Come on, now—be careful there!" Mr. Rossa warned as the boy squeezed past him up the ladder.

In fascination, Danny stared at the old, mysterious objects in the attic: broken chairs, a dusty lamp, boxes filled with yellowed paper paraphernalia. Thick cobwebs gilded everything—Danny wondered how the spiders ever found enough to survive up there; did they eat each other?

Mr. Rossa made his way over to a box of books in the corner, dribbling globs of melted wax on the floorboards. He bent over the books, spilling his globe of candlelight into the box. He squinted and ran his fingers over the cover of an old, hand-bound sheaf of parchments.

"What's that, Mister Rossa?" The old man looked up quickly, as if Danny had stopped him from entering a reverie. "Gosh, those books sure look old!"

The farmer smiled a little. "Do you know how to read, Danny?"

"I know my ABCs—and I know how to spell 'Danny.' But I can't read until I go to first grade, next year."

"Ah." Mr. Rossa looked back down at the books, paging through one so brittle that his gentle fingers plunged through a page with a puff of dust. The handwriting was old and faded, and illuminated with many stylized letters and illustrations, as if someone had painstakingly taken the time to make the documents beautiful for someone who could not read. "These are in Latin anyway." His voice was almost a sigh, and he dropped to his knees in front of the box, carefully shuffling among the parchments. The old man seemed to be sweating a little.

Danny fidgeted for a moment, losing interest in the books. He saw a painting hidden behind some piled, discarded clothes.

"Do you have a hero, Danny?" Mr. Rossa asked, slowly turning to look up from the books. His eyes were strange again, but Danny took sudden interest.

"Yeah! I like the Hulk—he's the best. And Spiderman." Danny began to sing quickly, "Spiderman, Spiderman, does whatever a spider can! Is he strong? Listen, Bud—He's got radioactive blood!"

Mr. Rossa frowned, releasing a long mouthful of air which rustled the strands of his once scarlet, now gray, beard. Danny stopped, and wondered what he had done wrong. "Do you have a hero, Mister Rossa?"

For a moment, he thought the old man was going to chuckle, but then the farmer forced his mouth into a wry smile, as if he knew something Danny did not. "Do you know who Frederick Barbarossa is, Danny?"

"Bobba Rossa? I know who Boba Fett is. He's from Star Wars."

Mr. Rossa sighed again. "Barbarossa was the king of a vast land, called the Holy Roman Empire ... oh, eight hundred years ago. He had flaming red hair, and a long scarlet beard. And the people loved him very much, for he was a strong emperor who had united the entire land. But the Empire had its enemies—the Infidels. So, Barbarossa gathered his army together and marched out on great wars, called the Crusades. He led his own armies to many great victories, farther than any other Crusade had gone—

all the way to the land of the Infidels, in Asia Minor. Barbarossa would have destroyed the Infidels once and for all." The farmer smiled, and Danny listened carefully.

"But then, one day Barbarossa led the vanguard of his troops to a river, the Calycadnus River. It had been raining for days on end, and many of the men had died from fevers caused by the dark and cruel gods of the Infidels. The bank of the river was muck, and the water itself was gray and thick, swollen with mud. The current was vicious."

Mr. Rossa seemed to be looking through Danny.

"It was early afternoon. The troops had just eaten a meal, partly of dry rations and partly of fresh food we had taken from villages along the way. The ford of the river didn't look passable, but Barbarossa was brave, and knew he needed to get his men across. They could never hope to take prisoners, so they killed them and threw the bodies into the current. The sky was heavy, as if the rains were going to come again—the army had to cross now.

"The Emperor, the red-haired giant, urged his horse forward, trusting in God to protect him. He would cross first, to show his men that it was safe, and then they would follow. The horse entered the river, trembling, afraid of the roaring water. The current sucked at the horse's legs, but Barbarossa—all dressed in his war armor and strutting in his imperial glory—urged his horse on. The water rose higher, until, near the center of the river, the animal was dancing on the slippery rocks of the channel, half swimming and half walking." The old farmer seemed almost breathless, but he continued to talk quickly, in a low voice.

"Some of the other soldiers entered the river, following their Emperor, struggling to keep control of the frightened horses. Others waited on the bank, watching and praying. Barbarossa drew his shining and deadly sword and raised it high so that the others could see him.

"Barbarossa's horse stumbled, became wild as it tried to regain its footing. The Emperor was flung from his mount as he grabbed for the reins. The horse thrashed and struggled, panicking, and was quickly drawn under, vanishing with the flow of mud and melted snow rushing down from the frozen mountaintops. Barbarossa knew how to swim, but his heavy armor dragged him down under the powerful current. He managed to keep a desperate grip on the hilt of his jeweled sword, as if that lifeline might save him. And then he vanished under the water, never to be seen again."

"Wow!" Danny let the word slither from his mouth.

"Now, a history book will say Barbarossa drowned that day. But the people, the soldiers, they all said that no, maybe he didn't die. Maybe the Emperor is still alive, sleeping in a cave somewhere up in the tall mountains of Asia Minor near the source of the Calycadnus River. He was a hero, so they built a legend around him ... and nobody ever lets legends die. They said Frederick Barbarossa lies sleeping beside a huge stone table somewhere deep within a holy cave; and one day, when his red beard has grown all the way around that table, he will wake up and save the Holy Roman Empire from all its enemies."

"Gosh!" Danny looked into the old man's eyes. "And your hero is Bobba Rossa?"

The farmer let a wry grin settle onto his face. "No, Danny—I *am* Barbarossa."

Danny's eyes widened as he drew a breath in astonishment, but then he narrowed his gaze; he tried to imitate the look Dad had given him when Danny said an invisible monster had broken Mom's lamp. "Aww, you're just kidding me!"

"Am I?" Mr. Rossa looked at him, but Danny couldn't tell if the farmer's grin was sly or smug. The old man raised his eyebrows, as if waiting for Danny to challenge him further.

"Oh, yeah? Well how come you didn't die in that river, then?"

"I was a hero, Danny. Heroes never die." It was almost a sigh. "We're not allowed."

Danny continued to look at the old man, not wanting to disbelieve the story because that would make the world less interesting, not even really caring if it were not true. Mr. Rossa kept staring at his own fingers, as if amazed they had suddenly gotten so old.

"How come you're not still sleeping in that cave? By the table? And how did you get here?"

"You can't sleep forever, Danny. Who's to say that I didn't wake up a century ago, and I've been around ever since? Nobody noticed me, and nobody believed anyway."

"And did you save the Holy Roman Empire from all its enemies?"

Mr. Rossa lowered his eyes. "It was already dead when I woke up again. The boundaries were all different ... the people were all changed—"

"Did you even try?"

"No." He searched for understanding in the boy's eyes, but Danny felt only disappointment. "I was just an ignorant king from the end of the Dark Ages. My solution to a problem was to gather up an army and charge with swords flashing. People don't do things that way anymore. How could I do a better job than the modern leaders, the very least of whom is more educated—and with an extra eight hundred years of experience to draw upon— than the most brilliant people I ever knew in my day? I decided it would be better to leave the people with their legend, and their hope, rather than destroying both."

Danny frowned, condemningly. "Well, do you at least go out and fight crooks and bad guys, like Spiderman does? Like all the Superheroes do?"

"Danny ..." The boy should have been impressed by Mr. Rossa's patience, but he was not. "The only reason we are heroes is because people make us into them. I'm still just a man inside—I can't wave my hands and make all the evil go away."

Danny stood up abruptly, looking uncomfortable. "I gotta go. My Mom'll yell at me for being gone so long."

Mr. Rossa frowned, as if trying to preserve the threads of his own confession. He picked up the candle, following Danny down the ladder. The porch door squeaked as the farmer held it open for Danny. "Come back again—anytime!"

Danny plunged into the alfalfa field, wading and running at the same time. He didn't answer immediately, until he could rationalize something in his mind. "Okay, I will." He started to go faster, calling into the wind ahead of him and hoping the words would drift back to the old man. "Promise!"

He wandered across the mountains of Asia Minor, got passage on a creaking ship up the coast of the Black Sea and then down the Danube. Many questioned him, but none believed his story. The Holy Roman Empire had been swallowed by history, as were the Crusades, as were the Infidels, as was Barbarossa.

Hoping to find something, he went across Eastern Europe, scavenged for some memories in his beloved Prague, and then moved southward to Rome. He read voraciously, discovered what had happened during his long slumber, and fell into despair. His beautiful Empire had turned cannibal and had fallen prey to itself. Even an Angel-gifted hero could not battle such an enemy.

For Danny, the summer was forever condensed into a day. The heart of the season struck when he had forgotten completely about his previous year in kindergarten, and first grade seemed infinitely far away. Danny's skin was blotched with freckles that hadn't been there a few weeks before. The alfalfa field had been cut and baled once already by the men who rented Mr. Rossa's land, and it had grown high enough to await its second cutting.

"I'm going to Mister Rossa's!" he called back at his mother as he let the door slam behind him. By now, he no longer really needed to tell her.

"You never watch cartoons anymore!" he heard her say, but he was already sprinting across the field....

Under the big boxelder tree in the farmyard, the two of them sat in the shade of the afternoon, watching the world, seeing nothing and everything at the same time. Mr. Rossa reached down to expertly remove a tall grass blade and stuck it in his mouth. Danny tried to imitate him, pulling up the grass by its roots and then slowly extracting the right part. The old man had once shown him how to whistle through a grass blade, but Danny had succeeded only in cutting his lips.

"Mister Rossa?"

The answer was a long time in coming. "Hmmm?"

"What's it like? Fighting in a big battle? I bet it's exciting."

The old farmer looked lost for a moment, and then let a smile spread slowly under his beard. "The first time I went out on a battlefield was the most terrifying experience ever. Even worse than the time I drowned. Just to look at the enemy army, and to see all those sharp swords—each one of them waiting to stick into your chest or chop your head off.

"I'll bet you didn't know I had my side cut open once, slashed right down the ribs all the way to my belly. Imagine looking down at your own innards, steaming up at you because it's a chilly morning. And then sitting there brave like a king, trying not to grunt as a healer sews your wound back together. Mind you, we had none of the anesthetics you have now. Here—I've still got the scar."

Mr. Rossa fumbled with the buttons on his shirt, exposing the thermal undershirt and part of his hairy chest. Danny saw a long white line, very straight and lumped together with scar tissue which looked centuries old. Just like the downstroke of a sword would leave.

"Your sword becomes the best friend you have in the entire world. After a while you forget that you might be ten seconds away from your own death, and you concentrate only on fighting. A red haze hovers around the edges of your eyes, slowly closing in, and pretty soon all you see is red. You're completely blind, but your arm knows what it's doing and you trust to your fighting instinct. And then, an instant later, sight floods back to you and you see all the trophies you've collected, all the heads in a pile. You go to your own soldiers, look at the comrades who didn't survive, the mangled ones with their mouths and their eyes and their wounds gaping open—and they seem to be angry at you because you survived, and they didn't."

Mr. Rossa paused for a minute and spat out his grass blade, breaking the spell. He looked at his hands, flexing them, and then ran his fingers through the once-red beard. "Ah, Danny, with you here I am older than I ever was before."

He traveled for years, north into France, then to England and Wales. An unwelcomed savior, he did various jobs, strenuous work even a battle-conditioned medieval king could barely endure. He married once, almost twice, but after several decades he had begun to realize the curse placed upon him by the Angel—he aged at only a sliver of mankind's rate. He had learned to keep his identity to himself, and he moved on as he grew restless with one place, as people noticed he had spent too many years looking the same age.

To Ireland, to a crowded, stinking steamer which carried him with a festering mass of other immigrants across the Atlantic to America, beyond the edge of the 12th Century's known world. He endured the abuse, traveled west from New York to try to start a farm for himself. He found this demeaning, for in his memories only peasants did such work. The horrors of the Dust Bowl nearly ruined him, and he moved back east, to the rolling hills of Wisconsin, on the outskirts of a small town where the people asked poignant questions. Lonesome, deserted by history, Frederick Barbarossa had decided to die here. After nearly a century of second life. And without a single friend to retell his story or remember him.

Danny turned the pages of the encyclopedia slowly, deliberately. He clutched the scrap of paper on which Mr. Rossa had printed "Frederick, Barbarossa."

"I want to look this up in the 'cyclopedia, Mister Rossa." he had insisted.

"Come on, do you think I'd be in there?"

"Of course! Everything's in the 'cyclopedia!"

Danny remembered the order of the alphabet, and he hoped to find a picture of Mr. Rossa. He had found the F volume and paged through it with the patience only a determined child could have, insisting on doing it himself, without asking for help from his mother or father who both sat in the kitchen finishing their lunch.

Danny crossed his legs in a lotus position. He finally found F-R and quickly proceeded through France, then Benjamin Franklin, and finally found Frederick I. And he saw the picture.

It was a crude drawing, a sketch simpler even than Danny imagined he could do—the Emperor Barbarossa riding like a superhero on a cartoon horse. Without a doubt, it was indeed Mr. Rossa. He stared at the picture, wishing he could read, and slowly realized that his parents' conversation had risen to the proportions of an argument.

"He's over there every day, all afternoon!" His mother shouted. "You aren't home often enough to hear him come up with words and ... and comparisons he has no way of knowing! That old farmer is telling him stories! It was almost better when he watched those crazy superhero cartoons—at least he only half-believed them!"

"Now wait a minute." His father's voice was calm, almost forcedly so. Dad always had a way of understanding the boy's point of view; Danny almost wondered if his father had been a boy once, too. "You're the one who wanted to move out here to the country. There's no one Danny's age within miles, no one who's even interested in the things he likes to talk about. Except for Mr. Rossa. They're keeping each other company. Besides, that old man is probably even lonelier than Danny is—"

"That old man is filling Danny's head with crazy stories! Do you know he's been telling Danny he's some German king who's been dead for centuries?"

"It is not a story!" Danny exploded into the dining room, still carrying the encyclopedia. He slammed it down on the table among the lunch debris. "His picture's right here, in the 'cyclopedia!"

"Daniel John!" his mother snapped, but Danny was angry enough to overcome his fear and awe of her.

"And he's not dead 'cause he's a hero, and heroes never die! Mister Rossa knows!"

His mother started to shout something else, but Danny turned and ran toward the front door where the screen let in the summer heat, but no breeze.

"Daniel John, you come back here this instant."

But Danny didn't listen, throwing the screen door shut behind him. "And besides, he's not a German king—he's a Holy Roman Emperor!" He began to run, charging through the alfalfa field which had been mown and raked, leaving the hay to dry in the sun before baling.

And he didn't stop running until he had reached the old farmer's peeling white door. "Mister Rossa! Mister Rossa!" He burst into the farmhouse.

Something was different. The house was quieter than the sound of soft breathing, and the sun seemed reluctant to penetrate the cream-colored shades over the windows. "Mister Rossa?"

The kitchen, the sitting room with its old wooden radio, the bathroom, and the bedroom were all together on the first floor, near the door, so that Mr. Rossa needed to take fewer steps. Now the bedroom was dim ... but Mr. Rossa always opened his shades early each morning.

"Mister Rossa?"

The old man lay on his bed, breathing slowly but not sleeping. The bed had been made, but the farmer was only half-dressed, as if he had realized he would never finish. Danny went close to him, saw that his hands were trembling, both his own and Mr. Rossa's. The old man's eyes were open, but glazed, exhausted—the fires within them which had always frightened Danny were now so dull that it terrified him even more.

"Mister Rossa ... what's wrong?"

The old man's breathing picked up, as if he had just noticed Danny, and he inhaled several times before answering. "I am very old, Danny ... even older than I had thought. I was frozen in what I had been ... you made me realize that I may be a hero ... but I am still very human inside. And that made me vulnerable. Thank you."

Danny gasped as he suddenly realized what was taking place. "Are you dying, Mister Rossa?" His eyes stood wide in the dimness, in his disbelief.

Mr. Rossa closed his eyes gently, wearily, and breathed deeply, with difficulty. "You can bet I'm going to tell that Angel a few things ... when I see him again."

"But you can't die! Heroes never die! 'Member? Remember! You said!"

He waited, and waited, but received no answer. He watched the old man's labored breathing. The eyes remained closed, but a thin, tired whisper flickered through his lips. "I think I need to sleep ... again."

"You promised!" Danny's ragged voice convulsed with spasms of sobs he wasn't supposed to express in front of a legendary king. Tears seemed to be streaming down his face. "You can't go to sleep! I don't want to wait a thousand years to see you again. You can't!"

Mr. Rossa opened his eyes again, looking at Danny from within himself, at some far-off place. "Remember, Danny."

The boy heard the words, although they had been barely spoken. He grabbed the old farmer's hand and buried his face in the wrinkled and musty shirt. "I love you, Mister Rossa."

The old man seemed to become completely lucid for a moment. Danny could see a reflection of the young Emperor, with fiery red hair and a fiery red beard, the leader of men, holding his sword high in the air.

"Danny ... my friend ... in my dresser ... bottom drawer ... it's yours." Strength in his voice seemed to drain into the air, leaving him no energy at all.

"What is it?" Danny whispered, but grief masked his curiosity.

The farmer didn't seem to hear him. He gripped Danny's hand so tightly it hurt, looking into the boy's eyes, "... best friend ..."

"You're my hero, Mister Rossa."

The old man was stricken with a spasm through his entire body. His loud gasping breaths were almost convulsions in themselves, keeping a different rhythm.

Danny wanted to cry out, but his vocal cords froze. This wasn't the way it was supposed to happen. He had seen people die on TV before. They said goodbye, or whatever they needed to say ... they closed their eyes and then breathed their last. Mr. Rossa's eyes were so tightly clenched that tears streamed between them. His teeth ground together, and a continual force of shudders rippled through his body.

But Mr. Rossa was already dead. The spirit had left his mind, and his body hadn't yet accepted the fact. Danny slid to the floor, beside the old man's bed, and cried and cried until Mr. Rossa's body settled into a peace. And Danny continued to sit, staring at the farmer who told so many stories, until his tears had dried by themselves.

Finally, he got to his feet, sniffled a few times, and wondered what to do. He went slowly to Mr. Rossa's dresser, almost afraid. The old chest of drawers sat dusty in the shadows, cluttered on top with odds-and-ends, treasures of a sort. The handle of one of the drawers was broken off.

He bent to the bottom drawer and pulled it open, surprised to find it lined with plush red velvet in imperial splendor. And inside the drawer, nestled among the velvet ... it had been lovingly polished and oiled over the years, more than a memory, more than a story. Danny trembled with his own awe and reached down to lift up Barbarossa's sword, his own sword, the Emperor's sword. He smiled broadly and silently vowed to care for it.

I love reading alternate histories, but they can be very difficult to write. Not only do you have to research the real history well enough to get all the details right, you also have to extrapolate your own alternate timeline and convey it in a way so the average reader can understand what's real and what's changed in the alternate history.

Oh, and it also has to be a good story.

For the anthology Trouble in the Wind, *authors wrote alternate takes on warfare and pivotal events in history. My friend Kevin Ikenberry is not only a military historian but also a retired military officer. He came up with an ambitious twist on the Napoleonic Wars, a real historical event where Napoleon had almost been assassinated. Imagine how world events would have changed if Napoleon had been killed in the Russian campaign.*

I had studied Russian history in college and was fascinated by the Napoleonic Wars, and this was a story I wanted to work on. Ike and I took the idea and explored what would have happened if that bullet had actually hit its target.

A SHOT HEARD 'ROUND THE WORLD
(WITH KEVIN IKENBERRY)

Dusk
5 December 1812
Near Smorgon, Russia

Antoine de Montagne nestled his chin against his chest, somewhat into the fold of his officer's coat as the march stopped for the fourth time in the last hour. With his eyes closed, the din of the retreat faded to a soft roar as his desire for warmth and rest overtook his senses. A tight hand grabbed his right arm and jerked him upright.

"Captain de Montagne." The voice was low and firm. "You would do well to keep your bearing."

Montagne blinked and stared into the face of General Caulaincourt, Napoleon's second in command. The man's face contained a tight smile, but his eyes were chips of dull ice. "My apologies, sir."

"Sleep will come for us, Captain. But not quite yet. We have a mission to undertake," Caulaincourt said. He leaned closer. "The Emperor wishes to depart for Paris immediately; within the hour. I have arranged the Imperial Guard Horse Chasseurs to meet us at the front of the retreat. He will move along the line via sleigh and then east to Ashmiany. As a translator, you will accompany us."

Montagne brightened and felt ashamed for it. There would be warmth and sleep yet. A sleigh would speed him home, and his service could end in dignity rather than mired in the mud with dysentery or some other disease ravaging his body. In his joy, a concerned question formed. "Why not Colonel de Fleur?"

Caulaincourt flashed a thin, vindictive smile. "The Emperor is disappointed with the Russian response to his demands for surrender, and so he wishes his Translator General to suffer a bit for his failures. As you are the only other officer fluent in the Slavic and German dialects he could encounter for the first part of the journey home, he has chosen you to translate for him."

Montagne flushed with pride. "I understand, General. I shall do my best."

"I know you will, Captain de Montagne," Caulaincourt replied. "I will rejoin the Chasseurs, select a guard force for our journey, and will accompany the Emperor as well. You wait here and join the Emperor's sleigh. Leave your horse with one of the lieutenants."

"Yes, sir," Montagne said. "I will collect my things and be ready."

Caulaincourt nodded and turned his eyes to the ragged march. "Tell no one of his plan. The *Grand Armeé* will learn tomorrow."

Montagne squinted. "Sir? The rumor is a *coup d'etat* took place in Paris. They say General de Malet has aspirations for the throne? Is it true, sir?"

Caulaincourt's thin smile broadened slightly. "Nothing travels faster amongst an army than rumor, Antoine. There is business the Emperor alone must attend to, and that is all you need to know. Our very government is at stake. Be ready to leave when the Emperor arrives. He will want to move quickly. There is peril at every turn."

So it is true. Montagne couldn't help but smile at the general's casual use of his first name. *And I must ride with a surly Emperor all the way to Paris.*

"Will you assume command here, sir?"

"No." A quiet storm passed over the general's face. "General Mamet will take command. I shall accompany you in the sleigh once the Chasseurs are briefed and prepared to undertake the escort mission."

Montagne said nothing. There wasn't a proper reply to the general's words any captain could utter. "I shall be ready, sir."

Caulaincourt nudged his horse and moved down the line to the east. Montagne saw him speak with several other officers as he moved forward. Caulaincourt exemplified leadership, and Montagne would have followed him anywhere. For a moment, he wondered if any of the officers whom Caulaincourt spoke to knew of Emperor Napoleon's journey home. A freshening breeze pushed cold air past his tight collar and down under his wool coat, making him shiver. Montagne's saddle bags and bedroll sat astride his horse; he would need nothing else for the journey.

Chin tucked into his collar again, he began to realize that departing with the Emperor might indeed get him home soon. Perhaps even in time for Christmas. What a present that would be! Faint cheers filtered forward from the rear of the formation and there could be no other explanation than the Emperor passing his troops in review.

Montagne patted the horse's neck and prepared to dismount. The closeness of the cheers caught his attention and he turned. The small sleigh carrying Emperor Napoleon approached and slowed to greet him as the sporadic musket fire from the near-constantly harassing Cossacks erupted toward the rear of the march.

Montagne dismounted, collected his bags, and passed the reins to a young, shivering lieutenant before turning toward the Emperor. The twin, black horses of the Emperor's team pulled a rickety wooden sleigh devoid of any of the rich trappings the great man often enjoyed during travel. The driver sat on a pedestal behind the passenger compartment under the light of a single lantern. *Necessity versus comfort.* The front rails of the sleigh came up to Montagne's chest. Above the withers of the two horses was a crook used to hold a bell. It sat curiously empty as he stepped behind the horses toward the passenger compartment.

Montagne saluted crisply and held the pose until Emperor Napoleon glanced at him and gave a half-hearted salute out of annoyance. Montagne felt his legs perceptibly shake. He'd never been in the presence of the Emperor, having only seen the great general and leader from a distance during the marches. His face was calm, almost idyllic, in the midst of the chaotic movement home. Even as the musket fire from the French infantry roared through the approaching night, the Emperor seemed completely at ease. At his left shoulder sat another captain, wearing the shoulder brocade of a personal aide-de-camp.

Montagne boarded the sleigh and sat in a small, curved portion of the sleigh barely deep enough, or wide enough, for him. Facing the rear, he stared into the faces of Emperor Napoleon, his aide, and the driver perched above them on an elevated seat.

The aide nodded a cool welcome. "You are the translator, yes? Captain de Montagne?"

"That's correct."

Napoleon's eyes flashed to him. "You are fluent in the languages of these heathens?"

"I am, sir," Montagne swallowed. "Russian, German, and several of the Slavic dialects."

The Emperor squinted at him, and there was distrust in his voice. "How did you come to this ability?"

"My parents traveled extensively in this region, sir." Montagne replied. "My father is a professor at *École Polytechnique.* He teaches history."

Napoleon harrumphed loudly. "Perhaps I should have had you craft the surrender of Czar Nicholas. A fluent son of a historian might have done a better job. Nicholas might have capitulated instead of refusing to fight."

Montagne met the Emperor's eye but said nothing in reply, as discretion required. Truth be told, the region surrounding them had never truly been peaceful and likely never would.

A violent flurry of rifle fire erupted somewhere behind them—sporadic, harassing fire of the Cossacks. The brief attack ended after two methodical volleys from whichever company honored the threat and ended it, as they always did. The harassers vanished into the night.

"Damned Cossacks," Napoleon said. His face screwed up in disgust. "Men without honor never stand and fight."

"Shall I send a messenger, sir?" the aide-de-camp asked.

Napoleon shook his head. "They will fire and flee. Let them go."

With the crack of the driver's whip, the sleigh lurched forward.

The route of march for the *Grand Armeé* wound through deep forests along paths barely wide enough for the army to pass in their standard formation. As such, the Emperor and his commanders directed the artillery to move forward and set the pace, which in the deepening snow seemed fittingly glacial. Still, the troops cheered their Emperor and he seemed to relish seeing them all again before leaving them in the midst of the brutal Russian winter.

There was no conversation that included Montagne. The aide and Napoleon communicated quietly, reviewing notes and dispatches. The younger captain's black hair came to a point between his eyes and his sullen face bothered Montagne for a reason he couldn't quite identify. Every time the aide's eyes flashed to meet his own, the distrust became palpable. Montagne turned his thoughts to his birth home in the South of France. There were no vicious winters there. He couldn't remember ever seeing his breath in the cold until they'd moved to Paris for his father to join the faculty of *École Polytechnique*. They'd spent two months of every year at their summer home in the hills above Nice. He hadn't visited there for four years or more, and the sudden longing for the warm sun and beautiful beaches on the nearby coasts threatened to bring tears to his eyes.

His reverie ended with the sudden stop of the sleigh. He rocked backward, slamming his shoulder blades into the curved railing. Napoleon and his aide pitched forward in their seats. The look on the Emperor's face changed from annoyance to rage. He stood abruptly, casting aside the blanket of furs from across his lap.

Montagne saw the Emperor's eyes flash across the formation and lock onto the nearest officers he could see.

"You! Get your men and push this sleigh. Now!"

A horde of soldiers splashed through the mud and leaned against the sleigh. Montagne stood from his seat, ready to jump out and assist them, but Napoleon barked, "Sit down!" and he sat like a scolded child.

Eventually, with numerous men grunting and pushing, the sleigh cleared the far side of the creek, but did not proceed further. The driver shouted at the soldiers, but to no avail.

Still standing, Napoleon took in the scene. He bellowed at the driver, "Move!"

The driver struggled with the reins. "Sir, we must halt the army. We cannot pass here because of the aid station. The trail is too narrow."

Napoleon surveyed their surroundings and pointed at a sparsely wooded area across the muddy stream where fresh stumps poked through the snow. "There! Take us up that hill and we will go around."

Montagne recognized this place from their march months before. The *Grand Armeé*'s supply trains had cleared paths through the forest as they moved and sometimes paralleled the route of march. In this case, they had cut a wagon-width trail through the narrow growth of birch trees to get the supply trains to this particular ford. If memory served him correctly, there would be another cut area on the far side.

The aide turned to him in concern. "Sir, you will be away from the army. We do not know where the trail may lead."

Napoleon gave his aide a dismissive glance and looked at the driver again. "I know *precisely* where that trail leads. Go around the aid station."

The driver shouted commands to the marching army. They milled about and gradually parted to allow the sleigh through. A few soldiers stared at the sleigh with harsh glances while most gawked, wide-eyed at their beloved leader standing in his sleigh and directing them as a conductor would an orchestra. The driver guided the sleigh into the hastily created path, through the creek bed, then successfully onto the other side.

As they climbed the small, sparsely forested hill on the narrow trail, Emperor Napoleon sat down and brought the blankets over himself again. He glanced at his aide. "Ensure the driver understands to find the first cut back to the *Grand Armeé*. We camped in this place on the march to Moscow, and I recall an access on the far side of the clearing where the wagons were able to move around the swollen creek during the summer. Now it is frozen mud. The damned thing slows me down again!"

His aide relayed the instructions to the driver and Napoleon looked across to Montagne. In the orange light of the solitary lantern above and behind them, his eyes were flinty. "General Caulaincourt informed you of my intent?"

"He did, sir."

Napoleon turned to stare forward. "I cannot fight a war in two places. Therefore, if the Russians do not wish to fight, they are not worth the efforts of our armies. In Paris, I will expunge my detractors, reconvene the government, and we will focus our affairs elsewhere. To hell with this place."

Montagne fought against asking the question on his tongue. With the advance of the *Grand Armeé*, most of Europe had fallen under French rule. Aside from Russia, which Emperor Napoleon had now apparently removed from his aspirations, his only other possible target for conquest would be England. Yet the British were embroiled in an armed dispute with the American colonies, who were allies of the French. The Emperor said no more; instead, he closed his eyes and lowered his face into the protective warmth of his collar.

The weather changed and large flakes of snow fell in ethereal curtains. The fresh precipitation muted the sounds of the army behind them as they crested a small hill that led to a clearing. The driver turned to follow the tree line, stark white birches with naked branches. Montagne leaned over the side of the sleigh to peer into the darkness. With the nearest lantern hanging above him, Montagne could see only a few yards in front of the horses. Their steps faltered and slowed. As the crack of the driver's whip sounded, the horses reared and skidded to a halt in the snow, Montage saw a single, bearded man dressed in heavy furs blocking their path. A Cossack.

He held a rifle in his hands.

"Allez!" the driver called to the man and waved his whip as if to sweep the Cossack from the narrow path. Montagne spun in his seat to peer between the horses at the scene. The lone man did not move. He stood in a narrow space at the edge of a wider clearing. Two trees, barely far apart enough for the sleigh to pass, rose on either side of him.

Again, the driver called and actually cracked the whip over the horses. Unable to move, they whinnied and stamped their hooves only a few feet from the Cossack. Montagne glanced back to the Emperor, who sat with his eyes closed as if trying to sleep. The aide looked up from his notes and met Montagne's eyes. After a moment, the aide slid the papers into a case and reached for a pistol tucked into the blankets at his feet. He nodded at Montagne. Taking his cue, Montagne stood in the sleigh and turned to face the Cossack.

"Move," he called to the man in Russian. The Cossack did not move, and he tried again in several dialects, including Latin and Greek. The fur-adorned man remained still, his rifle trained on the driver. He did not even look at Montagne nor did he speak.

In the silence, Montagne heard approaching riders. The team of horses pulling the sleigh startled and quivered in the snow. A thunderous roar of voices screaming something unintelligible raced into the clearing from the right.

More Cossacks!

Montagne ducked down in the sleigh. The aide handed him a pistol and crouched, assuming a protective stance in front of the Emperor. Montagne did the same and watched the Cossacks charge out of the night, directly at them. They raised their voices in an unintelligible scream, and Montagne raised his pistol and trained it on the closest targets.

Steady. Be steady.

The twilight reflected off the low clouds providing just enough light to see as dozens of riders waving rifles rode down upon them. He whirled to his left, to the near side of the clearing, at the thunderous sound of more horses approaching. Montagne saw the lone man no longer stood before the sleigh and realized what the Cossack had done.

An ambush! Here is where we will die.

The familiar shapes of the Imperial Guard Horse Chasseurs charged into the clearing and raced toward the galloping Cossacks. Several fired rifles from horseback, which were unlikely to hit anything. The Cossacks, however, returned the gesture both at the cavalry and at the sleigh. Rounds impacted the small sleigh near where he crouched, and Montagne dropped toward the floor next to the aide. Napoleon did not. The Emperor sat rigid in his seat, his eyes following the attack with a critical gaze.

The Chasseurs met the Cossack charge in the middle of the small clearing. Men on horseback joined in hand-to-hand combat. The guards, swords in hand, hacked and swung at the Cossacks who defended themselves with their rifles and what appeared to be axes. Men fell from their horses. More rifle fire filled the small clearing. Another surge of Cossacks charged into the fray threatening to overwhelm the small detachment of cavalry; they were closer, and faster, than the first charge. The aide stood, centered his pistol, and fired. One of the lead Cossacks tumbled into the snow.

Emboldened, Montagne rose from his crouch and aimed.

With the barrel centered on the Cossack closest to them, he squeezed the trigger. In the burst of smoke from the barrel, Montagne expected to see a similar result, but the rider screamed and brandished an axe high above his head as he closed the distance to the sleigh.

Montagne ducked into the sleigh and the aide handed another loaded pistol to him.

"Fire, Montagne! Keep firing!"

He took the weapon, resumed his firing position, and felt a strange calm wash over him as he again centered the barrel on the target and fired. The rider tumbled into the snow not forty feet away. He felt the aide tap him on the leg with the other pistol, again loaded and ready to fire.

So fast?

Voices yelled from the forest to his right and snapped his thought off like a dry twig. A regiment of infantry ran up the snow-covered hill and took up firing positions at the edge of the tree line. The driver sat frozen, watching the battle before them. Napoleon's aide sat next to Montagne, his eyes on the dim battlefield.

A volley of rifle fire tore into the Cossacks. Montagne flinched at the closeness of it all even as he raised a pistol and fired again. This time, the aide joined him. The Cossacks whirled as one and charged down on the exposed infantry, for the moment, forgetting their target. A second volley was fired at almost point-blank range, and many Cossacks and their horses crashed into the snow, but not all of them. The maniacal attackers tore into the infantry. Riflemen came up with bayonets and stabbed at them, eventually knocking them from their horses, but not before there were more casualties.

The French Chasseurs circled fand regrouped in the center of the clearing and charged toward the Cossacks fighting the exposed infantry. As if in a dream, the cavalry closed the distance at surreal speed. Every weapon was clearly visible, sword or rifle, as they brandished and fired. The Cossacks roared in defiance and whirled against the guards before turning back to the east and galloping for their lives. Some fired over their shoulders in a hopeful attempt to take down one of the guards, but they soon hunched forward on their mounts and ran.

"Driver!" Napoleon roared as he stood abruptly behind Montagne and the aide. "Move!"

Startled to action, the driver raised his reins and prepared to snap them across the backs of the team when a single rifle fired from darkness.

BOOM!

Montagne felt the rush of air as a musket ball rocketed through the air past them. He flinched, eyes closed, expecting to feel the impact. A heartbeat passed, then he opened his eyes and turned to the wide-eyed aide. The lone Cossack stepped out from behind a large tree, his musket barrel curling smoke into the night air. It dawned on Montagne that the weapon wasn't pointed at either himself or the aide. Nor had the Emperor been struck.

As one, they looked at the driver on the seat behind the sleigh. The top of the man's head was missing.

Montagne raised his pistol and pointed it at the Cossack as he stepped once more into the narrow path. The Cossack angrily slammed his musket into the snow. He simply stared at the sleigh for a long moment. Montagne hesitated to pull the trigger.

He wishes to die.

"Your army plundered our homes. They drank themselves into a stupor while they burned my family alive in my barn. Imagine losing everything to a people with whom you had no quarrel. You wanted a war, but leaders never feel the pain of the innocents who die at their hand. Now, you will understand the toll."

The hair on the back of Montagne's head stood erect as he translated. Napoleon's stern face sneered and his teeth bared. "Get that fucking peasant out of my way! Kill him now!" Napoleon screeched, pointing at the Cossack.

BOOM!

Montagne flinched as the sound seemed to come from extremely close behind them. Napoleon's face grew still, and he tucked his right hand inside his jacket in a characteristic gesture. Montagne saw the Emperor look down at his hand. He removed it from the jacket and Montagne saw bright red blood. Napoleon reached for the sleigh's curved railing with suddenly trembling hands.

Beyond the sleigh, a fur-clad shadow fled into the darkness. Montagne turned the pistol on the target, centered, and fired in one smooth movement. The figure fell forward into the snow.

BOOM!

The aide fired his pistol seemingly next to Montagne's ear. He whipped around to see the aide had executed the Cossack, and was now lowering the pistol. There was movement between them. The aide snatched at the Emperor's shoulder but missed. Napoleon pitched forward against the railing of the sleigh and fell forward, tumbling face first into the snow.

"Montagne! Help me!" the aide called as he leapt from the sleigh into the snow.

Montagne knelt in the snow next to the aide. The other captain cradled the Emperor's head across his legs and peered down into his still face. Montagne stared into sightless eyes for a long moment and turned his face up to see Caulaincourt shuffling toward them.

In that moment, words failed him. His ability to translate quickly and correctly vanished. Emotions overwrote his abilities. Mouth agape, he closed it and mentally shook himself to report.

"Sir, the Emperor is dead."

Caulaincourt removed his ornate headgear and placed it over his chest. The man's eyes closed in silent prayer. Montagne tried to pray but could not as the company of infantry swarmed protectively around the sleigh. Several of them moved into the forest and retrieved the body of the Cossack he'd killed. As they laid the body next to the man, he saw the size difference and felt tears forming in his eyes.

My God. The Emperor is dead and France is in disarray. I failed to protect him.

And I have killed a child.

What have I done?

Montagne closed his own eyes and tucked his chin to his chest. He knew the others would assume his grief was for their Emperor, and while some of it certainly was, he felt more for those displaced and affected by war. People whom armies and generals never considered.

Teeth clenched together, Montagne fought for control and, when he had it, opened his eyes to find Caulaincourt staring at him. The general's eyes were somber, but focused. He knelt next to Napoleon's body and grasped the dead man's right hand affectionately.

They sat in silence for a moment, eyes on their fallen Emperor, until the infantry returned and ringed them with quiet murmurs of shock and dismay. He found his voice. "What should we do, sir?"

Caulaincourt made eye contact with Napoleon's aide-de-camp first. "Load Emperor Napoleon's body into the sleigh. You will proceed to Ashmiany for new horses and provisions. I will meet you there and escort the Emperor's body personally. We will change the horses and proceed with all possible speed to Paris."

The general cleared his throat and spoke in a louder voice.

"Lieutenant Moreau? Summon the commanders to the front of the march immediately. I will meet them there. Have General Mamet report directly to me here. For the rest of you, I am giving you an order you will follow immediately and without fail. Speak not of what has happened here under penalty of death. The army, and the world, cannot know what has taken place until we decide to tell them. Do you understand?"

Amidst the murmurs and quiet assents, the aide replied in a loud, clear voice, "Yes, sir." He got to his feet and called for the infantry to assist him. Caulaincourt stood and motioned for the translator to step to the side.

"You did well, Montagne."

He took a breath and replied slowly. "I killed a child, sir."

Caulaincourt snorted. "That child killed your Emperor. His cowardly action has taken a great man from the field. Without him, France as we know it could crumble. Our enemies could pounce upon us and wipe us from the Earth in the coming days."

The enormity of what he'd seen finally cleared in Montagne's mind. The war in Spain would certainly falter as would the actions of the French fleet. The loss of Napoleon could embolden the British to attempt an invasion of Europe. Given the state of the *Grand Armeé*, there would not be much of a fight. With discord rampant in Paris, and the Emperor dead in the Russian snow, what might happen to the very world around them stunned Montagne to silence.

"We must keep our thoughts present." The general took a deep breath and exhaled a cloud of steam into the frigid night. His normally calm, almost placid face appeared more troubled than when on the march. "You are fluent in English, as well?"

The question momentarily stunned Montagne. "I am, sir."

Caulaincourt took a moment to assemble his thoughts. He turned to Montagne and pulled him farther from the crowd, his voice low.

Caulaincourt sighed and looked up into the darkness. "A war on two fronts did this. We pushed too far east. Our appetites were too large. Our enemies continue to wear us down from all sides and we cannot maintain constant warfare at sea and all across Europe forever. The toll is too great."

The usually calm, composed general seemed on the edge of either anguished weeping or incalculable rage. Caulaincourt closed his eyes for a couple of seconds. When he opened them, his composure had returned combined with a sureness, a confidence, Montagne hadn't seen before. The general's eyes were clear and bright in the near darkness as he turned back to face Montagne.

"You will escort the body to Ashmiany with me and then you will acquire horses and proceed to Calais will all possible speed."

"Calais?" Montagne blurted. Caulaincourt glared at him, and he apologized. "My apologies, sir."

Caulaincourt continued, "You will proceed to London on my personal orders and relay a message to their monarchy directly. I will compose it and you will personally deliver it to King George III, or his Prime Minister, in London. Is that clear?"

Montagne's mind whirled. Was Caulaincourt assuming command of the *Grand Armeé*, or the entire French government? Would he plead for peace? Would he capitulate to the powers that wished the *Grand Armeé* to return to their borders?

He nodded. "Yes, sir. I will proceed directly."

"Meet me at the head of the march in an hour's time, Montagne. Do not be late. The balance of our future depends on you."

They arrived at Ashmiany shortly before midnight. The French encampment there was small as most of the logistical stores to feed the approaching army pushed to the east ahead of them. The tiny, war-torn village would be glad to see the French retreat. With the army only six hours away now, the tents and wagons would be loaded and gone within a day's time. None too soon for the displaced villagers cowering in their homes.

The aide disappeared to coordinate with those in charge regarding the logistics of the return. Montagne stood by the sleigh, stamping his feet against the cold for a moment before two soldiers arrived to guard the sleigh. Each of the men glanced at the wrapped bundle on the floor of the sleigh for a moment and then took up positions on either side of it, facing away. Satisfied, Montagne moved up a slight incline and found the paddock. A lone sergeant guarded the horses. As he approached, the man stood and saluted.

"I bear a message from General Caulaincourt and require two horses on his orders." Montagne said. For the first time, he was aware of both the placement of his sword and his officer's pistol under his coat as well as the critical nature of his mission.

"Yes, sir," the attendant said and disappeared into the makeshift shack to gather the saddle and tack.

"Where is the quartermaster?"

The sergeant pointed down the incline to the familiar wagon trains. Two privates, likely roused by the sergeant, appeared in the doorway. One was thin and gangly with a speckled complexion, the other portly with dark eyebrows and sullen eyes.

Montagne pointed at the gangly one. "Go to the quartermaster and draw ten days' rations and water."

One private disappeared and Montagne stared at the other one. "Fetch the horses. The fastest you have."

Suddenly alone outside the paddock, Montagne turned to gaze over the small village which the logistical forces of the *Grand Armeé* called home. Though the hour was late, the village buzzed with activity. Armed men ran from point to point as if preparing a defense. From here, he would press on to Miedniki and on to Vilna. Each had a small French logistical garrison to support the needs of the army as it retreated toward France.

Another sergeant approached and saluted. "Sir, we are preparing for an attack. Local outposts have been harassed by the Cossacks since dusk. It is best you arm yourself and report to headquarters."

Montagne bristled. "I will do no such thing. I am under orders from General Caulaincourt in command of the *Grand Armeé*. As soon as I have a proper mount, I must depart. Prepare your defense, sergeant. My mission remains unchanged."

The man uttered *"Mon dieu"* before turning back toward the village and sprinting into the night.

As Montagne stood waiting for his horses, the cold suddenly seeped far inside his coat and shoes. He grew anxious to be off on his mission, and he looked into the paddock several times, until finally the sergeant appeared with his horses. Down the hill, the gangly private and two other figures moved toward him, each carrying a sizable load. They divided the load between the two horses, and when the mounts were ready, Montagne did not hesitate. He swung into the saddle on the black gelding and did not look back as he galloped off for Miedniki.

Two days west of Vilna, the forests gave way to large expanses of dormant grasslands. Under their intermittent blanket of snow, the fields showed the marks of couriers and small units of the French army along the route of march as they coordinated the retreat of the main effort.

Montagne followed the trail west as fast as his horses could go. Every couple of hours, he dismounted and led them through the fields and occasional stands of forest to rest them and get his own blood flowing. Fatigue tore at him from all sides. Stopping to sleep for any length of time seemed out of the question. Every time he'd come across an encampment, he'd been too awake and refreshed to feel compelled to stop. During the long night, he'd almost fallen from his saddle twice before finding a dilapidated barn. He'd lain down in the old, musty hay for an hour at most before guilt propelled him onto the horses and moving further west.

As he rode, paying attention to the horses and his pace, Montagne's mind tried to grasp the situation. Somewhere to the south, Caulaincourt and the body of the Emperor moved at high speed to Paris. He tapped the reassuring lump under his jacket of the general's note for the British monarchy and resisted, again, the temptation to read it even under the pretense of committing it to memory.

No. Montagne shook off the thought and lowered himself from the saddle to walk alongside the horses for a while. *The general trusted me to deliver his message. I must trust he knows what he is doing.*

He swung his right leg up and over the horse's back as the black gelding flinched backward. Montagne ducked and reversed the movement, reaching his leg toward the ground as the whistling hum of a near-miss shot through the space where he'd been a second before. The crash of a musket firing sounded through the strand of dormant trees he'd been about to enter. His heart racing, Montagne withdrew the pistol from under his coat and visually checked its readiness. Thankful for war horses familiar with the sound of weapons that didn't spook easily, Montagne used them for cover and looked toward the sound of the shot. In an instant, he saw a silhouetted rider on a pale horse gallop west and away from him.

He stood frozen in the snow for half a minute, trying to calm both his racing breath and his frantic mind. Had he been followed? Why would someone shoot at him? As he crossed eastern Europe, every dark corner of forest and wide-open plain had kept his eyes darting back and forth except for this one. He'd failed to stay alert and it almost cost him his life. Montagne rubbed the several days growth of beard on his chin and closed his tired eyes. He leaned his forehead against the horse's hide as he fought against the fatigue threatening to undermine his ability to focus on the work.

The Emperor is dead. The toll has been too great.

You must not fail.

He heard Caulaincourt's voice in his head. The implications of the general's unread message weren't clear to the translator, but there were two possibilities he surmised. Surrender to the British demands and an end to the war in Spain was certainly a possibility, though Caulaincourt's own feelings about the British matched the fallen Emperor's own, and that meant surrender was out of the question. If not surrender, then was the message one of peace? Cooperation? Something else?

His eyes snapped open. "I have to ride," he said to the wind. "For France, if not for me."

Survival instincts initiated, Montagne grabbed the leads for his horses and led the pair as fast as he could run into the protection of the strand of trees his attacker had vacated. In the dark, cold forest, Montagne stamped his feet and gazed for several minutes in all directions before climbing back astride his mount and pushing west once again.

Friendly way stations grew more numerous as he rode, and he traded horses several times in the ensuing days. Yet his own fatigue wore down on him unlike anything he'd ever experienced in his service. The forests and hills of Germany slowly became the rolling terrain of eastern France. At Roubaix, he turned northwest and made for the coast. The grasslands were brown with winter. He thought again of the sun and warmth of the family lands above Nice, and he longed to turn toward Paris and ride further south without looking back.

As he rode, Montagne wondered if Caulaincourt and the other leaders shared his fatigue, and not just with the war, with the struggle and upheaval of his country. He'd been ripped from his chosen studies and placed into the armed service of his country by a man seemingly hell-bent upon destruction at all costs. Emperor Napoleon would be equally celebrated and scorned for centuries to come. The suffering of so many would be forgotten.

Perhaps it's time I leave this all behind. For good.

The enormity of the thought struck him as the pre-dawn twilight spread over the sprawling coastal plain of Calais. Fishing boats crowded the harbor afraid to move into the channel and the constant swarming presence of the English fleet. Montagne believed it would be easy to find a patriotic fisherman to risk delivering him to the British.

At the last post, just as the sun rose to the east, Montagne surrendered his horses and sought out the quartermaster for rations and additional loads for his weapons only to be directed toward a distant, quiet tent. As he approached, Montagne listened to the whisper of caution from his mind and drew his pistol before he stepped inside. A lone, dark figure sat on a stool. He looked up and raised a pistol, pointing it at Montagne's chest. Montagne's own pistol was trained on the young man's smiling face. The two stood for a moment in awkward silence.

The Emperor's aide laughed and spoke in fluent English. "Captain Montagne, I'm afraid I must relieve you of that note. His Majesty will never receive it as long as I live."

Montagne smiled at the man's audacity. "Because of your loyalty to the Emperor?"

"No, my duty to the Crown." The aide stood and stepped closer. "I give you this chance, Montagne. Where is the message?"

"Go to hell," Montagne said and pulled the trigger. He squeezed his eyes shut expecting the report of the aide's pistol pointed at his chest. When it didn't come, Montagne opened his eyes and saw the aide lying on his side grasping for the pistol that had fallen from his grasp. Montagne stepped forward, kicked away the pistol, and knelt.

The aide coughed and blood sprayed from his mouth. Still, the man sneered as he struggled to speak. "France will fall, Montagne."

"Perhaps," Montagne replied. "But not today."

Finding a boat to traverse the channel took considerable effort. Not many sailors were willing to entertain the certainty of intercept with the British navy even while traveling under a flag of truce. War made cowards of dishonorable men. Montagne, in his addled state, wandered through the docks. Morning should have been a busy time along the docks in the wide, sure harbor but the vessels remained in their moorings as if frozen. The few fishermen at their boats watched him with uneasy eyes. Most looked away when he acknowledged them with a nod and a hopeful smile. Others turned their backs on him. When they did, he realized how much war had changed him. As a young officer, the idea of a Frenchman turning his back on the army, and a representative of the Emperor himself, would have angered him beyond the edge of reason. But the near-constant warfare had taken too much of a toll on the populace. He understood that toll for the first time in his life. His own commitment to the mission would have waned save for his respect for Caulaincourt and his own dreams of returning home to a land at peace.

An older man with a shock of white hair under a black knit

cap merely squinted at Montagne's request. He nodded and pointed at the small, single-masted boat. Before Montagne could even settle himself in the small bow, they were under sail across the placid harbor. Montagne lay in the ship's tiny bow to sleep.

Near noon, a rough hand shook him awake. Montagne sat upright at the whistle of a single cannonball arcing over their heads into the ocean. Over the stern, where the rudder sat unmanned and amidships, a warship approached. Montagne struggled to stand. He waved his arms.

"Sit down," the old man called over his shoulder. "I've hoisted the proper flag. They'll take you aboard, Captain. Just negotiate my freedom."

Montagne looked up at the simple white rectangle floating in the wind where the sails once billowed. As the warship came alongside, he looked up to see British soldiers pointing their rifles at his chest, careful sneers on their faces.

They collected him from the fisherman and roughly hauled him aboard what appeared to be a French-built *Pallas*-class frigate flagged as a British warship. His feet had barely touched the deck when the ship's captain, a pleasant-faced man with dark, windswept hair appeared in front of him.

"You're in quite the mess, sir," he said with a grim smile.

Montagne straightened. "If you'll permit me to come aboard, Captain," he said in fluent, British-accented English, "I am carrying a message from General Armand-Augustin-Louis de Caulaincourt, the Commander of the *Grand Armeé*, for the eyes of King George III only."

The ship's captain blinked but said nothing. "Can you elaborate further?"

"I appreciate your discretion, sir. That is a conversation best held in private. Your quarters, perhaps?" Montagne asked.

The captain nodded stiffly. "I am Captain Murray Maxwell of the *Daedalus*."

"Antoine de Montagne, senior translator for General Caulaincourt," Montagne said. He kept his gaze stern as if asking the young captain to say nothing more. "Sir, if you would, please release the fisherman; I traveled under the flag of truce to be here. Your quarrel is not with him or his meager catch."

Captain Maxwell nodded. He turned to a burly sailor with a trimmed beard. "Master at arms, release the fisherman. Take Captain de Montagne to my cabin. Post two guards at the door. I shall join him shortly. Mister Mowett? Make sail and continue the trials."

Montagne heard the crew spring to action as he found himself escorted belowdecks to the captain's cabin and an uncertain future. He didn't have to wait long.

The promise of delivering critical intelligence to the Admiralty, and the king himself, kept Maxwell firmly in Montagne's confidence. Upon hearing the news of Emperor Napoleon's death in Russia, Maxwell called his sailing master. Maxwell interrupted the sea trials for the newly commissioned *Daedalus* and reversed course for England with all possible speed, yet he told no one of Montagne's news or mission. The seas were rough during the transit, but Maxwell's treatment of Montagne never deviated from genteel and pleasant. Montagne wondered what the crew discussed in hushed tones as they glanced at him during his time on deck, but no one said anything to him save for the ship's captain.

They anchored in Portsmouth two days later and, circumventing the authority of the port commander, Maxwell arranged a coach and escort for himself and Montagne to London. Montagne had said nothing to anyone besides Maxwell about the demise of Napoleon and it became clear Maxwell understood the information's impact on all of Europe. The young ship's captain climbed aboard the coach to complete the last leg of the journey with Montagne.

The coach arrived in London in the late afternoon of Christmas Eve. The slushy thoroughfares were crowded as families with children moved from place to place, enjoying the holiday cheer.

Montagne thought of his own family in the South of France and his desire to join them as soon as possible. As much as he wanted to believe his time in the army was drawing to a close, and that the constant wars of the Emperor's rule of France would fade into a lasting peace, the churning in his stomach told him that unless a miracle occurred in the next few hours, he was still in the center of an enemy's country and too far from home.

Montagne watched the faces of excited children as the coach made its way to Buckingham Palace. Wearing his British naval uniform, Captain Maxwell swung out of the carriage at the palace gate and spoke to the guards, who in turn dispatched a runner to the palace. Montagne fought crippling anxiety and the fatigue of the previous fortnight as they waited for a response. At last, the *Daedalus*'s captain climbed aboard, and the carriage passed through the fortified gates.

Captain Maxwell turned to him, both flushed and relieved. "His Royal Highness, the Admiral of the Fleet, and Lord Liverpool, the Prime Minister, are both present, as I'd hoped." Maxwell lowered his voice, as if someone might be eavesdropping. "The Admiral of the Fleet is one of King George's sons. His Majesty has been ill for some time, and Lord Liverpool effectively runs the government and our war efforts. I said nothing of the contents of your message. I merely implied the news would be of critical importance."

"There have been rumors in France for some time regarding your king's health." Montagne smiled. "I am indebted to your trust and courtesy, Captain Maxwell."

The young officer smiled in return. "I hope the larger conflicts between our countries find a peaceful resolution. Without trying to sound naive, I believe you and I could be friends in other circumstances."

"Let us hope that peace comes swiftly."

Once the driver parked the carriage in front of the main palace entrance, they exited together. Several armed guards surrounded them with weapons at the ready. Maxwell stared at the sergeant of the guard in charge who nodded. They were ready to proceed.

Maxwell gestured Montagne forward and fell into step at his right shoulder. "Come, Captain de Montagne." The guards pressed in, accompanying them. Montagne drew a long, deep breath and tried to still his thrashing heart. Even after two years in the *Grand Armeé*, during countless actions and marches close to the front with artillery and musket rounds passing overhead, he had never experienced such abject fear.

They will take me and execute me without listening to a word I say. Caulaincourt's message, whatever it is, will be lost and forgotten.

The sudden urge to laugh at the terror in his bones almost overtook his senses as they stepped inside. Entering the ornate palace, Montagne kept his head and eyes forward, refusing to be distracted by the furnishings of King George's residence. The escorts directed them into a wide corridor where two gentlemen stood waiting for them. Both were older, distinguished men wearing powdered wigs that likely covered hair of a similar color. One wore the traditional dark blue dress uniform of an admiral of the Royal Navy and the other a dark, traditional jacket with a ruffled shirt underneath. The admiral was stout, if not a bit rotund, unlike the sailors of the *Daedalus* and others whom Montagne had observed along the shores of home. This man had likely never seen a posting at sea because of his lineage.

The escorts retreated to a watchful position around the four men. Captain Maxwell clicked his heels together and saluted. Unsure of the customs and courtesies, Montagne nodded and bowed very slightly at the waist to both men.

"Your Highness, Lord Liverpool. I am Captain Murray Maxwell, of His Majesty's Ship *Daedalus*. Allow me to present Captain Antoine de Montagne, translator for General Armand-Augustin-Louis de Caulaincourt, Commander of the *Grand Armeé*."

His Royal Highness, the Admiral of the Fleet, frowned at Montagne. "What news do you have that is so critical to interrupt the preparations for our Christmas celebrations, Captain de Montagne?"

"You said Caulaincourt is in command of your army?" Lord

Liverpool questioned immediately. His gaze intensified on Montagne. "I do not understand. Has there been a change in command of the French forces?"

Montagne nodded. "Sir, Emperor Napoleon is dead."

"What?" Lord Liverpool gasped. The men looked at each other.

Montagne met their shocked expressions. "He was killed by Cossack irregular forces outside of Smorgon, Russia on the fifth of December as the army retreated from Moscow."

The Admiral of the Fleet harrumphed and looked at Lord Liverpool. "This is a ruse."

"Sir, with respect, I was with the Emperor as he died. There was news of a possible *coup d'etat* in Paris. As the Russian campaign stalled and the *Grand Armeé* ran low on provisions, the Emperor ordered our withdrawal. During the retreat, the Emperor told General Caulaincourt he could not govern France from the front and proceeded home. As he started his journey, Cossacks attacked. He was killed in front of his aide-de-camp, General Caulaincourt, and myself. I can personally verify that he is dead."

The Admiral of the Fleet turned to Lord Liverpool, and they stared at each other for a moment. His Royal Highness asked, "And what of the aide?"

"He died at the Emperor's side. Only General Caulaincourt and I survived the attack," Montagne lied. Their question had been far from innocuous and confirmed the true identity of the man he'd executed as a spy in Calais.

Liverpool deftly changed the subject. "What is the message General Caulaincourt asked you to deliver to His Majesty? Let us see it."

Montagne reached into his pocket and withdrew the small, wax-sealed roll of paper. "General Caulaincourt was adamant this be seen by King George III or yourself first."

"And Napoleon is really dead?" the Admiral asked again, as if he couldn't believe it.

Montagne nodded. "If all has gone well, General Caulaincourt has returned to Paris. As for the status of the French government, I cannot say."

Lord Liverpool nodded to his counterpart. "As the Prime Minister, I am charged with handling all matters of importance for the Crown while His Majesty is ill. As you are aware, His Royal Highness, the Admiral of the Fleet, is Prince William the Duke of Clarence. While not the heir to the throne, he will review the note as well. Is this acceptable, Captain de Montagne?"

Montagne considered the situation and knew he had no alternative. "Of course, sir."

Lord Liverpool extended a hand, palm up, to Montagne. "If you please?"

Montagne extended the rolled message to the Prime Minister. Lord Liverpool took the message, broke the wax seal, and unrolled it.

As he read, the older man's mouth fell open slightly. He laughed once, and then again, before almost clutching it to his chest. "General Caulaincourt says he is returning to Paris with the intent of dissolving Emperor Napoleon's government and establishing peace through Europe. He says the Emperor's death at the hands of Cossacks has challenged his own personal convictions for warfare," Liverpool said. "From what I know of the man, I am inclined to believe him."

The Admiral of the Fleet harrumphed again. "We must be careful in our dealings with General Caulaincourt. With the French government in disarray, anything could happen ... as we've seen over the last several decades."

"Indeed. However, if this is a legitimate and honorable expression of his intent, there are great possibilities. Has our blockade been established at the American colonies?"

His Royal Highness nodded. "They should be in position. I await the confirming dispatch from Admiral Warren any day now."

Lord Liverpool's eyebrows rose, and a hint of a smile played on his lips. "How quickly can you sail a diplomatic mission to Paris?"

"Two days. The family's Christmas celebration must be preserved. I can have a ship dispatched and at the ready." His Royal Highness, the Admiral of the Fleet nodded. Where there had been doubt in his voice before was sudden enthusiasm.

"Begging your pardon, sir," Captain Maxwell spoke. "The *Daedalus* is docked in Portsmouth now and is ready to sail. I would be honored to transport the diplomatic party."

Lord Liverpool brightened. "Done! Captain Montagne? Will you accompany the party and assist with the presentation of terms?"

"Terms?" Montagne squinted and hastily added, "Sir?"

Lord Liverpool nodded and handed the note to His Royal Highness. "General de Caulaincourt has offered, in an attempt at peace, his full cooperation and diplomatic influence. You are aware we are in armed conflict yet again with our former colonies in America?"

Montagne shook his head. "I was only aware of naval actions in the Atlantic, sir."

"Well, we have seen several engagements with the Americans on the ground and they've held a significant advantage. That ends now. Once your navy and logistical support is withdrawn from America, we will see just how much resolve our former subjects have." He smiled again and glanced at His Royal Highness. "We shall recall Lord Wellington from Spain and instruct him to provide a thorough and complete invasion plan for the colonies. By summer, I will walk that ground myself and take their surrender personally. I've heard their capitol city is quite beautiful. Perhaps a proper flag flying over it will complete the scene?"

The Admiral of the Fleet beamed. "Quite right. His Majesty will be most pleased."

Lord Liverpool smiled at Montagne and Johnson. "You've delivered quite the Christmas present, gentlemen. Please join me for Christmas dinner tomorrow. You should have enough time to have your uniform laundered, *Colonel* de Montagne. And you as well, Captain Maxwell."

Montagne blurted. "I'm sorry, what did you say, sir?"

His Royal Highness turned the message to Montagne, where he read Caulaincourt's flowing script promoting him officially with the duties of Translator General of *la Grand Armeé*. "I take it this is a surprise?"

"Completely, sir."

Lord Liverpool laughed. "A commanding general's staff should always carry appropriate rank for their office, especially when they've performed their duties as honorably as you have. We would never shoot the messenger, Colonel de Montagne, whether it's Christmas or not. I trust you have a family, yes? Tell me about them over a glass of wine, and we'll toast a new peace for Europe and a bright new future."

This was my first collaboration with Rebecca, right after we got married. She had been working on an eerie, atmospheric idea for a story, inspired by the Beatles' haunting song "Julia." When she got stuck, she asked me to work on it with her, and we developed a story that is very different from my other work.

Around the same time, my friend Janet Berliner invited me to contribute to an anthology she was editing with Peter S. Beagle, The Immortal Unicorn—*stories not just about actual unicorns but the metaphor and symbology of unicorns.*

The character of Julia seemed to fit with the theme, a metaphorical unicorn, and Janet and Peter included "Sea Dreams" along with more traditional unicorn stories.

SEA DREAMS

(WITH REBECCA MOESTA)

Julia called me tonight as she has so many times before. Not on the telephone, but in that eerie, undeniable way she's used since we met as little girls, strangers and best friends at once. It usually meant she needed me, had something urgent or personal to say.

But this time I needed her, in a desperate, throw-common-sense-to-the-wind way ... and she knew it. Julia always knew.

And she had something to tell me.

Alone in the tiny bedroom of my comfortably conservative Florida apartment, I felt it as surely as I felt the cool sheets beneath me, and the humid, moon-warm September air that flowed through my half-opened window. At such times, common sense goes completely to sleep, leaving imagination wide awake and open to possibilities. And she called out to me.

Julia had been gone for five years, gone to the sea. Others might have said "drowned," might have used "gone" as a euphemism for "dead." I never did. The only thing I knew—that anyone could know for certain—was this: Julia was gone.

It had begun when we were eleven. That year, my parents and I left our Wisconsin home behind to spend our vacation at my grandmother's oceanside cottage in Cocoa Beach, Florida.

I had grown up in the Midwest, familiar with green hills and sprawling fields, but nothing had prepared me for my first sight of the Atlantic: an infinite force of blue-green mystery, its churning waves a magnet for my sensibilities, a sleeping power I had never suspected might exist.

Excited by the journey and the strange place, I was unable to sleep that first night in grandmother's cottage. The rumble of the waves, the insistent shushing whisper of the surf muttering a white-noise of secrets, vibrated even through the glass ... and grew louder still when I got up and nudged open the window to smell the salt air.

There, in the moonlight, a young girl stood on the beach—someone other than grandmother, her friends, and my parents, talking about grown-up things while I patiently played the role of well-behaved daughter. Another girl unable to sleep.

I put on a bikini (my first) and a pair of jeans, tiptoed down the stairs, and let myself out the sliding glass door onto the sand. As I walked toward the ocean, reprimanding myself for the foolhardiness of going out alone at night, I saw her still standing there, staring out into the waves.

She seemed statuesque in the moonlight, fragile, ethereal. She had waist-length hair the color of sun-washed sand, wide green eyes—I couldn't see them in the dark, but still I knew they were green—and a smile that matched the warmth and gentleness of the evening breeze.

"Thank you for coming," she said. She paused for a few moments, perhaps waiting for a response. As I carefully weighed the advisability of speaking to a stranger, even one who looked as delicate as a princess from a fairy tale, she added, "My name is Julia."

"I'm Elizabeth," I replied after another ten seconds of agonized deliberation. I shook her outstretched hand as gravely as she had extended it, thinking what an odd gesture this was for someone who had probably just completed the sixth grade. Which, I discovered once we started to talk, was exactly the case—as it was for me.

We spoke to each other as if I had been there all along and often came out for a chat, not like strangers who had just met on the beach after midnight. Within half an hour, we were sitting and talking like old friends, laughing at spontaneous jokes, sharing confidences, even finishing each other's sentences as though we somehow knew what the other meant to say.

"Do you like secrets? And stories?" Julia asked during a brief lull in our conversation. When I hastened to assure her that I did—though I had never given it much thought—she fell silent for a long moment and then began to weave me a tale as she looked out upon the waves, like an astronomer gazing toward a distant galaxy.

"I have seen the Princes of the Seven Seas," she said in a soft, dreamy voice, "and each of their kingdoms is filled with more magic and wonder than the next.... The two mightiest princes are the handsome twins, Ammeron and Ariston, who rule the kingdoms of the North."

She had found a large seashell on the beach and held it up to her ear, as if listening. "They tell me secrets. They tell me stories. Listen."

Julia half-closed her green eyes and talked in a whispery, hypnotic voice, as if reciting from memory—or repeating words she somehow heard in the convolutions of the seashell.

"They have exquisite underwater homes, soaring castles made of coral, whose spires reach so close to the surface that they can climb to the topmost turrets when the waves are calm and catch a glimpse of the sky...."

I giggled. Julia's voice was so earnest, so breathless. She frowned at me for my moment of disrespect, and I fell silent, listening with growing wonder as her story caught us both in a web of fantasy and carried us to a land of blues and greens, lights and shadows, beneath the shushing waves.

"Each kingdom is enchanted, filled with light and warmth,

and the princes rarely stay long in their castles. They prefer instead to ride across the brilliant landscapes of the underwater world, watching over their realms.

"Their loyal steeds are sleek narwhals that carry Ammeron and Ariston to all—"

"What's a narwhal?" I asked, betraying my Midwestern ignorance of the sea and its mysteries.

Julia blinked at me. "They're a sort of whale—like unicorns of the sea—strong swimmers with a single horn. Ancient sailors used to think they were monsters capable of sinking ships...."

She cocked her head, listening to the shell. Her face fell into deep sadness for the next part of her story, and I wondered how she could make it all up so fast.

"The sea princes enjoy a charmed existence, full of adventure—they live forever, you know. One of their favorite quests is to hunt the kraken, hideous creatures that ruled the oceans in the time before the Seven Princes, but the defeated monsters hide now, brooding over their lost empires. They hate Ammeron and Ariston most of all, and lurk in dark sea caves, dreaming of their chance to murder the princes and take back what they believe is rightfully theirs.

"On one such hunt, when Ammeron and Ariston rode their beloved narwhal steeds into a deep cavern, armed with abalone-tipped spears, they flushed out the king of the kraken, an enormous tentacled beast twice the size of any monster the two brothers had fought before.

"Their battle churned the waves for days—we called it a hurricane here above the surface—until finally, in one terrible moment, the kraken managed to capture Ammeron with a tentacle and drew the prince toward its sharp beak, to slice him to pieces!"

I let out an unwilling gasp, but Julia didn't seem to notice.

"But at the last moment, Ammeron's brave narwhal—seeing his beloved prince about to die—charged in without regard for his own safety and gouged out the kraken's eye with his single long horn! In agony, the monster released Ammeron and, thrashing about in the throes of death, caught the faithful narwhal in its powerful tentacles and crushed the noble steed an instant before the kraken, too, died."

A single tear crept down Julia's cheek.

"And though the prince now rides a new steed, his loyal narwhal companion is lost forever. He realizes how lonely he is, despite the friendship of his brother. Very lonely. Ammeron longs for another companion to ease the pain, a princess he can love forever.

"Ariston also yearns for a mate—but the princes are wise and powerful. They will accept none other than the perfect partner ... and they can wait. They live forever. They can wait."

We watched the moon disappear behind us and gradually the darkness over the ocean blossomed into petals of peach and pink and gold. I was awed by the swollen red sphere of the sun as it first bulged over the flat horizon, then rose higher, raining dawn across the waves like a firestorm. I had never seen a sunrise before, and I would never see one as beautiful again.

But with the dawn came the realization that I had been up all night, talking with Julia. My parents never got up early, especially not on vacation. Still, I was anxious to get back to my grandmother's house, partly to snatch an hour or two of sleep, but mostly to avoid any chance of being caught.

I knew exactly what my parents would say if they knew I had gone out alone, spent the quiet, dark hours of the night talking to a total stranger—and I wouldn't be able to argue with them. It did sound crazy, completely unlike anything I had ever done before. Irresponsible. Even thinking the terrible word brought a hot flush of embarrassment to my cheeks.

But I wouldn't have traded that night for anything. Though I resisted such silliness for most of my life, that was the first time I ever experienced magic.

The vacation to Cocoa Beach became an annual event. Even when I went back to Wisconsin, Julia and I were rarely out of touch. My parents taught me to be practical and realistic, to think of the future and set long-term goals. Julia, however, remained carefree and unconcerned, as comfortable with her fantasies as with her real life.

We wrote long letters filled with plans for the future, and the hopes and hurts of growing up. We weren't allowed to call each other often, but whenever something important happened to me, the phone would ring, and I would know it was Julia. She knew, somehow. Julia always knew.

During our summer weeks together, Julia spent endless hours telling me her daydreams about life in the enchanted realms beneath the sea. She had taught herself to sketch, and she drew marvelous, sweeping pictures of the undersea kingdoms. After listening to her for so long, I gradually learned to tell a passable story, though never with the ring of truth that she could give to her imaginings.

From Julia, I learned about the color of sunlight shining down from above, filtered through layers of rippling water. In my mind, I saw plankton blooms that made a stained-glass effect, especially at sunset. I learned how storms churned the surface of the sea, while the depths remained calm though with a "mistiness" caused by the foamy wavetops above.

I learned about hidden canyons filled with huge mollusks, shells as big and as old as the giant redwood trees, which patiently collected all the information brought to them by the fish.

Julia told me about secret meeting places in kelp forests, where Ammeron and Ariston went to spend carefree hours in their unending lives playing hide-and-seek with porpoises. But the lush green kelp groves now seemed empty to them, empty as the places in their hearts that waited for true love....

One day we found a short chain of round metal links at the water's edge. What its original purpose was or who had left it there, I could not fathom. Julia picked it up with a look that was even more unfathomable. She touched each of the loops again and again, moving them through her fingers as if saying some magical rosary. We kept walking, splashing up to our ankles in the low waves, until Julia gave a small cry. One of the links had come loose in her hand. She stared at it for a moment in consternation, then gave a delighted laugh. She slid the circlet from one finger to the next until it came to rest on the ring finger of her right hand, a perfect fit.

"There. I always knew he'd ask." Julia sent me a sidelong glance, a twinkle lurking in the green of her irises. She loosened another link and slipped it quickly onto my hand.

"All right," I sighed, feeling suddenly apprehensive, but knowing that it was no use trying to ignore her once she got started. "Who is 'he,' and what did he ask?"

"I am betrothed to Ammeron, heir to the Kingdom of the Seventh Sea," she said proudly.

"Sure, and I'm betrothed to his brother Ariston." I held up the cheap metal ring on my finger. "Aren't we a bit young to get engaged, Jule?"

Julia was unruffled. "Time means nothing in the Kingdoms beneath the sea. When a year passes here, it's no more than a day to them. Time is infinite there. Our princes will wait for us."

"You really think we're worth it? Besides, how do they know whether or not we accept?" I challenged, always adding a completely out-of-place practicality to Julia's fairy tales. But my sarcasm sailed as far over Julia's head as a shooting star.

"Wait," she said, grasping my arm as she swept the ocean with her intense gaze. Suddenly, she drew in a sharp breath. "Look!" Her eyes lit up as a dolphin leapt twice, not far from where we stood on the shore. "There," she sighed, "do we need any more proof than that?"

Even in the face of her excitement, I couldn't keep the slight edge out of my voice. "I'll admit that I've never seen dolphins leap so close to shore, but what does that have to do with—"

"Dolphins are the messengers of the royal families beneath the sea," she replied in her patient way. Always patient. "One leap is a greeting. Two leaps ask a question. Three leaps give an answer." She flashed a smile at me. There was certainty in her voice that sent a shiver down my back. "And now they're waiting for us to respond!"

I struggled for a moment with impatience but couldn't bring myself to answer with more of my cynicism. I tried my most soothing voice. "Well, I'm sure Ammeron will understand that you—"

But she wasn't listening. Before I could finish my thought, she was running at top speed along the damp, packed sand. I looked after her, and as I watched in amazement, she executed three of the most graceful leaps I had ever seen, strong and clean and confident. I knew I would look foolish if I even tried something like that. I'd probably fall flat on my face in the sand.

By the time I caught up to her, Julia was looking seaward, ankle-deep in waves, with tears sparkling on her lashes—or perhaps it was only the sea spray.

In her hand she held two more of the metal links from the chain she had found. Silently she handed me one of the links, then closed her eyes and threw the remaining one as far into the water as she could. I did the same, imitating her gesture but without the same conviction.

"Elizabeth," Julia said after a long moment, startling me with her quiet voice, "you are a very sensible person." It sounded like an accusation—and coming from Julia, it probably was.

We moved to dryer sand and sat for a long time watching the waves, letting the bright sun dazzle our eyes. Perhaps too long. But Julia's hand on my arm let me know that she saw it, too.

Far out in the water a dolphin leapt. Three times.

Our lives were divided each year into reality and imagination, north and south, school and vacation, rationality and magic, until we finished high school.

I planned my life as carefully and sensibly as I could. My

parents had taught me that a woman had to be practical—and I believed it. I chose my college courses with an eye toward the job market, avoiding "frivolous" art and history classes (no matter how much fun they sounded). After all, what good would they do me later in life?

My one concession to the lifelong pull the ocean had exerted on me, was that I chose to go to school at Florida State. Luckily, it was a perfectly acceptable school for the business management and accounting classes I intended to take, so I wasn't forced to define my reasons more precisely.

And it allowed me to see Julia more often.

Julia, on the other hand, always lived on the edge of reality. My parents disapproved of her, and I grew tired of defending her choices, so we came to the unspoken agreement that we would avoid the subject entirely ... though even I couldn't help being a bit disappointed in my friend. To me, it seemed Julia was wasting her life at the seaside.

I tried to help her make some sensible choices as well. She wasn't interested in college, preferring to spend her days hanging out near the ocean, making sketches that she sold for a pittance in local gift shops, doing odd jobs.

I convinced her to learn scuba diving. With her love of the sea, I knew she would be a natural, and in less than a year she was a certified instructor with a small, steady business. I even took lessons from her, as did one of my boyfriends, though that ended in disaster.

As for romance, I occasionally went out on dates with men I met in classes, since I felt that our mutual interests should form a solid basis for long-term partnership, but my dating resulted only in passionless short-term relationships that usually ended with an agreement ent to be "just friends." I never let on how much these breakups really hurt me, except to Julia.

After each one, I would call Julia and she would meet me at the Original Fat Boy's Bar-B-Que, waiting patiently while I drowned my sorrows in beer and barbecued beef. Then we would drive to the beach, where I'd cry for a while, tell her the whole miserable tale, and vow never to make the same mistake again. Sometimes she drew tiny caricatures of my stories, forming them into comical melodramas as I spoke, until I was forced to acknowledge how silly or inconsequential each romance seemed as I dissolved into laughter and tears.

Julia dated often, drifting through each relationship with little thought for the future, until the inevitable stormy end—usually (I suspected) sparked by Julia's spur-of-the-moment nature and consequent unreliability that frequently frustrated men. Somehow on those nights, she would call to me and, no matter where I was, I would feel the need to go walking on our beach. And she would be there.

Once, particularly burned at the end of a tempestuous relationship, she asked what she was doing wrong—a rhetorical question, perhaps, but I answered her (as if I had had a better track record in love than she). "You're spending too much time in a fairy tale, Jule. I used to really love your stories about the princes and the sea kingdoms, but we're not kids any more. Be a little more practical."

The ocean breeze lifted her pale hair in waves about her face as her sea-green eyes widened. "Practical? I could say you're living in just as much of a fairy tale, Elizabeth. The American Dream ... following all the rules, taking the right classes, expecting to find treasure in your career and a prince in some accountant or lawyer or doctor. Doesn't sound any more realistic to me."

I felt stung, but she just sighed and looked out to sea, getting that lost expression on her face again. "I'm sorry. I didn't mean to dump on you like that. Don't worry. I guess I shouldn't be so upset either. It doesn't really matter, you know. After all, I'm betrothed to the Prince of the Seventh Sea."

And I managed to laugh, which made me feel better. But Julia had a disturbing ... certainty in her voice.

The last time I ever saw Julia, her call was very strong. I was studying late on campus preparing for a final exam when for no apparent reason I felt an overpowering need to get away from my books, to talk to Julia. It had been months since I'd seen her.

No—she needed to talk to me.

Even though there was a storm warning in effect, I ran out the door without even stopping to pick up a jacket, got into my car, and sped all the way to Cocoa Beach. As I sprinted down to the beach behind Julia's house, I saw her standing on the sand. Dimly silhouetted against the cloudy sky, wearing nothing but a white bathing suit, her long hair blew wildly in the wind as she stared out to sea. It reminded me of the first time I had seen Julia as a little girl, standing in the moonlight.

When I came to stand beside her and saw her startled expression, I abruptly realized that something was very wrong: Julia hadn't expected me.

"You called me, Jule," I said. "What's going on?"

"I ... didn't mean to." She seemed to hesitate. "I'm going diving."

Then I noticed the pile of scuba gear close by, near the water. I understood Julia's subtle stubbornness enough to realize that she placed more weight on her feelings than on simple common sense, so I stifled the impulse to launch into an anxious safety lecture and kept my voice neutral. "I know you have plenty of night diving experience, but you shouldn't dive alone. Not tonight. The weather's not good. Look at the surf."

For a while, I thought she wouldn't answer. At last she said softly, "David's gone."

"The artist?" I asked, momentarily at a loss before successfully placing the name of the current man in her life.

She nodded. "It doesn't really matter, you know. He fell head-over-heels for a pharmacist. It hit him so hard, I almost felt sorry for him. Don't worry; I don't feel hurt. After all ..." Her voice trailed off. Her fingers toyed with the plain metal ring that hung from a silver chain around her neck. She had kept it all these years.

Her face was calm, but the storm in her sea-swept eyes rivaled the one brewing over the ocean. "After all," she finished with an enigmatic quirk of her lips, "I think tonight is my wedding night."

Uneasy, I tried for humor, hoping to stall her. "Don't you need a bridesmaid, then? I'll just go get my formal scuba tanks and my dress fins and meet you back here, okay?"

After a minute or so she looked straight at me, clear-eyed and smiling. "Thank you for coming. I really did need to see you again, but right now I think I need to be alone for a while."

"I'm not so sure I should leave," I said, stalling, reluctant to let her go, unable to force her to stay. "Friends don't let friends dive alone, you know?"

"Don't worry, Elizabeth," she said, barely above a whisper. "Remember, no matter what happens ... I'll call you." She put on her diving gear, letting me help her adjust the tanks, kissed me on the cheek, and waded into the turbulent water. "I'll call you in a week—probably less. I promise."

As I left the beach I looked back every few seconds to watch her until I saw her head disappear beneath the waves.

Later, Julia's tanks and her buoyancy compensator vest were found in perfect condition on the shore a few miles away. And a plain silver neck chain. That was all.

That was five years ago. And tonight, when I needed her the most, I heard her call again.

Now, sitting on the damp sands, I listen to the hushed purr of the waves and stare at the Atlantic Ocean under the moonlight.

At times like this, here on the beach where Julia and I used to sit together, I wonder if I really was the sensible one. Yes, I made all the "right" choices, earned my degree, found a suitable job, got a comfortable apartment—though no dashing prince (accountant, lawyer, or otherwise) seemed to notice. I had been supremely confident that it would only be a matter of time.

But then, with a simple blood test, I ran out of time. Next came more tests, then a biopsy and a brief stay in the hospital. And behind it all loomed the specter of more and more time spent among the other hopeless cancer patients, walking cadavers, with the ticking of the death watch growing louder and louder inside their heads.

I would rather listen to the ocean.

It wasn't fair!

I raged at the universe. Hadn't I done everything right? Then why had I fallen under a medical curse, with no prince to kiss my cold lips and dislodge the bit of poisoned apple from my throat?

I needed to hear Julia's stories again. I longed to know more about the princes and their sea-unicorns, the defeated kraken, the tall spires of coral castles, in that enchanted undersea world where everyone lived forever.

I found a seashell on the shore, washed up by the tide, as if deposited there for me alone. I picked it up, brushing loose grains of sand from the edge, held it to my ear ... and listened.

Far out in the water, I saw a dolphin make a double jump, two graceful silver arcs under the bright light of the moon.

My heart leapt with it, and I stood, blinking for a moment in disbelief. Then, feeling surprisingly restless and full of energy. I decided to go for a run along the beach.

And if I happened to leap once, twice, or three times ... who was there to know?

When I went back to college to get my MFA degree, I took various English and creative writing courses. In two of those classes, among the required reading was the short story "The Things They Carried" by Tim O'Brien—which is a very popular text in literature classes.

In a different course on flash fiction, an assignment was to write a very short story about warfare. Having just read "The Things They Carried," I decided to use the model in a fantasy setting with a medieval palace coup instead of the Vietnam War.

THE THINGS THE
PRINCESS CARRIED

His sword broke as he shoved shut the heavy door to the princess's quarters. It was the last instant, and the blade drove back the furious rebels long enough that Dane could kick one of the dead bodies out of the doorway. He slammed the wooden barricade and jammed the crossbar in position. It would hold for now—but not for long.

"They'll break through soon, Princess," he yelled over his shoulder, wiping blood from his face. "And they'll kill you. The castle is already on fire."

"We can get out through the passageway by the hearth," she said. "It leads out to the woods."

The loud *thunk* of a battle-axe struck the other side of the door. Dane heard shouts, more blows with the axe. "We have to survive in the deep forest. Take a few things you need, but we have to *go!*"

He had served as personal guard to the princess for five years. She trusted him, and she did exactly as he told her, without arguing, without weeping. She seized a satchel and ran around the room, while Dane yanked a blanket from the reading bench, colorfully embroidered, beautifully dyed. He spread it out and dumped candles, grapes, cheese, and bread from the plate holding the princess's dinner. He had lost his sword, but carried a knife at his side. He threw in a letter opener, long and silver, which could be used as another weapon if necessary. The gold candlesticks from the table could be sold if he needed to bribe anyone. The princess also had a jewel-encrusted mirror, which might serve in a pinch.

Axe blows hammered the door, splintering the wood. He gathered everything in the blanket, using it as a makeshift sack.

"I'm ready, Dane." The princess stood clutching her satchel, wearing only a lounging robe and rabbit-fur slippers. Together, they ran through the gap she had opened next to the hearth, leading into the secret passage. They fled into the dark and shadowy ways of the castle.

When they escaped from a small doorway beyond the walls, the princess finally began to sob. The castle was in flames behind her, the rebels shouting, glass smashing. "My father's dead, isn't he?" she asked, already knowing the answer. "And my mother?"

Dane had never hidden anything from her. "They killed the king and queen first. That was the start of the ambush. They had traitors in place. I barely got to you in time ... but we aren't safe yet." He hurried with her deep into the forest, following trails known only to him and the deer. They had to stay off the main roads, keep themselves hidden. They couldn't trust anyone, but Dane remembered an old hunter's shack he could find in a day or two.

Tonight, though, would be cold and difficult. Sleet already pelted down.

They talked little, not facing their terrible situation. The princess was nearly suffocated by the horror of what had happened to her parents, to the kingdom, to her life.

Dane found a rock overhang, where they took shelter. As the princess sat back, shivering in her fine lounging robe, he gathered a pile of dry twigs and kindling, then took out the knife he had brought as well as the small chunk of flint he always carried with him. With repeated *snicks* of the blade, he struck a spark that caught on the dry grasses, and soon they had a fire.

He opened his blanket satchel to sort through the items he had brought. He handed her the letter opener. "In case you need to defend yourself, Princess." Together, they shared the grapes and cheese, relishing the food for now. In the coming days, Dane would use his knife to kill small game animals, maybe fashion snares to catch a rabbit. It would be hard to survive and remain hidden, but they didn't dare ask for help.

The princess shivered, despite the fire, and Dane finally looked at her slippers, her robe. "Is that all you brought? You'll freeze!"

"Sorry," she said. "I only had a minute. I couldn't think."

He yanked the embroidered blanket and draped it over her shoulders, hoping it would keep her warm enough. He didn't dare make too bright a blaze.

He finally opened her satchel. This was all they had between the two of them to survive until they could find a loyalist camp. When he looked at the items, he was shocked to see what she had gathered in her desperate moments.

"Those are letters," she said, "written by my father to me. Another note from my mother. It's the last thing I have from them."

Dane picked up a hoop with a half-finished piece of embroidery of a bird. "What can we use this for?"

"It's what my mother and I were working on." Tears welled up in her eyes.

He found a pearl necklace, a bracelet, a brooch, nothing supremely valuable in jewels or gold, but apparently with some kind of sentimental attachment. He also found a rag doll, a ribbon collar from the small pet dog she once had. Dane couldn't keep the dismay from his voice. "We will barely survive, Princess! We might well die out here! How can we use this ..."

Anger flared in her eyes. "That is all I have left, my memories, my childhood, my loved ones." She tugged the blanket closer around her shoulders. "They are important things."

Dane wanted to scold her, but it had always been his job to be the practical one, to protect her, to remember the obvious things she simply didn't think about. It would do no good to rail at her.

"And this," the princess said, plucking one piece of jewelry, a heavy gold ring with an inset ruby. "Do you know what this is, Dane? You've seen it often enough." She sounded defiant, held up the ring. "This is my father's ring, the royal signet ring. He knew about the rebellion and gave this to me for safekeeping. This proves that I am the rightful heir. If the rebellion fails, then with this ring I can claim the throne." She leaned closer to the fire, so the flames reflected on the ruby. "Even though I had only a small satchel and a few minutes, I managed to carry the entire kingdom with me."

I can write heart-wrenching tragedies or dramatic thrillers, but as Heath Ledger's Joker asks, "Why so serious?" Sometimes, you just need to be funny.

There was a time when I really needed to write a light and heartwarming story. A terrible sequence of events made 2019 the worst year of my life. First, we had to put down our beloved cat Newton. Then a few months later, my son died. Then my dad died, and just over the cusp of the new year, my longtime friend and collaborator Neil Peart died after a long struggle with glioblastoma.

In the middle of that, I couldn't bring myself to do any writing. But —just what the doctor ordered—I was invited to an anthology edited by Laurel K. Hamilton and William McCaskey, Fantastic Hope ... *stories that were specifically* filled with hope.

I needed that. And I needed to laugh. And Dan Shamble always makes me laugh.

So this story was my first new writing in a long time, and my first new Dan Shamble story in years. "Heart of Clay" was a great way for me to get back on track.

HEART OF CLAY
A DAN SHAMBLE
ZOMBIE P.I. ADVENTURE

—I—

It makes me feel all hollow inside, Shamble," said Officer Toby McGoohan, my best human friend, as we looked down at the mangled corpse of the golem on the grass of the overflow parking area.

Someone had opened the clay guy's chest from the base of his throat down to his waist, splitting him like an orange. He was completely empty inside.

"Not a good time to joke, McGoo." I tilted my fedora and scratched my forehead around the hard edge of the bullet-hole scar from the night I'd been killed.

McGoo pulled out his notebook. "I always make jokes. You know that." He wore his usual blue patrol officer's uniform and cap from the Unnatural Quarter Police Department. At his side he carried a .38 Special police revolver and a .38 Extra Special loaded with silver bullets for troublesome monsters. His belt also had pepper spray and a squirt bottle of holy water. "These days, if I don't think all the ghosts and goblins are funny, I might get nightmares."

I knelt down on stiff knees next to the dead golem. Despite

lingering rigor mortis, my joints worked rather well once I got warmed up. I decided it was time to get a top-off at the embalming parlor again.

I touched the clay of the body. It was still soft and pliable, but drying out. From the hardness of the stone, the coroner could determine the time of death. According to the three letters imprinted on his forehead, his name was Joe.

Golems were hard-working but downtrodden, second-class citizens even among the unnaturals, fashioned by wizards and animated to do the dirty jobs that even slime demons liked to avoid. Since all golems looked alike, and because they often had trouble distinguishing themselves from one another, each golem had his name imprinted right on the forehead.

"I wonder what he was like," I pondered.

"He was probably like a golem, Shamble." McGoo used his radio to call in the report. Backup would arrive soon, but there was no emergency. Joe had been murdered out in the vacant parking ground for Dred's Real Renaissance Faire, but the Faire's gates had been long closed for the day when Joe met his untimely end.

As I looked at the dead gray mud of the corpse, I muttered, "Ashes to ashes, dust to dust." I ran my fingers along the skin, smearing a soft line. "And Play-Doh to Play-Doh."

"They can just scrunch up the clay again," McGoo said. "Moisten it with a little water and squish it into shape. Reanimate another golem."

"But it wouldn't be Joe anymore. And you know Robin would give you one of her famous stern looks if she heard you talking like that."

Robin Deyer was my human lawyer partner at Chambeaux & Deyer Investigations, a firebrand attorney who fought for all the unnaturals that had returned to the world after the strange and improbable event called the Big Uneasy. Robin was a lovely and intelligent young African American woman; I thought McGoo had a crush on her, although the chances of those two opposites having a relationship was about as unlikely as ... well, as anything else in the Unnatural Quarter.

"Not the stern look!" McGoo cried. "Point taken. It's a murder, plain and simple, and we better solve it."

I lurched back to my feet, drawing in a deep but unnecessary breath. My lungs no longer needed air, although it did make talking a lot easier. "Sounds like a job for a zombie detective."

McGoo looked up at the lights of the Renaissance Faire camp that had taken over the empty land outside of town, saw the smoke of cookfires, watched the nocturnal monsters dwindle down to lethargy as the day grew brighter. He glanced at the dead golem again. "Whew, and this is the second one in a week."

—II—

The dragon was the star attraction, no doubt about it, but Dred's Real Renaissance Faire had jousting matches, swordfights, minstrels, jesters, elaborate costumes, and souvenirs to fit any budget, so long as it was high. Food vendors served fantastical concoctions for all digestive systems, whether carnivorous, demonic, or health conscious. One pushy vendor offered me a brain gelato and didn't want to take no for an answer.

I'd been meaning to take Sheyenne, my ghost girlfriend, here on a date, and now I had a reason to go to the Renaissance Faire because of work. Sheyenne glowed with ectoplasmic delight when I bought tickets for all of us, including my partner Robin and cute little Alvina, the ten-year-old vampire girl who was either my daughter or McGoo's. (We weren't sure who was the real father, since we had both been embarrassingly involved with the mother, back in the day. But based on her cuteness and intelligence, I was betting on my genetics, not his.)

Sheyenne had altered her spectral form to look like a regal lady with her blond hair done up in extravagant braids. Her gown came out of a Disney princess movie.

"You look gorgeous," I said.

Not surprisingly, she shimmered. "Thank you, Beaux. I

wanted to look the part." I wore my usual fedora and sport jacket with the stitched-up bullet holes.

Inside the main entry gates, Talbot & Knowles had set up a medieval-looking tavern with a wooden sign that said YE OLDE BLOOD BAR, where they filled tankards of blood for rowdy vampires, and also served coffee, iced tea, and soft drinks for their less sanguine customers. I treated Alvina to a unicorn frappé, which was more sugar and caffeine than hemoglobin, but it made the girl even cuter than usual with her pigtails and a grin that showed off pointy fangs.

The Faire was gaudy and colorful, filled with noise, delightful diversions, and expensive things at every turn. After all the mythical creatures had returned, thanks to a cosmic alignment and accidental virginal blood sacrifice, the vampires, ghosts, mummies, werewolves, zombies, ghouls, trolls, gremlins, etcetera, congregated in the Unnatural Quarter, a place where they could feel at home.

But other mythical creatures, especially the dragon, the wizard king, enchantresses, and Jabberwocks, took their lives on the road. Dred's Real Renaissance Faire performed around the country, and they were doing quite well on their month-long stop here in the Unnatural Quarter.

"Can we watch the jousting?" Alvina asked.

"People just go there to see knights crash into each other," I said.

The little girl beamed. "Sounds great!"

I looked at the program. "Next match is in half an hour."

As Robin walked with us, I could tell the wheels were always turning behind her dark eyes. I had told her about the murdered golems, and now we saw numerous golems hauling barrels, tightening ropes, lugging heavy sacks, emptying dumpsters, scrubbing Porta Potties. I was sure some of them had known the two eviscerated victims.

The crowd around us paused and pointed into the sky. Robin glanced at her watch, and her face flashed a real smile. "Stop right here. This is a good place to watch."

"What is it?" I asked. "And how much does it cost?" It was an instinctive question here at the Renaissance Faire.

"Every hour on the hour, Dan," Robin said. "The dragon!"

At the far side of the site, beyond the crew tents, storage areas, and dumpsters, a scaly monster lurched into the sky, flapping broad wings as large as billboards. The dragon—named Alice—had a long, barbed tail and a sinuous neck, as seen on all the posters. Her eyes flared scarlet fire as she swooped over the Renaissance Faire and then dive bombed, letting out a roar as she streaked over the heads of the cheering spectators.

Alvina laughed. Sheyenne drifted close to me, and I could feel her thrumming spectral presence.

"We're safe," Robin reassured us. "The dragon may be powerful, but city ordinance limits her destructive activities."

Alice did a cartwheel in the air to more cheers, then cocked back her neck and opened her jaws wide. I thought she was going to breathe fire, but instead she released only a series of humorous smoke rings. After a five-minute performance, the dragon glided overhead, tipping her outstretched wings as if in a bow, and circled back to her large tent the size of an aircraft hangar, where she reportedly kept her treasure hoard.

"Can we have a dragon, Dan?" Alvina asked.

"We don't have the room in our apartment," I said, though I hated to disappoint the kid.

"Please? I'll take care of it, I *promise!*"

"It would be too big, honey," Sheyenne explained.

"Let's just get a little one. Hatched from an egg. If we go to the Humane Society ..."

"Little dragons grow into big dragons," Robin said.

"Let's start out with a salamander," I suggested. "Maybe we can work our way up."

That satisfied the girl, and we went off to find the jousting field.

As we went around back of Ye Olde Blood Bar, a golem waiter with a tray—Jim, according to the name on his forehead—was delivering dirty tankards to another golem, Don, who was wearing an apron and yellow dishwashing gloves. Standing at a large barrel of sudsy water, he sloshed the tankards in the soapy water to remove the bloodstains, then dunked them in a separate rinse barrel.

Since we were away from the crowds, I paused to do some detective work. "Excuse me, gentlemen. Are you aware that last night another golem was found murdered in the parking area? His chest had been pulled open, and he was empty inside. His name was Joe."

"Oh ... Joe," the golem said, sounding sad. "Joe was a good guy."

"What about your working conditions here at the Faire?" Robin asked. "Why would someone murder golems?"

"We just do our work," said Don, the golem with yellow dishwashing gloves. He dunked a tankard in the soapy water and swished it in the rinse barrel before setting it on a wooden drying shelf. "Whenever a master hires us, we're just putty in his hands."

I remembered the hollowed-out clay corpse. "What's inside a golem? Why would anyone want to take it?"

Both Jim and Don answered in unison. "We have a heart of clay." They each brought a hand up to their chests. "And Art has the heart of a lion. Art will save us all."

"Who's Art?" I asked.

Alvina tugged on my hand. "We have to get to the jousting."

"Just a minute, honey."

"Art is Art," said the golems. "He will free us."

"Is Art another golem?" Robin asked. "How do we find him?"

"You will find him," said Don and Jim.

When Alvina kept tugging, I realized that we really did need to go or we would miss the beginning of the joust.

Thankfully, it was a cloudy, gloomy day, so all types of unnaturals could enjoy the spectacle outside. Golem ushers herded the crowd to bleachers on the edge of the jousting field. On opposite ends, two armored knights sat on black stallions that pawed at the ground with sharp hooves. The knights wore full regalia, visored helmets, and doublets that should have borne the insignia of noble houses but instead sported corporate logos, the sponsors of the jousting teams. Each jouster held a long wooden lance.

On a raised reviewing stand beside the bleachers stood a man with curly, golden locks, wearing a jewel-studded crown and impressive black velvet robes. The black velvet was adorned with painted images of sad-eyed puppies and Elvis Presley. When the crowd was seated on the bleachers, the regal-looking man raised his hands, as if expecting roars of approval. He got a smattering of applause.

"I am Mortimer Dred, king of the Real Renaissance Faire." When he raised his hands higher, his ballooning black velvet sleeves dropped down to his elbows, revealing scrawny arms. "All fantasy-based unnaturals are here to perform for your entertainment, and tips are gladly accepted." The next round of applause was markedly subdued.

"Today's first match is between two of our greatest jousters. Sir Anatomy of Bone!" One of the knights raised the squeaking visor of his steel helmet to reveal a skull, grinning to hear the loud whistles that greeted his name. The skeleton knight opened his metal chestplate to reveal an empty rib cage.

"And on the other end of the field," King Dred roared, "Sir Fangsalot of Jugular!" The second knight doffed his helmet to reveal the pallid skin of a dapper vampire, a widow's peak, and slicked-back hair. He flashed his fangs.

"Those aren't real names," Alvina said. "They're silly stage names, like in WWE."

The kid was smart. Very smart. Took after me.

The skeleton knight lowered his lance, pointing it at his opponent. The vampire knight showed no concern about the long wooden stake pointed toward his chest.

When the Renaissance king waved a pennant, the two knights kicked their horses and charged directly toward each other like street racers playing chicken. The hooves pounded, the audience held their breath. We all stared, tense. The riders came closer and closer.

Out of the corner of my eye, I watched King Dred hurry down the steps of the reviewing stand, as if he had an important appointment. I turned back to the charging horses. The lances were leveled, the demonic horses were reckless. The two knights seemed not to care for their own lives or safety.

At the last moment, Sir Fangsalot raised his shield, knocked the threatening wooden staff to one side, but held his own pole firm and plunged it through the armored chest of Sir Anatomy. The lance skewered the skeletal knight and knocked him off his horse. He landed with a clamor of armor on the jousting field.

The crowd's gasp was like thunder. The vampire knight rode past and wheeled around, holding up a gauntleted hand in triumph. "Victory is mine!"

The skeleton fumbled on the ground, grabbing at his metal chestplate, barely able to move due to the long lance thrust directly through him. He pulled his armor plate open to reveal that the wooden shaft had passed harmlessly between two widely-spaced ribs.

"You hit no vital organs!" shouted Sir Anatomy. "I demand a rematch."

"It's all fake," said Alvina, "like WWE."

"All in good fun, honey," said Sheyenne. "No real knights were hurt during the performance."

Golems lumbered onto the field to extricate the long lance from Sir Anatomy. They rounded up the snorting demon horses and started to prepare the field for the two o'clock jousting round.

Having finished her unicorn frappé, Alvina was hungry again. Leaving the jousting field, we strolled among the vending stalls, sniffing the odors, some delicious, some nauseating.

I heard subdued shouting up ahead, clearly an argument that was not part of any performance. My eyes were drawn to pointy objects at a sword vendor's stall. A scrawny old gremlin with patchy fur and immensely thick glasses squirmed on a stool behind a counter, surrounded by broadswords, throwing daggers, battle-axes, and morning stars. A sign in front of the stall promised *Gifts for the whole family!*

King Mortimer Dred loomed in front of the stall, waving his arms. "I want that sword! You were supposed to hold it for me."

"Sorry, sir," said the gremlin in a raspy voice. "We can't do layaway plans."

"I am the Renaissance king," Mort insisted.

The gremlin leaned forward like an astronomer peering through a telescope, but he couldn't see much through his glasses. "I told you last week, and the week before, that someone already bought the sword." He gestured toward his gala of weapons on display. "But I have plenty of others. Why not choose a different one?"

"Because a different one is not Excalibur."

Attracted by the shouting, Robin, Sheyenne, and I approached the stall, ready to help if the situation grew ugly.

"Can I have a sword?" Alvina asked. "A long, pointy one?"

"Not today, honey," Robin said.

The gremlin brightened, sensing new customers. "I am Noxius, purveyor of sharp objects! I have blades of every shape and design, ranging from mortal combat weapons to kitchen cutlery. Talk to me if you see something you like." He leaned forward on his stool, peering down at Alvina. "How about a double-bladed battle-axe for the cute little girl?"

"Oh, so now you can see just fine?" Mort huffed.

"She's cute," explained the gremlin.

Alvina grinned bashfully, showing her fangs.

I butted in. "What seems to be the problem?"

Robin said, "I know several members of the Unnatural Quarter's Better Business Bureau."

"I should file a complaint!" Mort glared at Noxius. I saw that the painted puppies and Elvis figures on his black velvet robes were quite well done. "Excalibur is missing, and I need to find it. The sword belongs to me! I am the proper king!"

The gremlin shrugged. "First come, first served. The dragon lost the weapon from her hoard, fair and square. She just can't resist a bet."

Mort clenched his hands and worked his jaw. His eyes became

very hard. "That damned Alice and her gambling problem." He leaned over the rickety wooden counter, and the gremlin flinched behind his thick glasses. "I'll buy it back. I'll pay you double. Just tell me who has it."

"I told you before, they all look the same to me," said Noxius. "Couldn't read his name."

"Why would a golem want a legendary sword in the first place? What are they going to do with it?"

That immediately piqued my interest. "Excuse me, sir? I'm Dan Chambeaux, zombie private investigator, and this is Robin Deyer, my partner at Chambeaux and Deyer Investigations. Could you tell us more?"

Mortimer Dred gave us a dissecting look. Alvina waved, and the king didn't find her endearing. "I'll do more than explain to you—I'll hire you! If you're a detective, I need you to find Excalibur, the sword of kings. He who holds the blade, rules the land ... and the Real Renaissance Faire. I will pay you greatly if you find it for me."

As our business manager, Sheyenne immediately took charge. Somehow she produced a sheet of paper from her medieval costume. "This is our client engagement form. If you'll fill this out, Mr. Dred, we can begin our investigations right away."

—III—

As a zombie detective it's my passion to solve crimes, like golem murders. I liked keeping innocent monsters safe and helping my BHF McGoo. But we did have to pay the bills.

"We'll find the missing sword," I promised.

"Always take care of the client," Robin said, satisfied, "but our real work is in the name of justice."

"And keeping our business afloat," Sheyenne added. The two didn't always see eye to eye.

"Don't forget about my college fund," Alvina said.

Since Excalibur had been part of the dragon's treasure hoard until it fell into the hands of the gremlin sword vendor, we decided to go ask Alice. The little vampire girl was eager to meet her very first dragon, even though fantastical beasts were commonplace in the Unnatural Quarter.

Outside the main exhibition area, the dragon's tent was impossible to miss, being big enough to hold a giant flying reptile with elbow room to spare. We made our way through the hubbub, passing a fire eater who was being heckled by an actual fire demon, and a juggler who was a multi-armed squid creature wearing colorful medieval clothes.

Before our band of merry friends could get there, however, we encountered an unexpected attraction. Standing on a wooden crate, a golem raised clay fists to the sky and shouted in a hollow voice that belonged at a political rally. "Golems have been downtrodden for too long! We will no longer let our mud be trampled underfoot and tracked all over the house. We were made to serve, but we were not made to suffer. Golems have rights."

"Serve, not suffer," the crowd chanted.

I saw a handful of curious onlookers like ourselves, but most of the crowd consisted of golems dressed like peasants, laborers, beasts of burden. One wore a low-bodice dress with rounded clay breasts scrunched up in a bad imitation of a lusty barmaid.

"Serve, not suffer!" they chanted. Someone bellowed, "Three cheers for Art."

They all yelled, "Art! Art!"

The golem speaker stood straight-backed, strong and confident, his clay smooth and moist. The name "Art" was imprinted on his forehead. "I am on a crusade for my fellow golems. We want better conditions at the Real Renaissance Faire."

"And in the whole Unnatural Quarter," called another golem.

There was something about Art. Though most golems were subservient walking lumps of mud, this one was a *leader*, filled with charisma.

McGoo sidled up to me, dressed in his beat cop uniform, which meant he was on duty. I shuddered to imagine him in a Renaissance costume. "Hey Shamble. Seen anything suspicious?"

"If you don't see something suspicious in the Quarter," I said, "then that in itself is suspicious."

He tipped his cap toward the golem firebrand still shouting from his soapbox. "Who's that?"

"A rabble-rouser," I said.

"A crusader for justice," Robin interjected.

"That's what I meant to say," I corrected myself. "His name is Art."

McGoo nodded with mock seriousness. "You could frame him and hang him on the wall." When I responded with a blank look, he added, "Then he'd really be *art*." McGoo waited for me, or anyone, to laugh. He was about to explain the cleverness of his joke when fortunately we were interrupted by several huge ogre guards bent on violence.

"Break it up! Break it up!" The ogres' voices sounded like rocks rattling out of a gravel truck. They carried thick spiked clubs.

The golem workers scattered, knowing they weren't supposed to be on a coffee or crusading break. The burly ogres elbowed people aside as they pushed their way toward the defiant Art, swinging their clubs.

One of the smaller golems, obviously a convert to Art's cause, threw himself in front of the ogres, and they squashed him, bending his body and smooshing his shoulder and arm as they knocked him with a club. The damaged lump of clay twitched and crawled away.

McGoo charged in. "Hey, I'm law enforcement here. I'm a peace officer."

"We're chaos officers," said the nearest ogre. "Private contractors."

Art sprang from his soapbox and ducked down as he melted into the milling crowd. He ran a palm over his forehead to smear out the letters of his name, leaving only a blank gray patch as he disappeared.

The ogres—generally about as bright as golems—were easily confused.

After the impromptu crowd dispersed and the ogres strutted

in circles holding up their heavy clubs in search of something to do, I nudged Alvina along. "I better get you away from this."

Robin's nostrils flared, and she flashed a venomous glance at the ogre guards. "We were all a witness to that!"

While McGoo went to have stern words with the over-enthusiastic ogres, I hurried my companions toward the big tent on the outskirts. "We're off to see the dragon."

—IV—

Two more security ogres stood outside the dragon's tent, though I couldn't understand why an enormous creature like Alice would need bodyguards.

"To keep the paparazzi away," said one of the ogres.

"And autograph hounds," said the other. "Now, piss off."

Robin was incensed, but I tended to be calmer, more relaxed. After coming back from the dead, I found it easier not to be bothered by little things. I stepped forward. "We've been hired by King Mortimer Dred to investigate a missing sword that recently belonged to Alice. We're here to interview her."

Alvina piped up, "It's an important part of the case."

Sheyenne produced a copy of the client engagement contract, which enlisted our services for locating the sword called Excalibur, and thrust it in front of the ogres. "See, here's proof." They squinted, tugged on their drooping fat lips, and pondered. Ogres were too embarrassed to admit they couldn't read, so they let us pass.

Reptiles had a certain smell about them, and even though my senses were dulled thanks to the embalming process, I could instantly tell that some giant lizard lived within the tent. Of course, I could *see* the huge dragon, which was my second clue. Alvina pinched her fingers around her nose.

"Oh, visitors!" boomed the dragon in a lilting female voice. "I'm on a break between performances." Alice leaned forward with a gigantic scaly head, slitted eyes the size of basketballs, and fangs that would have made a great white shark pee in the water.

Her green and gold scales were like garbage-can lids. "Did you come to interview me? King Dred likes the publicity, but he never sends the press anymore." She snorted. "Once, I ate a reporter who asked an embarrassing question. Is this a softball interview?"

Alice settled herself on top of a pile of treasure—gold coins, chains, chests of jewels, battered suits of armor, swords with gem-inlaid hilts. The wealth I saw was enough for a comfortable retirement account, even for a long-lived dragon, but the amount did look a little disappointing. When Alice shifted her position, coins, chains, and gilded blades rattled beneath her. "Is this my good side?" She turned a head the size of a rowboat.

"We're here to talk to you about a sword, ma'am," I said, using my best professional P.I. voice. "The Renaissance king hired us to find Excalibur."

Alice grumbled. "Excalibur, Excalibur! I have plenty of treasure, and all anybody wants to talk about is Excalibur."

"Isn't the sword famous?" I asked. "From a movie, or something?"

Alice blinked her huge eyes. "You don't know the story of Excalibur?" Sheyenne and Robin both looked at me in surprise.

Alvina sighed. "Excalibur was the sword of King Arthur. Only the rightful king can draw it from the stone." The little vampire girl was constantly getting her information from the internet, so she was better informed than I.

"That must be why King Dred wants it," Robin said. "It legitimizes his rule over the Real Renaissance Faire."

"Isn't it all just fun and games?" Sheyenne asked. "Costumes and jousting acts? It's not a real legendary sword."

"After the Big Uneasy, who knows what's real anymore?" I asked. "If dragons can be real, then Excalibur can be real." I turned back to Alice. "So, can you tell us what happened to the sword?" I stepped closer, trying to be congenial. I could smell the dragon's breath.

"Excalibur was part of my hoard. So many riches! Once, I needed seven warehouses just to keep my treasure, but, alas, much of it is gone now, dwindled away." She raised her head and snorted one small smoke ring. "This losing streak is bound to end soon, though! I'll win it all back. I know I will." She flapped her giant wings, rattling the tent fabric overhead, then settled back onto the mound of gold and jewels.

Robin thought she understood. "You gambled away your treasure?"

"And Excalibur?" I added.

"I still have some riches." The dragon sounded defensive. "A big win is right around the corner. I know it. Dragons can sense these things."

Sheyenne drifted close and whispered in my ear. "The dragon has a gambling problem."

Dragons also had extremely acute hearing, as I should have remembered from *The Hobbit*. "Yes, I have a gambling problem—I admit it! It's the thrill, the risk ... and the winning." She clacked shut her fanged jaws. "Texas Hold 'em is my preference, though it's hard to hold the cards with big claws like these."

Alice raised a huge scaled hand. "I lost a chest of gold and Excalibur two weeks ago in a big game. That gremlin is a good player! Noxius would win a few hands, then I'd win, then he'd win a few more. He'd egg me on until I bet the whole pot." The dragon snorted smoke, flapped her wings, and tried to settle down. "I don't know how he can even see the cards with glasses that thick, but I kept raising the bet, because I *knew* I was about to start a winning streak!" Her slitted eyes had a disturbing obsession. "I'll win it back—I'll win it all back."

"You need help, Alice," Sheyenne said in a sincere voice. "It's an addiction. Gambling makes you lose everything."

The dragon hung her head and her groan of sorrow was a rumble deep in her throat. "I know ..." Then she perked up. "Would you like to play a round now? Who's got a deck of cards? I could use the practice!"

"Sorry, ma'am, I'm on the job," I said. "We need to find Excalibur."

"Talk with Noxius. He put it up for sale in his sword vending stand."

"He did. Sold it to a golem, but we don't know which one."

"Sure you don't want to play a game? Not even one?" Alice whined. "Low stakes, I promise! A buck a round. I'll bet on anything." She sounded desperate.

Sheyenne looked concerned. "I think the Unnatural Quarter chapter of Gamblers Anonymous accepts legendary creatures."

The dragon's need was so great she actually trembled. "It's a terrible disease." She closed her basketball-sized eyes. "Go away. I need to rest before my next performance."

Out of courtesy, we hurried out of the tent.

—V—

Rettop the Cavewight had hands like lawn rakes covered with thick mud. A big grin crossed his pale, sallow face. Sitting on a stone bench next to a wheelbarrow of fresh clay, he whistled as he worked. He pumped his potter's wheel with his feet and slapped on more mud, building up a mound that he shaped into a circular vase. His hands and fingers were so large he could manipulate a lot of mud at a time.

Werewolves, ghouls, and vampires watched him with interest as he shaped the sides, pulled up a fluted oblong container, then poked his fingers down inside to make it hollow, expanding the waist. Next to his potter's wheel sat a table filled with his wares, pots, vases, and ashtrays.

"Can you make canopic jars?" asked a curious mummy.

"One of my specialties," said Rettop. "I take commissions."

Alvina had paused to look at a crudely fashioned flowerpot. She looked up at me with those big eyes. "I'm thinking of getting a present for you and McGoo. Father's Day is coming up. How about an ashtray?" She picked up a lumpy object that looked like a project I had made in third grade.

If my heart was still beating, it would have been filled with joy. "That's beautiful."

"I'll take you shopping separately, honey," Sheyenne said. "We'll make it a surprise for both daddies."

With a loud muttering the crowd parted, and a damaged golem lurched forward, twisted and misshapen. "Rettop! Need repairs! Now!" The deformed golem could barely move, trying to get its clay legs to work. I realized it was the golem smashed by the security ogres at Art's rally. His name was Tony, according to his forehead.

The Cavewight clucked his pale tongue against crooked, brown teeth. "What a shame! That's why King Dred keeps me around. Step right up." He helped the golem to his potter's wheel and let out a long sigh. "I just want to make vases and pots, but I spend half my time repairing damaged golems." He clucked his tongue against his teeth again. "Let me see what I can do."

With spatulate hands, the Cavewight seized the golem's chest and shoulders, then worked like a chiropractor, twisting him, straightening him. The clay was pliable enough that Tony eventually straightened. He took palmfuls of fresh clay, using it on the golem instead of his pots. "Lucky you got here in time. If the damage had been more severe, your animation spell might have been broken." He slathered Tony's skin, bulked up his back, added to his biceps, even finished with a flourish of a cleft in the golem's chin. "There, good as new!"

"About those canopic jars?" said the mummy, his rattling dry voice tinged with impatience.

Then, not far away, someone screamed a high terrified shriek, which was always a good way to get attention.

As a ghost, Sheyenne could move faster than any of us, and she streaked away, waving for us to follow. Robin and Alvina bolted, and I shambled as quickly as I could, getting my body warmed up. Being a detective, I was great at solving mysteries, but chase scenes and action-packed brawls weren't my specialty.

A crowd had gathered by the dumpster bins behind Ye Olde Blood Bar. McGoo was already there, trying to hold off the crowds. A banshee barmaid with big hips and a layered skirt screamed and screamed, breaking nearby windows and nearly deafening us all. Sheyenne hovered in the air, her translucent form sparkling with intense anger. McGoo was red-faced.

Sprawled on the ground in front of the dumpsters were two more dead golems, side-by-side, their arms at odd angles and their chests split open, the clay pried apart and leaving them hollow: Don and Jim, the golems we had met earlier. Don still wore his yellow dishwashing gloves.

McGoo bent down beside the eviscerated clay figures. "It's too late."

"Why would anyone want to kill golems?" Robin asked. "And why open them up like that?"

More clay figures had gathered around, still riled up from Art's crusade. "Serve, not suffer," one grumbled. I heard the same words muttered among the others.

"Something bad is happening here, McGoo," I said. "Somebody's cracking open golems, like shucking oysters and hoping to find a pearl."

I could tell my best human friend had had enough. He bellowed, loud and clear, "Four golem murders in two weeks! This is a crime scene. This entire Renaissance Faire is a crime scene!" He pulled out his radio and called to request backup—all of it. "By order of the Unnatural Quarter Police Department, I declare this Faire closed. All the public must leave immediately in a calm and orderly fashion."

Security ogres lumbered in to see what the fuss was all about. "Knock some heads!"

"No, no, just a peaceful evacuation," Robin insisted. The ogres looked disappointed.

McGoo said, "Call King Dred. I want all Faire employees together on the jousting ground. I need to interrogate everyone." Sighing, he looked at me. "This is going to be a long day."

—VI—

Squad cars arrived before the Faire workers organized themselves on the jousting field. The security ogres got into several brawls (with each other, since they'd been given orders not to harm the paying customers), and eventually all of the patrons made their way to the overflow parking lot, creating a huge traffic jam as they headed back to the Unnatural Quarter.

King Mortimer Dred stood on the reviewing stand as if this entire meeting had been his idea. McGoo and I sorted the Faire workers by species so we could interrogate them better. Robin made sure that every accused monster was properly read its rights. Sheyenne had gotten a treat for Alvina, roasted frogs on a stick, because the little girl was hungry.

Trolls, mummies, and werewolves in blacksmith aprons gathered around, as well as Noxius the gremlin and Rettop the Cavewight. The vampire and skeleton jousters stood shoulder-to-shoulder, and I realized that they were actually close friends, not mortal enemies as the audience had thought. Even Alice the dragon thundered in, landing not far from King Dred's reviewing stand. Twenty or so golems crowded together, identical except for their various Renaissance costumes.

McGoo strutted in front of the reviewing stand. "Now that you're all here, I've got—"

"I'll take it from here," Mort boomed from the platform above. When he lifted his hands, his black velvet sleeves fell down to his elbows again. Thunder sounded across the sky, and dark clouds began to form. "I am King Mortimer Dred, your boss." He strode down from the reviewing stand and marched onto the field, heading straight for the gathered golems.

McGoo and I hurried after him, trying to regain control of the situation. "What are you doing, sir?" I asked.

"We have this handled," McGoo said.

King Dred ignored us. As he walked past the nearsighted gremlin, he grabbed the furry creature by his scrawny neck and dragged him to stand in front of the golems. "Now that you're all here in one place, I can get this done in a far more efficient manner. I need Excalibur. I know one of you golems bought it. I know one of you is hiding it." The king glowered, and his eyes crackled with sparks.

I looked at the smooth clay golems and wondered where in the world they could manage to hide something as large as a sword.

"I demand to know which one of you has Excalibur!"

After a long, petrified silence, one golem pushed forward from the back. He seemed taller than the others, exuding power. It was Art, the leader of the golems' crusade. "And I demand justice for all golems!" he said. "We will serve, but not suffer."

The wizard king seemed shocked and intimidated. "You demand nothing! Where is my sword?"

"The sword belongs to the rightful king," Art said.

"Or it belongs in my treasure hoard," the dragon piped up, "until I lost it in a poker game."

"Lost it fair and square," chirped Noxius.

"I am the king of the Real Renaissance Faire. I, Mortimer Dred, must draw the sword from the stone as was foretold in the legend."

Without flinching, Art placed a gray fist against his soft clay chest. "What if the sword is inside the stone already?"

I suddenly figured out the only place a golem could hide something as large as a sword, and I knew that Mort Dred understood it as well. "He was looking for the sword!" I said to McGoo, who clearly hadn't yet received the same revelation. Now the murders all made sense. "Excalibur! Art has it."

Like a flasher about to tear open his trench coat, Art plunged his clay fingers down the soft clay of his chest as if pulling a zipper, then he stretched his clay torso apart, opening himself up to expose a golden hilt and the polished steel of a sword blade that ran all the way down inside his back. Excalibur! The legendary blade hidden inside the soft stone body.

"I have Excalibur," Art declared. "I *am* Excalibur! The sword is in the stone."

The Cavewight cackled. "It fit perfectly. I thought it was clever." He held up his splayed hands and waggled his long fingers. "Sealed it right in there for safe keeping."

"It's mine!" Mort lunged forward to grab the golden hilt that protruded from Art's open chest. "Mine!" He pulled at the sword, struggling to draw Excalibur out of the golem's body.

The other golems shifted angrily, getting riled up. The Renaissance Faire employees watched, and even the dragon Alice peered down as Mort yanked, tugged, dug his feet in the ground and pulled, but Art held the sword inside him. Mort strained to wrench the legendary blade free, but it wouldn't budge.

Finally, red-faced, weak-kneed, and exhausted, he staggered back. His golden crown hung askew on his head.

With perfect timing, Sheyenne appeared in front of him, holding a piece of paper. "You engaged our services to locate the sword Excalibur, Mr. Dred. There it is! Our work is now complete, and here's our invoice. Payment is due upon receipt."

Mort flew into a rage. His curly, golden hair crackled, and his crown popped off his head like a champagne cork as his body filled with sorcerous energy. "I am King Mort Dred, and I am also a great wizard. I call upon the powers of dark magic to give me the sword that is my due. I need Excalibur!" He raised his hands, and lightning crackled from his fingertips. Angry black thunderheads gathered. The ground began to shake.

Art stood fearless with Excalibur still protruding from his open chest. He wrapped a clay hand around its hilt. "I do not have a heart of clay. I have the heart of a lion! I should be king."

"I will destroy all of you," Mort screamed, and thunder cracked around him for emphasis. "I will shatter every single golem and take the sword from the rubble of your bodies." He lurched back to summon a huge blast of terrible energy.

Knowing what I had to do, I didn't hesitate. I shambled forward, raised my voice. "You look extremely powerful, King Dred. I bet a hundred dollars that no one can stop you."

Mort let out a maniacal laugh. "Of course not—"

Then a huge reptilian foot stomped down on his head, a dragon's claw that smashed with all the weight of an enormous monster. The blow crushed the Renaissance king into a puddle of bones and flesh.

Alice let out a roar, and her slitted eyes were wide and bright with delight. "I'll take that bet!" she said. "Did I win?"

—VII—

Afterward, McGoo and I wrapped up the case while Robin wrote notes on her yellow legal pad for the final summary. Sheyenne took Alvina to get another sugary treat, while we arranged a petty-cash invoice to pay back the hundred-dollar bet.

McGoo scrutinized the red stain and the crumpled black velvet robes. The painted puppies looked extra sad now. "We know Mort Dred was the murderer, tearing open golems in search of the sword hidden inside." He wiped his shoe on the grassy ground to get rid of goop he had inadvertently stepped in. "Nothing left to arrest, though."

"Case solved," I said. "My two favorite words in the world."

"I like Payment Complete," Sheyenne said, leading Alvina back from a vendor with a frozen blood-pop. "Maybe we can get the Renaissance Faire treasurer to pay our bill?"

Robin shook her head. "Mr. Dred engaged us as a personal matter, not as a corporate contract with the Faire itself."

Moving proudly among his fellow golems, Art met each one, read their names aloud from their foreheads. The hilt of Excalibur still protruded from his chest like a badge of honor. He had also retrieved the golden crown worn by King Dred, and now he placed it on his own head, the king of the golems and possibly king of the Real Renaissance Faire.

Art said, "Serve, but not suffer. We must have rights for all golems."

Robin walked among them, listening to their grievances. "We can file a formal motion, and I'll approach the proper governing bodies. I will help ensure that you have good working conditions and proper maintenance."

"I'll help with the maintenance," said Rettop. The Cavewight was busy making commemorative clay medallions to sell to everyone present at the event.

"And regular mud baths!" said the golem Tony. Robin dutifully wrote it down.

Alice flew overhead, thrilled now. Without her knowledge, King Dred had claimed the dragon's entire treasure hoard as collateral, which he leveraged to finance the Real Renaissance Faire. Now that Dred had been properly squashed, Alice found that she now owned the entire operation. She was so ecstatic she did barrel rolls and loop-the-loops in the air.

"She still needs counseling for that gambling problem," Sheyenne said, "or she'll lose it all again."

Art strode up. "I will be her business advisor. Instead of the Real Renaissance Faire, we will call this the *Fair* Renaissance Faire, so that all can feel good about themselves when they attend."

The armored vampire knight and the skeleton knight joined each other on the jousting field, practicing with their swords. The dragon crashed down in front of them, and the two costumed knights ran forward to challenge her in a mock battle. With a beat of her wings, Alice knocked them both flat, but the unnatural knights sprang to their feet and ran into the melee, all in good fun.

"I still want a dragon," Alvina said.

"Maybe when you're older, honey," Sheyenne said.

"You could have one at McGoo's apartment for the nights you stay with him," I suggested.

He glared at me. "Let's start you out with a salamander first."

When my writing career was just getting established, I had an annual tradition of spending the holidays with a group of writer friends up in Eugene, Oregon. I lived in the San Francisco Bay Area, where I worked as a technical writer for a large research laboratory—in other words, I had a "real job"—but I very much wanted to be a full-time writer and worked diligently at my stories and novels.

Each year I drove up Interstate 5 along the spine of California to Oregon, sometimes in questionable mid-December weather, but I didn't want to miss my holiday gathering. One year I even took my fiancée Rebecca Moesta with me.

One of the Eugene locals would act as the host, and we'd get together the day before Christmas for conversation and cooking. Some people baked cookies or other desserts; I always made my famous lasagna. (Yes, turkey or ham might be more traditional, but we were a group who broke with traditions—we were writers, after all—and formed our own traditions.)

After the late afternoon feast, we passed out gifts. In keeping with being starving writers, no gift could cost more than a dollar, which forced us to do some imaginative shopping.

After the gift giving, we sat around the fireplace for the highlight of the evening—the true sharing of gifts among writers. We had each written a new story specially for the occasion, and we went around in a circle, reading our stories aloud. Some were heartwarming, some were scary, some magical, some imaginative, some haunting. Each writer had their own particular spin on the holiday season.

We were all new writers, learning our craft and learning the business. We poured our hearts and our energies into these stories.

In the years since, members of that group have become international bestselling authors, New York Times bestselling authors, winners or nominees of almost every award in numerous genres, from the Writers of the Future Award, to the Hugo, Nebula, World Fantasy, Philip K. Dick, Bram Stoker, Shamus, Edgar, Pushcart, Endeavor, Sidewise, Scribe, Locus, Mythopoeic Society, Romantic Times Reviewers' Choice, and Theodore Sturgeon Awards (and probably many others). Some have become publishers themselves, or movie producers, record producers, game designers.

Maybe there was magic in those Christmas Eves after all.

This was a novelette I wrote for that gathering, one of my most heartfelt stories. It goes beyond the Christmas spirit to the core of what it means to be a writer.

THE GHOST OF CHRISTMAS ALWAYS

"After she died I dreamed of her every night for many months, sometimes as a spirit, sometimes as a living creature, never with any of the bitterness of my real sorrow, but always with a kind of quiet happiness, which became so pleasant to me that I never lay down at night without a hope of the vision coming back ... And so it did."

— CHARLES DICKENS, IN A LETTER TO THE
MOTHER OF MARY HOGARTH, 1842

STAVE I

Mary was dead, to begin with. And yet each Christmas Eve her ghost came to haunt Charles Dickens. He waited the year round for the one night he could see her again, if only for a brief time.

Dickens gripped the arms of his chair, then let his eyes fall half-closed. Across from him, aromatic smoke came from a fire in the sitting room hearth. On the mantelpiece sat a scrolled ivory-and-gold clock with slim hands reaching toward midnight, when Mary would come. Wind rattled the window panes, pushing winter cold into the great house on Devonshire Terrace. The

Dickenses had added mahogany doors, marble mantels, and carpets to their new home—such extravagance was expected from the author of *Nicholas Nickleby*, *Oliver Twist*, and, of course, *The Pickwick Papers*.

But on the silent night before Christmas, the house felt like a deserted stage in the theater, filled with props and costumes but no actors. Mary had never lived here with them. His young sister-in-law had died before the unparalleled success swept over Dickens's life.

He stood up from the chair, brushed at his robe, and walked to the mantel. Dickens had urged the four children, his wife Kate, and the maid to retire early this night. None of them would suspect why he wanted them fast asleep. Beside the clock stood Mary's portrait, painted by Phiz, the artist who illustrated so many of Dickens's installments. After Mary's death had devastated him, Dickens begged Phiz to do the portrait from memory, as a special favor. Now Dickens touched the lines of her face, the soft eyes gazing at something unseen but wondrous, the curves of her dark hair. Sweet Mary Hogarth, the delightful sister of his moody and shallow-minded wife. Kate would be snoring upstairs, grossly pregnant with their fifth child. She would carry out the same chores on Christmas day as she did every day. She had no broader imagination, doing only what she felt her wifely obligations demanded. Not like young Mary, who was always so bright, so fascinated.... "Can't you gaze at that portrait any time, Charles Dickens? I have only a short while here with you."

Dickens turned, smiling. He felt a rush of happiness. Mary Hogarth stood there, spectral and unchanged since her death six years before. She wore a shimmering white gown that reflected a light not from the fireplace and blew in a breeze that Dickens himself could not feel. "I was waiting for you," he said.

"Just as I wait for this one night when I'm allowed to see you again." She took a step forward but did not touch him. She made no sound as she moved. "This year I have a present for you, Charles, a gift I hope you will treasure as much as I treasure giving it to you."

He could not think of what to say. He, Charles Dickens, who spoke in front of great audiences, who played in the theater, who read his own sketches aloud to crowds from the streets, found himself unable to utter a simple sentence to the wavering image of a sixteen-year-old girl. He finally said, "Merely seeing you again is enough to make me glad for the next twelve months." Mary smiled and, keeping her gaze on his, reached forward to touch the clock. "But this is better. I give you Time."

"Time?" he asked, not comprehending but feeling his heart filled with wonder. "I do need more of it, with all my commitments."

"No," she said with a lilt in her voice that reminded him of the times that they laughed, Charles and Kate and Mary, when they went on outings to the theater. "I give you *your* time, Charles. Your past, your present, and what is yet to come."

Before he could say more, Mary turned the hour hand backward from midnight in a full circle until it reached eleven o'clock. As the hand touched the top of the dial, the chimes rang out. Mary extended her fingers to him. "Take my hand, Charles. Let me show you."

Eagerly he wrapped his fingers around her cold flesh, insubstantial but as strong and insistent as the wind. Mary led him to the window and drew back the curtains. The distant lights of London sprawled out below, making him think of the crowded streets, tall buildings leaning out over alleys, small fires, and candlelit windows.

"Step with me into the past," she said.

Fighting back the tremors of fear in his voice, Dickens asked, "Long past?"

"No. Your past." And she stepped partway through the window, through the sash as if it were no more than a bit of fog.

"Wait!" he cried, "I am mortal! I cannot pass through brick and stone and glass."

"Bear but a touch of my hand, Charles." As Mary said this, she gave a tug.

Dickens walked forward clad only in slippers and dressing

gown, blinking as he stepped through and out into a clear winter night. But he felt no cold, no wind, only astonishment, for he found himself many miles from his home on Devonshire Terrace.

STAVE II

Though it was dark, Dickens could make out the three-storey house before him, with glowing orange lights in several of the windows. By day he would be able to see the nearby Kentish countryside, Chatham, and the Medway Valley.

"Good Heaven!" Dickens cried, "I was a boy here! My father worked in the naval dockyard."

Mary just smiled at him and raised her hand. Dickens found that they floated off the ground, rising along the terraces and shingles, to one of the upstairs windows where a single light still burned.

"That was my room!" Dickens said, keeping his voice to a whisper.

"And here is someone you'll like to see, no doubt."

They pressed their faces close to the window, and Dickens noted that, though the winter air must be very cold, neither his breath nor Mary's left any frost upon the window.

Inside the room he saw a plump woman with grayish-brown hair tied neatly behind her head. She sat in a chair pulled near to a pair of beds in which lay a boy and a girl. Both children had eyes wide and mouths slack with rapt fascination and terror. The woman leaned forward to talk; her eyes squinted, and her face contorted as she spoke, waving her hands.

"Why it's old Mary Weller, our maid! Bless her heart—Mary Weller alive again!"

The maid lurched out in the middle of her story, splaying her fingers like claws.

Both children squirmed backward in their beds, defending themselves with nervous giggling.

Dickens, delighted, turned to the spirit beside him. "She used to tell us horrible stories about Captain Murderer! And how he'd indulge his taste in wives by killing them off and baking them into pies! Ugh—my sister Fanny and I used to lie awake shivering in terror every time she told us one of those stories. But I loved them. I used to make up my own."

Mary patted him with her cold hand. "You've been a writer since the time you were a little boy. Come with me, around the corner." They descended to the ground again, but when they turned the corner, Dickens found that they had reached an alley far distant from the old house. The light had changed to a gray wintry afternoon. People crowded the street, women wrapped in dark clothes tugging children alongside them on the frozen mud. Thawed patches of slush surrounded steaming piles of fresh horse manure. Dogs ran about, harrying burly men who carried packages and crates. Off to one side a man hauled a narrow pauper's coffin on his back, passing unnoticed through the streets. Signboards protruded out over doors proclaiming lodging houses, barbers, poulterers, a tripe shop, a sausage-maker.

"This is the Strand!" Dickens said, nearly letting go of Mary's hand in his excitement. "I got lost here one day when I was a boy."

"In fact, there you are right now." Mary indicated a small child gawking at the crowds, stumbling along with wonder-filled eyes. The boy looked as if he had been crying, but the tears dried to streaks in the cold air. "I had a shilling and fourpence in my pocket," Dickens said. "My godfather gave it to me. I knew I would be rescued somehow. And I was very hungry." They followed the boy, observing yet unseen by the pedestrians. Little Charles Dickens walked along, dressed in a warm jacket, bumping into unshaven men who ignored him. He stared from window to window in food shops, shuffling his feet, looking around. He kept walking. Finally, he stopped in front of a pile of cooked sausages in a window. A paper sign in front read "Small Germans, a Penny." The boy stared at the sausages, shivering. He licked his lips. He took a deep breath, mustering courage, and strode in. The shopkeeper squinted at him with an amused grin, but the boy seemed confident now that he knew what to ask for.

"If you please, would you sell me one of those sausages?" His voice sounded tiny as Dickens listened. The boy reached into his pocket and took out a single penny. The shopkeeper used his fingers to pick up one of the sausages from the back of the pile and plucked the penny from the boy's hand at the exact moment he surrendered the sausage. Charles Dickens felt his cheeks flushing with the delight of the memory. "The sausage wasn't very warm," he told Mary, "but it was one of the most delicious things ever to pass my lips. Of course, part of it was that I had bought it myself."

The boy wandered the streets again, in and out of yards and little squares, chased off by cooks he gawked at, bullied by a gang of young toughs who wanted the rest of the money in his pockets. The boy broke into a run, pushing through the crowds, splashing in the slush, until he lost the boys in a dark alley lined with dim counting houses where misers changed their gold.

The boy stood in the growing dark, looking unspeakably forlorn.

"Can we not help him?" Dickens said.

Mary shook her head. "No, Charles, we are here only to observe. You pity this boy now, but would you have traded that single day in your life for anything you can imagine?"

"No, never. It astonishes me even now to think of how much I used from that day in *Oliver Twist*, and in *Nicholas Nickleby*, and in half a dozen of my sketches for the periodicals."

"And you will continue to find ways to use it. You're a writer, Charles, heart and soul. Everything you experience is fodder for the tales that delight so many people."

As Mary spoke, Dickens heard a loud cough and saw a middle-aged man come up to the wretched boy and ask what was wrong. The man's clothes were drab and worn, but the brass buttons on his coat had been polished with care.

"That watchman took me home," Dickens said in a whisper. "I remember his cough, how he wheezed all the way. I was afraid I was going to catch the plague from him."

Mary strolled ahead, turning her back on the departing boy

and the coughing watchman. "Why don't you come around the corner with me? We'll pass another decade."

Still astounded, Dickens followed her as the scene once again changed. He found himself in a dark court, narrow but clean. Clouds the color of ice on a deep pond covered the sky. In front of a dark office, a young man strode by with a polished walking stick. He looked like a twenty-year-old dandy, with gleaming shoes, black waistcoat, and vest. His gray felt trousers were new and unwrinkled, his green cravat impeccably tied. The brim of a brushed top hat shaded his face. The young man moved with a nervous manner as he stopped in front of the dark office—and then Dickens recognized the mail slot and the stenciled letters above it that read EDITOR'S BOX.

"This is Fleet Street! That's me, posting my very first contribution for the *Monthly Magazine.*" The young man pulled out a long envelope and, trying to appear nonchalant, slipped it into the black hole of the mail slot before striding away. He rapped his walking stick on the cobblestones, swaggering but hurrying, as if afraid to be caught at what he had done.

"I paid half a crown for the next issue of that magazine, and there it was in print! One of my sketches, 'A Dinner at Poplar Walk,' I think it was. I remember how it felt to see my words in print for the very first time."

Mary's voice took on a tone of chiding. "And you didn't even receive payment for the piece."

Dickens laughed. "What did it matter then? I was speaking to a whole world of readers! People were reading what I had written. I walked up and down Westminster Hall for half an hour. My eyes could hardly see, I was so excited!"

"Yet now you grow angry at anyone who prints even a bit of your correspondence without offering you royalties."

Dickens stiffened. "They make enormous amounts of money off me just by placing my name on their masthead! Pirates have made me lose thousands of pounds by flaunting the copyright law."

She had touched a sore spot, but he did not want to ruin their short time together by arguing. He softened his voice to change the subject. "These memories are delightful, Mary. Show me more!"

Her expression remained solemn. "Do not thank me until you have seen them all. Some of them may not be so precious, though they are as important."

Dickens felt a chill from inside. "What do you mean?" His tone spoke plainly that he did not want to hear the answer.

"Our time grows short," she said. "Quick! You must see one last memory of your past."

As she led him down the street, the sky darkened into night, growing blacker with each step they took. Greenish-white glows from gas street lights made the scene shift with a harsh mixture of glares and shadows. As Mary hurried him along, Dickens saw the buildings again, recognizing the brick facade, the wrought iron fence, the decorative lintels and arches of Mecklenburgh Square.

As they approached, Dickens saw a tall man open the wrought iron gate in front of a three-storey brick home. He was accompanied by two women, one larger and hanging on the man's arm, the other thin and delicate with dark hair pinned up under a bonnet. The man gestured for them both to precede him through the gate, then caught up with them under the rounded arch of the doorway. They all seemed to be laughing and enjoying themselves.

Dickens stood trembling, refusing to go another step. Mary pulled at him, but he closed his eyes. "No, Mary! Oh no, no!"

But she was insistent and drew him stumbling toward the door. "Was I not always a good friend to you, Charles? Without this visit, you cannot hope to receive everything I bring to you."

She led him through the half-open door into the rented home where young Charles Dickens lived with his new wife Kate and her sixteen-year-old sister Mary.

"We had just gone to the theater, do you remember?" Mary said in a distant voice, as if she barely remembered herself. "It was late when we got home, about one o'clock in the morning. I had gone up to bed—"

"Stop!" he said. He had spent years with every detail of that evening pounding in his head, haunting his nightmares. There, in front of him, in the old house he and Kate and the children had left only a short time ago, he watched a younger, carefree version of himself removing his coat and handing it to the maid. He set his walking stick against the rail of the stairs, tossed his top hat behind him in a cocky gesture to hit the hat rack, but of course he missed and was just bending over to pick it up when he heard a choking cry from upstairs. Mary's voice.

It echoed in his ears, in his memory.

Sweating and shivering at the same time, Dickens watched himself, running up the steep staircase, grabbing the rail and launching himself upward with every step. "Mary!" his younger self cried in concerned surprise.

Watching the scene unfold again, the elder Dickens could not stop himself from shouting the same as he dashed up to the second-floor bedrooms. His footfalls made no sound on the steps.

Just inside the door of her room, Mary lay on the floor gasping, begging for help. Young Dickens sent for a doctor. His face was drawn and horrified. As he watched from his invisible vantage, the elder Dickens shook his head. "The doctor will not be able to do anything. They said you had a diseased heart, Mary. And now I have a broken one, all over again."

He turned to the spectral form of Mary, who watched without emotion the image of herself writhing on the floor. Young Dickens and Kate helped her onto the bed. She would die there the following day.

"This scene has haunted me more than any other," Dickens said. "Every letter I wrote for a year bore a black border in remembrance of you." He sighed, but it came out more like a moan. "When I was writing *The Old Curiosity Shop* and the time came when Little Nell had to die, I trembled for days beforehand, recalling your death. It cast the most horrible shadow upon me, and it was all I could do to keep moving at all."

Mary sighed, and he felt her spectral hand squeeze his. "Sometimes you are too sentimental, Charles."

Dickens saw that time had changed again. Mary Hogarth lay on her bed, but sunlight streamed through the windows, and the younger Charles Dickens held her in his arms, pulling the bedclothes over to keep her warm. He stroked her tangled hair ... and felt her die in his arms.

Dickens watched himself take her cooling hand between his palms and slip one of the rings off her finger. "I will wear this ring of yours until the day I might join you," he said.

Dickens the observer stared at the ring on his own finger, still there after six years. To crush away the tears he rubbed his knuckles against his eyes. His head rang from the memory. Then the ringing sound became the chiming of the clock, and he and Mary's ghost returned to the warm sitting room in Devonshire Terrace. After all this time and all the years observed, the hour of midnight was just striking.

STAVE III

Dickens drew a deep breath to drive back all the memories he had thought tucked away safe and sound. He warmed his hands over the fire in the sitting room, but his heart seemed to regulate its own warmth and chill. Exhausted, he shuffled back to his chair, but before he could turn round and sink into the cushions, before the clock finished striking the hour of twelve, Mary stopped him.

"We have no time to rest, Charles. This is a busy night for both of us."

He blinked at her, but now the delight of his reunion with Mary had been blunted by watching her death all over again. "I can't bear anymore of my memories just now. I'm afraid of what else you might dredge from the mud of my past."

He squeezed his eyes shut and tried not to think of all the things he did not want to see again, all the black shadows of his younger life. But Mary's voice grew lighter.

"Not your past, Charles. Now we will go and see who you are

right now. Until the clock strikes one, let us observe your present."

This baffled him, and he made sure to let her see it on his face. "What do you mean? I know who I am."

"Are you quite certain?"

"How can I not?"

In answer, Mary narrowed her eyes and looked at him with a penetrating gaze that made her seem centuries older than her sixteen-year-old form suggested.

"All right then, Spirit," he said submissively. "Conduct me where you will."

Mary went to the door of the sitting room and beckoned him. "Shall we go upstairs, then."

The hall was dim and orange, lit by candles Kate had left burning for him after she went to bed. The flickering light seemed to set off sparks from Mary's flowing white dress.

As they went up the stairs, Dickens felt light on his feet, and he wondered if he was really moving himself. When the fourth stair failed to creak under his step, he knew that this would be another shadow-show of visions, a theater performance Mary had staged for him.

She turned down the upstairs hall and opened the door to the wide Master Bedroom. By the sunlight in the window Dickens saw it was morning again, that very morning. Kate sat back in a rocking chair, working on another embroidered pillowcase; their maid Anne had drawn the pattern for it, as usual. Draped along the scrolled arm of the rocker hung limp bundles of bright threads. Kate shifted and tried to be comfortable, but her pregnancy made her look awkward no matter what she did. Her eyes, her cheeks, everything about her looked bloated, especially in contrast to the shining spirit of her sister. Kate's face looked like a poor reproduction of Mary's carved out of a potato.

Three of the four children sat in the room with her, little Katey and Mamie peered at a book showing sketches of knights in shining armor; baby Walter lay on the bed making sounds like the water draining out of a wash basin.

"Kate sits here all day and does nothing," Dickens said. "Not at all like you, Mary. She takes no interest in my activities—"

Mary cut him off abruptly. "What would you have her do? The baby is due in less than a month. She watches the children, makes certain they refrain from bothering you, though many times they bother her to no end. Do you even notice?"

Interrupting her, the door burst open and five-year-old Charley ran in with tears brimming in his eyes. The boy made hiccupping noises and brushed past Dickens, missing him by no more than an inch, but he did not even see his father. In his small hand he held a little white note and a pincushion.

Kate looked up from her embroidery, saw the note, and allowed a brief and surprising expression of anger to flicker behind her eyes. Dickens remembered writing the note himself and placing it on Charley's bed, after he had completed his daily inspection of the household.

"What is it, Charley?" Kate asked. Her voice sounded soothing. Mamie and Katie turned the pages of their book, studiously ignoring their brother's anguish, while the baby kept gurgling.

The boy had to snuffle twice before he could hand her the note. His mother had no chance to read it before he burst out, "I only forgot to put my brown shoes in their box. I left 'em by my bed. I was going to." He drew a shaking breath and tried to fend off his tears long enough to speak what disturbed him the most. "And tomorrow's Christmas!"

Kate shook her head. "Don't expect mere Christmas to make your father an easier man. What reason has he to be merry?" She smiled at the boy. "We'll have to make twice as merry ourselves!"

Dickens remained at the door, stung, as Kate heaved herself out of the rocking chair. She set her embroidery aside, fumbling but unable to catch a packet of bright green thread that unraveled and spilled onto the floor. She paid it no heed and gave the boy a gentle hug.

"Look at this, Charles," Mary's spirit said from across the room. She ran her translucent fingers over the frame of a small watercolor portrait showing the four children at play. "Do you remember it?"

Indeed, he did—it was the going-away gift from a painter friend when he and Kate had departed for six months to see America. Dickens insisted on leaving the four children behind, claiming that the stress of travel and the inconvenience of having them along would be detrimental to his own activities.

Kate had mourned the thought of being separated from her children for half a year and begged not to go, but Dickens went ahead with the plans, the arrangements, the packing. Finally, Dickens sent his ebullient actor friend William Macready to speak to Kate and, as instructed, Macready gruffly told Mrs. Dickens that a wife's duty was to accompany her husband wherever he wished to go, and to be happy doing it. Kate took only the watercolor portrait of the children to keep her company; she propped it up in their room every night during the journey.

"You dragged my sister against her will to a foreign land she had no wish to see. The sea trip was the roughest passage for years. You never asked her if perhaps she would like to include something in your plans. But instead you took her to see you speak, to see you read aloud and give performances on the stage. You travelled to visit Washington Irving and Edgar Allan Poe and Henry Longfellow, and what did she profit from it all? The chance to hear you quietly insult your hosts and America in general, to complain about conditions there?"

Dickens took a step back out to the hall, and Mary's spirit whisked across the floor, passing through Katie and Mamie by their picture book. The anger in her eyes frightened him. This was not the type of visitation he had expected at all.

"Can we not see something else, Mary? I beg you!"

"Of course," she said, passing him, and flowing back down the stairs. "Let's go watch the great Charles Dickens at work."

Still light on his feet, he dashed after her as Mary went down the hall to his writing study. Inside, he saw the new fire licking at fresh logs in the large fireplace. It was the first blaze of the morning, and he had added enough logs to keep it burning for a long time; he knew he was bound to be distracted by his writing and pay it no attention.

Dickens saw himself sitting at the desk, bent over a sheet of paper with pen in hand and inkwell nearby. A jumbled stack of papers lay at his left elbow, with one page nearly falling to the floor. A smudged thumbprint from a spilled drop of ink obscured a word in the margin. The only sounds in the room were the scratching of pen against paper, a rapid clink into the inkwell, the sizzling sound of the fire, and his own rapid breathing.

But as Dickens stood and watched the scene, he heard a rustle and saw little Mamie bundled in a blanket on the sofa. Her face had the rubbed-raw blush of one recovering from a fever. She propped a book on her bent knees. Keeping both eyes on her father at his desk, Mamie very carefully turned the page, as if terrified she might make a sound.

"I remember this day! A week ago—Mamie was sick, and I told her it would be all right if she wanted to rest in my study while I worked." He turned and looked to Mary for reassurance.

"You don't appear to be paying much attention to your daughter." Mary's voice remained cold.

The Dickens at the desk sprang to his feet and ran to a small mirror on the wall. He pushed his face to the reflection, opened his mouth, made bizarre contortions of his lips and eyebrows, then ran back to the desk. Picking up his pen, he scribbled down an entire paragraph without stopping, tilting the pen at an extreme angle to keep the words flowing without interrupting the sentence to dip into the ink again.

A moment later he stood up, went to the mirror once more, and proceeded to have a stop-and-start conversation with himself.

"It's nothing unusual," Dickens said to Mary. "Sometimes I get rather involved with my characters." But he felt his cheeks burning at this intrusion into a private moment as he worked. "It helps me stage some of my scenes."

But Mary seemed not at all concerned about that, looking

instead at the girl on the sofa. Mamie watched her father's actions, bewildered and frightened, but she made not a sound.

"Your children are afraid of you, Charles. They see you as a whirlwind, always busy, never to be disturbed. You're a great mystery to them."

"Nonsense, they love me. I am their father!"

"You are a stranger."

Upset and impatient, Dickens stepped back out to the hall, turning his back on the scene in the study. "I presume you have some design with these pantomimes, Mary. Get on with it."

She took his hand, and this time it felt colder than ever. "Follow me, then. We'll take a walk outside." She threw open the front door to a sunny winter's afternoon, and they set foot on a street deep in the heart of London. The great house on Devonshire Terrace vanished behind them as they stepped into the bustle of activity. Dickens saw that they left no footprints in the snow.

They moved unhindered by the constant stream of passersby, the businessmen, the beggars. Coming from behind, Dickens recognized the man stumping along at a furious, distracted pace. He was dressed in a fur greatcoat over a brown frock coat, then a waistcoat in red from which a gold watch chain dangled. Two linked diamond pins fastened an extravagant cravat poking up around his Adam's apple. Mary hurried up beside the man, dragging her companion along.

"What are you trying to show me here, Mary? I know I like to walk, sometimes as much as thirty miles in a single day. It helps me to plan my stories, to converse with my characters. And I know very well what I look like."

"Do you know what you look like?" Mary asked, pulling him around to face the image of himself. The man kept walking ahead, eyes cast down, with steam from the cold air spurting out of his nose. "Look closely. See yourself not posing for the mirror."

Dickens inspected the familiar clean-shaven boyish-faced man, with wide nose and thick lips, long brown hair curling around his ears. But then he saw the shadows under the eyes, the sagging weariness in his defiant stride, the hunch of the shoulders, the tight frown heavy on his lips.

"I thought you said this would be visions of the present," Dickens said. "Surely this must be me some years in the future."

Mary shook her head. "No, that is how you appear to others even now. You appear harried, overworked, with never enough time. Constantly pushing yourself beyond goals no man could meet."

"With good reason!" he said, turning defensively toward her. "Is it so quiet in the grave that you can't hear them shouting how Charles Dickens has lost his popularity? The last installments of *The Old Curiosity Shop* were selling a hundred thousand copies a week, but now *Barnaby Rudge* barely sells a third of that, even at its best!"

His eyes blazed at her, and he stopped walking. Mary faced him, as the other image of Dickens continued his lonely walk along the streets, muttering to himself.

"I took a year away from writing to travel in America, and when I returned I thought the public would be hungry for my work, waiting to snap up anything I might do. But my American Notes received nothing but a cool reception from my readers. They used to snap up every tidbit so eagerly—are they all tired of it now? This week's installment of *Martin Chuzzlewit* is selling only twenty thousand copies, no matter what I do."

Mary's face grew stern, an alien expression on the girl he had cherished for so long in his dreams and nightmares. "And how much time do you waste giving speeches, attending gaudy social events? And that's only when you're not losing your temper with your friends or shouting at your publisher or carrying on your endless fight for a reformed copyright law."

"The pirates are stealing me blind with bastard copies of my stories!"

"You don't seem to be doing much good work with the money you already possess. What good would you do with more of it?"

Dickens made no answer, but Mary had not finished taunting him. "You write weekly sketches, you work on two novels at a time, you write one-act farces and you star in them as well. No wonder your children don't know their father; no wonder dear Kate ignores you in simple defense against how you ignore her."

"But writing is my business!" Dickens said, crossing his arms over the gaps in his robe.

"Business!" cried Mary, "Mankind is your business. Don't you realize that a single story from you could do more good work than the House of Commons can manage in a year? In your constant challenge to produce more and more, you've forgotten what stories mean. Don't you remember your passion for a story that demands to be told? Or are you more interested in instant projects to increase your fame—if only for the moment?"

He stammered, "But, but that is not how I think of it at all."

Mary turned and pointed to the figure of Charles Dickens still striding away. "Look at him, walking as fast as he can but with his eyes to the ground. He'll reach his destination and go right past it without even knowing. You are a writer, Charles, surely you can appreciate such a metaphor?"

Dickens, feeling a heavy weight inside his chest, turned away. "I want to go back inside now."

Mary stopped in front of a leatherworker's shop and grasped the handle of the door. Behind the glass, Dickens could see only shadows of the proprietor and customers moving about. Before she opened the door, Mary softened her expression into gentle girlishness.

"Think of your children," she said, "and the story that Kate tells them of the three little pigs. Is it better to build a hundred huts of straw, or one or two fortresses of stone?"

She opened the door. "Stop writing books of straw."

He followed her inside, into his own sitting room again. The single chime rang out into the room as the clock struck one.

STAVE IV

"I have only one more thing to show you, Charles," Mary said to him. "A glimpse of things yet to come."

Dickens wanted to go nearer the fire but found he could not move. "I think I fear that more than the other images." He realized his voice sounded thin.

"But I know you must have good intentions in your heart." Mary's eyes twinkled, and she flashed a smile at him. Once again, she looked the playful sixteen-year-old, and his heart began to ache. "Stop your worrying. You may even enjoy this."

With a lilt in her step, Mary crossed the sitting room to a door Dickens had never seen before. It looked dark and narrow, perhaps a place where Captain Murderer would keep his blades for trimming wives into bite-sized pieces. Mary drew the door open without a creak. The firelight sparkled on the brass work of the knob, which was different from any of the ornate latches Dickens had installed on the other mahogany doors.

Inside, he could see a shadowy passage, lit by a white glow along the ceilings, as harsh as gaslight but not the same. Mary snatched his hand and drew him inside. He tried to resist, but his feet felt like leaden weights hooked to puppet strings.

The warm light of the sitting room hearth dwindled into nothing and vanished as they stepped forward. The air felt cool and smelled musty. The room was too dark to be observed with any accuracy, but Dickens glanced around, anxious to know what kind of room it was.

As his eyes adjusted he saw that the narrow walls were not walls at all, but shelves. Bookshelves, filled with row upon row of bound volumes. "What is this place, Mary? A library perhaps?"

She stopped in front of a long shelf and raised her hand. Around them the light grew brighter, and he could distinguish all the books of different heights and sizes, with cloth or leather bindings of black, blue, brown. "Have a look at this one, Charles." With a crook of her finger, she tugged the first volume on the shelf a little way out. He squinted down at the gold-stamped letters on the spine.

"Why, that's my *Pickwick*! In an edition I have never seen." He made a small groan. "Someone else has pirated it then!"

Mary's gentle laughter sounded like a bird in the forest. "Have you forgotten that we stepped into your future? Things yet to come."

Dickens ran his fingers over the spines. "And here's *Oliver Twist*, and *The Old Curiosity Shop*!" But as he continued down the line he stopped. "*Hard Times? A Tale of Two Cities? Great Expectations? Bleak House? The Mystery of Edwin Drood? David Copperfield?*" He looked at her, dazed. "Who are all these people? Where are these places? Did I write so many books?"

Mary seemed entranced by the delight she saw on his face. "Of course." He reached out to pull one of the books from the shelves, but Mary stopped him. Sliding the volume back into place, she shook her head. "That is forbidden. If you'd like to learn these characters and know these stories, then you must write them yourself. Only that way can you, and the world, have these books."

He continued to stare at his own name engraved on the spines as if on a monument, CHARLES DICKENS. The thought of all those novels whirled in his imagination; he felt his fingers itching to get back to his pen and paper. Then he remembered the other things Mary had showed him that evening.

"Here is something you will enjoy even more," Mary said as she turned to the opposite shelf, and he saw more books, so many that they were stacked on top of each other, piled up out of sight, causing the shelves to bow in the middle. His name appeared on many of those spines, often in the titles. "Biographies of you, critical treatises, textbooks. The scholars have had as much enjoyment chronicling your life as studying your novels."

Dickens could only gape in astonishment. He felt his vision going dim with euphoria. He had never imagined this, not even in his most pretentious fantasies.

Mary took down one of the tomes and flipped to a page, then began to read in the flickering light. "'Charles Dickens was a great English novelist and one of the most popular writers of all time. A keen observer of life, Dickens had a great understanding of people. He showed sympathy for the poor and helpless, and mocked and criticized the selfish, the greedy, the cruel.'"

She closed the book with a slam and a smile. "What you will find even more remarkable, I think, is that the passage I just read will be written *more than a century after your death*. Your own fame will outshine that of Walter Scott, and Poe and Irving and Longfellow, all those you so admire."

Dickens had to grasp at one of the shelves to keep from falling backward. By the stiffness he felt on his face, he knew he must be grinning like an idiot. But then a suspicion of her own words cast a cloud across his thoughts. "Answer me one question, Mary—are these the images of things that *will* be, or are they the images of things that *may* be only?"

Mary began to walk back down the long corridor of shelves toward the sitting room.

"Mary! Tell me!" His slippers made skittering noises on the hard floor as he ran to catch up with her.

She stood at the door out into the firelit room. "Perhaps. But you must remember that your writing is not about *writing*, but about people. As is your life. It won't matter how clever you are, how many projects you can juggle at once, how many instances your name appears in the newspapers. You have a power to move the world if you choose to do so. But will you make the effort?"

Dickens pushed back into the sitting room. "Yes, I will! I won't forget the lessons you taught me."

He felt like dancing. The hands on the clock had somehow returned to midnight, and as he looked the hour began to chime once more.

Mary stood alone in the center of the room, and her white gown took on a grayish tinge, as if shadows seeped into the fabric. Her skin seemed paler than before, with a shimmering quality like cheap candlewax running into puddles.

"Now I must leave you, Charles. My time here is finished. Look to see me no more. And look that, for your own sake, you remember what has passed between us!" She stepped backward toward the window, fading as she went. Dickens reached for her, but the euphoria made him numb to the thought of never seeing her ghost again.

"Wait!" he called. "You've given me a gift beyond measure. Isn't there something I can do for you? Some way I can repay you?"

Mary continued to dissolve into the air, but at the last moment she turned her gaze full on him. "Write me a Christmas story," she said.

And when the last stroke of twelve had chimed, her ghost vanished completely.

Charles Dickens remained before the glowing hearth for a full hour, watching the logs slump into embers, before he finally turned and left the sitting room, going to the stairs that led to his bed. Kate would be long asleep, but he would do his best not to disturb her. As his foot fell on the fourth step, the creaking wood reminded him that he was whole and substantial, and alive. As were his family and his friends.

A Christmas story? he thought. His head pounded with the dizzying memories of the evening, and he knew sleep would be a long time coming.

He wondered if he would get any ideas.

PREVIOUS PUBLICATION INFORMATION

"The Old Man and the Cherry Tree," first published in *Grue*, no. 3, 1986.

"Scientific Romance," copyright © 1998 by WordFire, Inc., first published in *The UFO Files*, edited by Ed Gorman and Martin H. Greenberg, DAW, 1998.

"Sea Dreams," copyright © 1995 by Kevin J. Anderson and Rebecca Moesta. First published in *Peter S. Beagle's Immortal Unicorn*, edited by Peter S. Beagle, Janet Berliner, and Martin H. Greenberg, HarperPrism, 1995.

"Short Straws," copyright © 1995 by WordFire, Inc., first published in *The Ultimate Dragon*, ed. Bryon Preiss, John Betancourt, and Keith R.A. deCandido, Dell Books, Oct 1995.
"The Shot Heard 'Round the World," copyright © 2019, WordFire, Inc. and Kevin Ikenberry, first published in *Trouble in the Wind*, ed. Chris Kennedy & James Young, Theogony Books, 2019.

"Splinter," with Rebecca Moesta, first published in *Renaissance Faire*, ed. Andre Norton and Jean Rabe, DAW Books, Feb 2005.

"The Things the Princess Carried," copyright 2024, WordFire, Inc., first publication.

"Time Zone," copyright © 2018 WordFire, Inc., first published online in *Daily Science Fiction*, 2018.

"Trip Trap," with Sherrilyn Kenyon, first published in *Dark Duets*, ed. Christopher Golden, HarperVoyager, 2014.

ABOUT THE AUTHOR

Kevin J. Anderson has published more than 180 books, 58 of which have been national or international bestsellers. He has 24 million copies in print in 34 languages.

He has written numerous novels in the Star Wars, X-Files, and Dune universes, as well as the unique Clockwork Angels steampunk trilogy with legendary Rush drummer Neil Peart. His original works include the Saga of Seven Suns series, the Wake the Dragon and Terra Incognita fantasy trilogies, the humorous Dan Shamble, Zombie P.I. series and The Dragon Business series.

He has edited numerous anthologies, written comics and games, and the lyrics to two rock CDs as companions to his Terra Incognita trilogy.

Anderson is the director of the graduate program in Publishing at Western Colorado University, and he and his wife Rebecca Moesta are the publishers of WordFire Press.

IF YOU LIKED ...

If you liked *Fantasy Stories Volume: 1*, you might also enjoy other WordFire Press titles by Kevin J. Anderson.

Our list of other WordFire Press authors and titles is always growing. To find out more and shop our selection of titles, visit us at:
wordfirepress.com

www.ingramcontent.com/pod-product-compliance
Lightning Source LLC
Chambersburg PA
CBHW050504110726
47899CB00005B/1325